I0678143

THE THIRTEEN TRIBES OF CAIN SERIES

Book One

The Forsaken

R.J. Craddock

Transcendent Books
Springville, UT

This book is a work of fiction. Any references to historical events, real people, or real locals are used fictitiously. Other names, characters, places, and incidents are a product of the author's imagination, and any resemblance to actual events or locals or persons, living or dead, is purely coincidental.

Copyright © 2013 R.J. CRADDOCK
Transcendent Books, Springville, UT.
Manufactured in the United States of America
All rights reserved, including the right of reproduction in whole or in part in any form.

Seventh Edition, July 2025
Also available in eBook form.

Follow R.J. Craddock on Facebook, Goodreads, Instagram, Pinterest, and Twitter for all news and events.
www.rjcraddock.com

Summary: Her mother is dead, her home destroyed. Five-year-old Gwen flees from disaster and stumbles into the human world. Unable to speak their language but capable of reading their thoughts, she tries to acclimate to society. However, her native tongue is magical, giving her the power to control the elements. Misunderstood, orphaned Gwen runs off in search of her kind. Until her dark gifts bring to light a horrible truth, forcing her to make a fatal decision. There is no going back from murder.

Cover design and illustrations by R.J. Craddock. Cover illustration copyright © 2013 by R.J. Craddock of Green Cloak Design.

ISBN-13: 9780615806488 (Transcendent Books)

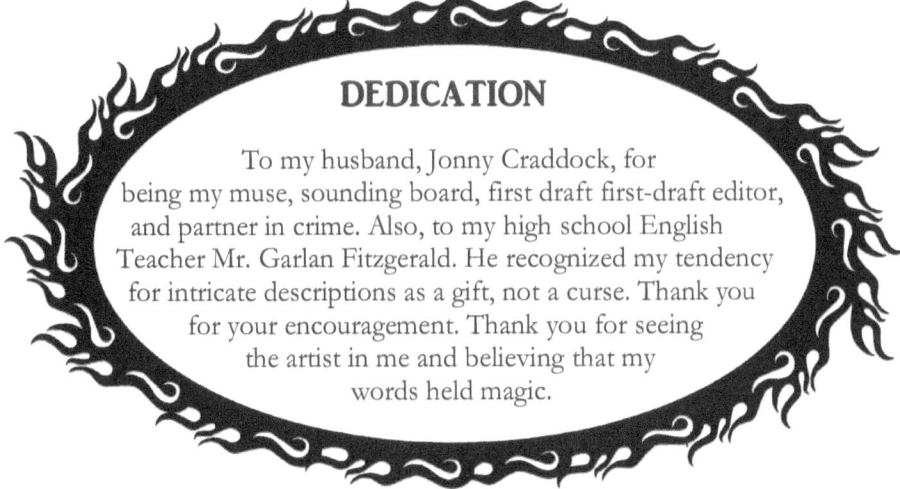

DEDICATION

To my husband, Jonny Craddock, for
being my muse, sounding board, first draft first-draft editor,
and partner in crime. Also, to my high school English
Teacher Mr. Garlan Fitzgerald. He recognized my tendency
for intricate descriptions as a gift, not a curse. Thank you
for your encouragement. Thank you for seeing
the artist in me and believing that my
words held magic.

The Forsaken

R.J. Craddock

CONTENTS

Prologue

Her innocence had drawn them to the woman. Tonight's prey was named Laura, and her ridiculous optimism made her perfect for their twisted little game. They had been at it all night, hunting her from dream to dream. The two friends, Deverick and Onan, liked to work as a tag team. First, Onan entered her subconscious, learning all he could about her hopes and fears. Then he became part of the dream, making himself one with her fantasy like the romantic hero, a dark, mysterious lover. Only after she had succumbed to his friend's influence did Deverick disturb her universe, rearranging the dream into something horrible and sickening: himself, the monster in the darkness that fed on her fear. Laura kept turning to Onan to rescue her, believing he was her hero, a part of her mind. She did not realize that he and the demon chasing her were in league with one another, best friends enjoying the simple pleasure of tormenting her. Even as children, Dreamwalking had always been their favorite forbidden pastime.

In her latest attempt to protect herself, their victim transformed the dream into a place where she felt safe: her childhood home, a simple brick bungalow in a nondescript suburban neighborhood. Behind her, Deverick became a pack of red-eyed savage wolves followed by a black tempest that devoured the blue sky as it moved toward her.

Suddenly, Onan swung open her front door. "Laura!" He

beckoned the confused woman, and, like a trusting fool, she ran to him and the refuge of the home she loved.

Once they were out of sight, the wolves melted away into a solitary man. Deverick laughed softly as he sauntered to the walnut tree in the front yard. He was a striking young man of twenty-two with a muscular build and a handsome face that was neither too masculine nor too pretty. His hair was black as night, his eyes blue and gold. All around him, the tempest still raged in Laura's dream world, engulfing the house in its shadow. He leaned against the tree trunk to wait. It was now Onan's turn to be the monster. A terrified scream came from within the small brick home. Deverick smiled, listening to the sounds of Laura's pain and horror as Onan had his fun.

Deverick felt no remorse. She was just a human and thus inconsequential. It didn't matter what they did to her. After all, it was only a nightmare. None of this was real. There would be no lasting damage done, no physical damage anyway. Nonetheless, she would awaken in the morning, terrified of falling asleep again. Usually, they only stalked their prey once, but perhaps they might visit Laura's dreams another night. The thought made Deverick smile again.

"Deverick!" He looked around him, knowing that voice too well to confuse it for something within the dream, but still half-expecting to see his mother standing behind him.

"Deverick! Get up, boy!" He felt the waking world tugging at him. With a groan, he turned toward the house.

"Onan," he called. "Sorry to interrupt, but I've got to go."

All at once, his friend appeared before him. A couple of inches taller than him, Onan looked fierce, his long auburn hair hanging wild and free, half-dressed with bloody claw marks across his bare chest. *Laura has more fight in her than I thought,* Deverick mused.

"It must be morning. My mother's come to wake me," Deverick confided, releasing an exasperated sigh.

"Old Mum again? Tell her I said good morning." Onan chuckled, his smile spreading to his light green eyes, the gold around the center lending him the feral look of a wild beast.

"See you tonight." The two friends clasped hands in farewell.

Laura's dream faded into a plain white room with only two doors standing side by side, one red and one black. With a wicked smile, Onan turned the gold knob on the red door, stepped through, and suddenly he and the door vanished from the dream.

Alone now, Deverick stood before the black door. This door represented the path back to the waking world, the door he must step through to reconnect his mind to his body. He could simply step out of the dream, but it was dangerous. There were far too many stories of dreamers like him who never found their way back, never to wake up again. Deverick opened the door and stepped across the threshold.

Sunlight rudely disrupted the stillness of the once-darkened room. Master Deverick Hawthorne stirred in his lush, silken bedding, shielding his eyes against the harsh light. A thin, feminine silhouette hovered before the glaring light in the window.

"Mother!" Deverick grumbled with a husky voice. "I don't have any appointments till noon. Let me sleep."

"This is not a day for slumbering in your bed like a fool," Lady Raizel Hawthorne retorted.

Deverick heard his Familiar Poe *caw* in agreement.

"Whose side are you on, Poe?" Shooting the raven perched on the mantel a scowl, Deverick pretended to reprimand his animal companion. Poe tilted his black feathered head to the side as if to say, *Does it matter?*

Deverick shuffled into a sitting position to look sternly at his mother with a groan. The look did nothing to intimidate the lady.

"All right, what have I done now?" he asked, clearing his dry throat.

His manservant, Reece, hurried to his bedside with an empty glass goblet, uttering a simple water spell. He handed the glass to his master, and the goblet quickly filled with water as if poured from an invisible source. Nonplussed, Deverick took a long swill. Other servants worked in his bedchamber as well. Several individuals diligently prepare breakfast for him and his mother, arranging it on the table beside the fireplace. At the same time, the rest scurried about the room collecting his belongings, gathering his clothes from the wardrobe, and packing them into many large trunks.

"All right, something's going on. Out with it, old lady." This earned Deverick a playful scoff of annoyance from his mother. He smiled mischievously at her, the glint of gold around the center of his sapphire eyes catching in the sunlight.

"The King is dead!" Lady Hawthorne announced in a half-whisper, glowing with exhilaration.

Dumbfounded, Deverick looked to Reece for confirmation. Taking Deverick's goblet, the thin, balding man nodded in affirmation.

After a momentary shock, Deverick turned his attention back to his mother. "But when? How?"

"Oh, that doesn't matter!" She gracefully glided across the polished wood floor to sit next to him on the edge of the bed. "The man was nearly ninety-eight; it was bound to happen sooner or later."

"Yes, but he looked not a day over forty," Deverick interjected, running his fingers through his black curly locks.

"Yes, well... *Kings* can afford those expensive potions, but only Vampires live forever."

"I know that. But still, I wasn't expecting—"

"Son, don't trouble yourself over the whys or the hows. Do you know what this means? You're now the King! He died without an heir, which makes you next in line."

Deverick gave himself a moment to let this sink in. Although he'd prepared his whole life for this day, he still felt numbed by the shock. *Am I ready for this?* Deverick asked himself.

Of course, you are, son. You were born for this! He heard his mother's answering voice in his head. Their eyes met in a look of understanding as she gave his hand a quick squeeze of encouragement.

"Now, there's a lot to be done before we depart. That's why we ought not to sit around wasting time. You must get to the palace by midday." She spoke aloud. Standing, his mother briskly walked over to the breakfast table.

Deverick threw off his blankets and gingerly got out of bed, massaging his lower back as he walked barefoot across the cold wood floor to join his mother. It was customary for them to have breakfast in this manner. After his father died, his mother started eating breakfast with him every morning in his room, leaving the grand dining hall unused except for special occasions. He thought of ending this tradition as he grew into a man, but he sensed that his mother was loneliest during the mornings.

He couldn't help envying men of the human world. In their culture, grown men didn't live with their mothers; they didn't have family members and servants barging in on them at all hours. He had heard that some bachelor's even had the luxury of sleeping naked; how he longed for that kind of privacy, that kind of freedom! But no, these thoughts would never do. If he started grumbling about his current situation, how would he ever come to terms with the life ahead of him?

The thought almost made Deverick trip on his feet before he sat across from his mother at the table. Poe, anticipating where his human half was going, swooped off the mantel to land on the table among the many food dishes. Like an excellent Familiar, he waited to be offered food and did not put his beak into the plate of eggs beside him. Deverick scooped some up for Poe and put them on a plate before him. His raven counterpart gave him a chirp in thanks and then gobbled his breakfast.

Ignoring his mother's pointed look of disapproval, Deverick glanced at the servants lined up along the wall, waiting to jump at their every command. His favorite food awaited him on the plate. His usual whims are anticipated and seen to by his manservant, Reece. The idea that he couldn't even be spontaneous with his choice of breakfast made him all the more melancholy.

He also realized there would be no more Dreamwalking with Onan, not tonight. Not ever. It would never do for the King to break the sacred laws. He would be held to a higher standard of conduct from now on. The personal lives of royalty were constantly scrutinized and exploited for political gain. Nothing was sacred, and nothing stayed a secret long when spies had magic to aid them. Even in dreams, walls have eyes and ears in the Wiccan world.

With a sigh of resignation, Deverick picked up his fork and dug into the last meal he would ever eat in the home of his youth.

A couple of hours later, Deverick found himself leading the procession of his household as they marched from Hawthorne Manor toward Black Lake. Poe perched comfortably on his master's left shoulder. Since they were trading the country manor for a grand palace, and none remained in the family but themselves, the old house would be closed up until they had use for it again. Servants levitated his bags, trunks, and other belongings with a simple spell as they followed behind Lady and Master Hawthorne.

The heir to the Wiccan Throne walked barefoot through the dew-covered grass, dressed plainly in a white button-down shirt and simple white slacks. He wore only his mother's family ring and the Hawthorne family medallion around his neck for jewelry. Ahead of them, two large tree trunks bent and twisted around each other, forming an arch beneath them. Passing through the arch, Deverick and the procession came to the shore of Black Lake.

"Time to make your own way, Poe," Deverick told the raven on his shoulder with a sad smile. "How I wish I could fly away with you right now," he whispered as he gently stroked the bird's sleek black feathers. Poe cawed and pecked Deverick's hair affectionately. Deverick extended his left arm, and Poe hopped up to rest upon his hand. He sensed the others around him, including his mother, getting impatient with this prolonged farewell. Quickly, the future king sent mental pictures to his Familiar through their telepathic bond. He clarified that Poe must fly to the Wiccan palace to meet Deverick. Poe flew into the blue sky above with another caw to signal his understanding. Deverick watched him leave with a restless sigh.

A flat stone disc rose out of the bank of the lake at the water's edge. Kneeling upon it, Deverick dipped his fingers into the lake, making a pattern in the murky water as it rippled. Muttering an old incantation softly, Deverick made the reflective surface of the water change. No longer did he see the blue sky above him and the woods surrounding his country estate, but an immaculate garden with a pure crystal fountain at its center. The white Wiccan palace looming in the background.

Standing, he stepped down onto the bank. Deverick knew that he would see the top of his family home above the tree line if he looked over his shoulder, but he fought the temptation.

"Here we go," he spoke under his breath as he walked into the water. The gritty soil of the lake bottom sloped gradually downward beneath his bare feet. He heard his mother step behind him and knew that the rest of the procession would follow in formation behind her into the water. He didn't hesitate as he went further into the lake, the water steadily rising around him until only his head was above the surface. He stepped over the drop-off and sank into the lake completely.

He was five the first time his mother took him to the Wiccan Kingdom, traveling by water. He remembered the peculiar feeling of nausea and disorientation that came from sinking and rising out of the water simultaneously. He felt himself rising magically back to the surface only a moment after his head submerged under Black Lake. As he emerged, the bright morning sunlight reflected off the crystal fountain, and the pure, clear water around him blinded him. The enchanted water dripped off as Deverick walked out of the fountain, leaving him completely dry.

Despite himself, he looked to the sky for any sign of Poe, although he knew there was no way the bird could've flown that far so quickly. Poe would never have attempted to travel by water. There were some things even a Familiar wouldn't do if their other half asked them.

Waiting for him by the entrance of the palace garden stood three of the previous King's royal advisors: Gregory Limrick, Delanie DuCall, and Calill Hardenbrook. They were all members of the first families of Wicca. This morning, the rest of the royal officers would be busy arranging the funeral services of the old king. Only these three were in charge of preparing the new King for the coronation.

While his mother and servants emerged from the fountain into the garden, Deverick strode to the three men. Limrick was in his fifties and an old friend of his father's. Hardenbrook was only a few years older than himself; they shared some mutual friends but weren't well acquainted. DuCall was Onan's father, a man Deverick had come to think of like a second father, especially after his own had passed away.

Deverick would've greeted them warmly like old friends, but DuCall spoke first.

"Lord Hawthorne, I must inform you that you have a challenger." The older, darker version of his son, DuCall, spoke in a cold, formal tone, his face devoid of emotion. Deverick had never once seen

Onan's father in all his life without a smile on his face. This demeanor did not suit the man he knew.

Something inside Deverick sank into the pit of his stomach. A challenger was the last thing he wanted to deal with today. He found it difficult to face the idea of being the sole person responsible for the welfare of an entire kingdom. Now he had to fight another man for the job; by tradition, it would be a fight to the death.

Lady Hawthorne stepped up to stand beside him, while he gathered his composure and reconciled himself to the situation. She took one look at her son's face and knew.

"I don't believe it. A challenger?" Turning her gaze on the three royal advisors, she added, "Who? Who would be so foolish?"

Deverick noticed a strange look pass behind DuCall's eyes, but it left just as quickly as it came. The other two seemed reluctant to speak. Both glanced at DuCall as if expecting him to answer. He said nothing.

"Perhaps we should go straight to the battle yard, my lord. Your challenger waits there now," Hardenbrook spoke up, his usual aristocratic air dispelled by the nervous quiver in his voice.

"Don't be ridiculous. We just arrived. I'm sure this contest hasn't been announced formally to the public yet. Why not hasten the coronation ceremony and pretend we didn't receive the challenge in time? No one but us will ever know," Lady Raizel suggested.

"The challenge has already been announced, my lady," DuCall said darkly, his face hard as stone.

"Yes, a small assembly has already gathered at the grounds to witness the proceedings. We were to bring you and Lord Hawthorne there as soon as you arrived," Limrick added in a cordial voice.

Lady Hawthorne opened her mouth to object, but one look from Deverick silenced her.

"Very well. Lead the way, gentlemen," the would-be King ordered.

* * * * *

Stepping onto the battlegrounds outside the palace walls, Deverick felt exposed before the growing crowd gathered. Two men stood in the center of the yard: one would be his challenger, and the other—dressed in his official uniform—was the palace guards' captain, who would oversee this contest of magical skill.

Deverick didn't recognize the man standing next to him. His challenger was young, tall, and strong of build. The man was dressed all in black, from the scarf wrapped around his head down to his shoes, as was customary for the rival to the throne. If this man won, he would strip Deverick's dead body of his white clothing and dress in them, taking his family ring and medallion as trophies—proof to all who saw them that he had defeated the future King.

Deverick wasn't afraid of a fight; he had defeated many over the years. He was considered the most powerful Wiccan male born in four generations. He mastered long forgotten spells, gifted with rare abilities. Wiccans as a people, were naturally arrogant and competitive, so no one believed he was unbeatable unless they fought him themselves. But this would be the first time such a challenge would result in death. He could've killed his past challengers, but it always seemed wasteful. Why kill one of his own? It was enough to humiliate his opponent to prove his skill. He didn't need to add bloodshed to enjoy the victory.

His mother squeezed his hand in encouragement or farewell; he wasn't sure which. Deverick left her and the royal advisors behind. Head held high and shoulders back, young Hawthorne crossed the yard, fully aware that every eye rested upon him. When he was ten feet away from the captain and his opponent, recognition dawned on him. His heart skipped a beat. His step almost faltered as he looked into the eyes of the man who came here today intending to take his life for the sake of a throne.

For the briefest moment, Deverick thought it might all be a joke, some big elaborate prank to congratulate him on his succession. But the dark look in his friend's eyes told him this was not so. The man standing between him and his destiny was the same man who stood by his side his whole life: Onan.

CHAPTER ONE

Miracle Child

Her eyes sting from the tears she cried an hour ago, the remnants dry upon her rosy, soot-covered cheeks. The lone black-haired five-year-old girl shivers involuntarily as she treks on through an endless snow-covered landscape.

Everyone is gone now, everything in flames. Nothing remains but ash and tears. She thinks to herself. *I must keep walking; there is nothing left to do.* All she can feel is the bitter cold as she trudges through the woods, the only living thing in an empty world of white. A mixture of glacial air and lingering smoke causes her lungs to ache. Her rasping coughs blow out in white clouds. Frigid and stiff, her body is as cold as the snow around her. She notices that even the morning sky above her is white, vast, and empty. She continues, her stockings soaked through, her feet numb.

She had lost one of her shoes a while back, walking over a bunch of fallen branches. Her foot slipped into a crevice, and when she tried to pull it out, her shoe did not come with it. Her little arms were too short to retrieve the shoe, so she simply left it there. Walking with one shoe proved uncomfortable, so she took it off her foot, clasping the lonely shoe against her chest.

The blackened, soiled clothes on her back are her only possessions in the world. Once sunny yellow and trimmed with frilly white lace, her short dress is now dirty with ash and dried blood. Its lace is gray and singed. Her gray stockings, once white, have holes burned away in places. Her green winter coat, musky with the smell of smoke, is still in pristine condition. Around her neck, she wears a gold chain necklace with an oval locket. Branded on the front is a symbol of a burning rose and the name Gwenevere. The locket is the only tie to her past, the only remnant of her identity.

She hasn't seen a single soul. No towns. No houses. No roads. She treks toward an unknown future, leaving behind her painful past. An image of her mother's beautiful face creeps into her dazed mind, making her want to start crying all over again. Fatigued, she holds back the tears.

"Crying never got the world to stop spinning," her father once said. Or at least she thought the man was her father. She only met him a handful of times. He always came to visit their little cottage late at night. She would see him only briefly before being sent to bed. He was always long gone before she awoke the following day. Nonetheless, she learned quickly not to cry, pout, or go to him for comfort. He was always serious, worried, and cold.

Why didn't he live with us if he is my father? Why does he feel like a stranger? Why wasn't he there when the fire ate up everything? A father should protect his family!

Her eyes water. She sniffles, forcing back the tears and pushing the memories away. It is better that she forgets them and leaves them behind her, so she does. With every step she takes forward, she puts more distance between herself and the world she once belonged. Hour after hour goes by, and fatigue makes it easier to shut out all thoughts and feelings. She thinks of nothing but walking in a straight line as the wind blows through her long, dark hair.

Brushing the errant strands out of her eyes, she saw a man. A tall, dark figure is lurking amongst the trees ahead of her. She was alone in the forest one moment, then the stranger just appears, watching her with a fascinated smile. She blinks several times, but the apparition remains. She hesitates only a moment and then continues forward. Not wanting to show her fear, she avoids his eyes.

He looks warm in his long, black trench coat, tall leather boots, and black suit. Yet, something about him is wrong. With a dark, unsettling determination, his gaze seems to follow wherever she moves. She senses his eyes on her skin, like ants crawling upon her. A bone-deep chill comes from his direction. And she thought she couldn't be any colder. Quickly, she deviates her course slightly off to the right to veer away from him.

As she comes closer to the dark stranger, he suddenly moves. The child bolts, breaking into a wild run. The forest becomes a blur around her as she speeds forward in a headlong dash.

Keep running. Don't look back. Panic carries her farther and faster than her weakened legs can on their own. The hood of her green coat flaps in the wind behind her. Coming over the crest of a hill, she trips on a rock, stumbles, and falls. Helplessly, she tumbles like a rag doll. The world spinning around her as she rolls down the hill, hitting rocks, tree limbs, and tree trunks. Sharp needles of pain shoot through her as the dead, dried plants along the hillside cut into her.

She lands with a thud, a loud, ringing crack echoing through her skull. She finds herself lying limply in the middle of a narrow canyon road. After the first wave of pain washes over her, she opens her eyes to see where she has wound up. The stranger in black is there standing at the crest of the hilltop, staring down at her. She goes cold inside, numb with fear as well as physical pain. Then he smiles at her.

"Gwenevere," a voice whispers in the wind.

All at once, he stands before her at the bottom of the hill, just across the canyon road. He smiles again.

"Don't be afraid, my child. I am your salvation." He speaks in a silvery voice. The sound makes her blood turn to ice, and fear beyond reason races through her. "Just ask, and I will take away your pain," he continues. His eyes are black as pitch, no light reflecting from the sun above. No pupils, just black emptiness.

"Who are you?" she trembles with a small voice.

"You can call me Luc—" Suddenly, a vehicle rounds the bend, coming toward them, catching them both off guard. *What is that thing?* Although loud and foreign to her, she finds this machine less terrifying to the man in black. Frantic for help, the girl struggles to her feet. Finding her legs unresponsive, she crawls toward the speeding car and away from the stranger with the soulless eyes.

Caw! Caw!

A raven swoops down from the white sky above to land right on the car's hood. It caws, flapping its wings wildly. The car comes to a tire-screeching halt mere feet from the lost child. The driver of the car pops out of the vehicle. Dark skinned, stout of build, and dressed in the oddest clothes the child has ever seen.

"You stupid, crazy bird. Get off my car!" the man yells at the animal, trying to scare it away by waving his arms. The bird caws loudly in his face before swooping down to land next to the frightened girl crawling in the road. She reaches out a small, shivering hand to touch the bird, with feathers the same color as her hair. However, it hops away, taking flight. Gone as quickly as it had arrived.

Seeing her there for the first time, the man rushes toward her, his young wife staring out the windshield in horror. The husband reaches for the child, and the girl crumbles into his arms, weak.

"Good God! What's happened to you? Where are your parents?" Looking into his warm brown eyes, the child feels warmth spread through her frozen flesh. A feeling of safety settles upon her. Turning to look over her shoulder, she begins to point at the man following her. However, the road and the forest behind her are empty.

"We're going to take you to see a doctor, all right?" the kind man asks, not waiting for her reply. He hefts her into his arms, carrying her to the car. After stowing her gently into the back seat, the man quickly takes his place behind the wheel.

"Well, did she say anything? What is she doing out here like this?" His wife turns to him, panicked. Also, dark skinned, her clothing and hairstyle equally strange to the girl. *No one wore those kinds of colors or patterns back home.* The child can't help noticing.

"She didn't say anything," he replies. "I think she's in shock." Calling back to the child in a reassuring voice, the man adds, "Everything's going to be all right, okay, sweetheart? You're going to be all right." He starts the car, speeding down the road toward town. The unusual motions of the vehicle and its incredible speed would intrigue the girl at any other time. Normally, her inquisitive mind would've needed to know the origin and purpose of the thing before entering it. However, the warm air around her and the hum of the engine soothe her curiosity, helping her relax.

"What's your name, honey?" With shock evident in her honey-colored eyes, the woman turns to smile weakly at the girl. The child only stares back at her, dazed.

The dark stranger in the woods had spoken to her in her speech, but this young couple speaks in a strange tongue, a language foreign to her ears. The friendly woman continues to talk to her, but the girl can't make sense of her words. She seems to be asking her a question, but the girl is too distracted to comprehend. Flurries of images pass through her mind, thoughts, and feelings that are not her own.

The woman chatters on, while the girl becomes oblivious. Fatigue finally overtakes her until the world around her grows still, dark, and empty.

* * * * *

How long has it been? She doesn't know, but the fog from her mind begins to lift. The child finds herself lying on a strange bed in a sterile, all-white room. She hears muffled voices and a peculiar rhythmic beeping sound nearby. Wrapped in several warm blankets, she feels strangely numb from her knees down. Her feet sting. She can feel ribbons of pain within, but she can't move them.

Worried, the child glances at her feet. They soak in a large bowl of murky water. She can't tell if it's warm or cold; she doesn't feel it on her skin. She realizes her stockings have been removed. In fact, all of her clothes are gone. Only a loose white paper-like robe covers her body. The little girl pulls the blankets tighter around her, looking about frantically. *Where am I? What's happening?*

She sees two women standing at the foot of her bed, speaking in voices she can't quite comprehend. The older woman is stocky, middle-aged, with dark hair and smiling brown eyes. She is dressed in a loose, matching green shirt and pants. She listens respectfully to the second, younger woman, who tucks a strand of red curly hair behind her ear. The redhead wears a white waist-length coat and flips through papers on a clipboard as she speaks.

"So, she has three broken ribs and a mild concussion," Doctor Thompson says. "Also, there's some smoke inhalation in her lungs, a few minor cuts, and bruises with abnormal scar tissue over her left breast. From the look of her, she probably hasn't eaten in days. And if that isn't bad enough, she has frostbite all over her feet." The lady informs the other.

"So, what do we do?" the older woman asks.

"Well, for now, I'd like you to up her pain meds and bandage her feet. Also, let's arrange to do some X-rays on her chest. Other than that, there's not much else we can do." The younger woman slips the chart back into the slot at the foot of the bed.

"Yes, Doctor Thompson."

Suddenly, afraid of these strangers, the girl tries to squirm away despite her injured legs, but they are like dead weights. Hearing the sound of sheets rustling, the nurse looks up to see the child staring at them with wild eyes.

"She's awake, Doctor," Nurse Sumpter announces.

The Doctor turns to look into the girl's round face. Her yellow-green eyes are confused, her long black hair is tousled, resembling a bird's nest, and her skin is pale as snow. *Poor little thing,* Doctor Renee Thompson thinks to herself. *She can't be any older than five, but she's so frail and malnourished it's hard to tell.*

"What's your name, sweetie?" The nurse flashes the child a kind smile. The little girl just stares up at her with a blank face.

"She tried to talk to me earlier, but I couldn't understand her," the Doctor informs the nurse. "She was half asleep at the time. I just assumed she was talking gibberish in her sleep." The nurse nods understanding.

"There's no need to be afraid, dear," Doctor Thompson reassures the child, stepping forward to pat the girl's hand. "We're friends." The child looks at her, puzzled, and scoots an inch or two away from her. She takes her hand out of the woman's reach. "Do you know how to contact your parents? Do you know your phone number or your address?"

"Who are you?" the girl asks in her tongue. The two women look at her oddly. She tries to tell them all about Mama, the fire, and the man in the woods, but they don't understand her words. They look as confused as she feels. They speak louder as if she is hard to hear, but the increase in volume doesn't make their strange language easier to understand. Once again, the girl sees strange images that flow from the others' minds into hers. She tries to shut them out to focus on what is happening to no avail. Frustrated, she shakes her head at everything they say until they stop bothering her.

Eventually, the two adults start talking amongst themselves. Then the woman in white lifts one of the girl's feet out of the bowl. The skin is white and waxy, but the toes are black as if someone dipped them in ink. The girl tries to move them, but they won't obey her. The woman gently places the girl's foot back into the water, commenting to the nurse, who nods at the instructions.

"I just hope they find her parents soon," the Doctor remarks. "Little girls need their mothers. She must be frightened to death." With that, she exits the room. The nurse wheels a metal cart with medical supplies over to the foot of the bed.

Pulling on a pair of latex gloves, the nurse notices the little green-eyed girl watching her suspiciously. The nurse slowly administers to the frostbitten feet, not wanting to frighten the child. Taking them out of the bowl, she sets the water aside on the lower shelf of her cart and dries them off with a rag. Suddenly, the girl reaches for her feet as if to touch them. While making a hushing sound, the nurse pushes her back down on the bed, soothing her. Reluctantly, the child relaxes and sits back to watch the nurse work.

She takes a tube of medical ointment and applies the strange-smelling cream all over the blackened extremities. The woman is incredibly careful and gentle with her task. Picking up a wad of bandages from the cart, the lady begins to wrap the feet. After a while, the child starts to find this process soothing.

When the nurse finishes, she leaves the room with her cart. The girl glances down at her bandaged feet. Wanting the pain to go away, she sits up, reaches out her hand, touching her bandaged toes. Closing her eyes, she sings in a cooing lullaby.

"*Dah-Day-Wente, Curea-Longa, Babeta-Lovota…*" The old familiar tune gives her comfort. Her mother sang it to her whenever she scraped her knee or became sick. Those words, and her mother's beautiful voice, had always made her feel safe and warm. Singing the lullaby now, she feels a contented warmth blanket her. The pain in her body fades away yet leaves her weak and tired. Before long, she slumps back down on the bed, sinking into the world of dreams.

* * * * *

Bright colors flash around her. She runs through a meadow of multi-colored wildflowers. A young boy is ahead of her. Laughing, he runs deeper into the meadow. The boy is older than she is, tall, blond, and blue-eyed, with a youthful impish smile on his face that seems to urge her to follow him. He keeps running, climbing up a steep hill. She finds it difficult to climb after him, but finally, she reaches the crest. The golden-haired boy waits for her to join him. When she does, he takes her hand in his and points to something beyond in the distance. Her gaze follows to a beautiful city grown out of the rocks, the trees, and the land itself. A magnificent white stone castle rests in the city's center, with many piers and towers rising into the sky as if reaching toward heaven.

It is the most beautiful thing she has ever seen. She steps toward the city, but the boy stops her, pulling her back to his side.

"No," he says in an urgent voice.

She looks up at him, confused. He repeatedly points to the city and the castle, shaking his head. "You can't go there. Not now…You must stay away from there."

He looks deep into her eyes to see if she understands. He takes her in his arms and hugs her, pressing her face against his chest. She feels comforted by his embrace, safe and protected by his presence. She longs to stay with him forever. He turns, pointing back the way they came, and nods in that direction.

"Go, Gwen. Run. It's not safe here for you now. Some will stop at nothing to hurt you. You must disappear. Your life and mine depend on it." He looks down at her, a sad yet loving gaze in his blue eyes with a golden circle around the pupils. Then he shoves her forward. Reluctantly, she obeys, walking back down the hill the way she came. She pauses as if to look back and ask him the many questions in her mind.

"Don't look back. Leave and only come back when I call for you, Gwenevere. Not before." She hears his voice over her shoulder.

She feels so confused, sad, and miserable to be leaving him. His rejection hurtles her forward, sending her running. Crying, she plows through the never-ending meadow. Before her, in the distance, a dark and ominous mountain looms, clouds hovering over its peak, its presence oppressive and haunting. She feels compelled by unseen forces to run to it, even though her heart screams for her to return to that magical city and the safe, loving embrace of the blue-eyed boy on the hill.

Disorientated, she wakes in the same stark-white hospital room in the hospital bed. After many panic-filled moments, she recognizes her surroundings, finally recalling everything that has happened to her in the last few days—the last lingering images of the dream lift like a mist from her mind. The one thing that she holds onto is the name the boy called her.

Gwenevere, he called me. Vaguely, she remembers having other names, too, but Gwen or Gwenevere is the most significant. It feels true to her. She reaches for her neck.

It's gone! Where's my necklace? Gwen looks about frantic until her eyes catch a glint of gold. She finds her large oval locket on the table beside her bed. Sighing in relief at its sight, she takes it. She opens the clasp to peer inside. Two locks of hair braided together are coiled inside. One is a lock of golden hair, delicate and soft, the other of deep black. They are intertwined, contrasting one another.

She closes the locket again to touch the engraved symbol across the golden cover. As she admires the locket, she tries to recall the boy from her dream. *What's his name? Did I know him before?* Something about him seems familiar, but… Feeling the dark images of her past trying to bubble up to the surface, she immediately shoves them away, not wanting the heartache that comes with them.

I don't want to be here anymore, She thinks to herself, looking about the strange, uninviting room. The same odd devices are nearby, beeping and buzzing, their purpose unknown to her. Tubes run everywhere; some are injected into her arm, and one coming out of her nose. Immediately, she begins to remove them.

"Don't move. You need to rest, sweetheart." Doctor Thompson sits next to the little girl's bed, waiting for her to awaken.

The Doctor moves from her chair to stand next to the bed. She wears her fiery-red hair up in a bun. Some runaway strands fall into her face, contrasting against her light brown eyes. A lovely display of freckles sprinkled across her cheeks and the bridge of her nose, making her skin seem fresh and rosy. She smiles down at Gwen.

"Do you want me to put that on for you?" She gestures toward the locket clutched in the girl's right hand. The child looks up at her, confused for a moment, and then nods her head. Doctor Thompson takes the locket and fastens it gently around the girl's neck, making sure not to get it tangled with the medical tubes around her face.

"Are you feeling better today?" Renee asks when the girl smiles, contented.

"I am Gwen. My family is gone, and I have no home. My feet are all better now. I am hungry. Where am I? Who are you? I want to leave now," Gwen rattles off in response.

The Doctor only hears, "*Me Gwen, femitie goona e me noni dwella. Mane fetta cura longa betta ou. Me henger. Ere me? Whoetta uon? Me levetta ou.*"

Renee smiles down at her and pats the child on the head.

While studying medicine at Berkley, the Doctor minored in foreign languages. She considers herself a gifted linguist. Despite this education, the Doctor finds this child's way of speech peculiar. The closest thing it resembles is baby talk. She can't identify the girl's nationality from looking at her either. Her skin is pale and creamy like milk, so she could be Caucasian, yet she has exotic green and yellow cat-like eyes that could've been Asian if not for the color, mixed with her jet-black hair, which suggests a Latin or Asian heritage. The Doctor knows for sure that she is a beautiful little girl. There is no doubt in Renee's mind that she will grow up to be a gorgeous woman someday, the kind of woman others will stop to notice.

The mystery surrounding this child puzzles Renee. It has been more than forty-eight hours since she appeared, yet the police have turned up nothing. They found only her other shoe and her footprints in the snow. Luckily, there has been no fresh snowfall. The police followed her tracks to find out where she came from but to no avail. The tracks suddenly stopped, as if the girl had fallen from the sky and landed in that very spot.

Her description has been sent out over the police radio. A picture taken in the hospital was attached to missing child flyers and sent to every station in the state. She was even featured in a bulletin on the six o'clock news. Still, no one called in. They have no leads, no clues, nothing at all. *It is as if the girl simply appeared out of the snow.*

The girl looks up at her and then points to her bandaged feet. They sit in a sling to elevate them. Renee is just about to tell the girl the sad news about her feet, even though she knows the little thing can't comprehend. When she notices the girl's feet move, her breath catches in her throat. She hurries over and unwraps the bandages carefully. Her eyes well up in astonishment as the fabric reveals the mystery within.

"Oh, my… that's impossible!" Just hours ago, the toes and half of both feet were completely black with frostbite; the feet had been stiff and without feeling. Now they are pink, soft, and perfectly healthy.

To emphasize this point, the girl wiggles her toes, laughing.

"*Dah-Day-Wente!*" she exclaims in her pretty little voice, pointing to her feet, face beaming with triumph.

"What? I don't know what that means. It's… it's impossible." Renee grabs the girl's medical chart and flips through it quickly despite knowing everything already in the file. *There has to be an explanation. Maybe they had the wrong diagnosis.* The damage to both feet was so severe that she and her colleagues agreed that amputation was the best course of action. *For her condition to go from one extreme to the next like this is just impossible,* Renee tells herself. A shiver danced down her spine.

One of the nurses on duty enters the room, making her rounds. When she sees the girl is awake and the stunned look on Renee's face, she immediately runs to the Doctor's side.

"Is something wrong, Doctor?" the nurse asks urgently. "Should I call for more help?"

"Who checked her bandages last?" Renee questions, trying to make her voice sound calm and professional.

"I did. Why?" The nurse glances at the girl's immaculate feet. "Oh!" The nurse exclaims, dropping a bedpan on the floor with a metallic clang.

Gwen still wiggles her toes with glee. *"Dah-Day-Wente! Dah-Day-Wente!"* she sings out, her pleasure showing from her head to her toes. She laughs, smiling, radiating pride as if she had just learned a new trick.

* * * * *

After all the tests are run twice, Renee has no choice but to accept that the impossible has genuinely happened. The news of the girl's miraculous recovery sweeps through the hospital like wildfire. Everyone on the staff and some patients come to see the miracle for themselves. The pretty little girl awes all. Some claim she must be an angel, that God has blessed her. Renee doesn't know what to think. As a doctor, she has dedicated her life to the pursuits of science and medicine. *Things like miracles don't exist.* But no scientific explanation can be reached. Ultimately, the hospital releases the perfectly healthy child to the authorities.

Renee knows something is different about this girl. Why this child unsettles her so, she can't quite explain. An unnatural feeling has taken residence in her gut—a feeling she can't seem to dislodge with all the logic in the world.

"Where will you be taking her?" Renee asks Mrs. Hewitt, the middle-aged social worker who has come to take the girl. The child stands beside Mrs. Hewitt, looking at them intensely as if trying to read their lips.

"She'll be put temporarily in the care of the sisters at the St. Paul's Catholic Orphanage until her family can be located," Hewitt replies matter-of-factly.

"Ah, God willing, that will be very soon." Renee offers. Smiling, Renee pats the child on the shoulder in farewell. *The girl seems very confused by the concept of a handshake.* The child just smiles uncertainly up at her. *I doubt she has any idea what's happening. How terrible it must be for her to be lost and have no way to communicate.*

"Good day, Doctor Thompson." The social worker gives Renee's hand a brisk shake. Before she can turn away, however, Renee speaks again.

"Do you know by chance if they've found a replacement for Doctor Stevens as the orphanage's physician? I remember hearing that he was retiring soon."

"Not that I have heard. Might you be interested in volunteering your services, Doctor?"

"Now that you mention it, I think I shall."

"I'll tell the sisters to expect a call from you." Mrs. Hewitt smiles politely before taking the raven-haired child by the hand leading her away.

As she watches them disappear from view down the hall, Renee thinks over her choice. If she takes the position, she would be required to visit the orphanage regularly to do checkups at their in-house clinic. There would be no compensation for her time. Not to mention that it would be additional responsibilities to her already busy schedule. *At least I can keep an eye on the girl.* Something demands that she do this. Turning into her office, she goes straight to the phone on her desk. *All I know is there is science and the unexplained. One way or another, I will solve the mystery of this nameless miracle child.*

CHAPTER TWO

Marianne January

The last few days of Gwen's life seemed like a circus of never-ending faces. She's been pulled this way and that, not knowing which way is up or down. After the commotion at the hospital, a profoundly serious and stoic face woman called Mrs. Hewitt came to take her to someplace called an "orphanage."

The social worker Mrs. Hewitt is a skinny, tall lady with a plain pinched face and short graying hair. A nasty bitterness hovers around her like a dark cloud of discontent as she maneuvers the stirring wheel, eyes plastered on the road ahead of her. She doesn't bother speaking to the child.

That's fine. Gwen shrugged. *I wouldn't know what she was saying.* Gwen rides the middle seat of the large, noisy metal contraption; the woman referred to as a station wagon. Before coming to this strange place, she hadn't seen anything like it. As far as she can remember, which isn't much, she and her mother had never traveled in such a manner. She marvels at the wonders around her seen through the glass window as they ride through town. Everything she sees is strange, mysterious, and wonderful to her. The city is unlike anything she has ever seen. The roads, the vehicles, the buildings, and even the people look foreign and magical. She can't decide where to look first. When they pull up in front of the orphanage, an old, turn-of-the-century mansion on the outskirts of town, she feels overwhelmed by all the dissimilarities to her world.

She is beginning to pick up a few words in these people's strange language. She now understands the basic meaning of the words: girl, child, lost, help, name, you, strange, miracle, impossible, feet, parents, and orphan.

Little Gwen looks out the glass windshield at the mansion before her. She will be living here in this imposing old building. *For how long?* This is the orphanage she gathers. This is where lost unwanted children like her stay.

Maybe I can talk to the other children better than the grown-ups, Gwen hopes.

The social worker gets out of her car and walks around to open the door for the newest tenant of St. Paul's. Gwen steps out, bringing along a red duffle bag. A present from the nurses at the hospital. They filled it with clothing and sanitary items they collected on her behalf. Gwen wears her old clothes. The yellow dress and green hooded jacket have been washed and mended, making her feel fresh and new. Her stockings were beyond repair, so she went without them. However, thanks to law enforcement's thorough investigation of the woods, she now has both of her shoes.

The bag is much too big for Gwen's small frame. Gwen is about to attempt to ask her current guardian for help with her bag when she realizes the lady is already headed up the stairs of the building. Quickly the child drapes the strap over her shoulder awkwardly. It takes considerable effort not to fall on her face as Gwen wabbles up the steps. Mrs. Hewitt waits for Gwen to join her at the massive double doors of the institution, not once looking down at her.

The lady wraps her fist against the dark mahogany wood three times before someone finally answers.

A pleasant-looking middle-aged woman opens the door in a black nun's habit. She smiles at the girl, nodding in acknowledgment as the social worker speaks. After exchanging words, the social worker introduces the new woman as Sister Debbie Bernard. The nun turns to Gwen and holds out a hand. At first, Gwen hesitates, but both ladies insist and gesture that she goes inside. Gwen takes Sister Bernard's hand, who leads her into the dark foreboding building. To Gwen's surprise, the social worker doesn't follow them. Instead, Mrs. Hewitt has already turned back to her car, with no backward glance in farewell. Quickly Gwen's newest guardian closes the door.

As the sister leads her down the long dark, paneled wood corridor, their footsteps echo on the parquet floor. Gwen can't help feeling a bit abandoned. Every time she meets someone new, it isn't long before they pass her on to someone else. Gwen hopes to stay in this place for a long while. She is already getting tired of coming and going.

Sister Bernard leads her into a large office at the end of the hall, where three other nuns await them. After entering, Sister Bernard gestures for Gwen to take the chair in front of the large desk. Directly behind them, a picture window looks out onto a courtyard where children play. With a sigh of relief, Gwen peels the bag off and places the duffle by the chair, before climbing into the seat. Sister Bernard then speaks to the other three nuns. She addresses the woman sitting behind the desk. Sister Bernard introduces her as Mother Sullivan. The other two ladies are Sister Mary Shaw and Sister Ellen Whitmore. The three Nuns all bow their heads to her in welcome. Gwen bows back, giving them a shy little smile.

"Thank you, Sister Bernard," Mother Sullivan announces in a calm voice of authority. "You may resume your regular duties now."

To Gwen's horror, Sister Bernard leaves. Gwen furrows her black brows in annoyance. Shaking off the frustration she pulls on the strap of her bag. After a moment's struggle, Gwen manages to get the red duffle up onto her lap. Satisfied, she turns her attention back to the three ladies before her. They seem to be waiting patiently for her to settle back into her chair. Gwen leans back into her seat, drawing comfort from the weight of the bag. *At least it can't leave me.* This sense of ownership settles her nerves.

Each woman in before her is different in every aspect. Sister Mary Shaw is a small, petite, young woman, perhaps in her mid-twenties—pretty, with a rosy-pink complexion, blue eyes, and blonde eyebrows and lashes. Gwen assumes that the woman's hair must be blonde, too, underneath her habit. Sister Ellen Whitmore is tall and thin as a rail, her face old and leathery, making her appear to be in her seventies. She wears a superior look on her face. Her condescending deep brown eyes stare, her brow furrowed tightly as she scrutinizes Gwen.

"So, this is the lost child from the woods?" Sister Ellen Whitmore asks rhetorically while the other two women nod in affirmation.

"What is your name, child?" Mother Sullivan questions. She is a large woman, tall in form and stature. She would be considered plump if it weren't for her remarkable height. Mother Sullivan looks to be in her fifties or sixties. Her face is neither handsome nor plain, just severe. She holds herself erect as if her spine is made of a steel rod. She has the demeanor of a queen.

"*Me Gwen, mane femitie goona. Whoetta uon?*" Gwen replies hesitantly.

The nuns look at each other, sharing the same questioning expression.

"They said she didn't speak a word of English, but I'll confess I didn't believe it," Sister Whitmore says in a dull drone.

"I am afraid we shall have to start from the beginning with this one," Sister Mary Shaw says in her soft, honey voice. Mother Superior nods while her eyes examine Gwen's face intently, searching for a flaw.

"With God's blessing, her relatives will come forth soon. However, since no one can understand a word she says, we shall have to give her a temporary name for the time being," the Mother Superior announces.

"Forgive me, Mother; I am still new to St. Paul's. What do we usually do in this situation?" Sister Mary Shaw inquires of her superior.

"We haven't had a case of true abandonment in some time, but, typically, the child will be given a proper name and a birthday based on the day they were first admitted into the orphanage," Sister Whitmore instructs, her low voice sounding bored.

"What letter did we leave off on, Sister Whitmore?" The Mother Superior asks.

Immediately, the thin old Nun hurries to a file cabinet next to the window, quickly retrieving a vanilla file from one of the drawers. She returns to the desk, laying the file open. Mother Superior pulls a pair of reading glasses from her pocket and scans the document.

"Ah. We left off with L, so that brings us to M," she announces, picking up a pencil and handing it along with the file back to Sister Whitmore.

"We already have plenty of Mary's and Maria's. What other names might you suggest, Mother?" Sister Whitmore inquires after reading the list of names in the file.

"Have we currently a Marianne?" Sister Shaw speaks up, peering at the document over Sister Whitmore's shoulder. Sister Whitmore immediately shuts the file, giving the younger sister a stern look.

"No, Marianne," she answers.

"Very well, then. And since she has no family name, we shall call her Marianne January for now," the Mother Superior dictates while Sister Whitmore scribbles it down on the ledger of names.

"And her date of birth, Mother?" Sister Shaw inquires.

"Today is January 15th, but if my memory hasn't failed me, we already have Stacey, David, and Angela with birthdays today." The Mother's superior looks at the thin woman standing beside her with a quirked eyebrow.

"That is correct, Mother," Sister Whitmore replies, not needing to check the records.

"How about the day she was found, then? That was the twelfth. I remember reading about it in the newspaper yesterday," Sister Shaw pipes in.

"Excellent suggestion, Sister Shaw. Put down January twelfth as her temporary birthday, Sister Whitmore." Sister Whitmore makes the note in the file and then looks up at the girl. Her eyes narrow.

"You are now called Marianne, child. You will answer to this name only and do as you are told." Sister Whitmore addresses Gwen with a firm set to her brow that says *nonsense won't be tolerated.*

Looking at the older woman, wide-eyed Gwen understands nothing.

"Give her time, Sister. This all must be too overwhelming for her still. I'm sure she'll get along fine once she is settled. I will personally keep an eye on her," Sister Shaw volunteers.

Sister Whitmore huffs in response.

With the significant business concluded, the three women discuss the particulars of the child's care. They decide her sleeping arrangement and who should be her tutor until Marianne catches up with the other children her age.

Gwen plays nervously with the zipper on the duffel bag in her lap. She listens intently to everything they say, willing her mind to understand their strange tongue. In this state, she sees images flashing before her mind's eye. Different images greet her as she gazes at each woman before her.

With the tall, skinny, wrinkled, old Whitmore, Gwen sees visions of the dorm rooms, the cafeteria, the classrooms, and the chapel. She even sees the grounds of the property. A feeling of distaste and arrogance saturates her being.

When she looks at the lovely young Sister Shaw, she sees images of the other children doing various things, from reading in class to running and playing in the courtyard. A feeling of gentleness and genuine love radiates from her.

Last, she looks upon the severe and intimidating Mother Sullivan. Gwen sees a collection of things from the woman's life. She sees the farm she grew up on, her family, her school, and the places she visited before becoming a nun. The images flutter through Gwen's mind, both familiar and unexplainable. Overall, she feels a deep, depressing emptiness from the Mother, a void in her soul that nothing but the church and her belief in God has filled.

As the nuns continue talking, she sees images of herself in the visions. Then realization sinks in; *I can see what they think.* Feeling relief in finally comprehending all the images she sees around everyone, her shoulders relax. She is the only one who can do this, or else someone would've figured out her name by now. *Can I use this to find out what they're saying?*

Suddenly, Sister Mary Shaw approaches, smiling sweetly.

"You're to come with me now, dear Marianne. I'll show you to your room," she says, addressing Gwen as if she understands her. The lady beckons her as she walks out of the room. Gwen follows quickly, eager to get away from the other two nuns. She already feels more at ease with Sister Shaw than anyone else she has yet met. Gwen nearly stumbles under the weight of the duffle as she catches up to Sister Shaw. The lady's brows furrow in concern. "Oh, you poor thing, here let me carry your bag for you." Quickly the young woman slides the strap off Gwen's little shoulder and hefts the duffle onto herself. With a reassuring smile Sister Shaw reaches a hand toward Gwen. Smiling appreciatively, the child takes her hand and the two continue further into the institution together.

Sister Mary Shaw shows Gwen about the orphanage, speaking nonstop about protocol, explaining this and that about procedure and operations. Not understanding a word, Gwen nods and tries her best to keep up with the lady's vigorous pace. Gwen tries to interpret all the woman's thoughts, but they fly by like leaves swirling in the wind.

Finally, Gwen is shown to her bedroom.

Four single beds sit in the room, each with its dresser beside them. Sister Shaw points to the bed nearest the window. Gwen takes this to mean that this is to be her bed. She also gathers that she must share the room with three other girls. Gwen has no time to unpack her things or get settled, for the nun quickly drops her duffle on the bed and turns, indicating for Gwen to follow, leaving promptly. Little Gwen, confused, hurries after the lady. She's afraid to let Sister Shaw get too far ahead of her, for fear of getting lost in this massive maze of stone and wood. To her relief the woman awaits her in the hallway, ready to take her hand once more.

Sister Shaw leads her outside to a courtyard where dozens of children play sports or talk in groups. Sister Shaw indicates that Gwen should join the other children.

"Now, Marianne, when the bell rings, follow all the other children into the cafeteria. That's where we eat breakfast, lunch, and dinner." Sister Shaw bends down to talk to Gwen, instructing her in a soft, tender voice. "Now go on with you. Make some friends, and I'll see you at lunch." She smiles. When the sister turns to leave, Gwen goes to follow her. The nun quickly closes the doors behind her, leaving Gwen staring at the old wooden doors, feeling wholly abandoned for the third time today.

Slowly she walks out into the middle of the courtyard, feeling the children's minds around her all at once, the hum of their collective thoughts overpowering. Several of them stop to watch her. Their stares seem to make Gwen's skin itch. They look at her, and she instantly sees what they are thinking. They are unkind things, dark feelings, and emotions that hurt as if yelled at her. The other girls dislike her, from the youngest, a year younger than Gwen, to the eldest, about fifteen. Something about her bothers them.

Perplexed, Gwen tries to understand why so many think she is pretty and then hate her for it. She searches the images transmitted from the boys and finds these even more unwelcoming. They are dark thoughts, strange pictures of touching, pushing, kicking, and feelings of pain, need, and loneliness.

I can't understand these people at all. She wants to give up, turn and run away, or find someplace to hide from the awful things she sees in these children's minds. Then she notices a peculiar boy.

A boy sits alone on a tree branch in the walnut tree near the courtyard's edge. He is large, with black, wavy hair hanging down in his face and around his shoulders. His golden eyes are all but hidden behind the curtain of his hair. The sleeves are torn off his blue t-shirt, with holes worn through the knees of the dark blue jeans that are much too short for his long legs. His toes protrude from a pair of old tennis shoes like homemade sandals. His demeanor is timid and afraid.

Curious, she walks straight to the tree, ignoring the other children. At the foot of the tree, staring up the thick trunk, she peers straight up at the atypical boy. His mind is different from the rest. Something about him tugs at her soul, calling her to him. He radiates feelings of emptiness, loneliness, and sadness.

She understands exactly how he feels. Compelled by a new sense of kinship, Gwen removes her green coat and drops it at the foot of the tree. She reaches above her head, grabbing hold of the lowest tree branch. It is challenging to climb in her little yellow dress, but she doesn't let it stop her. Some of the children yell up at her. It's probably better that she can't understand them because their words sound unpleasant.

The commotion below finally gets the boy's attention in the tree, for he stirs, looking all around him at the children below. Then, his eyes rest on Gwen. He stares at her wide-eyed as she climbs until she finally heaves herself onto his branch.

Her dress is ripped, and some of the lace is tattered. Her messy hair has twigs and tangled leaves, with her arms and legs scraped from the excursion. Nevertheless, she is beautiful. Her eyes glow from the exercise, showing green and yellow all at once. She gives him a dazzling smile. Straddling the tree limb, she scoots closer to him until they are face to face.

She reaches out a hand to him. Dumbfounded, he stares at it until he finally takes her hand in his. She gives it a vigorous shake sideways, sense this is what she's observed others do in this place. Reaching into the collar of her dress, she retrieves her oval-shaped locket. She holds it out for him to see. Pointing to the engraving, she says, "Gwenevere. Gwen." She points to herself emphatically.

The boy stares at her mouth agape.

He appears older than she, maybe nine or ten. He is tall and bulky with broad shoulders and chest. She senses his discomfort and panic at her presence.

Smiling, she leans closer to him and brushes the hair out of his face. Underneath the thick curtain of black, wavy hair, she sees the light brown skin and bushy eyebrows in the same black color as his long, thick hair. His golden eyes seem out of place with the rest of his visage, but Gwen sees honesty radiating from them.

She smiles at him again, feeling happy to have made a friend. She points to the boy, enthusiastically asking. "How long have you been here? What's your name?" in her own tongue. At first, he looks at her, surprised, but he slowly begins to smile. It is a strange, awkward smile, but it sends a sensation of warmth through her.

"They call me Adam here." To Gwen's astonishment, he speaks the words in her native tongue. Now it is her turn to look surprised.

"You talk like me!" she exclaims.

"Yes. How do you know to talk like that?" he asks. "I thought I was the only one. I can't remember where I learned it, but it's normal for me."

"My mother taught it to me. What do they speak here?" Gwen inquires, barely able to contain the joy bubbling up within her. "I don't understand it."

"They call it English. Most everyone here speaks it," he replies, running a hand through his hair and tucking the strands behind his ear.

"Where did you come from? Where is your mother?"

"I don't know." He shrugs. "I can't remember. I was dropped off at the orphanage when I was a toddler." His voice becomes sad and empty. Gwen feels his loneliness start to engulf him.

"My family is gone, too. I have no home."

Adam nods in understanding. He senses his impulse to hug her or reach out his hand to pat her on the back, but he still feels awkward.

"Why do you sit in this tree?" Gwen asks in a cheerful voice.

"The other children make fun of me because I am slow. They think I am dumb because it is hard for me to learn their language." Adam replies, "I'd rather be up here alone than down there with them," he adds.

"Oh. Well, I think it's pretty up here. I like how everyone else looks so small. It makes me feel like a giant," Gwen answers, again trying to distract the boy from his melancholy thoughts.

Adam is about to speak when suddenly the bell in the tower tolls.

"What's that?" Gwen asks, surprised by the strange sound. She covers her ears on impulse.

"The bell tower. It is lunchtime. Come on. I'll help you back down." He stands up, balances himself on the limb, and reaches down to help Gwen.

"I can do it myself," she answers confidently. Before Adam can protest, she leaps off of the branch. Falling downward, she catches one of the lower branches and then swings herself down to the next. Although she is still relatively high, she drops down, landing on her feet in a crouch on the ground below the tree's foot. She straightens up, smiling triumphantly back up at Adam.

His mouth gapes open. She breaks into a peal of laughter. Recovering from his shock, he looks around the courtyard to check and see if anyone is looking. By now, most of the children have already gone inside. The rest head for the doors, their backs turned to the walnut tree.

Gwen is startled when suddenly Adam jumps from the tree, falling straight down to the ground in a blur, passing perfectly between tree limbs to land right next to her at the base of the massive walnut. Gwen can't help but laugh. Adam smiles shyly, seeming glad to have impressed her.

"Adam! Marianne! Don't dilly-dally. Everyone's waiting for you."

They both turn to see Sister Mary Shaw at the door, beckoning them emphatically. Gwen picks up her green coat, and they hurry across the courtyard to the nun together. She gives them both a half-hearted reproachful look before ushering them inside.

After following the young nun through several corridors, they finally enter a large dining hall. Hundreds of children stand next to several tables arranged in three rows the length of the hall. At one end, doors lead into the kitchen. On the opposite end, another long table runs perpendicular to the other tables where the nuns, a priest, and the Mother Superior stand waiting.

Sister Shaw gives Gwen a gentle push forward before taking her place with the other nuns. Adam shyly takes Gwen's hand and leads her to the closest table. Blushing, he quickly releases her hand. Gwen goes to sit, but Adam stops her and points to the nuns at the end of the room. She notices all the children are watching the nuns, waiting for some signal.

Mother Superior nods her head curtly and takes her seat. Everyone follows suit, moving simultaneously. The kitchen's double doors swing open as if on cue. Several young women enter with serving trays balanced on one arm. These teens hurry around the room, handing out plates of food to everyone. The nun's table is done first, and then the children.

Gwen realizes that she hasn't eaten today as her stomach growls at the sight of the food. She had been given breakfast in the hospital but felt too nervous about going to the orphanage to swallow a bite. The food smells delicious, and now that she has found a friend, Gwen feels more at ease in this strange new world. When someone sets a plate of food down before her, she immediately reaches for the roll on her plate.

"Wait," Adam whispers. "We must wait for Father O'Brien to bless the food, and then we pray. After that, we eat," he explains to Gwen.

"Pray? What's that?" she asks, thoroughly confused. Adam smiles, enjoying the incredulous expression on her face.

"Don't worry. I'll help you learn everything you need to know," he says, reassuring her. "They have a lot of rules here."

Gwen smiles in appreciation and patiently folds her arms to resist the temptation to grab the food and duck under the table to devour it.

The serving girls head for the kitchen when the food is passed out, and the priest sitting next to the Mother Superior stands. The older man with warm smiling eyes wears all black with a white-collar. Gwen assumes that he is Father O'Brien. He faces the congregation of children and bows his head. Immediately, everyone else in the room follows his example.

Watching what Adam does, Gwen bows her head but keeps her eyes open as Father O'Brien begins to offer the blessing over the food. Gwen peeks out through her thick black lashes as the priest speaks in a soft yet firm voice, the meaning of the words evident in his tone of voice. Whatever he's saying makes him feel happy, humble, and respectful. Everyone in the room acts relatively quiet and reserved as if they are doing something important. Father O'Brien says, "Amen," and then everyone repeats the word at the end of the prayer. Gwen doesn't join not understanding what any of it means.

Once the prayer ends, everyone opens their eyes, including Father O'Brien, to eat their midday meal. Gwen reaches for the roll and tears into it with her teeth, chewing the warm, delectable bread with immense pleasure.

Adam and Gwen share little bits of conversation between them as they eat. During the meal, Gwen learns that Adam's full name is Adam Matthews, that he has been at the orphanage for almost six years, and that his birthday is March 21st. He calls it his false birthday because it wasn't the actual date of his birth but instead the day he was found on the orphanage's front doorstep. Adam also tells her that he is several grades behind in school and can't read or write like the other children his age.

"Can you read?" Adam asks. "You know, where you look at words in a book and know what they say to tell a story?"

"I don't know," Gwen replies. "I was in the hospital, and now I'm here. Don't know much else."

"Don't you remember anything?" Adam asks curiously.

Gwen shakes her head solemnly. Try as she might, Gwen can't recollect anything of the last five years. She vaguely remembers a fire and knows that she has no family left. All her memories of that family have faded to shadows, incomprehensible images of a broken past too painful to grasp. She has to start a new life—this is all in which she is confident.

At the end of the meal, as the servant girls clear the table, Sister Bernard stands, commanding the attention of everyone in the room.

"Children, as you may have heard, we have a new addition to St. Paul's. We do not yet know how long she will stay with us, but we would ask you all to make her feel welcome." She speaks, making eye contact with several children, her voice cheerful and kind. With a nod to Sister Mary Shaw, she continues. While she speaks, Sister Shaw hurries across the room to Gwen's side.

"Come with me, Marianne," she whispers, taking Gwen by the hand and leading her toward the front of the dining hall. She helps Gwen stand in front of the large table at the head of the room. She faces the multitude of children before her. Gwen holds tight to Sister

Shaw's hand, feeling strangely afraid of the things she might see if she looks into so many minds at once.

"Children, this is Marianne January. She is approximately five years old, and her new birthday is January 12th. She doesn't yet speak, so please be patient with her. Sister Shaw will tutor her until she can enter regular classes. Say hello to Marianne, children," Sister Bernard orders.

In unison, the children say, "Hello, Marianne," the sound of which makes Gwen shiver. She doesn't like being the center of attention at all. She doesn't understand why everyone keeps calling her Marianne. She opens her mouth to correct this misunderstanding but is cut off.

"You may go back to your seat now, Marianne," Sister Bernard informs her, bowing her head and smiling at her. Assuming that Gwen doesn't understand anything, she says, the nun asks Sister Shaw to escort Gwen back to her seat with a wave of her hand. Gwen tries to explain her name to Sister Shaw, but the nun just smiles at her sweetly. Having done her duty, Sister Shaw immediately returns to her seat at the head table.

Once sitting at the table next to Adam again, Gwen feels the anxiety welled up inside her fade.

The children are dismissed from their afternoon classes. The nuns stand, several leaving to resume their regular duties while the rest make a line at the front of the head table. Gwen watches as the children form several single-file lines in front of the nuns.

"What are they doing?"

"It's time to go to our classes. They're the teachers." Adam points to the line of nuns. "We must get in line with our class in front of our teacher. The teachers lead us to our classroom when all the students are in their classes.

"Which is your class?" Gwen asks Adam.

"We're in the special class for those behind the others. Sister Shaw is our teacher. She's nice. I don't mind not being able to read as long as I can stay with Sister Shaw," Adam smiles.

Gwen looks to the front of the room to see Sister Shaw receiving instruction from Mother Superior. Then, the Mother leaves the room with Father O'Brien.

"Come on; I'll show you where our class lines up." Tugging on Gwen's coat sleeve, Adam leads her across the room. They are the last children to line up, getting a few disapproving glances from the nuns. A stern look from Sister Whitmore silences the excited chatter from the children. Gwen notices the other children in their class, two girls and three boys of various ages. She is the youngest in the class.

All the classes wait for Sister Shaw to finish talking to the Mother Superior and take her place. Once she stands in her appointed place, the sister closest to the door leads her class out of the room. After that, each class departs one at a time, going down the line until it is finally Gwen's class's turn to go.

Gwen tugs on Adam's sleeve as they walk the halls toward their classroom.

"Adam, why are they calling me Marianne?"

"I was wondering that, too. Didn't you tell them your name is Gwen?" he whispers back.

"I tried," she replies, frustrated.

"Oh, well, I guess they gave you a new name. They did it with me, too."

"Oh, that's why you don't look like an Adam," Gwen whispers.

"What would you call me?" he asks over his shoulder.

"Don't know, but I'll give you a new name," she replies.

"I'll still call you Gwen if you want."

Gwen nods, pleased. She resolves that they can call her some made-up name all they want. She may be in a new world, and her life from before may be gone forever, but she will never let go of what she knows to be true. *I am Gwenevere, and I will never be Marianne January.*

CHAPTER THREE

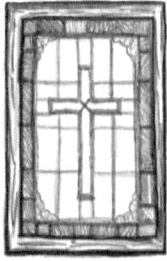

Endless Nightmares

Sunlight streams through the stain-glass window above, causing rainbow-colored lights to dance upon Gwen's notebook as she sits quietly at her desk. All around her, classmates sit hunched over, heads down, busy scribbling notes or reading passages from their textbooks. Beside her, Adam bruises himself over a simple math problem. He senses her eyes upon him and looks up.

The answer is forty-nine, Gwen tells him mentally, trying to explain how she solved the equation, but she didn't do any of the work herself. Over the last few months, she discovered that anything could be learned quickly if you can read minds. The real trick is discerning random things interrupting a train of thought. Then there is making sense of more than one mind at once. Shutting out the rest of the world to hear herself think is even more challenging. She had also discovered that she could talk to Adam inside his mind. This had startled her new friend at first but quickly he got used to the idea. Now they converse freely this way, only speaking aloud when they must to others.

"Thanks." Adam smiles before going on to the next problem.

Gwen looks down at her notebook, the assignment is complete, and every problem is solved perfectly. She has shown considerable progress in her brief time at St. Paul's, so much so that her teacher, Miss Shaw, mentioned having her transferred to the next grade level. This means she will have to get used to another teacher. Not that there's anything wrong with most of the nuns. They all seem genuinely nice. None are half as warm and kind as Sister Shaw, not to mention Gwen cannot imagine having Sister Whitmore as a teacher. She shudders involuntarily at the thought. Besides Adam, none of the other children has warmed up to Gwen. Adam will be left behind to struggle without her if she advances to the next class.

With a sigh, Gwen picks up her pencil and erases a few answers from her worksheet, rubbing out the correct answers to replace them with incomplete ones.

Satisfied, she begins drawing flowers in the margin of the paper. Running out of space, she opens her notebook to a blank page and begins sketching Adam. He looks almost comical with his brow furrowed and chin resting in his hand, glaring at his notebook as if staring down a fierce opponent. Gwen laughs and then looks around the room for another subject to draw.

Sitting at her desk at the head of the class, Sister Shaw's black and white habit gives an interesting contrast against the green surface of the chalkboard behind her. One errant strand of blonde hair escapes her headdress, draping across her face as she writes neatly in her journal.

Gwen marvels at her. Her every feeling and thought is open before Gwen's mind like a picture book speaking directly to her soul. She soon finds herself caught up in Mary Shaw's childhood memories. Before she knows it, Gwen is approaching her teacher's desk. The nun looks up at the young pupil.

"Do you... dream of her?" Gwen asks hesitantly, awkwardly speaking the unfamiliar words.

For a moment, Mary Shaw stares at Gwen, flabbergasted. "Why, Marianne, you can speak after all." She smiles at her brightly. "Now, what did you want to ask me?" the nun asks in a hushed voice to not disturb the rest of the class.

"Your mother died, and you were still a little girl. You dreamed of her a lot then. You woke up at night crying. I dream of my mother, too. And I cry, too. Do you still dream of her? Does it still make you cry?" Gwen asks tentatively, forcing the words out for fear of losing her nerve. Sister Shaw's face has gone ashen; her mouth is agape. Her mind goes blank with utter shock.

"Marianne, how did you... who told you about my mother?"

"No one. You were thinking about it and writing it down in your book," Gwen replies with a puzzled expression.

"Marianne, did you read it in my book? Did you look over my shoulder and read what I was writing?" Sister Shaw asks in a patient tone, obvious discomfort in her soft voice.

"No. When I look at people, I see what they think. I saw you thinking of her and when she died. She was old when you were born.

She had silver hair and blue eyes. You were the youngest in a big family and just older than me when she died of something called cancer?" Gwen says the last word as if asking a question since it is a term she has never heard before. She tries hard to think of her past and can't recall if anyone died of anything called cancer back where she comes from.

The nun's face goes even paler till she looks as if she might faint, her mouth working in unspoken words, her eyes wide.

"Are you sick?" the little girl asks, putting a hand on the young woman's shoulder to shake her awake from her trance.

Taking a deep breath, Mary Shaw closes her eyes a moment to collect herself. Gwen knows what the nun will ask even before the lady opens her eyes or mouth to form the question. "All right, Marianne, let's say I believe you. If you can read my mind, then tell me what—"

"Caramel," Gwen replies, cutting the nun short. "When you were a kid, your pet rabbit was named Caramel. Your brother ran it over with a truck on accident. After that, you made a pet of one of the chickens. You called it Honey. Your parents killed it and served it for Christmas dinner later. You were sad about it and refused to eat for days. That's when you stopped eating meat. You call yourself a vegetarian?" Again, a term Gwen's never heard before.

Sister Shaw's disbelief fades from utter shock to some semblance of acceptance. She smiles uncertainly at Gwen.

"A vegetarian is someone who doesn't eat meat, dear."

"Oh." Gwen thinks about this a moment before replying. "But

meat tastes so good."

Sister Shaw laughs despite herself. "Yes, to some, meat does taste good, but to others, it's—" She trails off, trying to think of a way to explain it.

"Oh, I get it. You don't like hurting animals, even eating them. It makes you sick?"

"Yes, it's something like that." Suddenly, the absurdity of the conversation hits the nun. She forces herself to think clearly and objectively about this unusual discovery in her new pupil.

"Marianne, do you know what telepathy is?"

Gwen shakes her head but instantly discerns the meaning from Sister Shaw's thoughts and blurts out, "Oh, you mean someone like me who can see what people think."

"Yes. How long have you been able to do this?"

Gwen shrugs. "It started when I met the couple that took me to the hospital."

"And you've been doing this ever since?" Gwen nods. "Can you read everyone's thoughts?"

"Yes. It doesn't always make sense, though. The things I see are sometimes confusing," Gwen explains as she struggles with the words that are harder to pronounce.

"And you didn't speak before because…?"

"You speak differently than me. But I've been listening and learning what you're all saying from your thoughts. I didn't want to say it wrong, so I didn't say anything."

"But you talk to Adam. I see you two chattering away all the time."

"He understands the way I talk. He can talk that way, too. He's been trying to help me learn English."

"And you're helping him, too? I've noticed he's doing much better in school since you came around." Gwen shrugs it off like it's no big deal. "How are you able to do that?"

Gwen looks down at the floor a bit sheepishly. "I've been telling him the answers and how everything should be done."

"You mean you've been helping him cheat? Are you whispering the answers to him during class or passing him notes?"

"No, I just think something, and he hears me in his head."

The young nun's eyebrows shoot up at that. "Oh," is all she can manage.

"Is that a bad thing?" Gwen asks.

"It sort of is. Adam needs to learn to do things for himself. You're not always going to be around to tell him the answers."

Gwen gives her an uncertain look at this but nods in agreement. "Marianne, have you told anyone else about this *talent*?"

"No, just you and Adam know. Should I tell Father O'Brien or the Mother Superior?" Gwen stumbles over the syllables in the word "superior" but manages to get the word out all the same.

"No, dear. It is best that you don't for now. I should tell you… telepathy is very uncommon. Most people don't even believe it exists. I've heard claims to the contrary, but it's never been proven."

"You believe me, right?" Gwen asks.

For a brief moment, doubt wafts through the young nun's

thoughts. Only the look of complete innocence and forthrightness on her pupil's face dispels this. Sister Shaw smiles and nods yes.

"I think you should try to learn not to do it if you can," she adds quickly. "A person's thoughts are private, and everyone should be able to keep those thoughts to themselves. Sometimes we think things we don't mean and would never say aloud. And we shouldn't be judged for those things, as long as we don't speak them and don't act upon them."

Gwen looks at her, a bit perplexed.

"Do you understand?" Sister Shaw takes one of Gwen's tiny hands in hers affectionately.

"Yes. I am trying. Sometimes it hurts to be in a room full of people. Everyone is thinking at once, and it makes my headache. I'll keep trying." A sudden thought occurs to her. "I'm sorry I looked into your past and saw your private thoughts. I didn't mean to."

"It's all right. You can always come to me if you need to talk to someone about your mother and your dreams." Gwen smiles brightly at this. Glancing up at the clock on the wall, Sister Shaw adds, "Now go back to your seat, Marianne. Class is almost over."

The girl turns to leave, then pauses a moment. She turns back to her teacher.

"Oh, and I renamed Adam. He's Raven now. He likes that better."

Sister Shaw gives her a conspiratorial smile. "Like the Edgar Allan Poe tale, *The Raven*?" Gwen nods. "I've noticed you like his books a lot." Gwen smiles

"And my name is Gwenevere, not Marianne. Please, call me

Gwen."

Sister Shaw nods slowly. "Okay, when it's just the three of us, I'll call you Gwen and Raven. I'll have to keep calling you Marianne and Adam, among the others."

Gwen sighs, exasperated, but nods agreement and says, "Thanks." Gwen almost skips back to her desk with a heart lighter than air. Raven gives her quizzical looks as she takes her seat.

What was that all about? he thinks.

I'll tell you about it at lunch, she thinks back, giving him a radiant smile. Raven shrugs and goes back to his math.

Maybe this place isn't so bad after all, she thinks. *Perhaps I'll feel at home here now that I have a grown-up on my side.* Gwen feels warmth spread within her as a seed of hope takes root.

* * * * *

The smell of pine hangs thick in the air. Soft soil feels cold under her bare feet as she wanders among the colossal shadows of tree trunks. High above her mid-day sky, sunlight sprinkles down through the leafy canopy. She basks in the warmth of its rays. Peace radiates from the forest as she wanders. She has nowhere to go and nothing better to do than to enjoy her lifelong playmate all around her: nature.

A cold chill comes over her as the symphony of sounds in the woods fade, till she is left alone in utter silence. She looks around, scanning the forest for danger or some sign indicating why she feels so vulnerable and afraid. All looks peaceful and still. Then, a new sound comes to her ears, something unnatural yet wild as anything living.

It starts in the distance, a soft rumbling that grows louder, closer. The sun beats down on her, its heat licking at her skin and making her dizzy. She looks about again, and suddenly, the forest is ablaze. The smell of burning foliage catches in her lungs. She bends over in chest-aching heaves. A cloud of black smoke eats up the beautiful morning sky, hiding the sun. Frantic, she looks for an escape. She spies a patch of blue sky over a flowery meadow just ahead. Coughing, she runs toward the sight. The wildfire rages as her feet try to outrun the deadly natural force.

If I make it to the meadow, I'll be free, she tells herself as she runs and stumbles forward. When she approaches the meadow, she picks up speed, her feet moving so quickly that they barely seem to touch the ground. As she bursts forth from the burning forest, she shoots off into the sky, leaving earth behind to soar into the heavens.

The burning woods and the open meadow quickly become a distant blur as she flies overhead, free, and unbound. Her fear fades in the warmth of the sun above and the cool breeze blowing against her. She laughs with delight as she twirls in the wind and loops in the air. She has never felt so free, so empowered. Smiling, she turns onto her back to gaze at the clouds. She contemplates soaring into them just to find out what clouds are made. A high-pitched scream pierces through the air and breaks her reverie.

Startled, she glances around. Another scream penetrates her ear. Before she can react, another voice joins the first, and then another, building on each other. Each cry of horror pounds against her eardrums. She instinctively puts her hands over her ears, trying to keep out the wails, but the sound can't be deafened. Panic grips her as she realizes that she isn't floating anymore. She's falling.

She grasps for a hold on something. Nothing surrounds her but air. She has nothing to grab hold of that might stop her deadly fall. Horrified, she tries to scream, but her voice is lost amongst the tumult of the phantom children's screams still encircling her. She looks over her shoulder to see the flowery meadow below, quickly growing closer. She'll hit the ground any moment now. She closes her eyes tight to prepare for the impact of death.

* * * * *

"Marianne! Wake up, Marianne!" a woman's voice yells.

She hits an unexpectedly soft surface with a thud, yet the wind still rushes out of her. The impact jolts her awake.

Gwen bolts upright, opening her eyes to a dimly lit bedroom. Confused and out of breath, she looks at the many wide-eyed stares of children and nuns. Lastly, her eyes alight on Mother Superior looming over her bedside in a robe and slippers, hair in a braid hanging over her shoulder, her expression mixed with confusion and fear.

"What's wrong?" Gwen asks after several deep breaths.

"You were floating!" Jill, one of her three roommates, squeals, looking disheveled in her pajamas amongst her wrinkled bedding.

"It's true!" Amy's shrill voice adds. She and Laura, her other roomies, cling to each other in Laura's bed across the room. Several other girls poke their heads in the doorway, chattering, and whispering. Even in her nightgown and bathrobe, Sister Whitmore intimidates and dominates the room so that the other girls dare not enter.

Against her will, Gwen hears the thoughts of those around her.

Freak!

She's not natural. Something's wrong with her!

I'm glad she's not my roommate.

Evil child.

She's got the devil's eyes!

We've got to get rid of her.

She and that boy are nothing but trouble.

I'm not sharing a room with that!

Gwen closes her eyes tight to focus on shutting out the hurtful unwelcome thoughts pushing in on her. They subside after a moment as she forces a mental wall between her mind and the others. Finally, she can think clearly.

"Well, Marianne, do you have anything to say?" Sister Whitmore demands. Gwen's eyes fling open, and she looks at them all, dumbfounded.

"I was just dreaming!" Gwen answers defensively. "Sometimes, I float. What's so wrong with that?"

Mother Sullivan looks down on her with a stern, grim look then turns her eyes to Sister Whitmore. "Sister Whitmore, please send for Father O'Brien."

Sister Whitmore nods, turning toward the girls hovering in the doorway. "Off to bed!" she orders, and, like roaches, the girls flee before her to their various rooms. She leaves the room, and a moment later Sister Shaw enters, dressed in her nightclothes, concern radiating from her as she rushes to Gwen's bedside.

"Mother, what's wrong? Is Gwen—I mean, is Marianne all right?"

"We may have a demon in our midst, Sister, and Marianne may be its unwitting host," Superior Mother answers with all seriousness and gravity. "After all that's occurred over this last year since this child has come to us, it seems very likely she may be possessed."

Sister Mary Shaw looks at her elder in shock.

"Surely, there must be another explanation, Mother. I have spent much time with Marianne, and I can attest that she is a good child. She may have peculiarities and a bit of a temper, but I firmly believe she is not—"

"She is! She is evil!" Jill announces, cutting off Sister Shaw. The two nuns gaze on the other girls, who still tremble, pale-faced and horrified as they look at Gwen.

Gwen forces the red-hot wave of rage in her gut to settle down, returning their stares with a disdainful glare.

Father O'Brien arrives with Sister Whitmore fast on his heels. She closes the door behind them. Father O'Brien looks tired but seems to have taken the time to put on his black suit and white collar, looking just as he always does.

"Now, what is all the fuss about, Mother Sullivan? Sister Whitmore said something about an evil disturbance?" Father O'Brien seems doubtful but becomes grave as he takes in the severe and frightened faces of the women and children around him.

"This child is possessed, Father," Mother Superior informs the priest, pointing at Gwen's chest with her boney, wrinkled finger.

"What evidence do we have of this?" he calmly asks the three nuns.

"She was floating in midair, Father. We saw it with our own eyes, and these girls will testify to have also seen it," Sister Whitmore answers.

Mother Superior nods.

Sister Shaw looks aghast.

"It's true, Father, and it's not the only strange thing she's done," Jill announces. The other two girls add their voices to the accusations, but the father silences them by raising a hand. He turns his gaze on six-year-old Gwen, a sweet, innocent-looking child, her green and yellow eyes still blurry with sleep.

"Now, my child, you've heard your accuser's claims. Is it true?" he asks patiently, no judgment on his face. Gwen peeks a moment into his mind and finds only tolerance and a sense of moral duty in his tired thoughts.

"I'm not evil or possessed. I'm no demon, and I've never seen one either. Sometimes when I sleep, I dream of flying. I can't help it if I float in my sleep. It just happens." Gwen thinks a moment before adding, "Besides, Laura snores in her sleep, Amy swears all the time when the nuns aren't near, and Jill's a thief. No one's calling any of them evil."

"I'm not a thief!" Jill protests.

"She tried to steal my locket!" Gwen shouts.

"And she used her evil voice to force me to give it back!" Jill shouts back, pointing at Gwen and looking at the grown-ups for support.

"So, you admit you stole from Marianne?" the priest asks calmly.

Jill's eyes widen, and her mouth clamps shut as she realizes her mistake.

"She was gonna give it back. She just wanted to see it for a minute," Laura speaks up in her friend's defense before quickly adding, "And I don't snore."

"Did Jill ask Marianne if she could see the locket?" the priest presses Laura.

"Yes, but she said no, of course. She always keeps to herself and only talks to her boyfriend."

Gwen glowers at her with disdain.

"And Jill still took Marianne's most prized possession without permission?"

"That's not the point!" Jill grumbles through clenched teeth. "She's a freak! She made her voice go all funny, and she controlled my mind. She made me give it back against my will. That's not normal. She's the daughter of Satan, I tell you!"

"That's quite enough, young lady," Sister Shaw interrupts with a voice of cold steel, standing up to stare down the three girls. "You will speak with respect in the presence of your elders, and you should not say such things about others when you are not blameless."

"Thank you, Sister Shaw. The children forgot their manners," Mother Sullivan says in a soothing voice. "The Father and I will conduct this interview. You may return to your room, Sister." The young Nun looks to her elder humbly and bows her head as she makes her way to the door.

"Please wait a moment, Sister Shaw, if you will?" Father O'Brien calls her, and she halts by the door to wait patiently. The priest turns to Mother Superior. "Mother, it is far too late to continue looking into this matter tonight. The children need their rest and if there is any threat of an evil presence here, I will need to consult with my elders first. If they agree there is cause for concern, they will send someone to investigate this disturbance and deal with it themselves."

"Of course, Father, which would be the best thing to do in this case. I fully support any decision the Church makes regarding this child."

"Also, I think it best that Marianne is separated from the other girls and put somewhere else for the time being." He glances down at Gwen and sees the hurt in her young face. "For the comfort and safety of everyone involved," he adds kindly.

"Just as I would've suggested myself, Father. I will take care of the arrangements."

"I think that perhaps the child should stay with Sister Shaw tonight until you can arrange another room for her."

"I would be happy to welcome Marianne into my quarters, Father," Sister Shaw speaks up from the doorway.

"Very well. We'll leave it to you, Sister Shaw, to see the child is settled comfortably tonight." The father nods in agreement and heads for the door, Mother Sullivan following on his heels.

"Now, back to bed with the rest of you. That means your own bed, Amy Tucker," Sister Whitmore orders the girls, waiting until Amy scurries across the room and huddles under the covers before leaving.

Father O'Brien turns to Mother Superior and Sister Whitmore by the door. "I think there needs to be some investigation into the actions of the other girls as well. It seems some need to be reminded why we do not steal from our neighbor." The two nuns nod in unison.

"I'll take care of that myself tomorrow after lessons, Father." Sister Whitmore gives him a thin smile.

The other girls each let out an involuntary squeak in panic, at Sister Whitmore's declaration. Gwen can't help sticking a tongue out at the others behind the adult's backs.

Father O'Brien, Mother Superior, and Sister Whitmore all head back to bed, leaving only Sister Shaw behind.

She turns to Gwen and smiling kindly; she crosses the room to her bedside. "Now come along, dear. Let's have a sleepover in my room. I've got a little couch on which you can sleep. We'll bring your blanket and pillow and anything else you need. We can come back for the rest of your things tomorrow."

Gwen nods in agreement. Avoiding the staring eyes of her frightened roommates, she slips out of bed and collects her locket and her shoes. Sister Shaw removes the blanket from the bed, folding it neatly before adding the pillow on top. She gathers a change of clothes for the child from the dresser and stacks them on top of the bedding. Taking this bundle in one arm, the young nun reaches her other hand out to Gwen, who accepts it gratefully.

"Goodnight, girls," Sister Shaw says farewell as they leave the room, Gwen closing the door behind them. They walk down the dimly lit silent hall, and Mary Shaw can sense little Gwen's tense muscles relax in her arm and hand. "Was it a bad dream or a good dream?" Sister Shaw's soft voice barely disturbs the silence of the sleeping orphanage around them.

"Both," Gwen replies. "They always start nice and end badly." She looks up at the nun with a bleak look in her eyes.

"Oh, come now." Sister Shaw gives her little hand a kind squeeze. "Don't worry about the others. They're just jealous. I wish I could fly, too."

Gwen smiles up at her at that. "I wish I knew how to do it when awake."

"Me, too! Let's hurry to bed then and get back to our dreams. The best thing about dreams is that they aren't real, but they can be anything you want. Remember next time it starts to get nasty, it's just a dream, and change it how you like."

"Okay, I'll try," Gwen replies.

"I'll race you to my room?"

Smiling at each other, the two quickly make their way to the nun's bedchamber, both feeling in better spirits. Mary Shaw is grateful to help the child she cherishes most of all the orphans in her care. Gwen feeling safer knowing she'll have a guardian to watch over her during the dark night.

Still, despite all the nuns encouraging words, a dark shiver runs down her spine. Gwen knows that her dreams are anything but normal; they are a world as real as the one she lives in by day. No matter how much the friendly nun might want to help settle Gwen's fears, nothing can eradicate that which always awaits her: endless nightmares.

CHAPTER FOUR

A Safe Harbor

A week later, Father Reitman, a church-appointed exorcist, arrives at St. Paul's. He is not alone. He brings a laywoman in the archdiocese, Sister Orich, who possesses a gift for discerning spirits, or so Gwen is told. Dr. Newman, a psychiatrist, and Dr. Thompson, the physician who treated her at the hospital. A short time after Gwen came to the orphanage, Dr. Renee Thompson became St. Paul's primary physician. The church has called upon these professionals to examine the child suspected of possession. However, Father Reitman will be the one who ultimately decides whether or not Gwen is possessed.

"Contrary to widespread belief, real exorcisms are rarely performed. A thorough process of elimination is undergone to determine if the telltale signs of possession can simply be explained by mental or physical illness," Sister Shaw said when she explained the entire process to Gwen.

Completing the first step in the investigation, Gwen is interviewed with those who claim to have witnessed her paranormal activities by Father Reitman and the psychiatrist, Dr. Newman. The testimonies of Mother Superior and the nuns seem very convincing. However, Gwen's roommate's tales come off as nothing more than resentment and common jealousy, making both the priest and the psychiatrist doubtful.

Dr. Thompson issues Gwen a clean bill of health. Afterward, the laywoman, Sister Orich, does her examination.

"Although I do sense a strong spiritual presence surrounding the child, I'm not convinced it is demonic in origin." Gwen hears Sister Orich tell Father Reitman from her art class down the hall. After a lengthy discussion with the priest and the psychiatrist, the three agree that "The only thing the child seems to be suffering from is the traumatic loss of her mother, a short temper, and social anxiety."

Unbeknownst to them, Gwen is privy to every thought and conversation despite everyone's efforts to conduct the investigation behind closed doors. The *"Exorcism Crew"* relays Gwen's judgment to Mother Superior, who replies. "I insist that I have seen the girl do unnatural things with my own eyes." this induces the priest to investigate further.

For three nights in a row, Father Reitman, or Dr. Newman, accompanied by one of the nuns, watches Gwen as she sleeps. However strange this is for her, eventually, Gwen dozes off. Every morning when she wakes, she expects to be condemned as a demon child for sleep floating. Yet nothing occurs the first night, the second, or the last night. The following morning, Gwen decides she's had enough and approaches the priest Father Reitman and makes a confession.

"I never did any of those things."

"You never spoke in a strange language and commanded things and people to move and do your will?" Father Reitman, a balding, spherical kind of man, asks.

"No. They made that up," Gwen answers calmly.

"But Mother Superior herself and Sister Whitmore claim they witnessed you floating in the air with their own eyes. The other girls might make up stories about you simply because of dislike, but nuns do not bear false witness." His belly jiggles, and his double chin dances as he speaks. Gwen tries to maintain her sober facade.

"That was a joke. While everyone was sleeping, my friend Raven and I set it up with strings."

"Mother Superior said she had to shout your name several times to wake you up. Then you fell rather suddenly to the bed. How did you do that without anyone seeing the strings?" Father Reitman asks, looking down his stubby nose at her.

"I was just pretending to sleep. The others didn't see me untie the rope before I fell. I didn't mean to scare the nuns; I just wanted to frighten my roommates. They don't like me much," Gwen confesses with fake solemnity.

The priest pats her down-turned head with a thick hand and bends down with difficulty, to look her in the eye.

"Children can sometimes be harsh, but that is no excuse for mean-spirited practical jokes. You've frightened half the orphanage with this possession nonsense. Not to mention you've wasted a lot of critical people's valuable time. Sometimes children act out like this to get attention, but I promise you, Marianne, it will not help you in the long run."

Father Reitman adjusts his suit jacket as he straightens to a standing position, looking gravely down on her. "Now, do you know the ten commandments, my child?"

Gwen nods with hands folded meekly and her head tilted just the right way to display childlike humility.

"Can you tell me which one tells us not to bear false witness?"

"The eighth commandment does," Gwen replies.

"You've disobeyed God's sacred command, haven't you?"

Gwen bows her head in false shame as a response.

"Then you will have to be punished for this grave sin. Children must learn early on the evils of telling lies." He sighs heavily. Gwen senses from his thoughts that her charade is working. He feels sorry for her, regretting the need to punishing such a sweet, innocent-looking child. "Come along, Marianne, you'll have to go and tell the truth to Father O'Brien and the Mother Superior. They will know how to handle this matter so that you learn never to lie again."

The priest turns, and Gwen reluctantly falls in step behind him. Gwen's feet grow heavier with every step down the long corridor toward Father O'Brien's office.

Her plan worked in a way. After seeing Sister Shaw's growing concern, she decided; *It's better to be known as a liar than evil or possessed.* Still, having to swallow her pride and openly lie to everyone, including Father O'Brien, whom she holds in the highest regard, galls her sensibilities. *It isn't my fault that I'm different from everyone else. Why should I have to suffer for it?* And suffer she will, she realizes, as it is Sister Whitmore's special duty to discipline the children of St. Paul's. It is a task she takes with immense pleasure.

Gwen has yet to visit Sister Whitmore's office, but she has heard plenty of stories from the other children, enough to make her sweat with apprehension as she walks toward her fate at the end of the hall. She knows that the truth will only get her into even more trouble, but still, it seems unfair that she's condemned no matter what she says.

* * * * *

Gwen's punishment is dealt with swiftly, and everyone is more apt to believe the lie than the truth. Regular disciplinary sessions with Sister Whitmore are prescribed for the next two weeks. Gwen is removed from the traditional quarters as well. Her new dwelling is a small, dark, cramped closet-size room in the attic where a bed and dresser can fit.

Sister Shaw, enraged, tries to convince the Mother Superior that a child as young as Marianne shouldn't be submitted to Sister Whitmore's cruel methods. However, Mother Superior won't budge. No one speaks openly of what happens behind the closed doors of

Sister Whitmore's office, but Sister Shaw is sure it involves some physical beating.

Every time they have an unruly child in their midst, it takes one visit to Sister Whitmore's office, and that child never acts out again. From then on, the once-disruptive child cringes in fear whenever the older sister comes near.

During Gwen's disciplinary sessions, Sister Shaw waits protectively outside Sister Whitmore's office. When Gwen exited the office at the end of their first session, she sensed Sister Shaw's surprise that she had not once cried out in pain. Neither did she cower; instead, she met Sister Whitmore glare for glare before walking down the hall to her class with her head held high. Gwen behaved in this fashion for the remainder of her punishment. She never once recoiled in fear as the others did when Sister Whitmore passed her in the hall. It seemed to Sister Shaw that the girl preferred the isolation from the others. After she was removed to the attic, there were no more strange occurrences for one entire year.

* * * * *

"There's a new boy," Raven whispers to Gwen during the mid-day meal. "His name is Douglas Williams. He's a couple of years younger than me." Raven points the boy out to her amongst the children at the farthest table in the grand hall. Gwen sees his back and shrugs, nonplused.

"Child services took him. His parents were drug dealers or something like that. They left him all alone and didn't come back for two weeks. He was half-starved when the postman dropped off a package at the door. I guess he looked pretty bad 'cuz he called the cops, and they came for him that night."

"I guess he's better off here, then," Gwen replies, taking a bite of her sandwich.

"He doesn't seem to think so. Sister Shaw said he hasn't been very talkative. She says they just released him from the hospital to the orphanage this morning, and all he's done since he got here is mope around. She asked me to try being his friend."

Gwen raises an eyebrow at this and then swallows a bite before replying, "Hanging out with us isn't going to make him popular around here."

Raven shrugs. "I told her that, but she still wants us to try being nice to him."

Gwen groans, annoyed. The two friends return to their respective meals.

* * * * *

One spring afternoon, several months later, Gwen leans against the walnut tree, reading a book, trying to pass the afternoon break alone as Raven has taken to bed with a nasty cold. All around her, the schoolyard bustles with youthful energy as her schoolmates play. Gwen shuts them all out, outwardly, and inwardly, trying to immerse herself in the words of Dickens. A boy, pretending he is just passing by, suddenly rushes to her side. She looks up and recognizes him as Douglas, the new kid. Without a word, Douglas quickly leans in and plants a kiss on her lips.

How dare he! Kill him, kill him now! Gwen hears the hiss of a voice in her ear, and a bone deep chill washes over her. In reaction she recoils, pushing the boy away from her with all her considerable might. With a terrified scream, Douglas flies backward through the air, landing on his back opposite the courtyard, over thirty feet away from little Gwen.

After a stunned moment of silence, all hell breaks loose as her schoolmates run away in a panic. The sister on duty runs to aid the fallen child. Douglas lies on the ground as if lifeless.

Father O'Brien is summoned, and the children are ushered inside as Douglas is moved into the infirmary. Soon after, Dr. Renee Thompson arrives to examine the patient. Sister Whitmore is sent to retrieve Gwen, who stands detached and stone-like under the tree watching the commotion. Her eyes dart about the courtyard as if fearing the shadows might come to life.

The nun drags the emotionless girl to her office at once for punishment. In the end, the doctor informs them that Douglas only suffers from a broken rib and a mild concussion. After wrapping up his side, she orders the boy to stay in bed for two weeks, but other than that, Douglas is fine.

Once Douglas fully recovers from his injuries, and they allow him out of his sickbed, he stays far away from Marianne. Outwardly she doesn't seem repentant for what she has done to him. Internally she is petrified of two things; the voice that had egged her on to attack Douglas and how violently she had reacted. If the voice hadn't enraged her further, she might have just slapped the boy or yelled in his face. Gwen doesn't bother asking herself whom the voice belonged. Somehow, she already knows. Despite not once seeing the man in black after that day in the woods, she has felt his presence ever since. Sometimes there was a black smudge in the corner of her eye, which evaporated when she tried to look directly upon it. At other times she felt the same indescribable chill he had given off. Once in a while, whenever she was alone, she heard someone whispering her name. Up till now she has told herself she was imagining things. Now she knows the truth. Whoever he was, he was no man of flesh and bone. The man in black with the black soulless eyes, was… something else. The realization leaves her feeling numb with fear.

The Douglas incident is the last straw for Mother Superior, who decides it's about time to get Marianne January adopted, out of the orphanage and away from the other children. No one but Adam is allowed to go near Marianne, afterward. The girl is forced to spend most of her free time in her room or Sister Shaw's office, helping her correct papers.

A few months later, a couple comes to St. Paul's looking for a young girl Gwen's age. They are a lovely God-fearing couple in their mid-to-late thirties who just lost their daughter a few years earlier. They have been unsuccessful in conceiving another child since. The nuns introduce them to Marianne. Her beautiful, angelic face and dazzling intelligence win the couple over in minutes. The nuns point out all of her good traits, telling how she excels in school, what an accomplished artist, singer, and reader she is, and how calm and refined a child she can be. In no time, the papers are signed, and Marianne is sent to her room to pack her things. She will live with the Harris family and be their little girl, now. All the nuns but Sister Shaw seem relieved to see her go. It's as if the whole orphanage heaves a sigh of relief as the dark-haired, wild-eyed girl walks out of St. Paul's front doors behind her new parents.

Heartbroken Raven hardly eats, stops paying attention in school, and never says a word to anyone—not even Sister Shaw. He reverts to his old habits, sitting in the walnut tree, a hermit once more.

A month later, the Harris family brings Marianne back. Despite sitting outside the office as her adopted parents spoke to the Mother Superior and Sister Whitmore, Gwen can still hear everything happening within. With her ability to tap into other's minds she can see the whole interview from Mother Sullivan's perspective as well.

"We admit that she's a sweet girl, but she seems to be constantly under a dark cloud." Mrs. Harris an overly tall curvy brunette woman explained to Mother Sullivan. "There might be something unnatural about her." Her voice had a sing-song air to it. As if she might start singing at any given moment.

"All sorts of strange things have happened in our home since she arrived." Her husband Mr. Harris added. His exaggerated mustache twitching comically as he spoke with animated hand gestures. "Now that we're expecting a child of our own, we just simply don't feel it safe to keep the girl."

"Now Sir I understand your concern but…" Mother Sullivan started to reason in a calm voice with her adopted parents. Inwardly the woman raged with strong emotions. *No, no, no. I will not let that little demon fox back into the Hen house with the rest of the chicks!*

Gwen retreats out of the nun's mind and stands. Sister Bernard sits patiently with her in one of the waiting area chairs. "Where do you think you're going Marianne?"

"Back to my room Sister." Gwen shrugged with a sway of her long black hair. Hefting her red duffle bag over her shoulder the child shuffles on down the hall. Sister Bernard called after her, but Gwen was too focused on escaping the painful words and thoughts of the four adults in the Mother Superior's office, to mind her. Sister Bernard didn't bother bringing her back.

Soon Gwen and Raven are reunited once more. Overcome with emotion, Raven cries and openly hugs his little friend, welcoming her home. The two of them become even more inseparable from that day, spending every available moment together. To all the nuns, Marianne doesn't seem the least bit upset to be back; on the contrary, she looks as happy to be rid of her new family as they were to be rid of her. Gwen settles right back into her old routine at St. Paul's as if the whole thing never happened.

* * * * *

Finally, Raven and Gwen graduate from the special studies class and join the other children. Sister Shaw is naturally concerned about the kind of trouble Gwenevere will get into under a different teacher. She said many a prayer, that all will go well.

Alas, it is doomed from the start. First, Gwen is put into Sister Whitmore's sixth-grade class with Raven. Gwen refuses to sit in the assigned seating, insisting on sitting next to Adam. Repeatedly she tells Sister Whitmore to call her by her real name. Also, she informs Sister Whitmore that she isn't to call Adam by the name Adam anymore and must call him Raven.

The nun sends Gwen to Mother Superior's office, who sends her to bed without lunch or dinner that day. Sister Whitmore suggests that the child be locked in her room without food until she acknowledges that her name is, in fact, Marianne. After two days, Sister Shaw convinces Father O'Brien to get Mother Superior to let Marianne out of her room. The girl still refuses to accept the name Marianne and corrects anyone who dares call her that name from that day on. She then calmly informs them that her name is Gwenevere, but they can call her Gwen.

Sister Shaw can't help being in awe of the girl and her robust and unyielding spirit. Some might consider this a fault, but she does not. Gwen fears nothing. She is a fighter, a conqueror, yet she can also be kind-hearted, loving, and devoted. Her sense of loyalty is astonishing. Sister Mary Shaw has always felt weak, timid, and afraid of others, especially Sister Whitmore. She believes that if she can emulate this little girl and be half the woman, she is at only seven years old, she could finally become the person she always wanted. Sister Shaw continues to take it upon herself to be Gwenevere and Raven's advocate in all things. Being like a mother, a sister, a teacher, and a friend to the two outcasts, made her feel for the first time that she is truly needed. As orphanage life continues to rage against them like the sea in the throes of a storm, Sister Shaw gives them a safe harbor.

CHAPTER FIVE

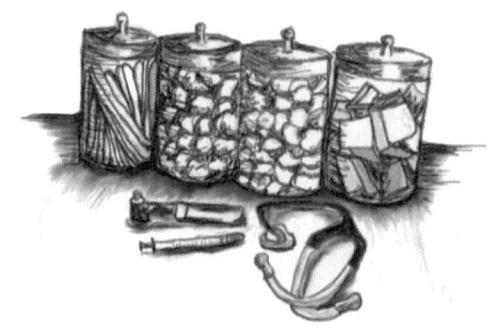

Unwanted and Shunned

Gwen wakes up one morning dreading the doctor's visit that afternoon. She doesn't like being touched, poked at, and most of all, punctured with needles. Gwen reminisces of all her past checkups as she gets dressed.

Over the last two years, Doctor Renee Thompson has been the visiting physician at the orphanage. She tries to seem nonchalant in her questioning of Gwen, utterly unaware that the seven-year-old can read her mind and thus is privy to every thought, emotion, or reaction in her wide-open psyche.

So it is that while the doctor tries to unravel the mystery behind the strange child, trying desperately to discover her every secret, Gwen has been the one getting all the answers while revealing nothing.

Gwen harbors no ill will toward the lady doctor but finds it annoying that the woman stares at her. Making her feel as though she is a fungus in a petri dish, some strange organism to be studied and torn apart. Doctor Thompson always listens with great interest to the nun's accounts of the strange occurrences that seem either to happen by Gwen's doing or around her. Gwen hates it when she probes for answers, trying to get Gwen to confirm the stories or confess that she has just been pulling pranks. The lady does not seem genuinely convinced by Gwen's confession to the exorcists, still suspecting her of holding some supernatural gift. Gwen can't tell which the doctor wants more: for Gwen to be extraordinary, be a fraud, or simply a naughty little girl who delights in frightening innocent children and dubious nuns.

Once dressed, Gwen heads down the long flight of stairs to get breakfast. She's gotten used to the repetitive routine of the orphanage. Every morning, she wakes up early to listen to the world around her and let her mind feel the essence of everything it touches. Practicing her unique gifts, she makes the bed levitate or reorganizes the books on her shelf using only the words of her true tongue. She also practices speaking, reading, and expanding her vocabulary in both her native language and English. It amuses her to think that while the other children below say their morning prayers, she is doing her own, quite different, spiritual worship.

With her morning meditation done, she joins everyone downstairs in the dining hall for breakfast. Naturally, she always sits with Raven at their own end of the table, for everyone else gives them a wide berth. Instead, they choose to cram together at the far end of their table, or smush tightly at another table. This suits them both just fine. Neither likes the company of others, while having them all at a distance makes it easier to talk about things that would only frighten an eavesdropper.

As the morning meal ends, the children march off to class. Raven and Gwen attend the same classes, for they have made sure to continually progress in their studies together. They're aware that this upsets the nuns, who constantly insist that Gwen should be in classes with children her age. Still, without Gwen sitting next to him in class, giving him the answers to quizzes, or encouraging him when he feels inadequate, Raven fails miserably.

After morning classes, they have a midday break. The children play in the courtyard or wander freely outside for an hour. Gwen knows the nuns invented the midday break so that they could gather together and have tea in silence, giving them a moment of peace from the constant insanity of the orphanage. It's suitable for the children, too, who love running around unsupervised for an hour. Otherwise, the children might go berserk if stuck in a classroom all day, learning arithmetic, or praying to this Saint or that. The daily break keeps the delicate balance of the institution in check.

At the end of the hour of freedom, the bell tower rings, and everyone scurries inside for lunch, and from there, they resume their school studies. The afternoon classes go on until four o'clock, when they are all escorted into the chapel for mass and then excused to their dorms to do their homework until the dinner bell rings at six o'clock.

Every other day before dinner, Gwen goes to choir practice. She has a remarkable voice and sings most of the solos. Often Gwen catches the choir director, Sister Mullen, thinking *If only the wee lass would behave as angelically as she sings.*

After dinner, everyone spends an hour in the large common room. The sisters occasionally have the children take turns reading from the Bible aloud in front of everyone. Still, most of the time, the children are allowed to gather in their groups about the room. Some groups play board games, read, do homework, or talk in low whispers while the sisters watch over them. A few Sisters wander about the room, some teaching knitting to a group of girls in the corner or joining the children in their games. Most of the nuns sit in their own part of the room, quietly discussing the day's business. Gwen and Raven often sit by themselves in their own corner. Raven carving something out of wood while Gwen curls up in a window seat either reading a book or sketching in her notepad.

At about eight o'clock, the sisters usher the children to bed. Seeing that the children brush their teeth and are in bed by eight-thirty, the lights are off, and all is still.

The night is Gwen's favorite part of the day. While everyone else sleeps, she, and Raven sneak out of their rooms and meet outside under their walnut tree. From there, they steal away into the woods surrounding the property to be free, to be themselves, far from prying eyes. They climb trees and leap through the forest's canopy like monkeys, wild and free. They have races, trying to beat each other's super speed. Raven always wins, but Gwen will beat him any day now.

She can feel it. Another one of their pastimes is hiking up to the waterfall high in the mountain. It would take any normal child hours to reach; it only takes Raven and Gwen fifteen minutes. They swim or dive off the rocks at the waterfall into the crystalline pool below. Sometimes Gwen dances nimbly on the water's surface, skimming the water like a nymph, light as air.

Behind the waterfall, there's a cave. They make this their fort, their secret place. Inside they stashed cans of food stolen from the kitchen pantry, some pillows, blankets, favorite books, paper, piles of wood to build a fire, and chalk with which Gwen draws on the walls. These decorations give their hideout a caveman like feel, only her drawings are much more sophisticated. This is their sanctuary. They dare not come here too often during the midday break. They fear the other children might follow them and find their special place. Since Raven is naturally nocturnal and Gwen has trouble sleeping; visiting the cave in the beautiful, serene cover of night is convenient.

Gwen daydreams of going to the cave as she and Raven devour their breakfast in solitude.

"The doctor's coming today," Raven comments, stuffing a spoonful of oatmeal into his mouth.

"I know. I wish she wouldn't," Gwen says, eating an apple, not savoring the taste. As Raven finishes his bowl of oatmeal, Gwen offers him hers. Raven smiles appreciatively and takes the bowl.

"Does she know that we're different? I mean, can you tell by her thoughts?" Raven scrapes the bottom of the bowl, cleaning it out with his spoon.

"She's not sure. She's still looking for concrete medical proof." After the oatmeal is finished, Raven pushes the two empty bowls toward the center of the table. "Can we go to the cave tonight?" Gwen asks.

"Of course, if we can get past Sister Whitmore." Raven glances over his shoulder at the nun in question, shivering slightly as her gaze passes over them.

"I know, she's starting to bug me. Since we stole the cheesecake from the cupboard, she's been poking around where she shouldn't. She thinks it's us, but she'll never prove it." Gwen and Raven share a conspiratorial smile.

The two misfits are like shadows in the night when they sneak into the kitchen, stealing away food from behind padlocked cupboards, fridges, and freezers. At first, the sisters thought it was vermin stealing their supplies until they realized the items taken were much too large for animals to carry. That's when they started locking up the food.

They locked the kitchen doors and windows when the thievery continued, but even that hadn't kept the thieves out. The two of them only occasionally stole food to help stock up their stash in case they needed to flee or finally decided they'd had enough of this place and ran. The thefts don't occur often, but it is a matter of principle to the Mother Superior— no one steals from her kitchen. Just recently, Gwen skulked into the kitchen and procured the cheesecake, a gift to Sister Whitmore for her birthday from the rest of the sisters. This had made the hunt for "the kitchen thieves" something very personal to Sister Whitmore.

Admittedly, they stole it just to spite Sister Whitmore. Tormenting her anonymously had long been their greatest sport. Unfortunately for them, she has taken it upon herself to sit as a guard outside the kitchen every night since. Her sentry makes their ventures out into the forest much riskier. Should she catch them, there would be hell to pay. Also, it would be all the proof she needs to accuse them of being the kitchen thieves.

Suddenly broken from her thoughts, Gwen looks up to see Raven staring at her from across the table. "Huh?"

"It's time to go to class now," Raven repeats.

Gwen realizes that the meal's remains have been cleared, and the nuns align in front of the large head table. Raven gets up from the table, and with a sigh, Gwen follows Raven to where Sister Bernard's class awaits. Whenever Doctor Thompson visits, she always comes during the afternoon classes, starting with the oldest class and working her way down. From class, the students are excused one at a time to the infirmary for their check-ups. Gwen is convinced the female doctor takes longer with her than anyone else, except maybe Raven, who has also become a curiosity to her because of his association with Gwen. She senses a peculiar connection between the two of them. Gwen forces herself to put the doctor out of her mind, letting herself get caught up in the familiar routine of daily life.

While helping Raven with his sixth-grade math homework, Gwen is finally summoned for her turn under Doctor Renee Thompson's stethoscope. Walking as slowly as possible, she drags her feet the whole way. Eventually, Gwen finds herself in front of the infirmary doors.

Turning the doorknob, she goes in. The tall, attractive redheaded Renee Thompson, MD, stands in front of the doorway to the private examination room. She smiles welcomingly at Gwen, stepping aside for her to enter the room. Gwen reluctantly enters. Crossing the room, she hops up on the examination table. The doctor closes the door before taking a seat.

She smiles at Gwen. As she lets her mind reach out to touch the woman's consciousness, Renee tries to think of nothing. Despite this, images flash in and out of view as the errant thoughts come unbidden to the doctor's mind. The Doctor has caught on that Gwen can somehow hear her thoughts or read her face. Sister Shaw would never betray her and Raven's trust. She has never given Doctor Thompson any information about Gwen, no matter how often the lady asked.

"How are you feeling today, Marianne?" Renee asks, trying to hide the anxiety in her voice.

"I'm fine." Gwen studies Renee with a suspicious look on her sweet doll-like face. "And it's Gwen, like I told you before."

"Oh, I must've forgotten. I apologize, Gwen." They stare at each other for a long while. Finally, Doctor Thompson breaks the silence, "So, Gwen, no colds, flu, headaches, chest pains, or soreness?"

"I'm fine."

"All right, but I still need to do a routine check-up to ensure all is well, okay?"

Gwen does as she is asked, following the light pen with her eyes, holding still as a tool is poked into her ears, and saying *"ah"* so the doctor can examine her mouth. Gwen hates the feel of the wooden stick pressed against her tongue.

"Lift your shirt, please," the Doctor commands, and Gwen complies shyly, revealing a strange scar over her heart. Gwen takes deep breaths when prompted, noticing how the Doctor scrutinizes the partially healed scar tissue. Gwen catches Renee's errant thoughts at the sight.

Over two years now, and that scar still looks new. It looks just like it did the first time I examined her in the hospital. It's still pink as if it just healed over. That isn't normal… Images of little Gwen scared in her hospital bed, form in Renee's mind. *I still can't get her to tell me how she got that scar.* Gwen tries not to cringe as Renee Thompson presses her cold metal stethoscope to her chest, listening to her heartbeat, then again when the doctor presses it to her back, asking her to take another deep breath.

"You can put your shirt down now," Renee instructs. Gwen lets her shirt fall back in place as she watches the doctor wheel her chair over to the counter. The lady retrieves an empty sterile medical cup.

Oh, pee-pee in the cup time, Gwen thinks dispassionately.

"Fill this for me, please," the doctor smiles, handing Gwen the cup.

Gwen takes the cup and scoots off the examination table with a sigh. She shuffles out of the room to the adjoining bathroom. The whole thing is humiliating. Gwen only keeps going to these check-ups to keep Sister Shaw happy, who constantly lectures Raven and her about the importance of good health. Plus, it would look suspicious if she refused examination.

At first, Gwen hadn't minded her check-ups. It wasn't until she started catching colds and getting other various illnesses soon after the doctor's visits that Gwen became suspicious of the red-haired woman and her cold, white hands. Granted, the first sicknesses were caused by the vaccinations she was given. They caused her to get sick before her body could adapt, developing immunities, so it hadn't been the doctor's fault she got ill. Yet she caught the Doctor thinking once how peculiar it was that Gwen got sick like everyone else. Gwen tried to sing the healing lullaby, the one memory that reminds her of her mother, but it did nothing to break the fevers or cure nausea, diarrhea, and stuffy, runny noses. It does ease pain or soreness in her body, heals cuts, and wounds, reduces headaches, and calms nerves. It's as if it only works on the exterior of her body but is useless against the tiny, microscopic viruses that attack her internally.

* * * * *

After Gwen leaves the examination room, Renee relaxes, slumping into her chair. Her gaze falls on the tongue depressor she just used, sitting on the top of the garbage in the trashcan. The urge to set the trashcan on fire comes over her to get rid of the evidence, but she shakes it off. *I'll just take the trash out with me when I leave. It's not as if anyone will ever suspect what I did.* The chances are that the virus won't take effect, and all her preparation will have been in vain. Due to Gwen's aversion to needles, she had no choice but to contaminate her orally instead of injecting the deadly virus straight into her bloodstream, which would've been much more effective. Now, all she has to do is wait.

So far, her experiments have not proven anything conclusive. The first time had been merely by accident when she gave Gwen the essential vaccinations on her first check-up after leaving for the orphanage. Soon after, Gwen fell ill. It suddenly occurred to Renee that this was an excellent opportunity to observe how human or superhuman the child was. She hypothesized that if the girl had some strange power, she would heal herself again or get over the sickness faster than most. Gwen did not react to the viruses any differently than any other child her age might have to the doctor's disappointment. Curiosity piqued, she launched herself into a full-on experiment. After that, she exposed the child to multiple other diseases, from the common cold to chickenpox and measles. The research subject wasn't responding as she had hoped. The doctor couldn't tell from any research so far that Gwen is anything more than an ordinary girl. This isn't the conclusion she was looking for. Renee still can't explain how the girl's feet miraculously healed from severe frostbite a couple of years ago.

This time is going to be different; she hopes. The other experiments had been superficial infections, nothing that would cause permanent physical damage, nothing life-threatening. She reasons that the girl has not healed herself because she knows she will get over the sickness in time. This time, she will have to do something to save herself again, as she did before. Her chances of surviving the virus are slim without being hospitalized. The girl might still die from it if she doesn't take it upon herself to heal her body. And when she does, Renee will have proof that the frostbite incident hadn't been a miracle, but the act of some paranormal gift the girl possesses.

It has to work this time, she tells herself, trying desperately to suppress the guilt welling up inside her. Renee realizes she can't face the girl again without giving everything away. She isn't wholly convinced that the telepathy rumor isn't just paranoia on the nun's part. The way Gwen looks at her makes Renee feel like she is in her head.

Quickly gathering her supplies into her medical bag, she grabs the trash bag out of the waste receptacle and heads for the door.

I'll just tell the sisters that I got an emergency page from the hospital, that I'll come back another time, she decides, feeling relieved at the plausibility of the lie. She leaves the infirmary.

A moment later, Gwen returns from the bathroom with a securely contained cup of urine held at arm's length in one hand. She goes into the office and stops, confusion causing her to pause. Not only is the doctor gone, but there's no sign that she had ever been in the examination room. Gwen turns her attention to the cup in her hand.

"What am I supposed to do with this?" she asks aloud in the empty room. Gwen notices that the trashcan has fallen onto its side, empty. Making up her mind, she stands the trashcan on its end and puts the urine sample in the bottom of the liner-less trash bin. Seven-year-old Gwen leaves the infirmary completely puzzled, wondering what had happened to the strange Doctor Thompson.

* * * * *

By evening, Gwen is confined to her bed. All through the afternoon classes, her temperature rose till she felt dizzy and feverish. After dinner, she vomits several times before passing out in the common room from pure physical weakness. For days, Gwen doesn't leave her bed. Delirious with a fever one moment and cold shivers the next, she begins to hallucinate in a half-waking dream. The doctor is called in on the third day. Doctor Thompson gives her an antibiotic. Sister Shaw, who takes it upon herself to act as the girl's nurse, receives some pills to give Gwen for her fever.

"I'll be back tomorrow to see how she's improved," Doctor Thompson tells Sister Shaw, knowing the medicines are all placebos. They will not affect the disease whatsoever.

When Gwen still doesn't improve, they move her to the hospital with Doctor Thompson to oversee the child's care.

By the sixth day, it's clear to Renee that she has made a terrible mistake. Gwen isn't going to heal herself. She will die if Renee doesn't give her the antidote soon, and even then, there's a chance that the virus will mutate, and she will be unaffected by the medicine.

Waiting for a moment when Gwen is alone, Renee administers the vaccine to the child. Staying by the girl's side all night and praying—even though she doesn't believe in a God—asking for forgiveness, help, and begging the Lord to save the girl from death's cold embrace. By the evening of the seventh day, Gwen's fever finally breaks. Color returns to her face as her vital signs stabilize.

Doctor Renee Thompson heaves a sigh of relief and asks another doctor to trade her patients. The whole ordeal has shaken Renee to the core. She became a doctor because she loved science and medicine and wanted to do good in the world. However, what she has done is inhumane, immoral, and evil. She has gone against her Hippocratic Oath.

After that, a new doctor does the rounds at St. Paul's. Renee Thompson stays at the hospital in town with a renewed interest in her work. She never goes near Gwenevere again.

* * * * *

It takes Gwen a month to fully recover from the deadly illness, spending most of this time confined to her hospital bed. She spends time reading old paperbacks that the nurses have donated to her. By the time she feels well enough to return to the orphanage, she has regained most of her strength but is still in a daze as to what has happened.

Gwen looks about her hospital room as she gets dressed. She has no possessions but the clothes on her back and her new collection of paperback novels to take with her. No "get well soon" cards, balloons, flowers, or well-meaning gifts signify that anyone noticed she had even been ill, let alone had almost died. Not that she had expected any great outpouring of love, but it feels odd to leave the hospital empty-handed after such an extended stay.

A kindly young nurse named Madeline Wilkes walks her down the hall to the outpatient desk. While waiting for the elevator, Gwen spies Doctor Thompson speaking to a first-year resident. Their eyes meet before the doctor nervously hurries away in the opposite direction for a moment. Gwen brushes off the incident and takes the elevator down to the lobby with Nurse Wilkes. When she steps off on the first floor, she half expects Sister Shaw to be waiting at the front desk. The lobby is empty. The petite Nurse Wilkes ushers her to a chair and goes to the front desk to speak to the security guard on duty, a tall, thin, Black man in his thirties.

Nurse Wilkes kneels next to Gwen's chair. "Someone should be here soon to pick you up, dear. Is there anything else you need?"

Gwen shakes her head.

What a poor, sad little thing, Nurse Wilkes thinks as she pats Gwen on the knee. Gwen hides her irritation behind a blank face. Madeline Wilkes bids her farewell and then takes the elevator back upstairs to resume her duties.

At first, Gwen passes the time by trying to read the magazines lying about. She counts how many people pass through the lobby as she waits. Finally, she starts listening in on the security guard's thoughts as he leafs through a magazine but blushes when inappropriate images of women float through his mind. Quickly Gwen shuts him out, closing her mind completely. Restless, Gwen looks up at the clock on the wall. She's been sitting here for over three hours.

When the security guard gets a phone call, Gwen takes the opportunity to go out onto the front curb through the revolving front doors. No car waits outside. As she turns to head back inside, Nurse Wilkes exits the building with her coat thrown over her scrubs, her purse in hand.

"Hey, what are you still doing here?"

"I guess they forgot." Gwen shrugs, feigning disinterest.

How pathetic. Doesn't anyone care for the girl? Nurse Wilkes thinks privately in her mind, unaware that Gwen can hear her as clearly as if she were screaming her thoughts aloud. She hesitates. "Well, my shift's over. What do you say you let me give you a ride home?" She smiles good-naturedly. *Oops, I shouldn't have said home; I don't want to rub in that she doesn't have a home. I don't want to upset her,* Madeline thinks, scolding herself.

"Thank you. I would walk, but I don't know the way," Gwen confesses as she follows Madeline Wilkes to her car, staring at her back until they climb into Madeline's gray Volkswagen Jetta.

"Oh, don't be silly. A little thing like you shouldn't ever go walking about all alone. Besides, the Orphanage is on the other side of town, on the edge of the woods. It would take too long and wouldn't be safe."

Flashes of images of the nurses standing around sharing tidbits of gossip pour from Madeline Wilkes's open mind. Gwen catches disjointed bits of conversation. Mostly the gossip she gleans is that everyone at the hospital had noticed the lack of sympathy shown to little Marianne. *There I go, putting my foot in my mouth again. Don't remind her of her time lost in the woods; it can't be a good memory for her. How frightening that must've been. How awful it must be to be so alone and...* Gwen shuts the mental floodgate tightly, wanting none of this woman's sympathy or pity.

Maybe it would've been better to walk after all than listen to this. Gwen turns her gaze out the window, trying to hide her watery eyes by watching the city go by, remembering her first car ride from the hospital to St. Paul's as they drive. Outside it starts to rain. Gwen observes that somehow it always rains when she's feeling down as if her emotional state summons the gloom all on its own.

Gwen says nothing, only speaking when prompted by Nurse Wilkes for directions. Nurse Wilkes tries to engage Gwen in conversation once they leave the town and head into the surrounding countryside, but Gwen only gives the cursory one-syllable answers. Finally, they pull up in front of the orphanage. With red duffle in toe, Gwen hurries out of the car and into the building before the well-meaning nurse can speak or think again.

When Gwen walks into the big front entryway of St. Paul's Orphanage, no one is there to welcome her. Slightly wet from the rain, her shoes squeak on the parquet floor as she passes several of the sisters' private offices and many classrooms on her way to her bedroom. Everyone stops what they're doing, silently watching her walk by, but no one says a word to her. Gwen doesn't even look in their direction. She heads straight to her room, walking up the back steps to her little attic dwelling.

Opening the door to her cramped apartment, she notices that no one changed the linens on her bed or bothered to dust or clean while she's been gone. She sits down on her bed, feeling how utterly alone in the world she is for the first time. Gwen is a solitary creature by nature, so she has never really noticed how everyone avoids her or how little she matters to them until now.

It strikes her that she could have died, and no one would have cared. No one would mourn her passing. She goes cold, feeling empty inside. *Maybe I am pathetic after all.* She puts her head in her hands and begins to sob.

The sound of footsteps running up the stairs startles her. She looks up, and a moment later, her bedroom door flies open to reveal Raven standing in the doorway. His face shows a mix of relief, joy, and loneliness.

"You are home!" he exclaims, a smile wide across his tan face.

Gwen goes from the darkest pits of hell to absolute joy, floating on a cloud at the sight of his happy, familiar face. She flings herself into his arms, nearly knocking the older, taller Raven over with the eagerness of her embrace. He warms her in his arms in a welcoming hug, holding her there, his chin resting on her head.

"I'm sorry they wouldn't let me see you. Everyone said you were contagious, and no matter what I did, no one would let me leave. I'm so glad you're okay!" Raven weeps into her hair.

"It's okay. I'm home," she whispers into his chest, tears of joy spring to her eyes that she quickly suppresses.

"Don't ever leave me again, Gwen. I can't stand being here without you." The desperation in his voice makes her heart ache.

"When I leave this place, I'm taking you with me," she announces.

Raven steps back to look down at her.

"You promise?"

"I promise. No one will ever separate us again." She smiles sadly up at him. "You're the only one who gets me, Raven. You're a part of me. We're two of a kind."

"Yeah… I know." Raven smiles shyly, feeling suddenly uneasy with their sentimental exchange. "Hey, do you want help unpacking your bag?"

"Sure." Gwen hefts the red duffle bag up onto the bed. Unzipping it, she turns to Raven. "I've got a ton of new books. Most of them are on the romantic side, but there's some action in them, too. Here, I think you'd like this one." Pulling one of the paperbacks out of her bag, she turns it over to show him the cover.

"*The Pirate's Lover*?" He makes a quizzical expression.

"There's this great scene where the first mate cuts the captain's head off and tosses it overboard to the sharks."

Raven looks at her doubtfully.

"Not if it's got…" Raven hesitates as if struggling to find words, his dark skin turning red.

"No, there's nothing naughty in it." Gwen snorts. "Some nurse went through all the romance novels with a black marker and got rid of all that stuff," Gwen explains, opening the book to show him the censored pages.

"Okay, we'll start it after we put your stuff away," Raven smiles, relieved, his face returning to its natural color. He finds places for all of her new books on the shelf while Gwen stuffs her clothes into the dresser.

Gwen suddenly realizes that she will never have a home like most children. She will never have parents, brothers, sisters, uncles, aunts, and grandparents. Raven is her best friend, family, and home, and he will always be there to love her. It doesn't matter how the rest of the world sees her or what they think. Let them all recoil from her, scorn her, taunt her, and call her names. She does not care.

To Raven, she will always be someone special, someone who matters. His love will protect her forever from the misery of being cursed, unwanted, and shunned.

CHAPTER SIX

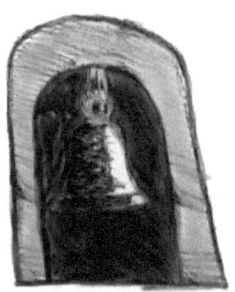

The Boy in the Tower

Gwen and Raven return from their nightly visit to their secret cave behind the waterfall, suppressing giggles as they sneak back into the orphanage just after two in the morning. They enter through the back door of the chapel, going into the balcony. A small door there leads to the attic loft, which runs the entire expanse of the orphanage. They follow it to Gwen's small attic bedroom, adjacent to the loft by a narrow flight of stairs. From there, they go their separate ways. Gwen returns to her bedroom, leaving Raven to sneak back downstairs and to his room, just two doors down from the base of the steps.

Gwen changes into her nightclothes, some pajama bottoms, and an oversized T-shirt. Getting into bed, she pulls the covers up around her chin.

"*Darkana,*" she chants in her native tongue, and the lights in her tiny, closet-size bedroom turn off, throwing the room into total darkness. She rolls onto her side and attempts to fall asleep.

She tries to think pleasant, soothing thoughts as she lies there, but she keeps feeling distracted as though something beckons her back into the waking world. She sits up in bed and looks about the dark room with an exasperated sigh.

"Go back to sleep, little one." A familiar voice breaks the silence of her room. With a gasp Gwen turns quickly to see the man in black leaning casually against her window seal. Despite being backlite by the soft moonlight, Gwen can still make out the wicked sneer on his exquisitely handsome face. Amazingly, his pitch black reflectionless eyes are visible if only by comparison to the rest of the shadows. She has no doubt that even in the darkest of settings his eyes would be the purest and deepest black imaginable. "There's nothing to be concerned with dear. Nothing that is any of your business anyways." The man in black adds in a honey-vinegar tone, both soothing and mocking all at once. With a twitch of her hand, she turned on the light switch from across the room. The fluorescent bulb in the fixture above her throwing her small room into warm light. The man in black is nowhere in sight. Gwen sits there a moment frozen in place, the hairs on her skin static as if caressed by a rubber balloon.

Gwen has half a mind to demand the specter show himself again and demand to know what he wants. She decides against this, feeling that talking to him might encourage him. She resolves to ignore him, instead. Not bothering to turn off the lights, Gwen settles back into her bed. This time she pulls the blankets over her head firmly. After a while she begins to doze off.

Until an eerie sensation washes over her as if something terribly wrong is about to happen. As if doused in ice water she snaps fully awake. Compelled, despite concern that the man in black might return, Gwen gets out of bed to see what the matter could be. *If he says it's nothing to worry about than that probably means, it's a matter of life or death.* She reasons with herself as she steps into her slippers and throws on a robe. She decides to wander around and follow her instincts. Somewhere in the orphanage, someone needs her help. *But who and why? And why is it my problem?*

It isn't. she hears his voice in her head this time, his visage not appearing again.

I'm not listening to him. I don't trust him.

You don't even know him, the man quips, his hiss of a voice tickling the inside of Gwen's ears. *What have I ever done to make you distrust me?*

Gwen refuses to acknowledge this question and reaches for the doorknob. The door begins to open only to be suddenly pushed shut with a violent gush of air. The doorknob unyielding in her grasp. She struggles fervently, pulling and straining with all her might to open the door. Still, the door remains immovable. Knowing full well it isn't locked, Gwen grits her teeth and tries again, this time using the true tongue as an aid.

"Op-eina!" Gwen growls and all at once the door pops open, Gwen nearly falling backward onto the floor. Quickly she stumbles forward and slips out the door before it slams shut, trapping her inside her room. She glares back at her bedroom door before hurrying away.

Gwen creeps down the back stairs, her feet light as air on the old, creaky, wooden steps. She expects to find that she had awoken someone and to see some children or a nun at the foot of the stairs. However, all is still. The orphanage tranquil. Quietly she passes Raven's room on her way down the hall. As she scurries through the night like a shadow, all her senses search for the origins of the peculiar premonition. A deep, oozing sense of dread begins to creep over her as her search continues without any success. *What if I don't get there in time? What if I am too late?* She thinks as she passes the doors leading to the outside courtyard. *What if I'm just being silly, and there's nothing wrong? What if the man in black is just toying with me?*

Suddenly, she hears a sound outside. Frozen in place, she waits, reaching out again, this time with her mind, looking for a human presence nearby.

In her mind, she finds Douglas, the strange, hostile boy who once stole a much-unwanted kiss from her. She has barely thought of him since that day a year ago when she injured him in defense of her person. When he finally recovered and the bandages came off, he wisely chose to maintain his distance from Gwen.

The emotions racing through the boy's mind now alarm her. She feels pain and humiliation with dark; depressing thoughts of death and blood. This is startling enough, but then Gwen sees some of Douglas's recent memories.

She sees flashes of images. First, she sees Douglas sitting, trembling in fear, waiting outside Sister Whitmore's office to be punished for starting a fight. Then he's in her office, the sister looming over him, saying unspeakable things to him, making him feel uncomfortable and afraid. Then, she's touching him in places he doesn't want to be touched, most of all by her. Gwen feels his horror and shame as she witnesses through his memories the things Sister Whitmore did and made him do to her. Gwen doesn't fully understand what she sees but knows by the revolted and violated feeling that crashes upon her that it isn't right or natural.

She can feel his anguish, his shame, and his self-loathing. Most of all, she feels his overwhelming desire to die, to erase himself from the face of the earth.

This is why I was summoned here, what I have been sent to prevent from happening.

In a flash, she throws open the doors to the courtyard running down the steps into the yard, looking around frantically for the boy that should be there. It isn't until she looks up that she sees him. He stands in the chapel's bell tower, high above on the ledge, looking down at the ground in a most solemn and melancholy manner.

Gwen freezes. She doesn't want to startle him. He hasn't noticed her standing there yet. However, she has to do something. Gwen walks slowly toward the chapel, never letting her eyes lose sight of Douglas as she tries to sneak closer. She quietly creeps around the back of the church to the back door that she and Raven used only half an hour earlier. Opening the door wide enough to squeeze herself inside, she enters the chapel. She desperately hopes he doesn't jump while she's sneaking about. Fear and adrenaline rush through her as she makes her way up the steps toward the bell tower. Her heart pounds frantically in her chest; her breath catches in her throat as she rounds the last curve in the staircase and ascends to the top. The large bell blocks her field of vision. Slowly she walks around the landing surrounding the bell, still anxiously holding her breath as she comes toward the front, frightened she might not find him there. His body broken on the ground below, instead.

Douglas's thin, tall silhouette stands against the night sky. Gwen almost releases a sigh of relief but holds it in, less the sound startles Douglas, causing him to slip and fall. She slowly approaches the boy, coming up from behind him; his back slouched over and his head downturned. With shaky hands, she reaches out slowly toward the boy. Suddenly, she wraps her arms around his chest and pulls him toward her to safety.

Douglas lets out a yell of alarm as the two topple backward. Gwen lands on her back with Douglas's weight crushing her beneath him. Gwen groans in pain, desperately pushing him off of her so she can breathe. Startled and scared, Douglas rolls off her, scrambling to his feet. He turns to confront his assailant.

"What are you doing here?" Douglas demands.

"Trying to help you!" Gwen shouts back at him as she gingerly gets up off the floor, dusting herself off.

"Why would you help me? You hate me!" the nine-year-old boy quarrels back, unable to hide the instability of his voice.

"I don't like you, but that doesn't mean I want you to jump off a building," Gwen tersely replies.

Douglas becomes quiet, struck by her blunt words. Shame shows on his face. The hopeless air of someone who doesn't want to live anymore hangs about him. His life had never been easy, but the latest injustice is too much to bear on his own, and he dare not tell anyone what happened.

What does this girl know anyway? She doesn't care. Douglas thinks *if she knew... she would've pushed me off the bell tower herself.*

"No, I wouldn't. And I do know. It doesn't matter how I know; you just have to trust me," the skinny seven-year-old says in a sympathetic tone.

Douglas looks at her, dumbfounded. Stammering, he says, "Bu—but... how did you know?" he starts to say, and then changing his mind, he says, "What wouldn't you do? What do you know?" he questions, challenging her.

"You were just thinking that I would push you off the bell tower if I knew what Sister Whitmore did to you," Gwen says bluntly, not knowing how to be delicate.

Douglas gives her a skeptical look.

"What? How could you know that? No one could know...." Douglas is surprised when Gwen suddenly rushes toward him, placing her hand firmly over his mouth to stop him from speaking.

"I told you not to worry about how I know! You wouldn't believe me if I told you anyway," she says in a harsh whisper. Stepping back, she removes her hand from his mouth and instead takes his hand in hers and turns as if to lead him away. Instantly, Douglas yanks his hand back from Gwen's grasp, jerking her backward. Furious, she spins around to confront him.

"I'm not going anywhere!" Douglas protests.

"You can't kill yourself," Gwen counters. "I won't let you!"

Douglas laughs at her and turns to get back onto the ledge but stops abruptly when Gwen steps in his path.

"It isn't your fault. This doesn't fix things. I don't know how you feel, but—"

Just let him jump. He wants to. He'll be happier when he's dead. The man in black's voice echoes in her head, looking over Douglas's shoulder she finds the man standing next to the massive bell. His hands stuffed into his pocket as if talking about something as ordinary as the weather. Smiling conspiratorially, he begins to walk toward Douglas. *Better yet, why don't we push him? You'll be putting him out of his misery. He'll thank you for…*

"Shut up! Will you go away already!" Gwen blurts out aloud unintentionally.

"What?! You shut up. I'm not bothering anyone." Douglas responds in outrage. "No one asked you to butt into my business! You want me to leave, then fine! Just get out of my…"

"No, I'm sorry." Gwen grabs both his arms tightly in her fists. Her face urgent she continues, "I wasn't talking to you. I was talking to him!" Suddenly a surge of energy shoots from the boy's skin into her hands and up her arms. The world around her fades into a blur.

Before Gwen's mind's eye, she sees an image of a handsome middle-aged couple come into focus. The husband is tall, dark-haired, and athletic with a ready smile. His wife a petite, little blonde with a sweet disposition. They stand in the Mother Superiors office, looking out the window at the orphans as they play in the courtyard. Mother Superior and Sister Shaw stand next to them. They are all speaking together, but Gwen can't hear the words. She is distracted by the blonde woman and the thoughts that stream from her consciousness through the vision. She is watching the boys at play when she notices Douglas pass. His solemn demeanor and striking resemblance to her baby brother, who died when she was a teenager, catches her eye. She suddenly needs to know why this boy is so sad? Wondering what he looks like when he smiles. She wants to make him smile, care for him, and keep him safe. The woman turns to her husband.

"That's the one, honey. That's the one we want." She points to Douglas.

Mother Superior tries to dissuade the woman, telling the couple about Douglas's past and destructive behavior, but the wife just smiles and shakes her head in response. Her mind is made up.

"You know he looks a little like Tommy, doesn't he?" the husband comments to his wife. She looks up at him and smiles.

"Yes, he does," she replies.

The vision fades away, gone as suddenly as it had come, leaving Gwen feeling dazed and disorientated.

"What was that?" Gwen says aloud, wobbling a little as she feels the world begin to spin around her. Suddenly, she finds herself on the floor, Douglas kneeling beside her.

"Are you okay?" he asks with genuine concern.

"I think so. I just…saw the strangest thing," she replies, shocked.

"What do you mean?" Douglas tells her, clearly agitated. "There's something wrong with you. You're not normal. One second, you're talking to me, then you're telling me to shut up saying you went talking to me, although I'm clearly the only person here." He adds. "Then you went all still, and your eyes rolled into the back of your head,"

"I did? Oh, sorry, that's never happened to me before." Gwen tries to brush the whole thing off. She gets to her feet. Douglas stands up, watching her suspiciously. Gwen ventures a glance around but the man in black is not present. Obviously, the boy hadn't seen him. She decides not to bother mentioning the specter again, less she lost all credibility in Douglas's eyes. "I'm just tired. It's late. Come on, let's go back to bed." Again, she grabs his hand in an attempt to make him follow her.

"Why?" Douglas makes Gwen stop and turn to face him. Not wanting him to get away from her, she holds his hand. Embarrassed by the physical contact with Gwen, Douglas shakes her hand off forcibly. He grimaces in disgust, even though he feels quite the opposite.

"Give me one good reason why I shouldn't jump," he demands, staring Gwen down, determined to scare the little girl away.

"Because she needs you as much as you need her," Gwen replies calmly, not intimidated by Douglas's cold manner.

"What are you talking about?" Douglas shouts, exasperated and surprised by her strange response. "Just leave me alone!" He turns his back on her, determined that this time he will jump even if he has to do it with Gwen watching. He doesn't care anymore. He has had enough.

"Soon, a couple will come. She'll see you, and she'll love you right away. You'll remind her of her little brother Thomas. He died when he was your age. They won't care where you come from, what you've done, or what's been done to you. They'll adopt you just as you are," Gwen prophecies.

Douglas stops dead in his tracks, his back still turned away from her. He looks out of the bell tower at the orphanage and the courtyard below.

"I'm not sure what will happen after, but she seems nice, like someone who'd be a perfect mom. I think you're going to be happy with them," Gwen replies, feeling suddenly jealous of the glorious future Douglas has before him, something Gwen knows she will never have. It hasn't bothered her before, but she feels utterly unwanted and alone in the world just now. She shakes off the thought. *Now isn't the time to feel sorry for myself. I still haven't fulfilled my obligation to save Douglas. This is my top priority at the moment.* "That's a good enough reason, isn't it?"

Slowly, Douglas looks over his shoulder at Gwen.

"How can you…?" Douglas begins to ask, but Gwen cuts him off.

"I told you, just trust me. I just know things sometimes. It doesn't matter how or why!" Gwen shouts at him, losing her patience.

Douglas doesn't know how to react; stunned and speechless, he stands there. After several minutes of silence and Gwen's anger finally subsides, she steps forward and takes Douglas's hand again. This time he doesn't resist and lets Gwen lead him back around the massive bell and down the stairs from the bell tower to the chapel below. All the while, they hold hands; Gwen is leading the way. They leave the chapel through the back doors and walk around the building to the courtyard. As they walk across the yard toward the large double doors leading into the main hall, Gwen can tell he's about to ask her a question. She gives him the time to build the courage to ask it, even though she already knows what he'll say. Gwen reaches out with her free hand to turn the knob when Douglas stops her.

"Um…Gwen, can I ask you something?"

"What?" she whispers, afraid their voices will wake someone. Although no one seems to have heard them even though they had been shouting a few minutes ago.

"Do you like me?" he blurts out. Gwen must resist the urge to laugh because of the strange blush that spreads over Douglas's face.

"I don't hate you. I told you that already," she replies, a little confused as to why it matters if she likes him or not.

"Well, then… can we be friends?" he asks eagerly.

Gwen shrugs. "Okay, as long as you don't try to kiss me again or touch me at all, for that matter." She turns to the doors and opens them, going inside, ignoring the deeper beet-red color spreading across Douglas's face.

He is mortified, but he knows he should have expected her to say something like that. He knows he should apologize. He should be afraid of her. After all, she broke several of his bones when she hurled him across the courtyard. He was hospitalized for two weeks. But she has shown a different side of herself tonight. She didn't have to come to his rescue. She could have left him to his fate, but she didn't. Even though he resisted her, she stayed, bringing him down. Whether she realizes it or not, she has been kinder to him in that moment than anyone else has in his lifetime.

He isn't sure whether he believes her about the couple she predicts will come for him. After all the other strange things he has seen and heard her do, it seems possible that she could be right. The thought fills him with hope like he has never known before.

Gwen hears these thoughts, knowing she ought to shut him out, but she can't help herself. Douglas hurries after Gwen into the orphanage, trying to catch up to her. With a new spring in his step, Douglas follows Gwen back to his bedroom door where she says goodnight, waiting for him to enter his room and close the door before returning to her own bed.

Douglas listens to her footsteps recede before quietly tiptoeing between his sleeping roommate's beds. He slips into bed, pulling the covers up over him. Douglas feels many emotions surging through him, making him feel anxious with excitement. No matter what tomorrow brings, he feels a sense of peace knowing that he now has a friend.

Gwen enters her room with quite a different feeling. *Why does it hurt to know that Douglas has been afraid of me? Why does it make me uncomfortable that Douglas now thinks of me as his new best friend?* She sits on her bed a wash in confusion. *I wasn't trying to be anyone's hero. I just did what I had to do.* Thus, distracted she doesn't bother to look around to see if the mysterious man in black is lurking in the shadows. Exhausted and emotionally spent she climbs under the bedcovers, wondering if she's gotten herself in over her head with Douglas.

"*Darkana*," she whispers, and the room goes dark and still.

* * * * *

Douglas plops himself down next to Gwen at the breakfast table the following day. Raven, sitting across the table, looks up at him, incredulous. He thinks, *What, is he lost?*

"Hi, Gwen." Gwen looks up at Douglas and stifles a groan.

"Hi," she replies. Raven catches her eye. "Um… hey, it's a long story, but…."

"Gwen and I are friends now," Douglas finishes for her, a smug look on his face.

"Since when?" Raven demands coldly. Gwen feels a wave of protective possessiveness rise within him as he remembers the "Stolen Kiss" incident.

"Last night," Douglas says weakly.

"What's that supposed to mean? If you touched her, I'll-" Raven clenches his fists as disturbing images race through his mind, Gwen privy to every one of them.

"Hey, quit it! It's not like that. I'll explain later, okay?" Gwen says through tight lips, her face a shade of red Raven's never seen before. She's not the kind to embarrass easily.

"I didn't do anything, Adam," Douglas mutters sullenly.

Raven shoots daggers at him with his eyes. Gwen gives them both a look that quiets them, each boy looking down at his breakfast.

While they eat, Gwen shows Raven the events of the night before telepathically, inserting her memories into his mind, and answering his occasional nonverbal question with thought. When the meal is over, and they separate from Douglas to go to their class, Raven knows everything. And several of the other children are whispering about the three of them eating together. Gwen tries her best to shut them out and focuses on the day ahead of her.

* * * * *

Later, Douglas sits near them in their shared classes and follows Gwen and Raven about during afternoon break. By lunchtime, everyone in the orphanage is talking about the strange change in Douglas; the boy once considered one of the worst bullies in St. Paul's.

Gwen hopes that Douglas will get tired of her and Raven's bizarre company and cease following them around like a lost puppy. As time goes on, she realizes that Douglas thinks that he is now a part of their gang.

It's odd for Gwen to have Douglas as a third wheel. After all, her and Raven's friendship is natural, forged by their common differences from the other children and the knowledge that they both come from the same mysterious society and share a language no one else has ever heard. Gwen doesn't have to try to be nice or sensitive about Raven's feelings. He listens to Gwen and follows her lead instead of being the center of attention. He speaks only when he has something important to say, letting her know if he doesn't share her point of view. For the most part, he is a terribly agreeable eleven-year-old boy.

Douglas is entirely different. Gwen has to try not to offend him, for he is headstrong, opinionated, sensitive, and irrational. The two frequently have heated debates about every topic under the sun. It seems they can't agree on anything, yet he hangs on her every word as though they're dripping with wisdom. Occasionally, he glances at her admiringly when he thinks she won't notice, but telepaths notice everything.

Raven can't stand Douglas's confrontational manners. Not that it bothers him when Gwen is blunt or abrasive. Somehow, it's endearing when she does it, but it's rude when Douglas acts this way. He hates how he stares at Gwen and fawns over her, always managing to put himself between Raven and Gwen. He misses the peace of the old days when it was only the two of them. When they could race in the forest, climb trees, and play in the waterfall. They rarely do any of those things now. They don't want to have to explain how they're able to do those things. Obviously, they're different. As far as they know, they're the only two people in the world who can run, jump, and climb like the Greek gods in the stories.

Douglas has seen enough of Gwen's peculiarities to suspect the truth and constantly asks her questions. Raven is the only one who really knows everything there is to know about Gwen. He likes it that way. The only other person either of them has ever confided in is Sister Mary Shaw, who is like a loving older sister with whom they know their secrets are safe.

* * * * *

The three of them sit under the walnut tree. With Gwen in the middle, Raven pulls up grass to her right with Douglas to her left, tossing a baseball in the air with one hand and catching it in the other. Gwen looks up from her heavily edited Harlequin paperback to see Douglas staring at her again. He smiles at her pleasantly. Gwen raises an eyebrow at him in response.

"Is that book any good?" Douglas asks.

Gwen shrugs, noncommittal.

"Then why do you keep reading it?"

"I finish every book I start," Gwen answers.

"Even if it sucks?" Douglas asks, disbelieving.

"Especially if it sucks."

"You wouldn't believe how bad some of those books are," Raven, looking around Gwen, chirps in.

"Why don't you two go do something useful instead of criticizing my book?" Gwen asks. She opens up the book to ignore them.

Douglas looks over to Raven.

"You want to play catch?" Douglas asks.

"Sure. Why not."

From behind the cover of her book, Gwen watches the two boys walk into the center of the courtyard. Douglas gestures to Raven to back up. Raven wanders fifteen feet away. Satisfied, Douglas tosses Raven the ball.

Gwen is pleased to watch the changes in Douglas. She never really noticed before what a loner he had been. She at least has Raven to confide in and Sister Shaw. But now that they're all friends, he seems to be a whole new person, although a bit irritating. He's almost enjoyable… sometimes.

Douglas has completely changed in his demeanor toward the other children as well. His manners and behavior are polite yet detached. He's open and friendly with Gwen and Raven just as long as Gwen agrees with him on everything. Which she never does.

Douglas even gets along with Raven as long as he stays out of his way when he wants to be close to Gwen, which she knows drives Raven crazy.

It gives her a funny feeling, knowing she's done something to help another. She stuck her neck out for Douglas and now must endure the consequences of her actions. *If only he'd stop looking at me in that peculiar way, everything would be just fine.*

Just then, Gwen decides it is a good thing that she followed her premonition to the bell tower that night. She will forever be grateful that she hadn't turned her back on the boy in the tower.

CHAPTER SEVEN

A Better Place

"**Y**ou can do nothing to stop her, Gwen. The Mother Superior will never believe you or Douglas."

Raven keeps his voice low as they make their way toward the Mother Superior's office. He looks about the halls suspiciously as if expecting Sister Whitmore to jump out from behind a bookcase. Suddenly appearing to stop them at any moment.

"Why not? If Douglas says it happened, she has to listen. Why would anybody lie about something like that?" Gwen turns to him, incredulous, yet continues walking toward her destination, not swayed from her task. "She can't know about this, I'm sure. I don't like Mother Sullivan, but she's honest and believes in what they're doing here. If someone's hurting one of the children, she has to protect them, even from one of her closest friends."

They turn the last corner into the main hall. Half a dozen offices line one wall. At the far end is the Mother Superior's office.

Raven shakes his head emphatically. "She'll never believe it of Sister Whitmore, and she'll never believe if it is coming from you or Douglas. Neither of you is her favorite, you know?"

"I have to try, Raven," Gwen replies solemnly. Raven hangs back as Gwen approaches Mother Sullivan's office and raps on the door.

A moment later, Sister Bernard, Mother Sullivan's current attendant, opens the door.

"What is it, child?"

"I have something to tell the Mother. It's very important." Sister Bernard looks over her shoulder back into the room, sharing a whispered exchange with the Mother, and then turns back to Gwen.

"You may come in, Marianne." She opens the door wide. Within, Raven sees the Mother sitting at her desk with a weary look on her face. Gwen pauses and turns to Raven, a question in her green eyes.

Raven instantly shakes his head and backs away. "I'll wait here for you." Gwen nods resigned. She enters the office as fearless as a warrior going into battle. Sister Bernard closes the door behind them, leaving Raven alone in the hall to await the outcome.

Ten minutes later, Raven hears raised voices within. In the next moment, the door to the office swings open. A very indignant Gwen is hulled by the collar out of the Mother Superior's office by the pale-faced Sister Bernard. Her ashen countenance in stark contrast to her black habit. The usually mellow nun gives him a tight-lipped glare as she and Gwen pass him down the hall. Gwen tries to reason with the nun but her demands to be let go and allowed to walk on her own are ignored. Raven stays back, wanting to follow Gwen but afraid to anger the nun further. However, in his hesitation, he's caught in front of the open door of Mother Superior's office. She stomps up to the office door, he catches a glimpse of the imposing woman's face before she slams the door shut. Her look of sheer hatred burns into his memory giving him a shiver.

Terrified, he hurries away down the hall after Gwen, only he never catches sight of her or Sister Bernard. At once, he goes to Gwen's room in the attic but finds it empty. After wandering the halls, a while, the bell for the midday meal tolls and he makes his way to the dining hall. Gwen isn't there. Raven settles down at their table to wait. After the food is blessed and served, he eats dispassionately, eyes constantly glancing at the doors for Gwen's entrance. She never comes.

"Where's Gwen?" Douglas inquires. Sitting a crossed the table from him, he looks to Raven expectantly. The older boy just looks back at his unwanted table guest for a long awkward moment. "Is something wrong? Is she okay?" Douglas questions further the idea of Gwen being in trouble clearly distressing to him.

"Whatever happens to her, it's all your fault." Raven replies with a narrow-eyed glare. With that he goes back to eating his lunch and ignores any further inquiries from Douglas. When the class bell rings Raven is grateful to get away from Douglas who relentlessly tries to get Raven to respond to him. Thankfully, they don't share any of the afternoon classes. Raven leaves Douglas perplexed and pale with anxiety.

With a hollow feeling in his gut, Raven goes about his afternoon classes without her, only to worry about her throughout the day when she still doesn't appear.

Only late that night when he sneaks up to Gwen's room does he finally find out what happened in that office.

He knocks at the door softly, not wanting to wake anyone. Suddenly, the door swings open all its own to reveal Gwen sitting on her bed in her pajamas with a notebook in her lap and a Bible lying open beside her.

"Come on in." Gwen waves him in. Raven takes a seat cross-legged on the floor, his face turned up to her expectantly.

Gwen ignores him and goes back to writing something vigorously on her notepad.

"I told you so."

Her pen stops mid stroke and Gwen glares down at him. Then she returns back to her work, leaving him to watch her downturned head for a while in silence.

"If you're not gonna tell me what happened, can you at least tell me what you're doing?" Raven probes.

Sighing Gwen sits up and looks down at him. "I'm drafting an essay on the book of Genesis. It's a report on what happened to the serpent that beguiled Eve in the Garden of Eden. It's supposed to teach me not to lie or deceive," Gwen replies with a smirk and a shrug. "I'm not so sure the Mother Superior understands the true meaning of the creation story," Gwen confides in Raven. "I might tell her so in my essay," she adds tersely.

"So, I take it she didn't believe you?" Gwen shakes her head in the negative. "And this is what they've had you doing all day? Couldn't you come down to eat at least?"

"Nope. Sister Bernard had me in the library studying the scriptures most of the day. She said I can eat when the essay is finished."

"Oh, well... maybe if we just keep Douglas out of trouble you won't have to worry about Whitmore anyway."

Gwen looks at him, stunned. "Wrong is wrong, Raven. She can't get away with it or she'll do it again. I'm pretty sure she has before."

This quiets Raven. Gwen goes back to working on her essay. After a long awkward silence, Raven gets up.

"Want me to go sneak something from the kitchen for you?" he asks.

"Sure, something from Whitmore's stash." Gwen smiles wickedly.

"Easy. I'll be right back." Raven closes Gwen's bedroom door on his way down the stairs. He quietly moves from shadow to shadow toward the kitchen, hoping that this whole incident resolves itself. At least for the moment, Gwen, is discouraged from her heroic efforts on Douglas's behalf.

* * * * *

A few months later, Douglas finds himself in trouble again. One of the other boys makes a snide comment in front of him about Gwen and it quickly turns into a shoving match. This gets the hotheaded Douglas sent to be disciplined. Gwen also finds a way to be sent to Sister Whitmore's office. An easy enough task for Gwen.

A few old wooden chairs sit just outside the nun's office. Gwen and Douglas occupy two of them. Douglas fidgets anxiously. Gwen, trying to remain calm for his sake, stays out of his head, not needing a reminder of why he's so terrified of Sister Whitmore.

The door opens, and the nun in question looms above them in the doorway, a tall figure in black. She points to Douglas with a cold expression.

"Douglas, you may come in." He stands reluctantly and follows the sister inside the office. Jumping out of her seat, Gwen follows fast on their heels and closes the door behind her before they have time to react.

"Marianne, you are to wait outside in the hall," Sister Whitmore commands sternly. Douglas nervously looks between Gwen and the elderly nun as he takes the chair in front of the desk. "I'll deal with you in a moment. Now leave," Sister Whitmore insists again in a far more intimidating voice. Gwen stands by the door staring the ancient, wiry old lady down.

"I can wait right here," Gwen replies. After several minutes of silence, angry stares, the sister gives Gwen a chilling smile.

"Very well, but you'll receive double the punishment for this," Sister Whitmore concedes and then goes on with her lecture for Douglas. Unable to get Gwen to leave the room, Sister Whitmore resorts to whipping Douglas's palms with a rod instead of paddling him or worse. Since Gwen is present, Douglas musters the strength not to cry out in pain when the rod strikes his palms, determined not to appear weak in front of her.

Once Douglas is finished, Gwen takes his place and receives her punishment from Sister Whitmore. She never flinches or makes a sound as her hands are abused. They turn red, welts appearing with every blow dealt to them. True to Whitmore's word, Gwen receives twice the usual lashes.

Afterward, Douglas boasts of her bravery to Raven, who's rarely ever seen the inside of Sister Whitmore's office. He goes on and on about how Gwen didn't cry out or make a fuss like other girls would have done.

The next time Gwen gets in trouble, Douglas suddenly shows up at her side outside Sister Whitmore's office, ready to repay his debt. Gwen smiles. When she is called in, Douglas goes in with her to face Whitmore together. This goes on a handful of times. Gwen is often sent to Sister Whitmore for speaking out in class or talking back to a teacher. Douglas is often disciplined for losing his temper or defending Gwen after the other children mock her. Gwen tells him over and over again to leave it alone, that she doesn't care what the others say or think of her. Douglas refuses to listen. He has become every bit as protective of her as Raven.

Raven can't stand another day of Gwen being paddled for Douglas's sake, of her being harmed because of that arrogant know-it-all Douglas! Raven enlists to help Gwen with her quest to get rid of Sister Whitmore.

Finally, he finds his chance when Father O'Brien returns from his mother's funeral, at which he presided. He has been gone a long time since his family all lived in the Midwest and he is called upon to give counsel and guidance to the family in their time of need. The moment he hears the sisters say the priest has returned, Raven goes to Gwen with the good news.

The next morning, Gwen, Douglas, and Raven sit in the line of chairs in the main hall just outside of Father O'Brien's personal office. The Father is already speaking with Sister Shaw, whom they recruit to help convince the Father of the truthfulness of their accusations. Even though she hasn't seen any proof herself, Sister Shaw believes Gwen implicitly, especially when she tells her that she has also seen similar images in Sister Whitmore's thoughts when they have been in her office. With some considerable coaxing from Gwen, Douglas confides in Sister Shaw the whole story of the sexual assault. Now it's up to Sister Shaw to convince the Father.

After what happened when Gwen went to the Mother Superior on her own, Sister Shaw advised that it would be better if she went with them this time. She also helped Douglas come to terms with the fact that he would have to make an official statement to the father and to the police.

Anxious, Douglas tensely rubs the floor in front of his chair with the toe of his shoe, the rubber of his soles leaving black marks on the polished wooden floor. His head turned down; he watches the marks appear as if this is the most fascinating sight in the world. Watching him out of the corner of her eye, Gwen can't help but feel sorry for Douglas. She wouldn't want to be in his place right now. She knows what it's like to have people doubt you, to be called a liar, but she can't imagine how difficult it will be to recount Sister Whitmore's evil deeds against him. Gwen shivers at the very thought of the things she has seen in his memories. If she doesn't want to re-live those dark images, she doubts Douglas does either. However, only he can tell his story. If not to have justice done, then to help himself come to terms with the encounter and put it behind him indefinitely.

Just then, the door to Father O'Brien's office opens and Sister Shaw exits, followed by the father himself. He is a tall, thin, kind, elderly man in his late sixties with a silvery ring of hair around his balding head, smiling eyes, and a friendly disposition. At the moment, however, Gwen notices that his face wears a grave expression. His manner is serious, yet calm and thoughtful.

"Douglas, would you step into my office, please?" he asks in a gentle tone that brings Douglas out of his preoccupied state. He turns to Gwen immediately.

"Will you come with me, Gwen?"

Before she can answer, however, the priest speaks up. "It is better we talk alone, Douglas. I need to be certain that this is true, and I need to hear it from you without anyone else influencing you," he tells him kindly.

Douglas looks up at the father and gulps. Standing, he passes Sister Shaw who gives him an encouraging pat on the back before he enters the office. Father O'Brien follows him inside, closing the door.

Sister Shaw takes the chair that Douglas vacated between Raven and Gwen, smiling reassuringly at both of them. They wait in complete silence for what seems like an hour before Douglas and Father O'Brien come out again. Douglas's eyes are red-rimmed and bloodshot. He sniffles and wipes his nose with a tissue, embarrassed. Father O'Brien whispers something encouraging to him, patting him on the back before he turns and looks at Gwen.

"I'd like a moment, Marianne. Please, step inside," Father O'Brien requests. He steps back into the office, fully expecting Gwen to follow him. Hesitantly, Gwen gets up from her seat, giving Douglas a quizzical look as she passes him, but Douglas only shrugs his shoulders in response. Gwen goes into the office, shutting the door.

Father O'Brien's office is simple with its dark wood-paneled walls, dark cherry wood desk, and furnishings. The father sits at his desk in his large leather chair, indicating for Gwen to take the chair in front of his desk. Gwen notices as she takes the seat the aroma of old spice and peppermint candy about the room. That's when she spies the candy dish on the corner of his desk, filled with the circular red and white striped treats. She resists the urge to swipe one from the glass jar and folds her hands in her lap instead.

"Let's cut to the chase, shall we?" Father O'Brien declares. "Douglas told me all about Sister Whitmore, but he also told me about an incident involving him and yourself in the chapel's bell tower. Is what he told me true?" he asks Gwen point-blank.

Gwen admires his straightforward manner but feels unsure of herself, hesitant to talk about the strange turn of events that brought her to Douglas's rescue at the right place and time.

"Well, what did he say happened?" she counters, not sure if she can trust the old man with the details.

"A lot of peculiar things, actually. He claims you showed up out of nowhere and saved him from taking his own life." He waits for Gwen to either confirm or deny this. She nods in the affirmative. "He also says you knew what he was thinking, and that, without being told, knew what Sister Whitmore had done to him. He also says you saw a vision of some kind?"

Gwen's face flushes as he lists the truth of these things, feeling betrayed and mortified that Douglas would tell him so much.

"Yes, I did those things." Gwen's whole body grows rigid with fear.

Father O'Brien looks at her, dumbfounded. Apparently, he expects her to deny the last part as Douglas's wild imagination. "Does this kind of thing happen a lot, Marianne? Oh, forgive me. I forgot you prefer to be called Gwen. Is that right?"

Gwen nods.

"Well, I've heard all the reports from Mother Sullivan, of course, but nothing odd has happened in some time. I'll admit I had almost forgotten all about your peculiar gifts until today. Am I to take it, then, that this sort of thing happens all the time, but that you've just chosen to be more discreet than you were in the past?" he asks her calmly.

"Yes. I don't want to scare anybody. The others are already afraid of me anyway. Why make things worse than they already are?" Gwen replies matter-of-factly.

The father just nods in response. As he sits, he ponders for a long while before he looks up at Gwen again. "Well, I'd like it if in the future you came to me when you had these premonitions or visions. I'd like to be kept informed of what else is happening around here, especially things about which I don't know." He pauses a moment. "Sister Whitmore doesn't have any other victims, does she?" Father O'Brien asks timidly as if he isn't sure he wants to hear the answer.

"There have been others over the years, but they're all gone now. Douglas is the only one recently," Gwen confirms.

Father O'Brien slouches in his chair with a sigh of resignation.

"I was afraid of that. Could you possibly give a list of names or describe the faces of the other children?" he asks.

"I know their names," Gwen replies.

Father O'Brien takes a notepad and a pen out of his desk drawer and slides them over to Gwen. Immediately, she begins to scribble down the names of the boys she saw in Sister Whitmore's thoughts and memories, shivering with disdain as she writes them all down. When she is done, Gwen looks over the list, checking to make sure she hasn't forgotten anyone and then hands the list over to the Father. His face falls into an expression of horror and disgust as he looks at the list of names, recognizing some of the most disturbed and rebellious boys who came through St. Paul. Shaking his head in acquiescence, he sets the list aside.

The father sits thinking quietly along moment. Unable to stand the silence, Gwen allows her mental barrier to fall away and peeks into Father O'Brien's thoughts.

Now I know there's some truth to these accusations. It is simply impossible for this girl to know any of these names. If there were even one false name on the list, someone who had never been at St. Paul's, then I could still have reasonable doubt but... sixteen accurate names? This can be no coincidence. With resignation Father O'Brien's eyes meet hers and he quiets the tumult of feelings raging in his heart to focus on the practical.

"Now, I'm going to have to ask you to keep silent on this matter, for the children's sake, not to mention the church's as well. It would be better if we leave this matter out of the public eye and just let the police handle it," Father O'Brien councils Gwen as he reaches for the telephone on his desk and calls the police department. While he waits for the line to pick up, he asks, "Have you told anyone else besides Sister Shaw and your friend Adam about this?"

"Yes. I went to Mother Sullivan first, but she wouldn't believe me," Gwen tells the Father.

"She wouldn't, of course. She and Sister Whitmore have been friends for a long time. They knew each other before they took the veil." He hesitates before asking, "Mother Sullivan didn't know this was going on, did she?"

"No. She thinks very highly of Sister Whitmore. She never thought anything was wrong," Gwen confides, wishing she could tell him otherwise so she could get rid of the unkind Mother Superior as well, but Gwen will not lie. It is beneath her and out of her character.

Someone at the police station answers the phone and Father O'Brien goes about the business of filling the detective in on the whole situation. He excuses Gwen with the understanding that she will have to give a statement to the police later that day, and possibly even be a witness if the case should later go to trial.

When Gwen finally leaves the office, she lets out a sigh of relief. *It's finally done with*, she thinks, feeling her duty to Douglas now resolved for the last time. Together, Sister Shaw, Raven, Douglas, and Gwen all wait for the police to arrive. Later, when Gwen thinks back on it, everything seemed to happen so fast.

The police come, and Sister Whitmore, who suspects nothing, is arrested. As a favor to Father O'Brien, she isn't handcuffed but simply escorted off the premises. The children stand in doorways and gather in the halls to watch her go. With a police officer on either side of her, Ellen Whitmore leaves the orphanage with her head held high and her face livid. No one but Mother Sullivan seems the least bit upset about Sister Whitmore's departure. The Mother Superior insists all the while that it is all a mistake and that three wicked, lying children simply fooled Father O'Brien.

Reluctantly, however, the Mother Superior is convinced after each name on the list is contacted, every one of them confirming that Sister Whitmore had indeed molested them. Some of the former victims come forward, willing to testify against the nun. Others choose to stay anonymous, just grateful to know that Sister Whitmore will finally get what she deserves.

Sister Whitmore has a private hearing and opts to take a guilty plea rather than fight the charges and drag everything out into a public court. She is convicted of sixteen counts of child molestation and sentenced to forty years in prison. After her conviction, she is officially excommunicated from the church. Despite all the churches best efforts to keep the matter out of the public eye. The story appears all over the local news outlets. Unfortunately, people become suspicious of all the sisters at St. Paul's after the word gets out. The orphanage is put under investigation for several months, but in the end, the police find nothing incriminating. They officially state that the institution was a sound, safe home for the children, and the sisters there were loving guardians and teachers. The circumstance of Ellen Whitmore's behavior was the act of an individual and does not reflect on the other Sisters at St. Paul's or Father O'Brien.

Eventually, things go back to normal, and everyone in town moves on passed the sensational news story about St. Paul Catholic Orphanage. Prospective adopting parents begin visiting St. Paul again, and life returns to the old ways: a steady routine of worship, schoolwork, and discipline.

* * * * *

Gwen is on her way back to her English class after her monthly visit with Father O'Brien, a tradition they started after the whole Sister

Whitmore affair. As she crosses the main foyer, she sees Sister Shaw escorting a young couple down the hall. Gwen stops and watches them. Smiling at Gwen, Sister Shaw passes by her, leading the couple toward the Mother Superior's office.

Gwen gasps, her mouth agape in amazement as the couple passes in front of her. The tall, dark-haired man towers over his sweet, little blonde wife, who turns and gives Gwen a polite smile before going on after the others. Gwen stands, frozen in place, unable to believe her eyes. It is the very same couple she saw in the vision six months earlier. She watches them enter the office at the end of the hall, dumbfounded. When the shock wears off, Gwen runs down the hall, turning down the next corridor toward her classroom on the other side of the building.

By the time she walks into class, she is out of breath, her cheeks flushed from the excursion. As she enters, Raven looks up, his interest piqued by the excited look on Gwen's face. Quietly, she makes her way to the empty desk in front of Ravens.

Trying to appear as if reading the assignment in her textbook, Gwen quickly fills Raven in, showing him the scene that occurred in the main hall. Raven is just about to respond back to Gwen when Sister Bernard suddenly stands, commanding the attention of the entire class.

"That will be all for today, children. Don't forget to read chapters nineteen through twenty-three tonight. There will be a quiz on them tomorrow. Class dismissed," Sister Bernard instructs. The children wait patiently until she's done speaking before they gather their belongings and hurry out of the classroom, eager to enjoy the midday break.

Gwen and Raven talk quietly about what she saw earlier as they make their way down the hall and out into the courtyard. They cross the yard to their walnut tree, their usual hangout spot. Just then, Gwen sees Douglas exit the building and head toward them.

"I hope you're right about those people. I'm kind of tired of Douglas hanging around us all the time," Raven admits to Gwen before Douglas comes in earshot.

"Hey, how was class?" Douglas inquires of Gwen, giving Raven a brief nod of recognition before standing next to her. Raven doesn't like how close Douglas stands and gives him an annoyed look, but Douglas ignores it.

"All right, but guess what?" Gwen says excitedly.

"What?"

"You're getting adopted today!" Gwen answers with a big smile on her face.

"What are you talking about?" Douglas asks incredulously.

"Remember the couple I told you about, the one in my vision?" Douglas just nods absently. "Well, they're here. I saw them go into Mother Sullivan's office ten minutes ago," she finishes, feeling rather pleased. Douglas stares at Gwen in disbelief.

"That's impossible. No one has visions. You just made all that stuff up so I wouldn't jump," he accuses her, barely able to keep control of his anger as he speaks in a harsh whisper.

Raven takes a few steps toward Douglas as if to warn him against yelling at Gwen, but she doesn't pay either boy any mind.

"Fine, don't believe me, then. But it's true. You'll find out soon," she adds.

"What if I don't want to be adopted? Huh? I like things the way they are!" Douglas retorts testily.

"Why?" Raven asks, surprised by the younger boy's statement.

"Because I have friends here. I don't know those people, and I won't know anyone wherever they live!" He all but shouts at Raven, who towers over both of them by several inches.

"So, you'll make friends," responds Gwen, feeling a little annoyed.

"I don't like being the new kid. Besides, making friends isn't that easy," Douglas admits, his temper cooling down. He hesitantly looks at Raven before stepping closer to Gwen to whisper something in her ear. Raven hears it anyway.

"I want to stay here with you, Gwen."

Gwen's face shows her discomfort. She stays silent for several minutes, Douglas fidgeting nervously. "You can't stay here, Douglas. Any of these kids would be glad to have this chance, to have their own family to love them. Don't be an idiot and throw it away!" she tells him bluntly.

"Don't you want me to stay?" Douglas asks. A pathetic expression on his face.

"No! You're not one of us! Raven and I are different. Someday we're going to leave this place and find our own people. You can't come with us!" Gwen tries to say it as gently as possible, but still, it sounds like a flat rejection.

Douglas's face goes red with embarrassment. Slowly, his face contorts in rage. "So that's how it is, huh? You'll take him with you, but you don't want me to tag along, is that it?" He all but spits the words at her, glaring all the while at Raven, who returns his gaze with an even more menacing glare of his own.

"Don't be stupid, Douglas!" Gwen steps between the two boys, and, losing her temper, she turns on Douglas, her yellow-green eyes flashing with emotion. "I don't hate you, but I never said we were friends! It's nothing personal. Raven and I aren't like the rest of you. We might not even be human!" she shouts at him. The hurt look on Douglas's face causes Gwen to instantly relax, letting her nerves unwind and her breathing to steady. In a calmer voice, she says, "You have a chance to have a real-life if you'll stop feeling sorry for yourself. Raven and I will never have that chance, so be grateful. At least someone wants you. No one will ever want us."

Feeling the tears gathering, Gwen turns and walks away at a brisk pace, not bothering to say goodbye to either of the two boys. She keeps walking until she finds the forest that lines the grounds of the orphanage. She knows she should stop, but she doesn't turn back. She walks aimlessly onward, trying to put distance between her and the truth. She will miss Douglas, but she said what was necessary. *It's better for him to leave, to go and live with that nice, young couple than to go with Raven and I on our quest. Who knows where we'll find our own kind, or how long we'll be searching?*

Pondering on the possibility of what they might find out there in the big wide world, Gwen stays in the forest for many hours. She does not bother to return for lunch or the afternoon classes.

Raven is relieved when she finally appears in the dining hall at dinnertime. He rushes to her as she makes her way toward their isolated table in the back of the room. "You okay, Gwen?" he asks, noticing the blank, cold look on her angelic face.

"I'm fine," she replies, taking her usual place on the bench. Raven sits next to her.

In minutes Sister Bernard approaches their table. "Marianne, come with me. The Mother would like a word with you." Sister Bernard's usual friendly tone is now stern as she takes Gwen by the hand, leading her up to the front of the dining hall.

Raven watches her depart, finding it strange that such a sweet, innocent-looking girl could get into trouble so often. He feels sorry for Gwen when she gets reprimanded before the whole assembly and sent to her room without supper, despite the protests from Sister Shaw and some of the other nuns. Gwen pauses at the door and looks at Raven. He gives her a conspiratorial smile. She returns it with a wan smile of her own before walking out the doors, heading back to her lonely attic bedroom with an empty stomach and tears in her eyes.

The rest of the day goes by painfully slow for Raven as he goes about his regular routine, awaiting the opportunity to slip away and visit Gwen. It isn't until after everyone is in bed and the lights are put out that Raven finally gets his chance. Careful not to wake his roommates as he slips into the hall, he makes a quick stop at the kitchen before going up the back stairs to Gwen's loft.

Balancing a plate of leftovers, a candy bar, and a can of soda in one hand, Raven uses his free hand to knock on Gwen's bedroom door. After a few moments, the door creaks open. Gwen peeks out at him suspiciously. Then, seeing the food in his hand, she opens the door wide to let him in. He steps inside and Gwen closes the door behind him. To his surprise, she is still wearing her clothes from that afternoon.

"Hi," Gwen says.

"Here. Are you starving?" Raven asks as he hands her the plate of food. She takes it and sits down on the bed to eat, eager to fill her belly.

"Thanks, Raven, I was hoping you'd come." She smiles weakly at him before she begins eating.

Raven sets the candy bar and can of soda on top of the dresser nearby before taking a seat on the bed next to her. They sit there in silence for several minutes.

"So, are you going to tell me what happened to Douglas?" Gwen asks in between bites of food.

"I thought you already knew," he replies, opening the can of soda and handing it to Gwen. She takes a long gulp of the drink.

"Tell me anyway. I didn't see everything that would happen, just parts," Gwen explains.

"Well, he was pretty upset when you ran off like you did."

"I didn't run off," Gwen interrupts him.

"Okay," Raven says to placate her. Gwen gestures for him to continue. "After you left, he didn't say anything to me, he just walked away. The bell rang and we all went back inside for class. I would've come to get you, Gwen, but I had a feeling you wanted to be alone. I'm sorry you got in trouble though."

"It's not your fault. I just needed to think about things," she reassures him.

"Okay." He pauses. "Well, later after classes were over, Douglas came up to me and asked if I'd seen you. I told him that you hadn't come back yet. He looked a little worried, but I told him you were fine. Anyway, he told me to tell you that you were right. He said that Sister Shaw got him out of his class and took him to the Mother Superior's office. The couple you told him about was there. After they talked to him a while, they asked if he wanted to go live with them, and he said yes. He was just gathering his things when he came looking for you. He left before dinnertime." While Raven speaks, he watches Gwen's reaction to his words, not certain if she is upset or relieved.

Finished with her food, Gwen sets the plate aside. She gets up and goes to the chest of drawers. Opening the top drawer, she retrieves a black canvas book and a wooden case. Before she sits back down, she grabs the candy bar and takes her seat next to him.

She hands the book and wooden case to Raven.

"These were on my bed when I got here," Gwen explains. She peels the wrapper off of the candy bar, breaks it in half, and hands part of it to Raven.

"Was there a note?" Raven asks, taking a bite of the candy bar before opening the wooden case. Inside, he finds a travel-size art kit filled with colored pencils, erasers, pens, a pencil sharpener, charcoal, oil pastels, brushes, and several little tubes of paint.

"On the inside cover of the sketch book," Gwen answers.

Raven opens it and reads the inscription he finds there.

Gwen,

I noticed how much you like to draw, so I got you this. I was going to give it to you for Christmas or for your birthday. However, I'm going to go live with Lisa and Matthew Engershaw now. I won't be around in January, so I'm giving it to you now. Have a happy eighth birthday, Gwen! Thank you for everything. I'll try to write to you often. I'll miss you!

Douglas Williams

P.S. I hope you'll still let me be your friend.

* * * * *

Winter is on the way. Gwen pulls a black woolen hood around her, her fur-lined boots keeping her feet warm as she walks the orphanage grounds. She kicks at the twigs scattered on the ground near the tree line of the woods.

She has to admit that she kind of misses Douglas. She enjoys the sketchbook and drawing kit he gave her, using it every day. Passing her time on lonely days in the courtyard drawing plants and trees, sometimes she even draws Raven and Sister Shaw.

Often, while she's outside sketching, she gets the strangest sensation that she's being watched. When she looks up, she sees no one, but whenever she passes the chapel, she feels compelled to look up at the bell tower. She half expects to see Douglas standing there on the ledge looking down on her.

True to his word, Douglas writes to Gwen once every week since he left. Gwen keeps his letters stowed away in her art kit, careful not to read them in front of Raven, ever the older brother, brooding and protective.

I never wanted to be Douglas's friend, so why do I feel such emptiness? From the first day he came to St. Paul's, he had been rude and obnoxious. After she saved his life and he began to hang around her and Raven, she found his company entertaining. He had a mind of his own and wasn't afraid to say what he thought or get the things he wanted, however abrasively he went about getting them. Gwen found in Douglas a temperament a little more akin to her own, unlike Raven, who is often too agreeable. *Sometimes it's nice to have someone to challenge you, someone who doesn't give you your way all the time. Not that I'm spoiled, far from it,* she tells herself as she walks between the barren aspen trees, the snow crunching as her boots leave white footprints behind.

Gwen places her gloved hand in her coat pocket, pulling out a folded letter. She opens it and reads it again.

Douglas gets along great with his new dad, who's teaching him to fish and hunt. He thinks the world of Mrs. Engershaw who's apparently a world-class cook. He's doing better in school now since he has a private tutor and he's even making a few new friends. Gwen tries to be happy for him. Some part of her is, yet still a bitter emptiness inside makes her angry at the entire world. She hasn't written Douglas back at all. His letters keep coming and she can't even muster the courage to pick up a pen. Every time she tries, she loses her nerve. *After all, what do I even have to write about?*

The bell tower rings the hour nearby and Gwen sighs. A cloud of cold mist forming before her mouth as she folds up the letter and stuffs it back into her pocket. Slowly she wanders back toward the orphanage. Its silhouette standing out against the purple sky of dusk.

"Why bother him with details of our pathetic routine?" she asks herself aloud. "Why tell him that I miss him like crazy? I can't even admit that to Raven. Why remind him of this place at all? He's better off in his world and I'm better off living in mine." She enters St. Paul's and makes her way through the halls toward her attic room. Gwen crosses the threshold and goes straight to the art kit.

Opening it, she gathers Douglas's letters in her hands and carries them across the room to dump them in the trashcan. She stares down at them a moment before she places the letter from her pocket on top of the rest. She feels a pang of regret but pushes it away. *It is better that he forgets me,* she tells herself. *After all, I'm stuck here, and he's free out there in a better place.*

CHAPTER EIGHT

A Peculiar Pair

G wen anxiously pulls at the hem of her skirt as she walks through the corridors of St. Paul, making her way toward the all-too-familiar office of Father O'Brien.

Everywhere she looks she sees the images from her nightmares springing to life before her waking eyes. She walks past a classroom and sees the room engulfed in flames, smoke billowing out of the open doorway into the hall. All around her, children wearing pajamas are running in a panic, screaming, and frantically clawing and shoving against one another to get out of the burning building.

She steps into the front foyer with trepidation, the walls, and the floorboards ablaze, the roar of the fire loud in her ears. She hears voices and turns to see some of the ghost-like shadows of sisters still dressed in their nightgowns. Trying to keep order the women usher children down one of the back passages and away from the inferno. Gwen's senses fill with the heat and the noise of the raging fire all around her. Her mouth goes dry. Every pore sweats with the imaginary heat.

A hand grasps her shoulder. With a shriek, Gwen whirls around to see Mother Sullivan looming over her.

"What's the matter with you, Marianne? Not up to some mischiefs again, are you?" Mother Sullivan questions with an interrogating tone while squinting suspiciously down her long nose. "Answer me when I ask you a question, child."

Gwen, still shaken by the images from her vision, has trouble finding her tongue. "I was just going to see Father O'Brien, Mother," she replies hesitantly. Just then, Father O'Brien steps out of his office. Gwen turns away from the Mother Superior and starts to walk toward the Father, but suddenly she becomes dizzy, her legs giving out beneath her.

Gwen finds herself on the floor, the Father by her side. He scoops her up into his arms. Carrying Gwen's slender, limp body, he takes her into his office and sets her down in the large, comfortable armchair next to the window. Feeling weak and nauseous, Gwen lies back in the chair and closes her eyes.

Father O'Brien turns to the Mother. "Quickly, fetch a glass of water, please," he orders, not bothering to see if she obeys. He focuses all his attention on Gwen. Reluctantly, Mother Sullivan leaves the room.

"What's wrong, child? Have you had enough to eat today?" Father O'Brien asks, gently.

"I've had another vision, Father." Gwen opens her glazed eyes, speaking in a distant voice.

"Have you, now? Is it the vision that's causing you to be so ill, my child?" Father O'Brien takes one of her hands in his and pats it tenderly.

"Yes, it was like this last time, but it went away. I've been having the same vision for a week." Gwen takes a deep breath to steady herself.

"Please, will you tell me what you've seen?" The priest asks earnestly.

"Fire in the hall, outside, in the classrooms, down the hall, all of St. Paul in flames." Her voice sounds dark and far away as she speaks.

"What nonsense!" Mother Sullivan exclaims. They both turn to see her standing in the doorway. The father retrieves the glass of water from Mother Sullivan, returning immediately to offer the refreshment to Gwen. She drinks, the cold liquid reviving her.

"It's true!" Gwen looks the larger woman in the eye with solemnity.

"Don't listen to her, Father. Marianne is a compulsive liar, a thief, and a cheater. I have tried many times to correct these flaws in her, but she is willful and bad-natured to the core. I will have her removed from your sight, and she shall not bother you again." Mother Sullivan moves to usher Gwen away. The father stands in her path.

"That will not be necessary. I will hear what the girl has to say. You may go, Mother." Father O'Brien dismisses the nun and gives Gwen his undivided attention. "Go on, Gwen, tell me everything."

Mother Sullivan lingers. "Her name is Marianne, Father."

"My name is Gwenevere." Gwen's irritation gives her strength. She sits up and glares at the plump Mother Superior.

"Don't worry about her, Gwen. Relax." The Priest pauses, waiting for Gwen to sit back in the chair and return her attention on him. "Now, Gwen, I need to know when the fire will happen, where it starts, and if anyone will be harmed," he instructs, his voice calm and soothing, and accepting.

"I don't know when, but I keep having the same dreams, the same images over and over again. So, I think it's going to happen soon." Gwen takes a deep breath. "I can't see where it starts or how, but the whole building will burn. I've seen the children and the sisters in their pajamas running through the halls, with smoke and flames everywhere."

"So it happens at night, then?" Father O'Brien interrupts.

"Yes," she replies.

"Does anyone get hurt?" he asks attentively.

"I can't tell. I've seen the Sisters trying to get the children out, but I don't see if anyone gets out of the building. I'm sorry, that's all I know," Gwen tells him hopelessly.

"It's all right, Gwen, you were right to tell me." Father O'Brien pats her hand. "I think I'll have someone look over the building, just to see if maybe there's a fire hazard or faulty wires somewhere. Who knows? Maybe it's something that we can prevent," he tells Gwen, trying to reassure her.

"You can't in good faith believe her, Father?" Astonishment plays across the older woman's wrinkled face.

"Of course, I do. She has foreseen things before, Mother, and she has yet to be proven wrong." He reaches for the telephone on his desk.

"But a child can't have visions. Only a holy servant of God can receive revelation and prophecy!" Mother Sullivan protests.

"God works in mysterious ways, Mother. We are all instruments in God's hands, doing His bidding. It would be unwise if God sent me a messenger and lives were lost because I did not heed His warning," Father O'Brien insist before dialing a number on the phone's keypad and putting the receiver to his ear. "You may go now, Gwen. Go lie down in your room and get some rest. I'll let you know if I find out anything. Okay?" He smiles at her reassuringly.

"Okay, Father. I hope they find something." Gwen gets up from the chair, feeling much more herself now, and hurries out of the room, wanting to get out of the office and as far away from the Mother Superior as possible. However, as soon as Gwen walks past the Mother, the large woman turns and follows her, pausing only to shut the office door behind her before she pursues Gwen. Before she knows it, the Mother Superior has her by the arm. The nun forces Gwen to stop in her tracks and face her.

"I have had enough of your treachery. You will march back into that office and tell the Father that you made the whole thing up!" the Mother orders.

"I will not. It's all true." Gwen glares at the older woman defiantly.

Somehow, Gwen doesn't see it coming. The Mother's raised hand hits her across the face with such speed and force that Gwen is knocked to the floor with the blow.

"You are a liar, Marianne!" She puts heavy emphasis on the name as she looms over Gwen. "You and your little friends concocted that lie about Sister Whitmore, and you will burn in hell for what you've done to her!" She spits the words down at Gwen, who stays on the floor, stunned. "I think you plan to start that fire yourself!"

"Why would I do that?" Gwen asks, aghast, as she rubs the tender welt on her left cheek.

"Because you are twisted, and because you are evil! You are unnatural. I know it! I've always felt it in my soul. Were it in my power, you would be thrown out into the streets to live in the gutter where you belong!" The nun grabs Gwen's arm and hauls her to her feet.

Gwen cries out in pain.

"You will go and tell the father the truth!" the Mother demands.

"No. You want me to tell a lie, and I am not a liar!" Gwen exclaims. This time Gwen is on her guard, and as the Mother raises her hand to strike the little girl, the child utters some words in her own tongue.

Suddenly, an unseen force pushes against Mother Sullivan, hurtling the tall woman off of her feet. She flies backward, hitting a cabinet along the side of the hall. The Mother Superior collapses to the floor wide eyed, followed by the cabinet as it falls on top of her with a crash, knocking her unconscious.

Gwen stands there for a moment, shaking, breathing heavily as shock and the overwhelming surge of anger and power inside overcomes her. Limitless energy pulses through her veins, her skin barely containing her. When she hears the sound of doors opening and footsteps approaching, she immediately comes back to her senses.

Gwen fights the urge to soar at her max speed as she runs down the hall, turning to go back down the corridor toward her room on the other side of the massive building. Gwen feels like her heart is beating in her ears, her mind reeling. Her core spirit burns with the need to burst.

She makes her way through the orphanage, ignoring the cries of alarm and startled glances of those she passes. Quickly, she runs up the back stairs to her bedroom and flings open the door. Once inside the room, Gwen moves with superhuman speed to gather all her belongings. She empties every drawer into the duffel bag the nurses at the hospital gave her three years ago. Tearing a page out of her black sketchbook, she scribbles a quick note, folds it up, and puts it in her pocket. Looking about the room, Gwen double-checks to make sure she has everything. Satisfied, she turns to run back down the stairs. She hurries to the second door on the left and knocks, hopping from foot to foot as she waits impatiently for someone to answer.

Finally, the door opens and a tall, young man about Raven's age answers. Gwen peeks through the doorway around him and spies Raven sitting on his bed doing homework. Gwen shoves her way past the boy in the doorway, deaf to his cry of protest.

Raven looks up and sees Gwen coming toward him, her hair disheveled, her face red with adrenaline. The wild, panicked gleam in her eyes startles him. He jumps to his feet, ready and alert.

"What's wrong? What's happened?" Raven asks his face serious and threatening.

"It's time," Gwen tells him. "Grab your things. We have to leave now!" she orders. Then she moves about the room gathering all the things, she can find that belongs to her friend. Raven, taking her lead, finds a backpack under his bed and begins shoving clothing and other items into it.

Mentally Gwen shares what transpired between her the priest and Mother Sullivan only moments ago. Raven takes this all in with shock and then understanding. His acceptance of her actions gives her a little relief from her guilt. The burden lighter for having expressed it in some way. At present, she is not sure she could speak of what occurred even if she wanted.

Gwen comes to him, handing him the armload of possessions she's collected. The two of them ignore his roommate, who keeps asking them questions and looking at them incredulously. When the backpack is full, Gwen turns to leave.

"Wait. Shouldn't we bring the blanket and pillow? You know, make a bedroll, or something?" Raven asks.

"Fine, but I didn't grab mine," Gwen concedes.

"We can go back and get your blankets, then," Raven assures her as he strips the bedding, laying it out on the floor so he can roll the pillow up inside the blanket. He takes his belt off of his pants and fastens it around the bedroll. With his bag in one hand and the bedroll over his shoulder, he turns to Gwen. She waits anxiously by the door, peeking out every so often to see if anyone is coming.

Together they leave Raven's room, his roommate watching as they depart. They start up the steps to Gwen's room to retrieve her bedding when they hear someone upstairs. They listen a moment and hear two sets of footsteps walking around in Gwen's room. They turn to each other, and, without saying a word, make a run for it. Going back the way they came, they run past Raven's roommate as they hurry down the hall, making their way toward the double doors that lead into the courtyard.

"Raven, wait!" Gwen comes to a halt in front of Sister Shaw's classroom. Raven stops several feet ahead of her. His eyes follow hers to the classroom door. Gwen can sense the young nun within. She struggles with the urge to knock but pushes the thought aside. Taking the note from her pocket, she shoves it under the door. When she straightens, Raven's eyes meet hers. A look of understanding passes between them, knowing that they may never see Sister Shaw again. They must leave the closest thing to a mother or family either of them has ever known. Raven takes Gwen's hand as they hurry down the corridor.

Somehow, without encountering anyone along the way, they make it to the courtyard, sneaking out the large double doors and into the open. Gwen scans the courtyard. Quickly, in a brisk walk, she leads the way across, heading into the woods that surround the orphanage.

It isn't until they are just within the trees that Gwen pauses a moment to look back. Raven stops, also needing to catch his breath. Together they look upon the old mansion that is St. Paul's Orphanage, perhaps for the last time. Strangely, neither of them is sad to be leaving behind the only home they've ever known. In a way, it isn't really their home. They are taking it with them because they are leaving together.

Just before they turn to continue on up the mountain, Gwen sees a figure run out into the courtyard, a young woman dressed in a nun's habit. Turning her back on the woman, Gwen follows after Raven. Gwen tries not to think of Sister Shaw, or how she'll worry about them. They have to leave. It's impossible for Gwen to stay now after what she's done. Besides, she can't stay in that place any longer. Everything about the orphanage smothers the life out of her. The feeling of freedom becomes stronger with every step she takes away from the building. She leaves all the feelings of being unwanted, misunderstood, and hated behind her.

It doesn't take them long to reach the waterfall, and soon they are safe inside the cave concealed behind it. They take off their packs and sit on the cold rock floor, resting their weary limbs. Gwen closes her eyes, letting the mist from the waterfall and the musky smell of the cave soothe her tattered nerves.

"We can't stay here long, you know?" Raven announces, bringing Gwen out of her thoughts.

"Why not?" Gwen asks disappointment showing on her doll-like face.

"Because they'll look all through the forest for us, and maybe someone will think to look behind the waterfall. Besides, we'll run out of supplies eventually, and then we'll have to leave," Raven explains.

"But where will we go?" Gwen demands, a hopeless panic washing over her.

"We can't go to town. They know you there. Maybe we can travel through the woods to the interstate. We can hitchhike to another town, maybe even another state." Raven sees the worried look on her face, her brow creased in concern. "Don't worry, Gwen, I'll take care of you. You'll see. We'll figure out a way to make money and find food." Raven tries to reassure her, but Gwen still seems doubtful of their future.

"How long can we stay here?" Gwen asks.

"I don't know, probably just tonight. Might even be a good idea to gather our stash and leave now."

Gwen thinks a moment and then nods. Together they begin the process of packing their hidden hoard of provisions. Most of the food is stored in boxes, the rest in plastic bags collected from their rare visits into town to the grocery store. They shove as much of the necessities into their bags with their clothes. By the time they're finished they have four over-flowing plastic grocery bags full of canned goods and other dry or non-perishable items. The rest they'll have to leave behind; they can't carry anymore with them.

"We'll leave tonight," Gwen announces.

"Then we should sleep now, so we can leave at dark," Raven suggests.

"Agreed." Gwen tries to smile, but it comes off as weak and tired.

Raven lays out the bedroll on the cold, dark cave floor. Raven lies down, adjusting himself to find a comfortable spot, and Gwen lies beside him, her back to him as she curls up to sleep. Raven hesitantly scoots closer to her, draping an arm over her. She snuggles up against him, and together they fall peacefully to sleep.

They awoke several hours later in full darkness, the cave a damp hollow void of blackness. Fumbling blindly on her hands and knees, Gwen finds a flashlight in one of their packs. Switching it on, Gwen scans the cave for Raven.

"Hey, get that out of my eyes!" Raven holds his hand before his face to shield it from the glaring flashlight.

"Sorry."

Raven grumbles something, stretching before he rolls up the bedroll.

"What time is it?" Gwen starts gathering their things.

Raven squints at his wristwatch in the dim light, with a flashlight in hand, Gwen makes her way to him, shining the light on his watch.

"It's 3:15." Raven looks up at Gwen. "Time to go."

Together they climb out of the cave and into the night. The waterfall laps into the stream, glistening in the moonlight. A strange light glows in the distance through the trees, making the otherwise night sky bright.

"Raven, what is that?" Gwen asks, pointing to the glow down below in the valley.

He looks at her, perplexed. "Let's go down and get a closer look," he says as he leads her down the mountainside.

When they are halfway down the mountain, Gwen gasps in horror at the sight below. The orphanage is on fire, giving off a golden glow with the entire building ablaze. Gwen scans the grounds around the burning building. To her relief, she sees a crowd of people standing on the edge of the property, watching as the fire engines pull up. Firemen run out, busying themselves with the task of stopping the raging inferno. The children and the nuns all stand in their pajamas, shivering in the night. She scans the crowd but can't tell from this distance if Sister Shaw is among them. Father O'Brien in his black suit is hard to miss as he talks urgently to a policeman near the front of the ever-dwindling mansion.

"How many of them are there? Can you count them all?" Gwen asks Raven anxiously.

"I think they're all there. Don't worry, Gwen, I'm sure Sister Shaw and the father got everybody out," Raven says reassuringly as he places a hand on her shoulder.

"Do you see Sister Shaw?" Gwen scans the crowd again.

"I think she just joined the Father." Raven points out the young woman standing next to the priest, the only sister wearing her habit.

The two runaways stay for several minutes, both silently watching the orphanage burn to the ground. After a while, Raven takes her hand in his.

"Come on, Gwen, we should be going. They have their hands full with the fire. No one's going to come looking for us now, at least not for a couple of hours."

Gwen nods. Turning, she lets Raven lead her as they make their way back up the mountain. Gwen finds herself wondering how the fire started. As if the universe answered her question, she suddenly sees an image in her head. A single candle left burning in the library with a stack of books next to it on the table. A figure steps out of the shadows. She recognizes the person as the man in black, the same strange specter that has occasionally hunted her ever since she was found in the woods three years earlier. Calmly, he reaches out a finger to push over the candle. The wick still lit, it rolls across the books, and then—as if by magic—the flame from the candle leaps into life, multiplying itself across the books, eating up the pages within. From the books to the table beneath it, the fire spreads, doing its lovely, deadly dance across the wooden surface, reaching out to the floor and the bookshelves nearby. The man in black watches with a satisfied smirk as the library burns around him. He then turns, fading into the shadows as if he were never there at all.

Gwen returns to the present, her head spinning from the vision, her heartbreaking for all those beautiful books now gone forever, never to reveal their mysteries again. Fear grips her as she realizes who the man in her vision might actually be.

Raven looks at her with understanding in his eyes, his arm around her shoulders to steady her. Without his support, Gwen might collapse. Raven doesn't ask what happened; he's seen her like this before. She's grateful, because she's not sure if she could explain it or if he'd believe her. Raven strokes her back, comforting her until the dizzy spell subsides and her face regains its color. Gwen smiles weakly and takes his hand.

Together they wander through the forest and on toward an unknown future. Gwen has no idea where they'll live or how they'll survive, but she takes comfort in knowing that they'll be together.

The world will never understand their friendship. Twelve-year-old Raven seems bulky, and awkward, next to the eight-year-old Gwen with her slender frame, blunt, and fearless nature. Looking at them, people won't see that the things that make them fit together are the very things that make them so different. They know that they belonged to each other, as two parts of one whole. Gwen knows the world will always treat them as outcasts, unfit for this world, unfit for each other, seen only as a peculiar pair.

CHAPTER NINE

Black Fur and Golden Eyes

The runaways wander through the forest for days, following an old map Raven had acquired from town the year before. They head toward highway 108 on the other side of the mountain. The harsh winter conditions make their journey difficult. The days are slightly more bearable than the bitterly cold nights, the sun hidden behind a sky of white. At night, the two of them share a bedroll, Gwen curling up into the warmth beside Raven's large, bulky frame. During the daytime, Gwen wears her winter coat along with several layers of clothing beneath it. Even that isn't enough. On the second day, Raven decides to give his extra-large coat to his friend. It doesn't matter to him. He doesn't feel the cold the way Gwen does.

Whenever Gwen loses the strength to move her frozen limbs, Raven carries her thin and fragile body like a porcelain doll in his arms.

They make camp at dusk because Gwen can't see in the dark. Raven builds a fire and sets up camp while Gwen finds something among their provisions to eat for supper.

For some time now, Raven has been noticing strange changes in him, things he at first dismissed as normal puberty—growing pains and all. It has become all too apparent that he is experiencing something quite different. His muscles ache as if they'll burst through his clothing. The need to move, to test the length and speed of his stride, to run wild through the forest, burns within. His skin is often feverish, but he isn't uncomfortable, as though his internal body temperature has risen to match his exterior. Hair suddenly springs out of every crevice and spreads across every inch of his body at a most alarming rate.

He's heard that most boys start to grow a little facial and chest hair at his age, but this is like animal fur. The hair on his head grows twice its length in a week. Raven ties it up in a Japanese topknot to keep it out of his eyes. His face, full of stubble, itches terribly. Even the way he sees the world around him has altered. His vision is so clear that he notices the tiniest speck of dust in the air. He sees twice as far as before. And at night everything glows from within as the world becomes a silvery mirror image of its daylight self. All of his senses are magnified, and his every desire is more acute. He feels like a wild beast confined inside a boy's body. Feeling the urge to hunt and kill creeps unbidden into every thought.

Naturally, he becomes frightened of himself, so much so that he dares not utter a word about this to Gwen. Instead, he suffers in silence, holding in the rage and the animal-like frenzy deep within.

Finally, on Gwen's false birthday, they see Highway 108 not too far off in the distance. Soon they will be in civilization. They look forward to finding something warm to eat, and maybe even find a place to bathe. Their moods are lightened considerably by the prospect. Gwen even finds the strength to run, skipping down the hill through the woods up to the busy road. Raven laughs at her giddy mood and follows close behind her.

"Finally, we made it!" Gwen exclaims as Raven dumps his backpack down next to her, stretching out the ache in his back.

"I told you I knew how to read the map. Didn't you trust me?" Raven asks, pretending to have hurt feelings.

"Of course, I do, but it just took too long. It didn't look that far on the map," Gwen protests. She sets down her own bags. Using the duffel bag as a chair, she sits on the side of the road and watches the cars as they approach.

"I've never hitch-hiked before," Raven admits to Gwen, watching the cars pass by dubiously.

"I think we just stick our thumbs out, or write where we're headed on a sign," Gwen replies. Standing up, she unzips her duffel bag and digs out her sketchbook and art case. She rips out a sheet of paper, takes a black marker out of the case, and holds the felt tip in her hand over the paper. "So where are we going?" Gwen looks up at Raven expectantly.

"Well, where do you want to live, Gwen?"

"How about New York?" Gwen answers with a big grin.

"What's in New York?" Raven asks.

"All sorts of things, and it's a big city, we should be able to find someone like us there. Don't you think?" Gwen replies.

"Sure. With a lot of people there, we might blend in better than places like this," Raven concedes. "Okay, if we're going to New York then we need to head south. It's a long way from here. We probably could hitch a ride to the nearest Greyhound Station and take a bus."

"But we don't have any money, Raven," Gwen reminds him.

"I've been thinking about that. You know how we stole the food from the kitchen back at the orphanage?" Raven asks.

"We borrowed. We never stole anything," Gwen protests.

"Fine, we borrowed. Well, I think we might just continue borrowing the things we need." Raven sees the look of distress on Gwen's face. "Just until we're old enough to work, I mean. Then, we'll go straight," he finishes.

"I guess we don't have any other choice, do we?" Gwen admits. "Okay, we'll borrow, but we can't get caught."

"Of course," Raven agrees. "So, why don't you write down 'Headed South' on that sign?" Raven instructs.

Gwen does as she's told and hands the sign to Raven. They wait for half an hour on the side of the road, holding their sign, many vehicles passing them. Raven begins to worry as darkness settles, and he hopes that he and Gwen might sleep some place clean and warm tonight. Just when they're about to give up, a middle-aged man in an orange rusty old pick-up finally pulls up to the shoulder of the highway. He leans toward the passenger side of the car and addresses them.

"How far south you two headed?" the stranger asks, peering at the two children from beneath a torn, old baseball cap. His face carries the tan of a laborer or farmer.

Raven, struck dumb by shyness is unable to speak to the stranger, feeling uncomfortable under his scrutinizing gaze.

"The next town ought to be fine, mister, if you'd be willing to give us a lift," Gwen pipes up, standing on her tiptoes to address the driver.

"Don't your brother speak none?" the driver asks, suspicious.

"He's not good around strangers. He's really friendly once you get to know him," Gwen reassures the man, giving him a big, sweet smile. With her foot, Gwen kicks Raven and gives him a sidelong look.

"We're looking for the nearest Greyhound Station." Coming out of his stupor, Raven forces himself to attempt civility.

"Oh, is that right? Well, there's one over in Lewiston. It just so happens that's where I'm headed. Why don't you two climb on in and I'll take you with me?" the pick-up driver invites.

Gwen looks to Raven. After a quick unspoken exchange with their eyes, they simultaneously nod to each other in agreement.

"Thank you, sir. We appreciate it," Raven replies, stepping forward to help Gwen into the pick-up. The vehicle has a small cab with a miniature back seat behind the driver. Gwen climbs over the seat and gets in back. Raven retrieves Gwen's duffel bag and tosses it over the seat. He stows his own backpack next to it in the back and then climbs into the passenger seat.

"You comfortable back there, sweetheart?" the driver asks, looking in his rearview mirror at Gwen. She nods. "All right, then." The driver puts the stick shift in gear, and they pull onto the highway, merge with the traffic, and head south.

Leaning her head against the window, curling up on the seat, Gwen quickly becomes lulled into a deep sleep by the gentle sway of the road, leaving Raven alone awake with the stranger. They pass several minutes in silence until the pick-up driver glances over at Raven.

"I guess I'll be the one to introduce myself first. I'm Rex Cutler. What's your name, son?" Rex asks congenially.

"Raven Mathews." Raven gestures toward Gwen with a nod of his head. "That's Gwen."

"What kind of name is Raven?" Rex asks curiously.

"That's what Gwen calls me," Raven replies a bit tersely, trying not to take offense by the stranger's jest.

"I didn't mean to offend," the man assures him. "Where you from?" Rex asks.

"Rumford abouts," Raven replies, not caring to mention the orphanage from which he and Gwen ran away.

"Oh." The driver thinks over this bit of information for a moment. "You're a little young to be traveling on your own, especially with a pretty little girl like that. I'd say you were thirteen, maybe fourteen to look at you. Am I right?" Rex inquires.

Raven stiffens, at a loss for how to respond. They hadn't really thought of what to say if anyone asked them who they were or where they came from. Silently, Raven wills Gwen to wake up and come to his aid, but she still snores softly in the back seat. Inside, Raven begins to panic.

What if he's heard of two runaways from St. Paul's? Surely someone's reported us missing by now, Raven thinks. Outwardly, he tries to maintain a blank face. He won't let anyone take Gwen back to the orphanage. She showed him what occurred between her and the Mother Superior. Although he believes she acted in self-defense, that it had been an accident, he knows that wouldn't matter to anyone else. He knows what the Mother Superior thinks of Gwen—to her, Gwen is an evil, bad-natured child, possibly of the devil. Raven knows that Mother Sullivan won't rest until Gwen's committed to some kind of nuthouse or a juvenile delinquent center. The thought of Gwen in a straitjacket, confined, locked away in a rubber room somewhere upsets him. Rage begins to well up inside him. He will protect Gwen, no matter the cost; no one will take her from him.

The man waits for Raven to reply, but when Raven remains silent, he changes the subject. "It doesn't matter, I guess. So, where you headed, Raven?" Rex asks, trying to sound easygoing.

"Why do you ask so many questions?" Raven asks in a low growl. His body stiffens with the effort of containing his emotions.

"Just making small talk, son. The road can bore a man to sleep, that's all," Rex replies. He is a bit taken back by the young man's behavior.

"It's none of your business. If you can't keep your questions to yourself, then you can let us out on the side of the road. We can walk to Lewiston," Raven tells the older man in a surly tone.

"Son, are you in some kind of trouble?" Rex asks, but he doesn't give Raven the chance to answer. "I heard the other day about some runaways in the area. A twelve-year-old boy and a little eight-year-old girl, supposed to be really pretty and talk older than her age." Rex looks over at Raven, a suspicious look crossing his face. "That's you, ain't it? I bet she isn't your little sister at all, is she? Did you steal that girl, boy? Where you taking that girl to, huh?" Rex's voice takes on a harsh accusatory tone.

"I don't know what you're talking about. Just pull over here. We don't need a ride after all!" Raven commands, giving the man a stern look. He reaches over the seat and shakes Gwen gently awake.

"Wake up, Gwen, we're getting out," he tells her as her eyes open. She stares at him a moment, confusion showing in her yellow-green eyes.

"No, you're not! I'm taking you two back where you belong!" Suddenly, Rex Cutler steers out of the main traffic, cutting off some other cars as he quickly makes a U-turn and heads back the way he had come.

"What's going on, Raven?" Gwen asks, perplexed. A stream of images invades her mind as she senses the thoughts and feelings of the driver. The things he thinks of Raven appall her. Apparently, the man thinks her best friend—the nicest, kindest boy in the world—is some kind of child molester. Gwen is just about to try and calm the driver down when she notices something strange happening with Raven.

"We're not going back there!" Raven shouts. He shakes all over as if he is having a seizure. His muscles are tense as he fights his own body for control. Gwen gasps in horror as Raven's features begin to change, his very form mutating before her eyes.

Hair begins to sprout out of his flesh as if by magic, covering him in a black-silvery fur. His fingernails grow, his hands becoming like massive paws. His golden eyes become animal-like as his nose and mouth become a muzzle, his ears becoming pointed and furry. Raven screams in agony as every bone in his body seems to realign itself, disjointing from its natural human form into that of a ferocious animal. Behind the wall of pain, he is vaguely aware of Gwen screaming his name, her little hands tugging at his left arm even as it distorts and reshapes itself. He can't comprehend anything else happening around him, the excruciating pain swallowing him whole into a cocoon of thoughts, feelings, and emotions that are not his own. He feels the feral animal instinct taking over his will, his human consciousness suppressed by an animal's need to hunt.

Gwen tries in vain to get Raven to respond to her, to look at her. However, he has transformed almost completely. He no longer resembles a boy. He is a wolf. All her attention focuses on trying to touch Raven's mind, completely forgetting about the man driving the truck.

She catches a sudden gleam of metal in her peripheral vision and turns barely in time to see Rex—whose face distorts in panic and fear—pull out a handgun and aim it at Raven. With a speed that even surprises *her*, Gwen grabs Rex's hand and yanks the weapon upward.

The explosion of sound is deafening as the gun goes off in their hands shooting a hole in the roof of the truck.

Rex yells in surprise as the truck swerves all over the road. He tries to regain control of the wheel with his left hand as he struggles with Gwen for the gun in his right. The truck veers off the road into the forest, jostling as it speeds over dirt and rock. Gwen lurches forward. Rex hits the windshield with a loud crack when the truck rams straight into a tree causing the vehicle to come to an abrupt stop. The handgun flies out of Rex's grasp and rolls under the passenger side seat.

Gwen rocks backward and hits her head on the back wall of the cab. Her vision blurs and the world spins around her. Gwen tries to regain control of her senses when she hears a low growling sound. Peering over the seat, she sees a large, silver, black wolf sitting in the passenger seat, its cold, gold-eyed stare directed at Rex. The man, barely recovering from the impact of the crash, turns and looks in disbelief at the animal only two feet away from him. The black wolf bares his teeth at Rex, his growl intensifying. In a panic, with a hand to his bleeding forehead, Rex opens the driver's side door and stumbles out into the forest, desperately fleeing from the creature. No sooner does Rex flee than the wolf pounces, leaping out of the truck through the open door and into the night after his prey.

"Raven, no!" Gwen yells. Still dizzy, she climbs over the seat, lowers herself out of the tall truck, and stumbles onto the ground. Her body aches all over. Gwen tries to chase after the wolf, but all she can see is the blackness of night. Ahead of her, she hears Rex scream. The sound causes her to quicken her pace. Howling sounds through the trees, echoing through the forest. Gwen runs blindly into the night. Trying to maneuver through trees and rocks, she hopes desperately that she isn't too late. Suddenly, she hears Rex scream again, this time closer by. She races toward the sound, her heart thumping out of her chest.

Coming around a thicket of trees, she enters a clearing. The moon peers out from behind the clouds, illuminating the clearing before her. Across the clearing, the grown man cowers, caught against a tree before the massive silver-black beast. Snarling, the wolf advances toward the man, readying himself to pounce.

"Raven! Stop it!" Gwen runs toward the monster, screaming in a panic, her voice shrill as tears come to her eyes. The sound of her voice startles the wolf, causing it to turn and look at the girl for the first time. She runs up to him, stopping only a foot in front of him. She falls to her knees, overcome with fear and desperation. "Please!" She begs the beast before her. He stares at her, his golden eyes searching her face, his head cocked to one side. Trying to recall her, puzzling out who she is and if she is a threat or a friend.

Trembling, Gwen reaches out her hand toward the animal with a friendly gesture, trying to beckon him away from his prey. The wolf moves hesitantly toward her, reaching out with his muzzle to sniff her out-stretched hand. Recognizing her scent, the animal relaxes. He presses his wet snout to her hand and nuzzles her affectionately. Gwen moves forward, running her hand along the creature's silky silver-black coat as she speaks in a soothing voice.

"It's okay, Raven. The man isn't going to hurt us. We'll just go back to the truck and leave. No one needs to get hurt," Gwen tells him. She reaches out with her mind, trying to sense the boy inside the animal's frame. She finds a tight net of emotions tangled around Raven's subconscious, cocooned within as if in a comatose state. The conscious animal side of his mind seething with rage is beginning to relent, and he becomes more docile, meek. Within his psyche she feels Raven awaken slowly, coming back to the surface, emerging out of the tangle of the wolf's instincts, thoughts, and emotions. Returning to her own self again, Gwen breathes a heavy sigh of relief.

Across the clearing, Rex Cutler trembles, his gaze transfixed by the little girl standing calmly as the dangerous wolf lays down at her feet, complacent as a puppy. Before his eyes, the creature seems to fold into itself, shedding its fur as its body contracts, mutating back into the naked form of the boy he had been prior.

Delirious, Raven awakens in the moonlit forest, lying naked and curled up at Gwen's feet. At first, he thinks he's dreaming, but in his dreams, forests don't smell of pine and rain. They don't feel this real. *How did I get here?* he thinks as his mind begins to register everything around him. The last thing he can recall is being in the truck with Gwen and that man. He had been angry about something…. oh, yes, the man was going to take them back to the orphanage. He had turned the truck around and then…Raven searches his mind for what happened next. All he finds is a disjointed collection of images that seem feral and inhuman.

Careful to shield Gwen from his nakedness, Raven raises himself up on his elbow and looks up at her. Her face pale in fear, yet when her yellow-green eyes look into his, her whole body seems to melt, the tension draining out of her. She kneels down beside him, concern and relief playing across her delicate face.

"Raven, are you alright?" Gwen inquires, pushing back the long black strands of hair that hang down around his face to get a better look at him.

"I'm fine, I think. Gwen, how did I get here?" He looks around at the forest, taking in the clearing and the man staring at him with a terrified fixation.

"You mean you don't remember? Not any of it?" Gwen asks, astonished.

"No, I... I can't. I mean, it's all... what I remember doesn't make any sense," Raven manages to stammer.

"You changed into a wolf, Raven," Gwen explains, awe in her youthful voice.

Raven looks at her, incredulous. "That's impossible. I mean, yeah, you do extraordinary things, but I'm just...." He trails off, not knowing what to say.

"You're just like me, only different." Gwen shivers as a gust of wind whips through the clearing, causing the branches of the trees to sway above them. "Aren't you cold?" Gwen asks, pulling Raven's overcoat off of her slender frame and draping it over his shoulders.

"No, I'm warm, but what happened to my clothes?" Raven asks shyly.

"I think they were torn apart when you morphed into the wolf,"

Gwen replies. She looks over at Rex Cutler who sits frozen in place, completely paralyzed by fear, staring at the two of them. "We need to get out of here, fast. The driver saw you change, too, Raven, and if it weren't for me, you might have killed him."

"I didn't hurt you, did I?" Panicked, Raven searches her face and arms for any sign of a bruise, scratch, or cut.

"No, I'm fine. But you sure scared me!"

"I'm sorry, Gwen, I had no idea I was capable of… *that*."

"It's okay. We'll figure it all out later, but we have to leave now." Gwen stands and walks across the clearing up to Rex.

"We need your pants," Gwen commands.

Rex Cutler just stares at the little girl, dumbfounded. Then, from behind the girl, he sees the boy rise to his feet and put on his coat. Suddenly frightened that the boy will become the beast again, the man nods dumbly and fumbles with the buttons and zipper of his blue denim jeans.

Gwen turns away, trying to avoid the sight of the man disrobing and also Raven's nakedness. She walks out of the clearing, back toward the wrecked truck and the mangled tree. The forest is dark around her. The moon pierces through the clouds. The barren tree branches cast shadows like skeleton fingers upon her. The forest is still and ominous as Gwen finds her way through the shrubs and rocks. Suddenly, Raven appears beside her, his unnaturally swift gait making it easy for him to catch up to her. He wears the man's pants and shoes, both of which are much too large, which surprises Gwen. She thinks of Raven as massive, but perhaps he is just big for his age. The thought causes Gwen to wonder how big Raven will be when he is a full-grown man.

"What happened to the man?" Gwen asks looking over her shoulder back the way they had come. The forest remains silent and still around them.

"He threw his shoes, pants and his shirt at me and ran deeper into the woods in his underwear like he thought I was gonna chase him down," Raven replies with an embarrassed blush to his tan cheeks. "I don't think he's going to come after us."

Gwen nods at this and the two of them walk side by side in silence for a while. Coming around a grove of trees, they spy the truck up ahead. Quietly, the two children walk up to the vehicle.

"I think we should take the man's truck, Gwen. He'll go straight to the police if we don't, and we can get to the bus station faster this way." Raven explains in a timid voice.

"Stealing food is one thing Raven but…"

"I thought you said we didn't steal that food we just borrowed it?" He interjects in a teasing tone.

Gwen gives him a look and shakes her head exasperated. "Fine we'll borrow the vehicle but only to get to the bus station. We need to ditch it as fast as possible."

"I totally agree."

Nervously the children get into the truck.

Raven climbs into the driver's seat and turns to Gwen. "Buckle up." He suggests as he does himself. He grips the steering wheel, and a sense of child-like excitement comes over him at the prospect of driving for the very first time. The keys dangle from the ignition. Raven turns the key, surprised and relieved when the engine turns over and roars to life. Recalling all the things he had observed over the years of watching others drive, he remembers to put his foot on the clutch and release the gas as he puts the stick shift in reverse. The vehicle lurches backward, the dented hood separating from the large tree trunk in front of it. The truck sputters and stalls a couple of times before Raven gets them turned around and headed back toward the interstate.

Soon they come to the spot where they swerved off earlier. Luckily, the road is deserted in both directions. No one seems to have seen them drive off the road before. Hesitantly, Raven pulls onto the freeway, crosses over the double line, and heads south toward Lewiston. At first, Raven is nervous, his body rigid and his knuckles white as he firmly grasps the steering wheel with both hands. After they pass several little green mile markers, he becomes more confident and allows himself to relax. Yet the impulse to check the rearview mirror lingers like an obsessive-compulsive twitch. To his relief, no one is in pursuit behind them.

Raven glances over at Gwen. She stares out the window in a daze.

"What are you thinking, Gwen?"

"I was wondering why that happened. What caused you to change like that?" Puzzlement fills Gwen's voice.

"I was afraid of what they would do to you if we got caught," Raven replies simply.

"Oh." She pauses to reflect on this revelation for a moment, then, she asks, "So you think it's caused by fear?"

"I don't know, Gwen. I thought werewolves changed in the light of a full moon," Raven replies sarcastically, laughing at the ridiculousness of it all. "What am I? A monster? Is this going to happen again? And if it does, might I kill someone? What am I going to do? I'm scared, Gwen. Tell me what to do." His voice trembles in fear, his eyes misty with the beginnings of tears as he turns a beseeching gaze on Gwen, looking to a girl four years his junior for guidance and reassurance.

Gwen looks him in the eyes, at a loss for the answers Raven seeks. Yet something inside her feels the need to be strong for him, to protect her friend from anything, including himself. Gwen reaches out, takes one of his big hands off of the steering wheel, places it in her delicate hand, and squeezes it affectionately.

"We'll find out what we are, Raven. I promise you. There has to be others like us, and I'll find them. Until then, don't worry about hurting anyone. My voice brought you back. I won't let the beast take over again."

The confidence in her voice soothing his frayed nerves, giving him a sense of hope. Smiling gratefully, he nods and returns his attention to the road. Raven drives on, letting himself momentarily forget the disturbing event that just occurred, and instead ponders the next obstacle facing them. How will they avoid being recognized when they get to town? And even more importantly, how will they get the money to purchase the bus tickets to New York? He cannot think of any solutions to their dilemma, yet he has every confidence that

Gwen will think of something. She always does.

* * * * *

An hour later, the old mangled pick-up truck pulls into the parking lot of a diner in Lewiston, Maine. Raven parks and turns off the engine. Starring out the windshield, he watches the people coming in and out of the diner. Lying on the seat next to him with her head in his lap is Gwen, fast asleep. Raven gazes down at her, a look of concern upon his dark countenance. Gently, he shakes Gwen's shoulder, rousing her. Moaning and stretching, she sits up and gives a large yawn, making a strange, high-pitched, girly sigh in the process. With heavily lidded, red-rimmed eyes, Gwen looks about, taking in their surroundings.

She looks to Raven. "Where are we?" she asks, her voice heavy with sleep.

"I thought we could use something hot to eat," Raven replies as an elderly couple walks past. The man peers at Raven in a suspicious way, probably thinking that Raven looks much too young to drive.

"Isn't that dangerous? They have missing children posters, you know? What if one's inside on the bulletin board or hanging above the register? Besides, we don't have any money," Gwen reminds him, anxiety resonating in her voice.

"Well, then, it's time we got some money, don't you think?"

"It won't be like stealing food from the kitchen, you know? This is more dangerous!"

It suddenly occurs to Raven that perhaps Gwen doesn't like stealing. She felt justified in taking food from the orphanage. The little bit here and there hadn't hurt anyone. What they have to do now is a whole other thing entirely.

"We don't have a choice, Gwen. We need food, and we need money to get to New York," Raven gently points out.

"I know," Gwen sighs.

Scooting across the seat over to the passenger door, Gwen opens it and hops out of the truck. Raven follows suit, meeting her on the sidewalk. The two of them walk side by side up to the front entrance of the 50's-style diner. Raven holds the door open for Gwen and then follows after her. A feeling of uncertainty settles heavy in the pit of his stomach as they enter the busy restaurant.

Inside, the diner is packed with locals scattered about, sitting at the counter or in the booths. Men, women, and children eat their evening meals while waitresses and busboys hurry about the cramped interior, carrying trays and dishes to and from the back doors leading into the kitchen. Behind the row of patrons sitting on bar stools at the counter, the fry cooks can be seen through a long, narrow passthrough. Systematically the cooks take order slips and produce plate after plate of hot, delicious food. The smell wafts through the diner to Gwen and Raven's noses, instantly causing their empty stomachs to rumble. The duo immediately makes their way over to the far corner and take a seat in an empty booth. A moment later, a waitress, a woman in her fifties with light blonde curly hair done in a bun and a bitter expression on her face, approaches their table with a notebook open and a pen in hand. The name on her nametag reads Beatrice.

"What'll it be, kids?" the woman asks, her voice dripping disdain as she forces a smile. She eyes Raven a moment, taking in his oversized clothing and generally disheveled appearance before turning a scrutinizing gaze on Gwen, who fights the urge to squirm under the inspection. She realizes that her own appearance isn't any better than Raven's, with her torn, grass-stained, light-blue jeans and old, faded green hoodie. With her hair matted and greasy from days without washing, Gwen can't help wondering if they smell as foul as they look.

Raven sits there, a little taken back by the woman's rude appraisal of them. The woman remains silent, waiting for them to speak. Gwen looks around and sees two menus tucked away in a cubby next to the napkins and salt and pepper shakers. Snatching one, Gwen flips it open and scans through its contents. She orders two hamburgers with fries and soft drinks and one chocolate shake. She glances at Raven for approval. He quickly nods, giving her an ambiguous expression. The sour-faced waitress scribbles down the order, giving them a long, measured, skeptical look before turning on her heels and heading back toward the bar. The second the woman leaves, Raven gives Gwen a questioning look, as if asking, *"Well, does she know?"* Gwen shakes her head *"No."*

"She was thinking that we're going to eat and then run off without paying the bill. It's called dine and dash," Gwen tells him.

"Where did you hear that?" he asks curiously.

"Just now… in her thoughts. No one else is thinking about us so I think we're safe."

Raven nods in understanding. He relaxes his posture a little, letting himself slouch in his seat; he entertains himself by drumming his fingers against the tabletop, rhythmically. Fifteen minutes go by and then Beatrice returns with a large tray. The middle-aged waitress sets their drinks and two plates in front of Raven and Gwen, giving the two travel-worn youths a long, stern look before leaving.

The hamburgers and fries look heavenly to Gwen, who immediately reaches out, taking the fresh, steaming-hot burger in her grasp. Gwen hesitates momentarily just as she brings the food up to her mouth about to take the first bite. She stops and looks across the table at Raven, who sits staring down at his plate, with a ravenous look.

"Raven?" He looks up, her voice breaking the spell.

"Yeah?"

"What are we going to do?" she asks, anxiety thick in her voice.

"I was hoping you'd come up with something," he admits as he shakes his head in defeat.

The uncomfortable sensation of being watched causes Gwen to look around the diner. She notices their waitress watching them from behind the counter as she pours coffee for a patron. Beatrice leans over and whispers something to another waitress standing nearby. All three adults stop and look in the direction of Gwen and Raven's table.

Gwen takes a bite of her sandwich, then another, chewing the food at a dispassionate pace, giving off the appearance of nonchalance.

"Eat up, Raven. Don't act nervous, just eat," Gwen instructs between bites. Grabbing a couple of French fries, she stuffs them in her mouth, relishing their warm, golden salty taste.

Raven finally begins to eat. He chews his food slowly, allowing himself to relax and enjoy every bite. They spend the remainder of the meal in silence, both retreating into their own troubled thoughts.

Gwen tries to look at the situation from every angle, trying to find a way around their obstacles. No matter how many scenarios she walks through in her head, no solution comes to mind. Gwen reaches down, grabbing for another fry to devour. Her hand touches the plate finding nothing. Looking down, she is astonished to see her plate completely empty. She has eaten it all. Raven is on his last bite of hamburger, a couple errant fries the only remnants of his meal on his plate. Reaching out for her soda, Gwen is surprised to notice that it, too, is all but gone. She sucks on the straw, slurping up the remainder of the sweet fluid until all that's left is ice at the bottom of her glass.

Just then, Gwen spies Beatrice walking up the aisle with their chocolate shake. She sets the shake and the metal cup down on the table along with two spoons and two straws. Reaching into her apron pocket, she retrieves a slip of paper. She pauses, looking between the two children, trying to decide who gets the bill. Deciding Gwen is the brains of the operation; she holds it out toward her. Gwen looks at the paper and then up at the waitress, who stares down at her in an intimidating manner. Acting as though she were unaffected, Gwen reaches out and takes the bill immediately, sliding it across the table toward Raven. He reaches out as if to take it, when suddenly the waitress places her hand on top of his. He looks up at her, his face white, panic clear in his golden eyes.

"When you're done, I'll be waiting at the register. It's right up front next to the door. If you're thinking of running, I'd think again. There ain't no way you're gettin' past me," Beatrice informs them in a hard, mocking voice, her hand still pinning Raven's to the counter. She gives them a bitter smile. "You enjoy that shake now." She finishes in a mock-friendly tone before leaving to return to her other customers.

Raven watches her go, lets out his breath, and turns to Gwen, fear written all over his face. "What are we going to do now? Can't you do something? I mean, can't you make her believe that a piece of paper is actually money or something like that?" Raven's frantic voice makes all his words run together as he speaks.

"I don't know how to do that!" Gwen replies, a bit annoyed. "Just calm down. I have an idea."

Raven listens patiently as she explains. "That might get us away from that crazy waitress, but it doesn't solve our money problems." Raven points out.

"What do you want to do, hold up the place? We're kids, Raven. Nobody's going to be afraid of us, let alone give us their money," Gwen snaps back at him.

"I know, but we have to buy those bus tickets somehow," Raven retorts before adding, "The Greyhound station is right across the street."

"Maybe we'll keep hitch-hiking, or borrow another car, or sneak onto the bus?" She is running out of ideas, and she knows it, but there just has to be a solution.

"Hitch-hiking didn't go so well, and *borrowing* cars is dangerous. We have to ditch the truck. That Rex guy's bound to report it stolen eventually." Raven drums his fingers against the tabletop, thinking. "I guess we can try to sneak aboard the bus," Raven reassures Gwen, who seems a bit overwhelmed. "I'm sure your plan will work, and we'll find a way to New York." Raven finds it odd to have their roles reversed; usually she's the one reassuring him. *After all, she is just a little girl. She can't be brave all the time,* he reminds himself.

While they wait for the opportunity to put Gwen's plan into action, they drink their shake, enjoying the luxury, for chocolate is something the nuns hadn't allowed the children to eat very often.

In the booth next to them is a family with children about their age. Gwen's been watching them, and notices that they are close to finishing their meal and leaving. She waits as the father, a big heavy-set man, gets up from the table and goes to the register to pay the bill while his wife gets the kids ready to go. Beatrice is distracted; her back turned as she talks to the cooks through the pass through.

Gwen nods to Raven, and simultaneously they both take off their coats and slip them under the table. Gwen wears a plain white t-shirt, while Raven wears the pick-up truck owner's flannel button-up long sleeve shirt. Gwen digs a hair band out of her pocket and quickly gathers all her hair up into a ponytail. Raven uses the melted ice in his glass to wet his hair down and slick it back. Just then, the mother and her children get up from the table. Raven and Gwen immediately fall in line behind them, blending in with the rest of the children.

They both try to remain calm, walking at a normal pace, and trying to behave as part of the family. The father waits, holding the door open for them. Smiling up at him, the mother exits, the children follow close behind. As Raven approaches the door the man nods to him, naturally holding the door open for him and Gwen just to be polite. Raven smiles back at the man and walks out. Gwen feels a sense of elation as she comes toward the door.

A hand grabs her by the arm and roughly hauls her back into the diner.

"Where do you think you're going?" Beatrice all but shouts at her as her fingers dig into the flesh of Gwen's arm. Gwen fights and struggles to get free. All around her, she can feel the customers and employees gawking, the chatter of their many voices sounding loud in her ears until she feels as though her head is going to burst. Gwen stops struggling and turns to behold a dark look of hatred on the middle-aged woman towering over her.

"Let me go!" Gwen commands. Her voice becomes deep and hollow, the sound filling the whole diner with its resonating tone. It penetrates all the spectator's ears, reverberating through their skulls. Beatrice releases her. Her eyes widen and her expression goes blank as she stands up, her gaze transfixed upon Gwen's yellow-green eyes.

Raven runs back through the door. He stops short when he realizes that everyone save Gwen is acting strangely. He looks all around the diner noticing that all present sit or stand stiffly, bodies erect, all turned toward Gwen, their faces devoid of feeling or emotion. Gwen is now their only focus, commanding their strict attention as they stare at her with wide eyes.

"What happened?" Raven turns to Gwen who looks around her in disbelief.

"I don't know. I mean, I did this once before, but it was kind of an accident."

"Well, what did you do?" Raven asks, perplexed as he waves a hand in front of Beatrice's eyes to see if she'll flinch or blink. She doesn't react, just continues to stare, transfixed.

"I just spoke, and this happened!" Gwen exclaims. She frowns at the kind man who still holds the door open and stretches out a hand toward him. "You can go now," she says, but he doesn't move. She says it again, this time staring deep into his eyes. Suddenly, he springs to life, startling both Gwen and Raven.

"Have a good night, miss," he says, smiling down to Gwen before he quickly exits to join his family, who await him outside. The door swings shut behind him, leaving Raven and Gwen to stare after him in amazement.

"Can you tell them what to do?" Raven asks, flabbergasted.

"I don't know," Gwen replies. She scans the rest of the occupants of the diner and is somewhat relieved to see that their condition had not altered. "Let me see if I can do it again," she says, planting herself right in front of the unfriendly Beatrice. Taking a deep breath, Gwen looks deep into her eyes, and using the same commanding voice she says, "Go open the cash register and give us all the money inside."

Just as the man had done, Beatrice springs into life, a cheery, cheerful disposition about her as she turns and practically skips back behind the counter. She pushes a few buttons, and the register springs open with a chime. The once-rude waitress reaches in, pulls out the entire cash till, and holds it out to Gwen, a big beaming smile on her wrinkled face.

Raven and Gwen exchange a look of awe. Gwen slowly smiles, a nervous laugh erupting as she reaches out and takes the cash from the waitress, who just stands their grinning at them like an idiot doll.

"Hurry, go get our bags from the truck!" Gwen orders Raven, who immediately rushes out the door to obey. While he is gone, Gwen is left alone with the mannequin-like people. All their eyes upon her make her skin crawl. Beatrice's unnatural smile makes her the most uncomfortable.

Out of the corner of her eye, she sees something move and turns to look out the glass window into the dark night. Suddenly, a man dressed in a fancy white suit appears on the other side of the glass windowpane. It is the man from the forest with the soulless black eyes. The same man that had appeared in her bedroom that night she found Douglas, who had discouraged her from helping him. The same man that started the fire in her vision. He smiles, and Gwen feels her inners turn to ice. She stares wide eyed at this apparition, feeling cold and ashamed as if standing their naked.

You are all powerful, aren't you, my dear? A voice like dark music in an empty room echoes in her mind. The man before her just smiles. His lips haven't moved, yet she hears his voice. *You can kill them if you want. Or just kill one. Just to see how it feels. You know you can do it. The power is there, just reach out…* He speaks of killing in a dispassionate tone, raising an eyebrow as if to issue a challenge.

Who are you? Gwen finds herself speaking in her mind, knowing somehow that she can't push him out of her head.

It only takes a minute for Raven to return, yet for Gwen, it feels like an eternity has passed. The bell of the diner's front door dings. Startled, Gwen turns to watch Raven walk into the diner, their bags tucked under his large arms.

"Here is your bag, Gwen." Raven hands it to her, his face flushed from running, his eyes alight with excitement.

Gwen glances back where the man in white had been standing, finding nothing but the dark, empty night behind the clear windowpane. She stares, shocked and unsure what to think.

"Gwen? You, okay?" Raven gives her a funny look, peering out the window to see what she's staring at and then back at her again when he sees nothing.

Gwen takes a breath and gives a forced smile. "Here, hold my bag open for me," she instructs. Raven complies.

Gwen empties all the money from the till into the bag, taking everything, even the rolls of pennies. She turns and hands the empty till to Beatrice.

"Thank you very much, Beatrice. You've been most accommodating!" Gwen says in a mock sophisticated tone, trying very hard not to bust up laughing, from hysteria or fear she's not sure which. Beatrice just smiles back, puts the till back in the register, and closes it.

"We better go before someone comes in and sees… this," Raven comments while making a sweeping gesture to encompass all the frozen people standing around them. Gwen nods in agreement. She has a tough time zipping up her bag full to bursting with her clothes and all the money. Together, the two of them turn to leave, but then Raven stops and turns to Gwen, "Shouldn't we do something? I mean, how long does this thing last?"

"I'm not sure. What, should I tell them all to go to sleep?" she asks, a bit uncertain.

"Yeah, that's not a bad idea. Then, when they wake up, no one will be sure if it was real or just a dream!" Raven replies.

I'm not so sure this isn't a dream, Gwen thinks to herself, fighting the urge to spare a glance out the window again.

"Here it goes, then." Gwen clears her throat and takes a few steps back into the diner, centering herself in a place where everyone can see her eyes, including the fry cooks who peek out through the window. "You will all go to sleep now. When you wake up, you won't remember me or the boy. We weren't here." Gwen looks to Raven for approval. He shrugs. Gwen is startled when people start dropping like flies. The patrons and employees all close their eyes. Their bodies go limp. Those standing collapse to the floor, hitting the tile with a loud thud. People sitting in booths slump over, their heads falling to the tabletops, some landing in plates of food. No one seems to be badly hurt. Beatrice lies doubled over the cash register, sound asleep, snoring loudly. Then all is still once more.

"Okay, let's go before something else happens," Gwen yells to Raven as she runs toward him and the exit. Together, they race from the diner, down the steps, and across the street toward the Greyhound station on the other side.

Panting, Gwen, and Raven approach the ticket office. A young man in his twenties sits behind the glass with a microphone and a register. He gives the two of them a curious look as he waits for the two youths to catch their breaths. Gwen is the first to regain her composure.

"When's the next bus to New York City leaving?" she asks the man through the hole in the glass.

"It leaves in fifteen minutes. You want two tickets?" He asks in a groggy tone. *Obviously, he's been here for a while.*

"Yes, two tickets to New York, please," Gwen answers. She takes off her duffel bag and begins to unzip it. She stops herself and then, looking suspiciously at the man, she steps out of his view.

"How much will that be?" Raven asks, trying to buy Gwen some time.

Gwen looks around, making sure no one is watching before she opens the bag and pulls out a large wad of cash. She quickly straightens and folds it, putting it into her front pants pocket.

"That depends. How old are you two?" the young man behind the glass asks Raven.

"I'm eighteen, and she's twelve," Raven replies nervously. Just then, Gwen steps up beside Raven, hearing the tail end of the conversation.

"Yeah, we're going to visit our grandma in Brooklyn." The attendant looks them both over skeptically. "I thought you said the bus was leaving soon?" Gwen asks suddenly, her impatience showing.

"Yeah, any minute now actually," the young man replies.

"Well, can you hurry, then? Our grandmother's really sick and we need to get there by tomorrow." Gwen tries to sound sad and concerned about her fictitious grandmother.

"Yeah, we're afraid we won't make in time if we wait till tomorrow," Raven speaks up, trying to aide Gwen in her charade.

"All right, then. One adult ticket and one child comes to $355.25 total," the young man announces, "Plus, I'll need to see some I.D.," he adds, addressing Raven.

"Come on, we don't have time for this. The bus could leave without us! Please, please, just sell us the tickets," Gwen begs. She takes the money out of her pocket, counts out the right amount, and hands the money through the hole in the ticket window to the attendant. He looks down at the money. With a sigh of resignation, he takes it, enters the information into his computer, puts the money into the register, and prints out the tickets. With a little smile for Gwen, he hands the tickets through the window to Raven.

"Thank you!" Gwen beams at him. With tickets in hand, Raven and Gwen make a mad dash toward where the buses are waiting. They find their bus terminal, the last of the passengers boarding the bus just as they reach it. Climbing aboard, they stop to show their tickets to the driver. She punches the tickets before waving them on. Bubbling with excitement and fear they make their way down the aisle. Raven selects a couple of seats toward the back of the bus for them. Stowing their bags in the overhead compartment, they sit. To Raven it seems as though Gwen can't contain her excitement as the engine of the bus roars into life and the vehicle pulls away from the station. He doesn't know that she can't wait to get away from the man in white. Whatever that was, either real or imaginary, she just wants to leave him and whole diner incident behind them.

Once they are onto the highway headed south, Raven heaves a heavy sigh and turns in his seat to look at Gwen. She leans back in her seat, a huge smile upon her angelic face. "We made it!" she exclaims in a whisper so that none of the other passengers overhear. She can barely hide the nervous panic bubbling beneath.

"Gwen, that was pretty cool. What you did back there, I mean," he compliments.

"Thanks." Gwen leans over, resting her head on his large shoulder. Raven smiles and settles into his seat, glad that the worst of their journey is behind them.

The gentle sway of the road lulls the two orphans into a well-deserved sleep, exhausted from all the excitement over the last several days.

* * * * *

Gwen finds herself carried away into a disjointed dream, hundreds of random images materializing before her. She sees Sister Mary Shaw back at the orphanage sitting at her desk correcting papers. Then she sees Douglas sitting at the supper table with his new family, smiling and laughing with his adopted parents. For the briefest moment, the man in white appears before her mind's eye, but quickly she pushes the image away, instead finding herself running through the forest, blindly following after someone in the dark. She comes into a clearing. The moon emerges from behind the clouds. Moonlight shines on the wolf before her, the beast staring at his prey—the poor man foolish enough to give them a ride. Gwen shouts, the meaning of her words lost in the reverie, but the creature hears and turns toward her. She wants to see past the monster before her and see instead the gentle, kind-hearted boy she knows, but, in the dream, all she can see is his black fur and golden eyes.

CHAPTER TEN

Coney Island Misfits

*T*hey are children of the streets, just two runaways melting into the nameless masses of the dirty, hungry, and undesirable homeless of New York City. Upon first arriving, Gwen is enchanted by the loud, vibrant city and all its many marvels. The money from the diner quickly runs out; Raven spends it upon Gwen's every desire. They spend their first week in a modest motel, which seems to them like a palace. They eat out at diners and fast-food joints every night and buy themselves some new clothes and other necessities. It's no surprise that when the week is up, they can no longer afford the motel room. They are thrown out to live on the streets, penniless once more.

Raven and Gwen try to make a decent life for themselves, taking advantage of the city's many homeless shelters. They find these institutions too depressing and quickly give them up for a life of peddling and pickpocketing. Gwen insists that they not look like the multitudes of homeless that plague the city, maintaining instead a clean, hygienic appearance. This proves beneficial for their enterprise as well as their overall health. Choosing for their dwellings abandoned warehouses, old buildings, and factories, they move every so often to keep from drawing attention to themselves. Together they set up a home and sanctuary similar to their cave back at St. Paul's.

During the day, they spend most of their time at the public library, searching for any information they can find of their own kind. From mythology, fairytales, legends, and history, Gwen delves into the printed works, searching for answers. Hundreds of stories tell of beings such as them, but how much of it is make-believe, she can't tell. She shifts her focus more to the locations of these stories. Since most of them take place in foreign lands across the sea, this is little help in their quest, but a few are based in America, and this, at least, is a start.

Gwen comes across many books about the Salem Witch Trials, enthralled by the many accounts of the Witches and their evil deeds, but not so pleased with their sad endings. *Am I one of their kind? Am I a Witch?* she considers. Perhaps it is just the teachings of the nuns that make part of her reject this notion as ridiculous, yet she knows firsthand that the unexplainable happens, and it often happens because of her. She has to know for certain what she is, and where she came from, so she continues her tireless search.

In the afternoons, the two find a street corner or a park and set up their operation. Gwen stands on a crate and sings, a hat placed at her feet for donations. Raven hangs back, pretending to be completely unassociated with the beautiful, black-haired girl with the voice of an angel. It doesn't take long for the citizens passing by to become distracted by the siren and stop to appreciate her musical performance. Only after a crowd has formed around Gwen does Raven make his way through the audience stealthily pilfering wallets, money purses, watches, and other valuables. His quick hand and his unassuming nonchalant manner make it possible for him to rob the crowd blind.

After he has a decent bounty in his jacket pockets, Raven walks out from the crowd again, stalking on down the street to a dark, secluded alley to go through the loot, dividing the valuables from the driver's licenses and credit cards. Gwen points out early on that credit cards and driver's licenses are dangerous since they can be easily tracked and shouldn't be taken. Respecting Gwen's good sense, Raven does as she suggests.

When the loot is separated, Raven puts everything back in its original place and stows all the stolen items minus the cash away in a brown paper bag to be anonymously dropped off at the nearest police station, post office, or other government offices later. Eventually, they will be returned to their owners. With no trace of where these mysterious bags came from, the police are left scratching their heads, leaving Raven and Gwen in the clear.

Although it isn't honest work, it is next to impossible for them to make a living otherwise. Gwen forces herself not to think of it as stealing, but as survival. With this little operation, they make a modest living, providing for their every need. They scavenge what they can dumpster diving, collecting small furniture items such as rugs, chairs, and cabinets to make their current dwelling cozy, even though they know they will have to leave it all behind when it comes time to move again.

Their simple existence offers little worries or cares outside of their need to stay together and out of sight from the authorities. They are content enough, maybe even happy. Occasionally, they go out of their way to do something fun, even if it means spending every last dime they have. At times, they spend all day at the movies, watching one movie after another, stuffing themselves with popcorn, hot dogs, nachos, candy, and soft drinks till they almost burst. They play in the arcade in the theatre lobby in between, and get their picture taken in the photo booth to commemorate the occasion. When the theater finally closes for the night, Gwen, and Raven walk home, light-hearted and giggling hysterically about nothing in particular.

After staying in New York, a year, Raven takes Gwen ice skating in central park for her ninth false birthday. Gwen is a terrible skater, falling constantly, leaving her hindquarters black and blue by the end of the evening, but she doesn't seem to care. Every time she falls down Gwen busts up laughing, often pulling Raven down with her. He smiles and laughs along. Afterward they have a snowball fight on their way home. Raven lets her win, of course. It's the best birthday Gwen has ever had, at least so far.

* * * * *

On a Friday afternoon in June, the two misfits take the subway all the way to Coney Island. Catching the D train in Harlem, where they currently dwell, they ride all the way to the end of the line, getting off at Stillwell Avenue. Thirteen-year-old Raven and nine-year-old Gwen find themselves following the crowds of people, caught in the tidal wave of tourists and locals alike all seeking the day's entertainment. Emerging from the station, they spot the Original Nathan's Famous Hotdog stand—more of a building that takes up a whole block than a stand as the name suggests. This is the first indication that they have arrived in Coney Island territory.

As always, Gwen did her homework on this New York City relic. She devoured every book about Coney Island the library has to offer. It gives her a kind of pleasure knowing so much about a place that she is only now, for the first time, laying her eyes on.

Coney Island once had been a peninsula named for the wild rabbits that originally inhabited the site. Over the years, it has gone from a beach resort to the first amusement park in 1895 to one of the world's most popular vacation spots to its current derelict state, half amusement park, half condemned wreck. George Tilyou, designer of Steeplechase Park in 1897, the first of the three original amusement parks in Coney Island, declared, "If Paris is France, then Coney Island, between June and September, is the world." At its height, between 1880 and World War II, Coney Island was the largest amusement area in the United States, attracting millions of visitors every year. At the time, there were three competing major amusement parks: Luna Park, Dreamland, and Steeplechase Park, as well as many independent amusement parks. All things come to an end, and Coney Island fell victim to the change of times, technology, better parks, street gangs, and a poor economy, leaving it as a historic relic of the New York of the past.

"Should we eat first?" Raven nudges Gwen as they approach the over-crowded hot dog eatery, breaking her from her historic contemplations.

"Yeah, I mean we have to eat at Nathan's. Did you know that Coney Island is the birthplace of the hotdog? In fact, this is the first Nathan's Famous Hotdog stand ever. It was built in 1916, founded by Nathan Handwerker and his wife Ida. Back then they only charged 5 cents a hot dog!"

Raven gives her a look, not needing to voice his thoughts. She can hear them loud and clear even if his face doesn't say it all.

"Hey, history isn't nerdy! It's cool," Gwen says in her defense.

Raven chuckles as they get in line at the world-famous hotdog stand behind an overweight woman and her ancient, emaciated husband.

Twenty minutes later they finish off their hot dogs as they walk past the iconic Cyclone Roller Coaster. Gwen fights the urge to casually mention to Raven that the ride is a New York City landmark, built in 1927, and one of the nation's oldest wooden coasters still in operation. Instead, she announces, "I'm ready for my first roller coaster ride. How about you?"

Raven looks up at the ancient wooden structure before them and gulps down his last bite of hot dog, stalling before answering. "I don't know, Gwen. I mean, shouldn't we start small, you know, with bumper cars and stuff?" Shielding his eyes against the sun, Raven looks up and down the street. "Didn't you say there's a kiddie park around here?"

"Yeah, on 12th street. If it's bumper cars, you want there's one at the Eldorado arcade," Gwen answers, looking bored as she tosses her hot dog wrapper into a nearby garbage bin.

"Come on, it sounds fun." Raven turns her in the opposite direction, tugging Gwen along after him toward the less frightening attractions.

"Big baby," Gwen grumbles beneath her breath, knowing his animal-like sense of hearing will pick it up.

"I'm only thinking of you. You're not ready for it. Girls don't like roller coasters, I'm told," he replies as his cheeks redden.

Gwen stops abruptly at this, putting her hands on her hips in a stance that says what she thinks of such a notion. "What, the big bad wolf is afraid of a little roller coaster?" she teases.

In response, Raven runs his hand through his shaggy mane with an emphatic, "No."

"Yes, you are. You're afraid," Gwen taunts, poking him playfully in the ribs.

"No, I'm not afraid of anything."

"Then come on!" Gwen grabs Raven by the shirt and hauls him back to the ominous Cyclone.

Nervously, they board the ride, sitting side by side, as the cars rumble into life. Gwen clutches the safety guard before her. The cold metal bar feels strangely reassuring in her hand as the coaster cars rapidly move along the track. After twisting bends, curves, and dips, Gwen finds herself sailing high above the beach, the boardwalk, and the other amusement parks below her. A world alive with color is far more beautiful from this far up. The gray water of the ocean washes upon the glittering sandy beach. The boardwalk becomes like an endless white divider between nature and the man-made attractions. The people below look like specks wandering back and forth along the faded carousels, rides, arcades, shops, and food stands.

The cars take a jerky turn, the wooden track giving a creaking groan, a telltale sign of the Cyclone's age, and then she and the other passengers plummet downward in an 85-foot drop. All around her the passengers let out shrieks of pleasure—yells of horror and excitement. Gwen gives in, adding her own squeals to the tumult of human voices carried on the wind rising and falling with the coaster's looping tracks. All too soon, the ride comes to a stop. Gwen's heart keeps racing on, still twirling along in the wind trying to rejoin her body. Gwen gives out a delighted little giggle and stumbles out of the car after the other passengers.

"Come on, Raven, let's get back in line. I want to do it again!" She looks over her shoulder, her friend nowhere in sight. Somewhere nearby, the sound of someone retching reaches her ears. Scanning the crowd, she finds the culprit hunched over a nearby trashcan. A group of teenagers pass him and laugh, shaking their heads and pointing in his direction, although Raven's too busy losing his lunch to care. He feels Gwen's soft hand on his back, running up through his swept back, moistened hair. He doesn't dare move, hiding his shame.

Eventually he rises from the trash, not meeting Gwen's penetrating green eyes. "I think there was something wrong with that hot dog," he mumbles as he heads toward the nearest bathroom. Sensing rather than seeing, Gwen follows behind him through the crowd. The invisible tether between them pulls her along after him. He leaves her outside as he hurries into the last stall to finish what he started.

About fifteen minutes later Raven emerges from the men's restroom ready to face the all-knowing, smirking eyes of a particular nine-year-old girl, only to find Gwen leaning against a lamppost with a large Sprite in her hand. She hands it to him without a sideways smile, jibe, or quip.

"For your tummy." Raven takes the drink and sucks in the cold lime soda. As it settles in his empty, abused stomach, he feels a bit refreshed and revived when there's no immediate threat of it coming back up again. Somehow, without any verbal agreement, they end up at the kiddie park. At first, even the bumper cars seem too perilous to Raven's condition.

The arcade amuses them for a while, until the bumper cars seem friendlier to Raven's stomach. Hours later, curiosity gets the best of them, or at least it gets the best of Gwen, and Raven finds himself being hauled along the crowded boardwalk once more.

They ride the famous B&B Carousel, tour the New York Aquarium, and go through a haunted house, which neither of the skeptical duo finds the least bit frightening. Finally, around seven o'clock, Raven has his appetite back and they grab a slice of pie at Totonno's Pizzeria Napolitano on Neptune Ave.

They still have a few hours to kill till the firework show on the beach at nine. Raven spots the freak show tent. He nudges Gwen. "I bet we could give 'em a run for their money." Raven thinks the better of this comment and cuts short a laugh. "Not that you're a freak, Gwen. I mean…"

She looks up at him through her lush black curtain of hair and smiles. "Nah, Raven, we're freaks all right," she laughs.

"What, it's not normal to grow fur or levitate?" Raven asks mockingly, a fake perplexed look upon his dark countenance.

Gwen giggles a little. "Come on, let's see what they got."

Inside the tent, they find seats among the curious audience waiting to see what goes for unnatural amongst humans. There are contortionists, bearded ladies, mutated versions of human beings, and the world's smallest man, but nothing in the show truly impresses them as true experts of the world of strange. When they leave the freak show, Gwen has an unsettling feeling in her gut.

"What's wrong?" Raven instinctively senses her mood.

Sometimes Gwen almost wonders if he's the one who can read minds. She shrugs, kicking a random soda can littering the street.

"Disappointed, I guess. I kind of wanted someone to ask us to join the show," Gwen admits.

"Yeah, somehow I don't think we'd fit in even there." Raven looks up the street spotting a strange sign in front of a shop. "Come on, I know what might cheer you up."

Curious, Gwen follows her friend up to the shop with a big palm painted above the words: 'Madame Fortune, Palm Readings and Tarot Cards.' Gwen quirks an eyebrow at Raven.

"Might be fun. After all, you never know, she might be the real deal. Like you."

"Yeah, right," Gwen scoffs, not wanting to admit that she's curious. "Why don't you go first, Raven?"

"We've only got so much money left. I'm not really into this kind of thing. I like surprises," Raven replies.

Gwen smiles wanly at this. "You think maybe she can tell me something about my past? I'd rather pay to hear about that," she admits, staring into the open doorway of the shop. It's dark inside, like the gaping hole in her memory. Her first five years on earth bring only a vacant void, an emptiness that aches in her soul and burns in her chest.

"Only one way to find out." Raven hands Gwen a bunch of wadded up bills. She pockets the cash, taking a nervous breath before stepping into that dark emptiness before her.

A few steps into the dim shop, Gwen finds herself standing in front of a tall counter, staring at the bottom of a pair of men's shoes which rest on the counter before her. She stands on tiptoes to see a teenage boy sound asleep, leaning back in an old office chair behind the desk.

Gwen peers around the tiny room, noticing the few shelves with books and random items on the wall behind the counter. A beaded curtain on her right leads into another room. When she notices a bell on one end of the counter, she reaches over and taps it with her palm quickly. It lets out a single high-pitched chime. The slumbering boy slumbers on, oblivious. Gwen tries coughing loudly, but nothing wakes him.

"Hello? I want to see Madame Fortune," she announces to her dim surroundings, hoping that the lady herself isn't taking a nap as well. She reaches out with her mind, probing further into the shop and finding a female personage in the back room. Her thoughts sound as loud as a blasting stereo to Gwen's ears.

That stupid, no good, lazy son of a bi—

Gwen hears the sound of the woman's feet approaching, and then Madame Fortune herself sticks her head out of the beaded curtain. Her round head is half-covered in strange gypsy scarves. Red, curly hair hangs from her ears to her shoulders. Harsh makeup covers the features of what might be a plain woman in her fifties, with visible wrinkles at the corners of her eyes and mouth. Gaudy jewelry dangles from her ears, neck, and wrists, emphasizing her gypsy persona. Her light brown eyes take in Gwen's small form in one glance and move on to glare at the sleeping boy.

Without a word, the madame reaches over and hits the bell several times in succession. Gwen flinches at the high-pitched ringing. The sleeping attendant springs into life, eyes wide and face alarmed, startled by the raucousness. His feet slip off the counter as he tumbles off the chair and onto the floor. A heartbeat later, he springs up, righting the chair to its original position and briskly dusting off his t-shirt. Madame Fortune gives him a gaze of cool disdain. This makes the youth go pale. Madame points to Gwen, and then abruptly vanishes behind the beaded curtain.

Gwen smiles awkwardly up at the scrawny teenager before her.

"I'd like to see Madame Fortune, please."

"Y—yes, of course. Would you like a tarot reading or palm? We also offer scrying and other forms of divination." He pauses. "Wait, aren't you a little young for this kind of thing? Where's your mom, anyway?" He looks her up and down as if just now fully conscious of the girl he's addressing. He even leans over the counter to look at her as if she were a roach on the floor, possibly contemplating whether he should squish her underneath his size fourteen shoe. Ironically, he has the same image in his thoughts as Gwen.

Gwen meets his incredulous expression with a cool glare, straightening her shoulders and raising her chin. "I don't have a mother, but I have money. I want to know about my past."

The boy hesitates a moment, a bit taken aback by her intimidating demeanor.

"Forget about him, child. Just come on back, dear," calls Madame Fortune from within.

Sheepishly, the lanky boy waves for her to pass through the beaded curtain. Just as Gwen passes out of sight, she hears him think, *whoa, she's got scary eyes. That's got to be the spookiest little girl I've ever seen. Wonder why she's so—*

Quickly shutting him out, Gwen focuses on her surroundings. Her eyes adjust to the dim light, the smell of incense tingling her nose. The simple inner room holds a round table with two chairs in the center of the room, the madame sitting casually behind it. Next to the wall behind her, a large chest sits beneath a long antique mirror on the wall above it. The mirror reflects the opposite wall, an identical mirror hanging there, the dual reflections giving the appearance of an eternity caught in glass.

An old glass display cabinet sits against the right wall with an enormous collection of different size crystal balls, scrying stones, colored candles, and other tools of divination. Four tall lamps give the room a soft, almost romantic, glow from their positions in the corners of the room. One ornate chandelier dripping in crystals hangs directly above the table, washing the green tablecloth in bright light. Directly beneath the light in the center of the table is a round shape covered by a black velvet cloth. The twin scents of incents and decay linger in the air.

If that's a shrunken head under that cloth I'm outta here, Gwen tells herself.

Madame Fortune waves Gwen to the empty chair across from her, her long fingernails making her hand seem almost elegant despite the clanging of the bangles on her wrists. Gwen walks toward the chair, trying not to be transfixed in the image reflected in the two mirrors. She sits, looking at the elderly lady before her.

What are you doing here, baby doll? she thinks to herself. Aloud, she proclaims, "I am Madame Fortune," pronouncing the title as if she is of French descent even though Gwen knows this not to be the case. "I understand you seek the secrets of the past?"

Gwen nods, unable to form the words to explain her complicated situation. If this woman really thinks she has divine powers, then she should be able to discern the whole truth about Gwen, the same way Gwen already knows so much about her.

Madame Fortune, Elise as she's called outside of the office, reaches for a deck of tarot cards sitting to one side of the table. She shuffles them whilst eyeing Gwen, considering her.

"Can you pay, my little cherub?"

Gwen suppresses her disdain at the pet name and reaches into her pocket, placing her collection of crumpled bills on the table. Madame Fortune quirks an eyebrow at the cash. *You shouldn't take money from a baby. But if she's here, there has to be a reason.* The fortuneteller's curiosity wins over her ethics.

"So, what will it be? The cards? Shall I read your little hands? Or the crystal ball?"

"I've done some reading on palmistry, and it seems to be all interpretation. How accurate are you telling someone about their past?" Gwen asks skeptically. She knows right away that the woman is impressed by her vocabulary, her intellect for one so young, and also a little annoyed to be interrogated by a mere child.

"Oh, so you know a little something of the art, do you? It's far more complex than you can comprehend, little one. But Madame Fortune stands by her readings. Palmistry is very scientific as well as spiritual. If you believe, then we can find the answers you seek."

Nodding, Gwen nervously wipes her hands on her blue jeans before placing them palms up on the table on either side of the mysterious, black-draped orb. Madame Fortune takes Gwen's left hand in her right hand, delicately tracing along the lines with her fingernails. The sensation tickles but Gwen forces herself not to retract her hand protectively.

Gwen is flooded with the woman's true impressions through the telepathic current between their minds while they sit silently beneath the bright crystal chandelier. Apparently, her hand is unusual. She has more lines in her hand than this woman has ever seen, especially in a child. The lines foretell of greatness, misery, tragedy, ominous events past, present, and yet to come, and numerous loves awaiting her in the future.

Gwen finds the last a bit startling, even more so than the coming tragedies. Finally, the fortuneteller looks up at Gwen, a peculiar expression wrinkling her brow. "May I see your right hand?"

Gwen nods as the fortuneteller shifts her body to focus her attention on her right hand. Gwen listens as the woman rambles inwardly about the possible meanings of the signs in her second hand. Together, they perplex the woman, yet they also excite her. *It isn't everyday someone like this walk into your shop, Elise. Don't upset her or she might not let you take pictures.* Calmly, the woman reaches for Gwen's left hand, holding each of her hands in her own, meeting Gwen's eyes only when her composure is intact.

"You're an old soul, that's for sure. You don't belong to this world, yet you are as much a part of the here and now as you are of the past. There's so much to see in your hand that it would take days to interpret it all."

That's why she wants to ask me if she can take pictures of them, Gwen thinks.

"But there are a few things I can tell you." Tracing a line with her long-lacquered fingernail from the bottom of Gwen's palm in an arch ending between her thumb and index finger, she continues, "See here, child. This is your lifeline." Gwen peers down at her palm to see the odd lines in the skin of her hand. "Most lifelines are continual, no breaks, or if there is a break, just one. You have three clear breaks."

"What does that mean?" Gwen looks up into the older woman's eyes, looking for an answer that might settle her nerves.

"There are different interpretations, but it used to be believed that a break in the lifeline was an indication of death, a short lifeline meaning a short life or untimely death." Madame Fortune sees the fearful look in Gwen's young eyes and hurries on, "Do not fear, child. This clearly can't be the meaning of these breaks. After all, a person cannot die three times, only once, and modern theories of Divination see these as signs of a drastic life change, not fatal."

Gwen releases a breath she didn't realize she'd been holding and collects her thoughts. "Can you tell when in my life these drastic changes will happen?"

"Not precisely, no. However, I would say that one has already occurred. When you were incredibly young, perhaps?" Madame looks to Gwen for confirmation.

"Yes, when I was five." The hush in Gwen's voice seems to heighten the tension in the atmosphere of the room. Madame waits for Gwen to elaborate, but when she doesn't, the fortuneteller nods, returning her attention to Gwen's hand.

"The next big change is coming soon; I think in a matter of years. And the last is very close to the end of your life."

"What can you tell me about my past? About whom I was or who I'm supposed to be?" Gwen asks, not able to hide the tremor in her voice.

"It's too complex to say all at once. I see a sad life full of heartache and trial. It might help to narrow things down a bit. What exactly is it about your past you want to know, dear? Pose this in a single question if you can."

Gwen thinks for a long moment as Madame Fortune waits patiently. *Just one question? I have a hundred questions that have no answers,* Gwen admits to herself. Aloud she says, "I want to know what happened to my mother. I mean, I want to know how she died. What happened that last night I saw her?"

The woman across the table looks a bit pale for a moment before her professionalism sets in, clearing her countenance. "I think maybe it would help to gaze into my crystal ball." The older woman glances down at Gwen's meager stack of money and adds, "Free of charge, of course." She smiles brightly at her.

"All right, let's give it a try." The lady watches as Gwen hides her hands in her lap.

Madame Fortune stands and crosses to her display case, removing a large white candle and a vial of Lemuria oil, and returns to the table. Setting the oil aside, she places the candle before Gwen. The redheaded fortuneteller turns her back on Gwen for a moment, returning with a long, smoldering incense stick. She uses this to light the candle, returning it to its original place before settling down in the chair again opposite Gwen. She retrieves a notebook and a pencil from a drawer on her side of the table and places these items before her. Unscrewing the cap on the vial of oil, she dips a drop onto her index finger, rubbing the oil into her forehead just above a spot in between her eyes in the place referred to as the third eye. Replacing the lid on the oil, Madame straightens her posture, squares her shoulders, lifts her chin, and takes a deep breath.

To Gwen's astonishment, the woman suddenly brings her hands together and claps twice. All at once, the four lamps in the corners and the chandelier above them go out, and the room plunges into darkness. The white candle burns before Gwen, giving off an eerie light encircling only the two of them and the tabletop in its glow. Finally, Madame exhales and uncovers the black velvet cloth from the object in the center of the table.

Gwen suppresses a gasp as the beautiful, iridescent, clear crystal ball is revealed. The candlelight reflects off its surface, showing points of rainbow-colored light within its depths.

"Now we may begin," Madame announces. "I need absolute silence." With this, she closes her eyes and begins to breathe in a rhythmic fashion.

If Gwen weren't telepathic, this would all seem very puzzling to her. Instead, she follows the woman's every thought, understanding that the fortuneteller is simply focusing her energy, grounding herself, and clearing negative energy from her mind to draw in positive energy. This allows her to open her third eye, centering herself.

Gwen tries to do likewise, calming herself from within, breathing in a soothing beat, trying to empty her mind, to be open to the process, to be ready for whatever happens next.

Madame Fortune asks, "How did this child's mother die? Please show me the event as it occurred that night." She speaks as if to the crystal ball, calling it by a strange name.

When the fortuneteller opens her eyes, Gwen is ready for just about anything, from spinning heads to speaking in tongues. All the woman does is turn her gaze into the crystal ball between them. She looks into a point of light on the ball that draws her eyes and gazes past it, seeing beyond.

Gwen melts into the woman's consciousness, willing herself to see through the eyes of Madame Fortune, ready to share the psychic's journey into the depths of the scrying stone. Gwen makes the full connection with Madame Fortune's mind, of which the older woman is completely unaware, her trance-like state making it all too easy for Gwen to have full access to her entirely. Elise's body begins to vibrate. Her skin becomes cold, and Gwen feels these sensations through the connection, as if they really happen to her.

Madame Fortune sees a mist smoking within the depths of the crystal. She keeps her focus just past the mist, letting it seep into her, careful not to be startled by it else she loses the connection and come out of her trance abruptly. The mist turns from white to dark gray smoke, an eerie haze in the iridescent ball. Gwen suppresses the urge to shiver.

Calmly and without breaking eye contact with the crystal ball, Madame Fortune picks up the pencil, poised to write down any impressions, images, colors, shapes, and sounds she might receive through the scrying stone.

All at once within the gray smoke, a young woman's face appears. She has long blonde hair, fair skin, and yellow-green eyes. She is utterly beautiful. Something about her visage tugs at Gwen's heart and mind, recognition beyond her mental grasp. The woman's face is replaced by a man's face, regal and proud, with a strong brow and a chin set in determination. His hair dark as night, his eyes unnatural like blue fire. His image invokes a childlike fear in Gwen.

Elise's left hand writes vigorously while her mental connection never breaks from the images before her. Gwen is too distracted by the phantoms in the crystal to pay attention to the words the fortuneteller scribbles. Gwen eyes remain transfixed as the gray smoke changes from orange to red, like a blaze. She can almost feel the heat of it, the turmoil within it, as images emerge in rapid succession.

A small hut sits in the woods, a meadow of wildflowers surrounded by a forest of burning trees. The blonde beauty lies lifeless in a pool of blood, a small child clutching her arm, a burning rose, violet eyes, a city carved out of a mountain side, a white tower encircled by smoke, and finally, a young blonde-haired boy walking in the snow in the middle of the night carrying a small dead girl with midnight-black hair.

Other images flash within the smoke, but are gone before Gwen can identify them, yet she knows that Madame Fortune after years of practice has missed nothing and will take note of them on her little pad of paper. The fortuneteller begins to speak, an otherworldly hollowness in her voice.

"For the child of the forsaken, the prince must die. For the child, the dead will rise. For the world, the child will die thrice, and in three days from the ashes will rise to claim the souls of men and heaven and hell will collide."

Stunned, Gwen snaps out of her trance, feeling ice cold as her consciousness settles back to reality. Her spirit awkwardly rejoins her body, like distant acquaintances reunited, every inch of her skin covered in goose bumps. She blinks several times, sucking in ragged breaths before focusing on the ever-still fortuneteller across the table. Her gaze is still focused within the ball, her eyes rarely blinking, her body relaxed fully in the trance.

"A child to be born of The Forsaken, to divide the worlds, an heir to Rose and Thorn. Power will be spoken in its voice, death in its words, hearts of men held in its hands meant to enslave all with its curse."

Gwen's blood runs cold. Her body quakes. Part of her feels the need to run, to get as far from this woman and her empty voice and those dark images as her feet can take her. Another part of her is stricken with the need to know all, stuck in her seat, unable to tear herself away.

Suddenly, Madame Fortune's voice changes, sounding like a young boy.

"Run, Gwen, run! Never come back! Never come back! Only death awaits you here!"

"Gwenevere! Gwenevere! Hail to the Rose and Thorn!" she cries in yet another voice. Next, she speaks in the voice of an elderly woman as she finishes with, "Beware the sister of lies, the mother of darkness, and the angel of death!"

The smoky mist within the crystal ball covers over the orb's surface, all images fading into gray. Slowly, the smoke clears to the faint white mist and then evaporates, leaving the scrying stone crystal clear once more.

Madame Fortune finally goes quiet. Her left hand ceases its scribbling, releases the pencil, and becomes still. Gwen senses Fortune leaving the trance and coming back to her normal self. She exhales. Closing her eyes, she allows her shoulders to slump and leans back in her chair, an air of exhaustion about her.

When she looks up at Gwen, Madame Fortune gives her a weak yet pleasant smile. She notices the pale, troubled look on the girl's face and turns instantly maternal.

"Dear, are you all right? Do you need something to eat? Or to drink, perhaps?"

Gwen leans back in her chair and nods, dumb.

The fortuneteller quickly retrieves a package of crackers with a cheese ball wrapped in plastic wrap, and a couple cans of Coke from the trunk against the wall. She sets them on the table. After opening the crackers, she unwraps the cheese and places a Coke in front of Gwen. The older woman then takes the other cola and pops it open, settling into her chair again.

Gwen looks at the food before her, a bit hesitant.

"Go ahead, kiddo. Crystal gazing can be rather exhausting. It helps to have a snack afterward to settle your nerves."

Gwen nods at this and reaches for her soda can.

After the two have eaten and most of their drinks are gone,

Madame Fortune finally turns to the business at hand.

"Feel better?" she asks, observing her briefly till she nods in affirmation. Madame Fortune turns her attention to her notepad, scrutinizing her own writing as if trying to interpret hieroglyphs. "Hmmm…" Elise rests her chin in her hand, her brow creasing in consideration.

"Well? What did you find out? I mean, the whole thing was kind of strange. You spoke in funny voices, different people's voices, and talked of a child and a prince and I don't know what any of this has to do with my mother."

Madame Fortune looks at her, pity crossing her brown eyes. She smiles a little too brightly for comfort. "Don't be afraid, dear. The speaking aloud happens often. It's really nothing to worry about. The process can be a bit confusing but I'm very practiced and made notes of everything I received through the stone." Gwen relaxes at this. "You wanted to know what happened to your mother, correct?"

"How she died, yes," Gwen confirms, impatience evident in her voice.

"But you were there. Do you remember nothing of this event?"

"Nothing," Gwen whispers.

Madame Fortune pats Gwen's hand, her face concerned. "Are you sure, then, that you wish to hear this? Sometimes we suppress memories for a reason."

Gwen gulps, turning her eyes away from the fiery-haired fortuneteller. "I'm ready to know. I can handle it now." Squaring her shoulders and straightening her back, Gwen meets the older woman's gaze. All at once, she doesn't look like a child but a strong young woman. Madame Fortune nods to her respectfully.

"All right, then." She clears her throat. "I had the impression that your mother lived in a secluded place, away from others almost as if she were hiding." She looks to Gwen, hoping this will jog a memory, but Gwen only looks at her stone-faced. The older woman turns to her notepad and continues, "You lived there in the woods with her all alone. Sometimes a man would come. I think he was your father, maybe." Again, she glances at Gwen, but this time she seems relieved. Now she carries on more confidently. "But he didn't live with you." Elise thinks a moment, staring at the far wall as if the answers will be written there. "He was important. I mean, he was powerful somehow. But there was another woman, a dark woman with strange eyes."

Gwen perks up at this, remembering the strange violet eyes that appeared in the crystal ball, feeling an icy shiver run through her flesh. She leans forward, her emotions a mix of excitement and apprehension.

"This woman, there's something wrong about her. She knew your mother very well, yet she hated her."

"Why?" The word slips out of Gwen's mouth before she realizes it.

Madame Fortune shakes her head, "I don't know, child. Jealousy maybe? Perhaps she, too, loved your father and wanted revenge."

Gwen's face poses the question her voice cannot, at which Elise frowns and nods sadly. "Yes, she's the one who did it. I'm sorry, but…" She pauses, and at that moment the room seems to hold its breath. "Your mother was murdered."

Gwen shakes her head emphatically. "No, I remember something about a fire. Did you see anything about that?" Gwen asks hopefully.

"Yes, but this other woman with the purple eyes, she was the arsonist. She only meant to hide the deed and burn the evidence."

Gwen goes pale. Every part of her turns cold and numb. Somewhere deep in her gut she feels the truth of this. Somehow, she has always known but hid the painful reality of it away so she wouldn't have to feel it. All at once, pain overpowers her, washing over her like a wave of molten heat, icy pain melting in her rage.

Madame Fortune looks hesitant to continue, biting her lip.

"What?" Gwen asks. "Is there something else?" Her voice carries a sharp edge, but she manages to contain herself.

The fortuneteller looks uncomfortable. Gwen senses that she's embarrassed, confused at what she's about to say. "I saw you, too. That night when your mother… you found her after it had happened. But the woman, she was still there and she…"

"Please, whatever it is, just tell me!" Gwen demands desperately.

"She killed you." Madame Fortune shrugs and testifies, "I saw it. And everything confirms it. She cut out your heart." Her voice trembles, her eyes watering. She wipes them away with the back of her hand, careful not to harm her well-manicured nails. "I'm sorry. It's just so vivid in my mind. It happened. I'm sure of it. You were young but I'm positive that you're the same child from the vision. There's no mistaking those eyes."

Gwen sits as still as stone, her face paler than a ghost. Her right-hand itches to touch the strange scar on her chest just above her heart. She feels the rhythms of its beat within her, listening just to reassure herself that it is truly there. She knows that she has a heart. Blood pumps through it and through her.

"You were just a baby. Why would someone do that to a child?" Elise asks. She seems on the verge of a breakdown, overwhelmed by the vividness of the vision.

Gwen reaches over and pats her left hand for comfort. "Hey, it's okay. Look at me, I'm fine."

Elise meets her eyes and takes a deep calming breath. "Yes, you are alive because he saved you."

"Who?" Gwen asks, eyes bewildered. "My father?"

"No. A boy hiding in the forest. He followed the woman there, but he didn't realize what she had done until it was too late, and then... everything was burning: the house and the trees. He had to wait until she left. He was afraid she might see him and..." Elise takes another calming deep breath and discloses, "He dragged you from the house before it collapsed into the snow."

"But what about my mother?"

"He was only nine, maybe ten years old. A very thin young man, and in no way strong enough to pull her out. It was you that he wanted. You were the reason he followed the other woman."

"Well, what happened next?"

Elise shakes her head in frustration. "I'm not sure. The images go hazy, jumbled. I saw him touch his hand to your wound, and then... everything became bright. A light overtook my sight, and the vision was gone. That's all."

The fortuneteller suddenly looks a hundred years older to Gwen, the utter exhaustion showing in the lines on her face. For a long moment, the two of them sit quietly, both lost in their thoughts.

"What about all that stuff that you said? Talking in those strange voices? What does that all mean? What does it have to do with my mother?"

Elise, seeming more herself, picks up the notepad scanning it for a moment. "Ah, here it is." She reads it aloud again.

Gwen listens to the words a second time, still perplexed by them. "You know, it sounds almost like scripture or a prophecy of some kind." She looks to the young girl across from her. "You know what a prophecy is, dear?"

"Yes. It's like someone seeing the future and making a record of it," Gwen answers.

"Exactly! Don't ask me what these means or what it foretells. It sounds ominous, though. It talks about a prince and the only prince I know of is the Prince of England."

Gwen feigns a weak laugh at that, trying to hide her uneasiness. "Is there anything more to tell me?" she asks hopefully, ashamed to admit that part of her wants a happy ending to dispel the gloom that hangs around her.

"Nothing conclusive, I'm afraid. If you want, you may have a look at my notes. Maybe there's something significant that I've missed."

At this, Madame Fortune rips the paper from her notepad and hands it across the table. Gwen takes it with timid hands. She nods and smiles weakly at her host as Madame Fortune stands. "Thank you." She leaves her money on the table and turns to go.

"Wait. You're welcome to visit me again if you like. We could try it again," Elise suggests.

"Yes, maybe. Thank you again." Gwen awkwardly waves goodbye and walks toward the beaded curtain, catching her image for a moment in the dual reflections of the mirrors on the two opposing walls.

Gwen perceives a glimpse of someone standing behind her, not the Fortuneteller, but a man in black smiling from ear to ear. Gwen gasps and whirls around to look frantically about the room. Startled, Madame Fortune watches her.

"Is something wrong? Do you remember something?" Elise looks about the room, too.

Gwen looks back into the mirror opposite her, seeing only her own reflection multiplied into infinity. "No, it's nothing. I just thought I saw something." Embarrassed, Gwen avoids the fortuneteller's questioning eyes and hurries through the beaded curtain. To Gwen's relief, the desk clerk is sleeping soundly again, and she slips out of the dark shop without question.

* * * * *

The sun hangs low in the sky, reflecting its golden rays over the waves as they crash upon the glittering beach, blanching the boardwalk and painting the faded amusement park in an orange glow. *Sunset isn't far off,* Gwen notes as she scans the street for her dark-haired friend.

"There you are!" Raven gets off a nearby park bench, the youths meeting in the middle of the street. "What took so long, Gwen? The fireworks will be starting soon."

"Sorry, Raven. It was more complicated than I thought it would be." Gwen falls in step with the older boy as he leads them back toward the center of Coney Island.

"It's okay. I was worried when you didn't come out after a while, though," Raven says, sensing her somber mood. Hesitantly, he asks, "So what did she say? Did you find out anything useful?"

"Kind of. Not what I was expecting, but… it doesn't matter now, I guess." Gwen tries to shrug it off, giving Raven one of her most dazzling smiles.

He isn't fooled. "Not good news, huh?"

Gwen's smile fades. She hangs her head, her long black hair hiding her face. Still clutching the paper Madame Fortune gave her, Gwen looks at it curiously.

"What's that?"

"Nothing," Gwen remarks, quickly folding the paper and stuffing it into her jeans pocket. Raven doesn't comment. Instead, he takes Gwen's hand in his, leading her through the throng toward the boardwalk and the beach beyond.

Already locals and tourists alike sit on blankets and under umbrellas along the beach waiting for the firework spectacle to commence once the sun goes down. Gwen eyes the crowded beach and suddenly wants nothing more than solitude. Raven seems to feel her mood and heads down the boardwalk toward the far end of the beach, hoping to find a less crowded piece of sand to call their own.

As they continue along the boardwalk, Gwen watches the boards beneath them, white and aged with sand dusting across the wooden surface. Through the cracks, she can see an empty space below, perhaps a dark retreat for wounded hearts and lost souls. Gwen stops unlinking their hands. Raven looking to his small companion curiously stops beside her.

"Come on," she mutters as she steps off the boardwalk and into the sandy beach. Raven trails behind. She walks along the boardwalk until she finds a gap wide enough. She gets down on her knees and crawls nimbly beneath the boardwalk. Raven watches this and laughs. It takes him a bit more maneuvering than Gwen, but he manages to squeeze himself beneath the boardwalk as well.

The sand in the underbelly of the boardwalk is cold and slightly damp. Bits of seaweed and shell lie beneath them. Gwen lies on her back and Raven does, too. They lay like this in silence for a while, watching the people pass by above through the slivers of fading sunlight in the cracks of the boardwalk. A deep melancholy radiates from Gwen, her green eyes staring off into a world only she can see. Determined not to disturb her, Raven forces himself to remain quiet and still, allowing her to be the first to break the silence.

After a while, sand seems to itch all the way up Raven's back, and something crawls across his leg. He tries not to wonder what kind of bugs and other vermin might hide under here as images of scorpions and crabs flash through his mind. Just when he thinks he can't sit there another moment, Gwen stirs in the dark next to him. Reaching into the neck of her shirt, Gwen pulls out her gold locket on its chain. She looks upon the engraving on the front, her name Gwenevere above a symbol of a burning rose.

She saw this image inside the crystal ball. Within the locket is a lock of her black hair, intertwined with a lock of golden hair that she now knows must have been her mother's.

"Hail to the Rose and Thorn," Gwen whispers absently as the images from the fortuneteller cloud her mind again, a confusing mess of half-truths and almost answers.

Suddenly, a loud crack and an explosion sound above them. A moment later a sparkle of light shoots into the sky, illuminating their hideaway through the cracks of their wooden roof. Gwen scrambles wordlessly out into the open air, Raven not a second behind her. The sky has surrendered to darkness with a few dim stars twinkling in the distant canopy. Raven dusts the sand off himself as he follows Gwen toward the dark waves along the shoreline. The lights of a boat can be seen floating in the ocean a few miles out from the water's edge. They watch as another skyscraper firework is launched from the boat. The sound of black powder booms, followed by the screech of the fiery plume as it soars into the sky and erupts into dozens of dazzling colors that seem to reach down toward them as they fall down to earth as ash.

Raven silently takes Gwen's hand, pulling her down onto the sandy beach. She smiles at him warmly then snuggles up to him, resting her head against his shoulder. Raven wraps an arm around her slim form, welcoming her into his embrace. In this manner, they watch the firework show, ooh-ing and ahh-ing in appreciation along with the other spectators. Forgetting their meager little lives, they bask in the multi-colored glow showering above them from the heavens.

Eventually, the fireworks crescendo ending in an impressive booming finale. Slowly, the beach clears as the spectators gather their belongings and move to exit the amusement park. Closing time has come to Coney Island, but the two orphans remain seated in the sand watching everyone pass them by.

Gwen watches a young family with three children. The son, about Raven's age, helps his father fold up a flannel blanket while his mother and sisters pack up an old, wicker picnic basket. There's nothing special about this family. They seem like simple folk just living a simple life. But to Gwen, watching them as they smile and laugh together, sharing a joke as they make their way up the boardwalk, they seem like an impossible fantasy. The youngest daughter, a girl only five years old, trips on her flip-flops and loses one of her shoes, falling behind the others. The father stops and goes back for her, picking up her tiny shoe and holding it out for his daughter to slip her baby-sized foot into it. She smiles up at him as he takes her hand firmly in his. Gwen feels her breath catch in her chest. Her eyes wet with tears. She looks away, unable to bear the sight of them another second.

Where was he when I needed him? Why wasn't he there when my mother needed him? The questions burn unspoken in her mind, searing her with bitterness. Gwen closes her eyes tight against the tears, willing them to stay put, forcing her emotions down into her gut where she hides everything away. Raven's warm hand brushes her face, pushing her hair back behind her ear. She knows he's concerned—scared even—of what she's not telling him, but she can't speak the words. She can't bring herself to tell him what she saw and heard. *Madame Fortune was right. We forget things for a reason.*

When Gwen finally gets to her feet, Raven follows beside her, casting a reassuring shadow as they walk past the rollercoasters and shops. Neon lights and signs twinkle out one by one. As they exit the park and cross the street toward the subway, Raven stops and looks back.

Today, for a brief time, they almost forgot how different they are from other children their age, what outsiders they really are. As the park closes, the other children get into their cars or board the train with their families, headed back to their beautiful homes.

Raven looks down at Gwen, both knowing that as lonely as they feel sometimes, they are grateful to have each other. Maybe that will make it possible to endure anything.

Gwen smiles up at him, a real smile this time. "Let's go home."

Together they turn their backs on the fantasy of a lost childhood, and hand in hand, leave the park as Coney Island misfits.

CHAPTER ELEVEN

Guardians

*T*heir lives settle into a routine. Breakfasting on day-old muffins and doughnuts that the corner bakery throws out. They shower at a nearby apartment complex gym, to which they gain entrance through a back window. Mornings pass in the library or in local bookstores. For their afternoons they go to the park, working the crowd. They treat themselves to dinner at one of the many restaurants in the neighborhood, ending the day back home in their little hovel where they currently squat. Living in this fashion, the years pass by without either of them noticing. In fact, if it weren't for the many physical changes Raven experiences, Gwen might have gone on believing that they would stay children forever.

Raven continues to struggle with the wolf deep inside. He finds himself unable to control his temper, often changing into his wolf form and destroying their home and their meager possessions. Frightened,

Gwen finds the strength not to flee, instead staying calm and focusing all her mental powers on penetrating the animal's mind to find her friend. In this manner, she is able to talk to him, to calm him, to help him manage the beast, to help him transform back into his human self. When Raven becomes the wolf, he feels an uncontrollable urge to hunt and feed on the flesh of other creatures. This terrible rage bubbles up from within and without Gwen's help, he never could overcome it. It frustrates Raven that he can't control himself. It becomes increasingly imperative that they find answers to their pasts and find their own kind. Raven hopes that his own kind can help him tame the beast within.

Gwen visits local bookstores and shops that claim to be a part of the occult or Wiccan hoping to find real Witches, but time after time, she is bitterly disappointed. She chats up the owners and the shop clerks as she browses the shelves lined with spell books and ancient magic relics, asking questions about the craft, getting many confusing and contradictory answers. She tries to test them by speaking in her native tongue, but they only look at her, confused, thinking she's mumbling or stammering her words. No one seems to know any of the spells she conjures. When she looks into their thoughts, she sees their typical human upbringings. They are clearly not her kind at all.

Still, Gwen buys several spell books, taking them home to test them for herself. Most are fake, the magical words meaningless, invoking no magic. She doesn't feel the fabric of the world around her alter when she speaks their words. She even tries to cast spells using potions, but to no avail.

Only rarely does anything in these books have any real magical value. In these cases, some of the rituals and sayings are incorrect and don't work completely. Gwen starts to realize that perhaps these books are the human interpretation of real Witchcraft. Maybe in the past an authentic Witch taught some humans the art. Over the years, as the practices of Wicca were passed down from generation to generation, more and more of the true words were lost.

* * * * *

Raven and Gwen, after leaving a basketball game, board a bus headed toward the heart of town where they plan to finish his fourteenth birthday celebrations over dinner. For this special occasion, Gwen chose a nice Chinese restaurant in an upper-class part of New York, far away from their current Bronx address.

When they step off the bus in front of the restaurant, Raven feels light and carefree. The day's revelry transported him into a higher plane of happiness, where all his worries and cares vanish into nothingness. He feels excited by the prospect of dining some place new, and Chinese is his favorite. He looks at Gwen, dressed up for the occasion wearing a cute, short black dress, a green cardigan, and her favorite black converse sneakers. Her hair is half-swept up in a French braid, everything about her perfectly angelic and sweet. Just looking at her adds immeasurably to Raven's happiness.

Raven steps up to the entrance of the restaurant and holds the door open for Gwen, who smiles appreciatively before entering. The matron meets them at the podium up front, hesitating a moment as she eyes the unlikely couple.

"Just two?" she asks, a slight Chinese accent to her voice.

"We're meeting our dad here. He should be here in a couple minutes. He's just running a little late," Gwen answers naturally, repeating the line they've used a hundred times before.

"You want to wait for him, then, before taking your table?" the middle-aged matron asks.

"Oh, no, we're pretty hungry. Dad said to go ahead and start without him," Raven answers, trying extremely hard to assume Gwen's natural mannerisms. Raven finds it ironic that Gwen, who hates lying, is such a natural at it, while he lacks the talent. He can't help but feel like everyone can see through his lies, which makes him nervous and fidgety. Gwen keeps reminding him that, unlike her, most people can't read minds. "As long as you keep your face neutral, no one will suspect a thing." Of course, that's much easier said than done.

The matron pauses a moment, looking between the two youths, a little perplexed, as though she's uncertain of their story.

"It's our dad's birthday, so we're treating him to dinner. Mom's going to come pick us up in an hour," Gwen confides to the matron with a little smile, making sure to add that they have money to pay.

"Oh! Yes, yes! We better seat you right away," the matron chirps in response. Beckoning them to follow her, she leads them to a booth in the corner. The restaurant is only half-full. Gwen called in advance to make sure. Neither of them likes crowded places. They prefer solitude, especially when they eat. There is something soothing and rather relaxing about eating a quiet meal in a calm environment. In Gwen's opinion, it makes the food taste better. It's something that she never felt in the dining hall back at St. Paul's. The atmosphere there had been loud and chaotic, which was most unappetizing.

With a sigh, Gwen takes her seat at the booth, Raven taking the seat opposite her.

The matron hands them each a menu. "What to drink?" she asks, giving her most polite little smile.

"Just water will be fine," Gwen answers as she flips through the pages of the menu, waiting for something to catch her eye. The matron is about to leave but stops and turns back.

"What name will your father give when he comes?" she asks.

"Oh. His name's Douglas," Gwen answers quickly. She gets a questioning glance from Raven across the table. The matron nods and hurries away.

"Why that name?" Raven whispers.

Gwen has no chance to respond as their waiter comes to the table carrying two glasses of water. He smiles at them as he places their drinks down. "Are you ready to order?" he asks. He is a pleasant-looking Chinese man in his early twenties.

Gwen knows that Raven has already chosen what he'll eat even though he hasn't opened the menu. He has this habit of always eating the same thing at every restaurant he patronizes. If it's an Italian place, he'll order lasagna. Mexican, and he'll order enchiladas. And at Asian restaurants, he always eats beef and broccoli stir-fry with slivered almonds, although he always orders the almonds on the side. This forces Gwen to make up her mind quickly since she doesn't want to keep Raven waiting.

Raven speaks up immediately, choosing, of course, the beef and broccoli. The waiter scribbles it down in his notebook, turning to Gwen with an expectant look on his face. Panicked, Gwen looks down at the menu and picks the first thing her eyes fall upon. She orders the Kung-Pao chicken and hands the waiter her menu. As soon as the waiter turns his back, heading to the kitchen, Gwen gives Raven an annoyed look. He shrugs in response, having heard her rant on his strange dining habits before. She rolls her eyes at him.

To pass the time while they wait for their food, Gwen writes a sentence on her napkin, beginning a story and then passes it to Raven. They are in the middle of this little diversion when a strange sensation comes over Gwen. She feels the fabric of space and time around her flex and stretch just as it does whenever she casts a spell, only this time it feels different. Perplexed, Gwen tries to sense its origin. She has never felt another person do magic before; in fact, she has almost come to believe that she is the last survivor of a dead race. Until now.

Reaching out with her consciousness, she encounters many beings nearby. She gets a sense of their minds without probing within and senses that they are magic wielders. She feels four of them walking toward her.

Gwen doesn't quite know how to feel about this sudden development. Outwardly, she goes stiff, sitting upright as though a rail is wedged up her spine. She stares at the front entrance of the restaurant, waiting for the four strangers to enter. *I wonder what other wiccans look like?*

Raven looks up from scribbling a line on the napkin to pass it to Gwen, noticing for the first time the look of severe panic on her pale face. Alarmed, he reaches out his hand to take hers. Startled by his touch, Gwen comes out of her trance and looks at Raven, perplexed.

"What is it?" Raven whispers across the table, fear edging his sharp voice.

"I don't know. Someone's coming," Gwen replies.

She turns her head as the front doors open. Raven turns in his seat to watch the newcomers enter the restaurant.

A family of four enters, all with dark hair, medium complexions, and the same gold and violet eyes. Nothing else about the group is remarkable or striking. They look like an ordinary family to Raven. Even their clothing is unremarkable, neither expensive nor cheap, basic in color and style. Raven turns to make a jibe at Gwen, something along the lines of how paranoid she's getting, when he notices the expression on his friend's young face. He can't tell if she's even breathing. Her eyes fixate on the group being led by the matron to a booth near the entrance.

Gwen is stunned to find that the group of magicians is a family.

The father is a man in his early forties, built like an athlete with broad shoulders and a thick, muscular frame. He has a thick mustache and beard and wears his brown hair short. The plain, thirty-something woman next to him must be his wife for she wears a wedding band. She also wears a bizarre engagement ring that looks like two snakes mating. She stands a head shorter than her six-foot tall husband, her hair curly and up in a ponytail, her clothes typical of the average American housewife. Their two children are teenagers, a boy, and a girl. The eldest looks sixteen. She's a tall, stick figure of a girl with short, curly-brown hair, with looks exactly like her mother. Their fourteen-year-old son looks like a miniature, hairless version of his father. Each of them is skinny, brunette, and ordinary, except for those gold and violet eyes.

Gwen has only recently begun to perfect her abilities as a psychic, seeing beyond thoughts and emotions coursing through mortal minds to see their auras. These orbs of energy surround every living being. Within each person's aura lies their true identity. Auras are both colorful and musical in nature. They aren't just orbs of stagnant light but vibrant, living, thriving extensions of the soul itself, each with its own pulsing rhythm like a heartbeat in a low hum.

Gwen has spent many hours staring into her mirror every night, examining her own aura in the hopes of understanding all its many mysteries, and also to better understand herself. Her pale green aura shimmers with a pearlescent light. Its ripple like a pebble skipping across a pond, never calm or smooth. Her rhythm is like unto the percussion section in a large symphony orchestra; numerous beats intertwined to make one intricate sound, which she finds both complex and beautiful. Accompanying all this is a lovely high-pitched tone like someone holding one perfect note for eternity.

Now she finds herself facing several entities with eerily similar auras. Each has a different color, vibrancy, rhythm, and hum, but every one of them have the same pearlescent glow. *This has to be the soul's magical essence*; Gwen thinks to herself.

Gwen begins to relax. When no one looks in her direction or notice her and Raven sitting across the restaurant staring at them. She quickly averts her gaze and shoots a warning glance at Raven. Immediately, he turns around and gives Gwen a questioning look.

"Well?" he asks, passing the napkin with their impromptu story over to Gwen.

She looks down at the napkin a moment, confused. She reads the last line of the story and picks up the pen to continue on with her own. "I think they're Witches or Wiccans."

Raven waits for her to elaborate but Gwen just bends her head over the napkin and writes. When finished, she hands the napkin and pen back to him, a calm expression upon her face.

"How can you tell?" Raven asks, incredulous.

"By their auras," Gwen answers. "Plus, I felt them use magic before they entered the restaurant. What spell they performed, I'm not sure. It's nothing I've ever felt before."

Raven senses a hint of jealousy in Gwen's voice. There's nothing she hates more than being ignorant and prides herself on her intellect and ability to learn new things with great ease. *Gwen must hate the idea of these strangers knowing more about magic than her,* Raven realizes. "Why don't you go over and introduce yourself or something?" Raven asks.

"What? We don't know them. I bet there are as many bad Witches as there are bad people," Gwen replies, a bit shocked by the lack of sense in Raven's suggestion.

"You've been looking for your own kind for years and now we meet some and you're not going to go talk to them?" Raven asks completely flabbergasted.

"No, I'm going to wait until they leave and follow them home. We'll observe them for a while. Maybe later, if they seem all right, we'll talk to them," she answers, sounding a little annoyed.

"Okay, whatever you say." Raven writes the last line of the story, finishing their back-and-forth tale, and hands it to Gwen to read over. "If you can tell that they're Witches, can't they tell that you're one, too?"

"I don't know, maybe. They don't seem to be aware of us, though."

Gwen risks a quick glance over at the family of Wiccans. They're ordering their food from the waiter. None of them look in her direction.

"Maybe they can't read auras or minds the way you do," Raven comments in a cheerful voice, trying to boost Gwen's self-esteem and reassure his own.

Just then, their waiter approaches the table with their plates. Smiling, he sets their food in front of them. "Enjoy your meal."

"Finally! I'm starved." Raven unravels the utensils tucked away inside his napkin and immediately digs into his food, shoveling it into his mouth with great eagerness.

Shaking her head in disgust of Raven's appalling table manners, Gwen looks about for the salt and pepper shakers, and spots them across the table. Completely by instinct, she whispers the words for movement, magically calling the salt and pepper shakers to glide across the table toward her plate. In that same instant, Gwen realizes that she made a terrible error. She suddenly feels a tightly woven spell converge upon her. Paralysis strikes her physical form as a mental block severs her from the source of all her magical abilities as if cutting a metaphorical umbilical cord between her and the power of the universe. As if the emptiness that she feels isn't torture enough, her mind is assaulted by the prodding of other beings forcing their way into her conscious, mentally raping her mind and memories. Gwen tries with all her mental capacity to fight off her assailants, to find a place to hide herself within her own mind, but they are working together. Alone she is no match for their joint mental attack.

Suddenly, Gwen's body starts to convulse in a seizure, her eyes rolling into the back of her head. Raven stares at her in complete shock and then rushes to her side, trying to aid her. Taking her into his arms, he tries to force her to be still, but she squirms ceaselessly in his embrace. He calls her name over and over again, but she doesn't answer. He lays her on the ground, shouting for help.

All around them, the other customers stop eating their meals and watch this shocking display. The matron and the waiter come rushing to help Raven. The matron sends the waiter to call 911. Amongst all the chaos, Raven looks up and sees the family of Witches sitting perfectly still in their seats staring at Gwen with cold, unfeeling expressions, watching them with their piercing violet eyes. Suddenly, he knows that he has to get Gwen as far from those people as possible. Gathering her in his arms, he picks Gwen up off the ground and heads toward the door.

Raven ignores the matron who shouts at him, telling him not to move the girl, and that he should wait for the ambulance. With a single thought in mind, he makes his way toward the entrance. The Wiccan family follows him with their staring eyes. When he is just about to pass them, Raven stares right back into their faces, giving them a challenging look. Suddenly, a look of shock comes over the daughter's face as she glimpses into Raven's golden eyes.

"Werewolf!" she whispers to the others, a look of dread distorting her face. The others all look at each other, then back at him, surprised. He growls and hurries into the foyer and out of the restaurant.

Rain pours from the sky, falling heavily on them as he continues quickly down the street, drenching the two of them within a couple of minutes. Raven dares not to get on the bus, afraid the driver will take one look at Gwen and demand that he takes her to the hospital or call the authorities himself. Even now, in this darkest of times, they must keep a low profile. Instead, he carries Gwen, cradled in his arms, running as fast as his legs will take him. Several pedestrians on the street gawk and cry out in shock as they watched this fourteen-year-old boy whiz past them at inhuman speed. He doesn't pay any mind to them. Home is too far away. He must find a safe place nearby to hide Gwen until she recovers. He only hopes that the Wiccans aren't following them. A terrible dread settles on him as he realizes that Gwen, whom he has always believed to be the stronger of the two of them, was bested by the brunette family of Witches.

How can I, a mere Werewolf, stand against Wiccans? What will become of Gwen if I can't protect her? If they take her, what evil will they do to her? All these thoughts race through his panicked mind as Raven runs in the rain.

Finally, Gwen's body begins to relax as the seizure subsides. She goes limp in his arms. Her eyes closing, she fades in and out of consciousness. Relief bubbles up inside him, so much that he feels as though he'll start to cry. He allows himself to recover, realizing he's run over twenty city blocks.

He looks over his shoulder back the way he came, relieved to see no one is following him. He stops a moment to catch his breath. Once calm, Raven begins to scan the area for someplace dry and safe to wait out the night. After several minutes of searching, he finds an empty office building. The front door is locked, so Raven carries Gwen into the alley alongside the building to try and break into one of the side windows or through the back door.

Walking in darkness along the alley, he uses his night vision to see everything around him. The sound of a girls' laughter pierces the silence of the alley, bouncing off the walls and carrying an eerie echo all around him. Raven stops dead in his tracks, a cold shiver running up his spine. Frantic, he searches the alley and rooftops for any signs of life but sees nothing. All of a sudden, he is knocked down by an invisible force, causing him to drop the unconscious Gwen. The momentum sends her rolling across the pavement until she comes to rest several feet away from Raven.

Regaining his footing, Raven spins around to face his attacker, yet the alley is empty behind him. Remembering Gwen, Raven takes a step toward her. A figure materializes out of the air, forming before his eyes as if dust in the wind gathering and shaping itself into human form. Raven instantly recognizes the man as the strange, bearded father of the Wiccan family from the restaurant. Gwen lies still as a corpse between him and the dark stranger.

The man gives Raven a wicked smile, his eyes dark and empty as he takes a step toward Gwen's unconscious body. Panic and rage boil within Raven.

"You stay away from her!" Raven bellows.

The man stops as he looks at Raven quizzically. Then, suddenly, his plain, curly-haired wife appears beside him, a smirk upon her lips.

"What's a dog like you doing with a Wiccan?" the woman asks, amused, speaking in the pure tongue, the language that only he and

Gwen shared.

"We're family!" Raven replies, walking slowly toward Gwen, never taking his eyes off of the two personages before him.

"Nonsense! Wiccans don't mate with animals. Your race is inferior to ours. The bitch and sire that raised you should've taught you this!" the woman taunts.

Enraged, Raven stops dead in his tracks. He tries to produce some kind of retort but can think of nothing. Instead, he lets his rage take control of him, letting out a low guttural growl at the pair.

The man grabs his wife by the arm and forces her to look at him. "Don't anger him, Sanindra," he whispers in a commanding tone. The woman gives her husband an annoyed look, yanking her arm free from his grip.

"We don't want a fight. We just want the girl," the man announces, trying to make his voice sound polite.

"Just walk away, wolf!" a voice commands. Raven turns to his right to see the son, a boy just his age, crouched upon a stack of old crates and pallets, staring at him with those vibrant, violet, trademark eyes of the family.

"What do you want with her?" Raven demands.

"It's none of your concern. This is Wiccan business," yet another disembodied voice answers from behind him. Raven whirls around to see their sixteen-year-old daughter materialize before him, standing dangerously nearby. Her presence and demeanor frighten Raven the most.

"She's not one of you. She belongs with me!" Raven tells the shorthaired girl before him. Ignoring them all, he goes to retrieve the fallen Gwen, but the boy suddenly appears in front of him, blocking his path. With a cry like a beast, Raven instinctively reaches out, taking the skinny boy in his clutches. He heaves him off the ground as if he weighed no more than a baby and hurls the unsuspecting boy through the air, removing him from his path. The boy crashes back onto the pile of crates.

"*Evata Madota!*" the boy's mother hisses at Raven. From her out-stretched hands, an orb of light materializes, shooting forth toward him.

He has no time to react. The orb hits him in the chest, a burning sensation like acid seeping into his flesh, muscles, and bones. The impact sends him flying backward through the air. When he finally lands with a hard, bone-aching crash to the pavement, he lies just within the mouth of the alley, thirty feet away from Gwen's motionless form.

Raven groans in agony as he struggles to regain control of his weakened, bruised body. The burning sensation within makes his mind feverish and incomprehensible.

"Hurry, grab the girl before he recovers!" the woman commands, her voice sounding far away.

Suddenly, Raven finds himself alert once more, the pain in his body nothing compared to his urgent need to protect Gwen. For the first time, he needs the strength of the wolf and longs for the fury of the animal inside him.

Mentally, he begins to summon the monster, willing the transformation that has always happened accidentally until now, to take hold of him and make him a killer. He finds it more difficult than he expects. But then, he's only spent the last several years denying his true nature. Raven tries harder, giving himself up to his emotions, letting all his rage, frustration, hatred, and love engulf him in a dark embrace. He slips away as a new entity takes hold of his mind, his body, and his instincts. He feels the monster claim him. As pain racks his body, his physical being re-arranges itself to match the dark, sinister mind now in power.

* * * * *

Gwen is jostled awake to find herself hanging over the bearded Wiccans shoulders. She glimpses his wife and two children following behind him as they make their escape with her as their captive. They freeze when a furious howl erupts in the alley behind them, their faces sharing identical looks of shock. Instantly, the mother turns to face the wolf, but she has no time to utter a spell before Raven leaps, biting down on her leg. The wolf yanks her off her feet and drags the Wiccan back into the dark alley. Her family, in shock, hears her cry out once more before the sound of crushing bones meets their ears. Then, all is silent.

Anger distorts her husband's face. Throwing Gwen down on the ground, he enters the alley with a warrior's battle cry, his children following after him to avenge their mother.

The impact of hitting the pavement jars Gwen into consciousness. She has a splitting headache, and a hundred aches and pains all over her body. Gwen tries to shake off a strange sense of disorientation.

Where am I? The glaring light from the streetlamp above her makes her eyes burn. She hears shouts, screams, and then a wolf's howl nearby. Startled, Gwen sits upright. She looks into the dark alleyway, listening for a moment. Again, a wolf howls into the night.

"Raven!" Gwen whispers.

She stumbles to her feet, the world spinning around her as she tries to make her way into the dark foreboding alley before her. As she walks, she regains her balance. Her head stops spinning, and her eyes adjust to the darkness all around her. Ahead of her, she sees human shapes moving and what looks like a creature on all fours, pouncing and snarling at them.

"Raven!" Gwen shouts. She begins to run, fear and love carrying her weak body beyond its own capacity.

Finally, she comes upon the beast and its attackers. Gwen gasps in horror. Before her is pure carnage; the lifeless body of the brunette woman from the restaurant rests at her feet. She lay like a broken doll, her broken arms and legs jutting out at unnatural angles, her throat crushed. Her hollow violet eyes direct their blank, wide-eyed stare up at Gwen. Her husband's remains lie scattered all about the alley at the feet of his two orphaned children, who fight earnestly with the creature.

The teenage brother and sister shoot orbs of light at the monstrous silver-black wolf before them, who lunges and snaps at them, dodging their supernatural missiles. The son is gravely wounded, his face scratched, his shirt in tatters with large gouges in his chest where claws have ripped into his flesh. Yet he still manages to hurtle orbs of fire, lightning, and air toward the wolf, keeping out of the monster's clutches. His unscathed sister is clearly the strongest magician of the family. She knocks the silver-black wolf off his feet, lunging at him with a silver blade, striking and jabbing at him when he's down. Then she leaps back to safety when the animal is on its feet again, ready for another attack.

This time the beast's speed and strength surpasses theirs. Lunging forward, the wolf's jaws come crashing down on the young boy's calf, yanking the screaming child off of his feet and dragging him within range of its razor-sharp claws.

"No, Raven! Stop!" Gwen yells out.

The creature stops. Its ears perk up at the sound of Gwen's familiar voice. It turns to look at her, still keeping its captive pinned underneath him.

"Please, Raven, leave them alone! They're only children!" Gwen walks toward him. "See, I'm all right. We can go home now," she says, trying to soothe the monster's fury.

Gwen is horrified to see how battered and weak Raven is. Singed patches of fur surround pink flesh where the Witches' fireballs have struck. Long gashes bleed where the blade cut, blood matting down his fur. He moves slowly; clearly, the fight has taken its toll upon him.

The sixteen-year-old Witch spins around, releasing a dark orb of silver light, aiming the sphere at Gwen's chest.

"Be still!" Gwen speaks, her voice taking on that same hollow tone that she had in the diner all those years ago. The sound carries loud as a megaphone, bouncing of the concrete walls and hitting their two attackers' ears. It penetrates their consciousness, leaving them in a state of hypnosis. The girl instantly stands bolt upright; a wide-eyed stare focused on Gwen's face. Her brother lay on the pavement similarly transfixed. Although her words give her control over the Wiccans, she is too late to stop the missile vaulted toward her.

The magic strikes her in the chest, absorbing into her flesh, draining her of all her strength. Gwen collapses in a heap onto the pavement.

The beast lets out a sorrowful cry, leaping off the boy to attack the girl who injured his Gwen. The helpless can only stand there as the beast pounces. He crashes down, pinning her to the pavement beneath him. The wolf opens his jaws and readies to tear out the girl's throat with its razor-sharp teeth.

As the paralysis fades away, Gwen tries to get to her feet. "No! Raven, stop!"

The wolves' golden eyes stay on Gwen's face as it climbs off of its prey and toddles over to her side. The wolf sniffs at her hair and face, licking her cheek with affection. Reassured that she is well, the wolf nudges her with his snout, rubbing against her like a puppy.

"Everything's going to be all right now," Gwen reassures, stroking the beast's silvery-black mane. With her mind, she delves deep into creature's subconscious, finding Raven within, racked with panic and fear. Slowly, she calls the boy out of the beast, feeling Raven become stronger and the monster becoming dormant inside of him. Within minutes, the animal curls up at her feet writhing in pain as it mutates back into its human form.

Averting her eyes, Gwen glances over at their enemies lying on the ground, their heads turned to stare at Gwen, their faces blank. "Now what do we do with these two?" Looking all about her at the remains of the two slain Wiccan parents, she adds, "And what to do about them?" Gwen already knows the answer. Behind her, Gwen hears Raven stirring. "Are you alright?" she asks without turning to look at her friend, whom she knows is completely naked after his transformation.

"I think so. How about you?" Raven gets to his feet as he sees the aftermath of his rage. "Oh, Gwen! What have I done?" he asks, his voice weak.

"What you felt you must. I would've done the same for you."

"What are we going to do? Surely, we can't hide something like this?" Raven asks, helplessness resonating in his voice.

"We can. No one can know what has happened. There might be others where these people came from. They'll hunt us down," Gwen informs him.

Raven walks up behind her, stopping just out of her field of vision. "I'll do anything you say. Please just make it all go away, Gwen." Raven's voice cracks as a sob breaks from within his soul.

Listening to her friend's misery, Gwen closes her eyes tight, fighting the tears. A single teardrop escapes and slides down her cheek.

"Gather all the remains of the dead together into a pile," Gwen instructs.

"What about the children?" Raven asks weakly.

"I'll think of something." Gwen listens as Raven scuffles away, leaving her to stand in the dark alley alone with her thoughts. Suddenly it's all too much for Gwen to bear. She, too, lost a mother a long time ago. Now and then, she still dreams or sees flashes of brief images and memories long forgotten, a face gone forever. Gwen fights back the tears that threaten to break free. Tonight's events have conjured two more orphans. Gwen tries not to imagine how they will feel when they come to.

"They won't have to remember a thing," Gwen whispers to herself, an idea forming in her mind. She turns, moving back into the dark alley, ready to do what has to be done and be gone from this place.

"Gwen, stop. Don't come any closer. I'm still naked," Raven announces, calling out to her from somewhere ahead of her.

"Well, what are we going to do about clothes? You can't wander around New York like that," Gwen replies, closing her eyes tight even though most of the alley is cast in darkness and shadows.

"I don't suppose I can borrow the boy's clothes?" Raven asks.

"No. They must return home looking the same way they did when they left. No one must suspect that anything's amiss," Gwen answers firmly.

"Obviously, you didn't get a good look at the boy's clothes. They're ruined, torn to shreds, and he's wounded pretty badly, Gwen. I think he might bleed to death."

"Oh no! I totally forgot about him. Fine, you can have his torn clothes if you want. I'll just have to find something else for him to wear," Gwen replies, then, continues, "I can't do anything with my eyes closed, though. Could you hurry and put something on already?"

"Oh, yeah. I gathered all the bits and pieces of the parents together. I had to throw up a few times, but I did it." Gwen hears the noise of his feet padding on the pavement and the sound of his movements as he wanders farther away from her down the alley to kneel besides the still hypnotized fourteen-year-old Wiccan.

Raven is about to unbutton the boy's pants but gets weird qualms about it. He turns toward where Gwen stands, whose eyes shut tight as she waits for him.

"You know, it's kind of weird undressing another guy. Could you maybe do it for me?" Raven asks, embarrassed.

"And what? You think it's not a problem for me?" Gwen replies, trying hard not to laugh at her best friend's shyness. She is certain his face must be beet red from blushing.

"Fine, I'll do it," she hears him grumble. "Man, this isn't easy with him like this. It's like undressing a doll!" Raven complains. "Okay, there. I've got his pants off. Just wait a moment and I'll be decent," he tells her. Quickly, Raven steps into the boy's pants, which were fine except for the large tear in the left leg, a massive bloodstain covering the lower half of his pant leg.

Raven looks down at the half-naked boy at his feet and sees the giant teeth marks in the boy's calf, the wound oozing blood. He becomes sick but his stomach is already empty. When he wretches, only stomach acid comes up. His head spins when he stands. Raven forces himself to look away from his victim and turn back to Gwen. She stands just behind him, her eyes wide open, a look of concern upon her pale face.

"Are you okay, Raven?" she asks, coming up to him and putting a hand to his cheek as if feeling for a fever.

"I'm fine. You need to heal him quick, Gwen. His wound is even worse than I thought. Do you think you can heal him like you've done to yourself?"

Gwen nods. Bending down beside the wounded boy, Gwen places her hands upon his leg, one on each side of the wound.

I hope this works, please work! Closing her eyes, she begins to chant the healing song her mother sang over her cradle and bedside. "*Dah-Day-Wente, Curea-Longa, Babeta-Lovota.*" With the magic of the words coursing through her, Gwen reaches out into his mind, searching for every wound and scratch in the boy's body, seeking out each one and healing it, scourging it of infection before moving on to the next. She continues to sing the lullaby in a low voice over and over again until she feels her own energy weakening. Finally, she lets the song fade from her lips and relinquishes her hold on the boy. Leaning back on her heels, she observes her patient. The boy before her is now unscathed, a healthy color in his cheeks, with no evidence of blood anywhere on his person.

"Will he be all right?" Raven asks from over her shoulder, bending over to see for himself.

"I think so. Come on, Raven, we have work to do, and we're running out of time." Gwen gets to her feet and looking around she spies the pile of dead body parts that had once been the boy's father. At the bottom lies the corpse of the mother. Gwen grimaces.

"Okay. I need you to get him some new clothes. Steal them if you have to, but please try to get something similar to what he already had on," she pleads.

"You act as though someone's waiting for them," Raven remarks.

"There is. It's a small coven but a vengeful one," Gwen replies.

Raven looks at her doubtfully.

"I was in his mind, and that's what I saw. Witches usually live in Covens, at least that's what I've read. This could mean thirteen Witches or more, I'm not sure. So, we need to make them forget they even met us, let alone everything that happened tonight. If we can do this without raising suspicions with their Coven, it'll give us more time to disappear."

"All right, I guess you're the expert," Raven admits before turning and heading out of the alley to complete his errand.

Gwen stares at the pile of human remains and focuses all her attention on a conjuring spell, one she has never used before. She witnessed firsthand the two Wiccan teenagers do many marvelous things. Until now, she never imagined such things were possible. Trying to remember what she heard and saw the siblings do earlier, Gwen casts the spell for fire. After several tries, an orb of burning light springs forth from her bosom, landing in the heap before her. Within seconds, the two corpses are alight, burning in the inferno before Gwen. She grimaces at the smell of burning flesh and hair in the air, trying to keep her own stomach calm.

Feeling pleased with her accomplishment, Gwen turns her attention to the two children. The siblings still lay on the ground several feet apart, the boy on his back, the girl on her stomach. Both stares, wide-eyed and awaiting her instructions. With a sigh, Gwen walks over to a spot that puts her in the eye-line of both teenagers. Immediately, both sets of eyes fix upon her face the moment she is in their field of vision. Taking a deep breath, Gwen prepares herself to reshape their thoughts, their memories, and their actions.

"Stand up," she commands, in the hollow voice of authority. Simultaneously the siblings obey, springing to their feet and standing at attention before her. The boy is not at all bothered to stand there in his underwear.

"You will forget everything that you just saw," Gwen says. Within moments, she replaces their memories, reshaping the events of the evening for them, telling them what to say and how to behave. By the time she finishes, Raven returns, now wearing a grey flannel shirt and brown boots along with the boys tattered jeans.

He stares at the burning pile of human flesh, wrinkling up his nose. "Aren't you worried someone will notice the smoke or at least the smell and call the fire department?" Raven asks.

"No, we're in the business district. These buildings are empty. It'll burn out before morning," Gwen assures him. "You got the clothes, I see."

"Yeah. Hey, can you just have him put these on himself now? I mean since he's up and all?" Raven asks.

"Of course."

Raven nods gratefully. He hands Gwen the pair of pants and t-shirt he has stolen.

"Elias, come here and take these clothes." Instantly the boy comes to life, walking up to Gwen. He takes the clothing from her outstretched hands. "Put them on. Throw your old shirt into the fire," she orders, pointing to the inferno ten feet away from where they stand. The boy obeys, changing into his new clothes, which to Gwen's relief not only fit, but were very much like the ones he had been wearing. When the boy is done, he walks over to the fire and tosses his torn t-shirt into the blaze. "Now come back and stand before me," Gwen intones. The boy listens and returns to his sister's side.

"Follow me." She turns, and the two of them follow. She leads them to the other end of the alleyway, coming out of the darkness into the lamp light. Raven follows close behind, looking about the alley and around at the empty street as if expecting another attack to spring at any moment.

Gwen continues giving orders. "You will wait here five minutes, then you will go across the street and go down into the subway. Once there, you will awaken from this stupor and remember nothing after leaving the restaurant. You will notice your parents are missing. You will not go looking for them, but instead, board the train and wait for them at home. Tell the others that you were separated and lost your parents, but not to worry because they should be home soon. Everything is going to be fine," Gwen promises once more, and then breaks eye contact with them.

Gwen turns to Raven, who stands leaning against the brick wall. In her normal voice she says, "Come on. Let's get out of here, fast!" She leads the way down the street, away from the zombie-like children, toward their own home. Raven catches up halfway down the street. They walk side by side, neither one caring to share their thoughts.

After a while, Gwen glances over at Raven and gasps. "Look at you! I mean, you look terrible. Why didn't you say anything?" Gwen exclaims.

"You needed my help. Besides, I didn't want to worry you. You seemed pretty stressed out already," Raven admits.

"Yeah, but Raven, you're losing blood. You've got cuts everywhere, and your hair!"

"What about my hair?" Raven asks in alarm.

"Well, parts of it are burned off, right down to your scalp. You look awful. Are you in pain?" Gwen reaches out a hand to touch the place above Raven's forehead where his hair should've been, touching the bare, scorched skin instead.

Raven flinches, recoiling from the searing pain. His skin is obviously still very sensitive. "Yes, I ache all over. But really, it's not too bad. Just don't touch me. I'm sure I'll be better after a good night's sleep," Raven insists.

"Nonsense. Sleep doesn't cure stab wounds and third-degree burns, you idiot. Come here and stand in the shadows for a moment so I can heal you," Gwen instructs.

"Really, Gwen, don't put yourself through—"

Ignoring his protest, Gwen grabs Raven by the arm and hauls him into the shadows of a nearby building. She places her hands upon his chest and chants the healing song. It takes a long time for Gwen to work through all the many wounds and burns, but eventually she heals them all, leaving her feeling completely exhausted.

"There. Feel better?" Gwen asks weakly.

"Yes, thank you. How do I look?" he queries.

"Still awful. I don't know how to re-grow hair, Raven. Sorry." Gwen gives him a fatigued smile and begins to stumble, losing her balance.

Before she can fall, Raven catches her. Picking her up off her feet, he cradles her in his arms. "You see! You take too much upon yourself, Gwen. You spend all your time watching out for me, but who's going to look out for you?"

"That's what you're here for," Gwen replies, smiling sweetly up at him. "Now, take me home. It's been a really long night."

"Yes, ma'am," Raven replies, smiling back at her. Raven carries Gwen all the way home. By the time he reaches the abandoned apartment building where they live in the Bronx, Gwen is fast asleep. Raven gently lays her down on her makeshift bed, a pile of old blankets and soiled pillows. Straightening up he looks down upon Gwen's angelic face as shame pierces his heart.

He'd come so close to losing her tonight. She'd been attacked, her life endangered, and he had been helpless to stop it. Yes, he had found a way to protect her, but at what cost? He shivers inside at the memory of the couple he had slain in her defense. He couldn't really remember their murders, but somewhere deep inside he knows what the animal did, and it isn't repentant of the deed. To the beast, they were threats, because they were threatening his cub.

"No," Raven realizes. "She's not my cub, she's, my mate." Over the last several years, he fell in love with his best friend, and now he knows that one way or another she will be his wife someday. Of course, she's still much too young, and he's much too shy to confess his feelings for her. Someday, he will.

Bending down, Raven kisses Gwen gently on the forehead before heading over to his bedroll. With a sigh, he settles under the covers, forcing all the memories of the terrible events of the night from his mind. He chooses, instead, to think of the future, his and Gwen's future together. Before long, Raven is fast asleep, dreaming of his green-eyed angel, knowing that they will always be each other's guardians.

CHAPTER TWELVE

The Meddling of Others

D r. Renee Thompson basks in the warmth of the sun as she strolls down the street, admiring the New York City architecture all around her. She finishes some leisurely shopping on 5th Avenue, and, having reached her spending limit for the day, decides to call it quits. She is staying at her sister's apartment in Greenwich Village. It's only a short walk away from where she ate lunch, so she figures she'll walk back instead of taking a taxi.

Renee thinks New York is beautiful in the summer. Hot, noisy, and full of life. She feels alive here and loves to visit her little sister regularly.

I should take Rachael out to dinner tonight; she thinks as she comes up to a busy intersection. She joins the large crowd of gathering pedestrians waiting at the crosswalk for the light to change. While standing there, pondering which restaurant her sister might enjoy dining at that evening, Renee stares into the crowd waiting on the opposite side of the street. She isn't looking at anyone in particular, just scanning the crowd, fascinated by the diversity of faces displayed there.

Then her eyes alight upon a young girl's face. Something about her is strangely familiar. Renee looks again. If she had to guess the girl's age, she would say eleven, maybe twelve. The girl is short, perhaps a little over five feet tall with long, straight, jet black hair, milky-white skin, and light eyes. Renee can't say the exact color of the girl's eyes from so far away, but they are exotic, almost feline in shape.

The girl's clothes are a bit boyish. She sports a faded black t-shirt, which carries the logo of the day's most popular rock band, under a green hoodie, with light blue faded jeans, and green low-top Converse sneakers. Her clothing hangs off of her slender frame, making it perfectly obvious that she is devoid of womanly curves. The mysterious girl waits impatiently. Obviously, she has some place important to be. Renee also notes that the girl seems to be alone, no one else in the crowd takes notice of her. Clearly, she is without a guardian. This also seems odd to Renee.

Finally, the light changes. The cars crossing their path stop and the crosswalk signals for foot traffic to proceed. Instantly, the crowd moves forward, carrying Renee off the sidewalk and across the street. Determined to figure out how she knows this girl, Renee keeps her eyes glued to the girl's face within the crowd headed toward her.

The girl has a calm, collected air about her as she walks across the street. For such a young and petite person, Renee is surprised at how easily the girl keeps up with the stride of the people around her. Obviously, she is either a native New Yorker or has lived in the city for quite some time. There's something commanding about the girl's walk, a kind of confidence rare in someone so young. Slowly, the girl comes toward Renee, every moment bringing them closer to the middle of the intersection and to each other. As she gets closer, the girl's features are more distinguishable: the beautiful shape of her face, the high cheekbones, the slender, straight nose, and her beautifully full lips. Renee knows now, without a doubt, that she has seen this face before…but where?

The girl approaches. Renee is about to pass by on the right. The girl is preoccupied, not realizing she's being observed until she passes Renee. At that moment, the girl looks up and glances straight into Renee's face. Renee gasps. *I know those eyes!*

Yellow just around the pupil, like an eclipse, the sun's rays shooting out from behind a black full moon. The color goes from yellow to a light green out towards the edge into a deeper shade of green. The effect is mesmerizing, even stunning to behold. They're peculiar eyes, the kind one doesn't often see.

Renee stops in the middle of the street, momentarily stunned by this revelation. The crowd of pedestrians pushes and shoves past her. Springing to action, Renee turns and heads back the way she came. Quickly, she finds the girl in the crowd, spotting the back of her green hoodie as it moves away from her. The girl is just stepping up onto the sidewalk.

"Marianne! Wait, Marianne!" Renee calls out, racing to catch up to the girl, who doesn't respond. She just keeps walking down the street.

"Marianne, please wait! Mari—" Renee finds herself struggling to remember the other name the orphan used. What was it? "Gwenevere! Gwen!" Renee shouts, the name practically leaping off the tip of her tongue.

Startled, the girl stops dead in her tracks and looks about, confused. Just then, the Doctor comes up from behind the young girl and rests a hand on her shoulder. The girl spins around in a panic at the touch, turning a dark glare upon the woman standing over her. Recognition settles in and her face blanches. Instantly, the girl steps back, shaking Renee's hand away from her shoulder.

"Gwen! It *is* you!" Renee shouts. "Where have you been? The police looked everywhere for you and for that friend of yours. Some thought you'd died in the fire."

"I'm sorry, but you have me confused with someone else. I don't know you."

Without a backward glance, the girl hurries away, immediately blending into the many pedestrians along the sidewalk. Renee won't be so easily blown off. Quickly, she chases after the girl, struggling to find her again among the crowded sidewalks of the bustling city. After chasing her former patient for several blocks, Renee is about to admit her defeat and give up.

As she turns to head back to her sister's apartment, she catches a glimpse of green in her peripheral vision. Renee takes a second look and sees the girl running across the street and into the park on the opposite side. Quickly, the doctor follows, making sure to maintain a far enough distance so as not to alert the young girl to her presence.

Gwenevere crosses the grass to an assembly area where a large stone statue sits on a stage in the center. Renee stays back, shielded from view by a tree nearby. She watches as Gwenevere scans the park. A young man, about fifteen or sixteen years-old, emerges from the many people walking along the jogging path. He cuts across the grass to meet Gwen.

Though it's been three years since she's seen him, Renee knows Adam Mathews at sight. She vaguely remembers that Marianne not only changed her own name but her friend's name as well, and for the life of her, she can't recall what that other name was.

From her hiding place, Renee watches as the two youths huddle together and converse. A very heated discussion ensues, the two friends very animated in their gestures. Clearly, something has upset them. As they speak, they both peer about, looking around suspiciously as if knowing they are watched. After a while, Adam manages to calm the distraught Gwenevere. Protectively he puts an arm around her shoulders and the two start walking away.

Afraid she might lose sight of them, Renee hurries after, making sure to follow far enough behind and to walk in a steady pace so as not to attract attention.

She follows them out of the park and down the street. At this point Adam hails a taxi and the two climb in. By the time Renee's able to get a taxi of her own, the other car pulls away from the curb, headed down the street. Renee jumps into the cab.

"Follow that cab please!" Renee instructs the cab driver, an elderly fellow, wearing a news boy cap backwards over his wavy gray hair. His expression is sour, his teeth incredibly yellow, the same shade of lemon lime soda. He shoots her a quick *'you've got to be joking'* look but complies anyway. The taxi takes off swiftly.

Renee's cab follows the children from uptown all the way down to the slums. The Doctor is shocked when the other cab pulls over in a decrepit part of town and the two orphans step out.

They can't possibly live out here, she thinks as she pays her driver and hurries out to follow them. Hanging back, she follows as the two children lead her back to their dwelling. Renee expects them to enter one of the many shabby apartment buildings along the main avenues. Instead, they keep going. Walking down many alleyways and side streets, they lead her to an old railway station. Hiding behind old cargo cars and trains, Renee slowly follows them to where old trains come to die, looking every bit like a train graveyard. Walking down the abandoned tracks with rusty old bits and pieces of locomotives surrounding her on both sides like statues, monuments to an era long passed.

Renee hides in one of the empty freight trains as Adam hoists Gwen into an open window of one of the retired passenger cars. Adam hefts himself up into the window after his friend. Renee stays there for a long time, not sure what to do next. Finally, the doctor comes to a decision. Being very careful to leave as silently as she came, Renee Thompson retraces her steps across the railway station, back through the alleys and side streets, until she finds herself once more on the main road where the taxi had dropped her off a half hour earlier.

The middle-class, white woman in the ghetto is intimidated by her surroundings, sure she will stick out like a sore thumb. Nevertheless, she acts calm and confident as she walks down the avenue, headed back toward the respectable part of town. Along the way, she passes by a group of young men dressed liked thugs, but she pays no mind to them, keeping her eyes ahead of her. She hears some of the young men shout expletives behind her. She neither responds nor looks back. To her relief, they don't follow her.

After what seems like an eternity, Renee spots a taxi coming up the street. Getting the driver's attention, she jumps out from the curb to wave it down before the vehicle can pass her. She sighs in relief as she climbs inside.

"Take me to the nearest police station, please," she tells the driver. A moment later, the taxi continues on. Renee feels a strange sensation as she leaves the two lost children behind.

* * * * *

"I didn't imagine her, Raven. I swear the woman I saw today was the doctor who used to come to St. Paul's. Doctor Thompson," Gwen repeats emphatically to her thick-headed best friend for what seems like the hundredth time.

"That's impossible, Gwen. I mean, how could she have found us? She was probably just a look-alike!" Raven retorts, obviously tired of the conversation.

"Who happens to know I used to be called Marianne?" Gwen asks.

"You probably remind her of someone she knows who's named that," Raven answers, a little uncertain.

"Oh, come on! That's a big coincidence, don't you think?" Anxiously, Gwen paces down the aisle of the passenger car.

Aligned on either side of the car along the row of glass windows are brown, leather-upholstered seats. Two of these seats toward the back have become their makeshift beds with blankets, pillows, and old couch cushions for extra padding. Near the front of the car, they improvised a little kitchen area with a big, metal drum that serves as a fire pit, a water basin, and pitcher on a discarded nightstand acting as the sink, with a miniature refrigerator for storing food. It doesn't work, of course, so the food is always warm, but at least it keeps the rodents away. It holds canned foods and other nonperishable items. Three milk crates are stacked nearby. Above the sink area, several mismatched pots and pans hang from hooks from the ceiling and wall. Their dishes hide in the nightstand drawers.

They have long since acquired the habit of always keeping all their clothes and most of their valuable possessions in two suitcases and a duffel bag, which they stow under the seats where they sleep.

This keeps them in easy reach just in case of an emergency, so they can grab the bags and run at a moment's notice.

Raven stands at the front of the passenger car, trying to light a fire in the metal drum, watching Gwen pace back and forth nervously out of the corner of his eye.

"Oh, I don't know, Gwen. What are the odds of Doctor Thompson being on the same street at the same time? She lives in Maine, for crying out loud."

"I know the odds. But I'm telling you, it was her!" Gwen interrupts him.

"Just calm down. We'll figure it out after lunch, okay?" Raven tries to placate her.

After watching Raven struggle to ignite kindling and newspaper inside the makeshift fire pit, Gwen strides up to the metal drum. Chanting a few words in the pure tongue, a ball of fire forms out of her outstretched hands, shooting it into the drum. Immediately the kindling catches fire and a moments later the fire is blazing. He gives her an embarrassed smile.

"I don't feel like eating right now. I think we should leave," Gwen announces.

"But I like it here. And besides, you said you lost her. She doesn't know where we live," Raven points out.

Walking over to the wall above the sink, he pulls down a grill rack and a cast-iron skillet from their hooks and places them on top of the metal drum. He retrieves a loaf of bread, a package of deli meat, and a block of cheese from the refrigerator. Placing the food on top of the refrigerator, Raven makes two sandwiches. He places them in the skillet to melt the cheese.

"I still think moving to another place would be a wise idea," Gwen reiterates. Her tummy grumbles as she watches Raven grill the sandwiches, flipping them over occasionally with a spatula from the nightstand drawer.

"But we just got settled here. I mean, everything's the way we like it. We have a water pump next to the main train station office, plenty of scrap wood lying around, a supermarket nearby, and we don't have any neighbors to spy on us. It's perfect."

"Yeah, except that it's cold at night, there's no bathroom, and we have to walk three miles to find a decent place to shower," Gwen grumbles. She sits down on one of the front seats to wait for Raven to finish cooking.

"You know, you could just sponge bath like I do," Raven replies.

"In the open by the railroad station, where anyone could happen by? No, thank you!" Gwen answers in a huff.

Raven chuckles. "You know, you can be so girly sometimes."

"I still think we should find a new place," Gwen repeats.

"Why? It's fun living in a train station. It reminds me of that book you read last year," Raven argues.

"You mean *The Boxcar Kids*?" she asks.

"Yeah, that was a good story," Raven replies defensively.

Gwen rolls her eyes.

"There aren't any happy endings in real life, Raven. There aren't any loving couples to adopt us, or beautiful homes in our story!" Gwen counters.

"I know that" Raven answers, a bit dejected.

Gwen sighs, sorry to hurt her friend's feelings. Raven is too optimistic sometimes, even unrealistic. It blinds him to the harsh reality of their situation. Gwen feels the burden of being the leader. The voice of reason rests solely upon her shoulders. Sometimes it's a little much for an eleven-year-old to handle.

"Please, Raven. I know you like this place. I just have a really bad feeling in my gut that if we don't leave this place tonight, something terrible is going to happen."

The sincerity in her voice and the frightened look upon Gwen's face, makes Raven soften. He feels himself bending, as he always does, to her will.

"Okay. But can't we at least wait until morning or something? I don't want to sleep under that overpass again. The bums there are all crazy and creepy."

"Not to mention ugly and smelly," Gwen adds, giving Raven a little smile.

"Then we could have all day tomorrow to find a new place. How about it?" Raven asks.

"I don't know, Raven."

"Please, Gwen? Just sleep on it. If you still think we should move on when we wake, then we'll go."

"And you won't complain?" Gwen asks.

"I won't, I promise," Raven agrees.

"Okay. I don't like it, but it does make sense to wait till morning," Gwen admits.

"Good!" Raven smiles satisfied that they have reached a compromise.

Raven goes to the nightstand and searches through the drawers. He comes back to the fire drum with two plates, balancing both in one hand. Using the spatula in the other, Raven scoops one sandwich onto each plate.

"Here. Lunch is ready." Raven hands Gwen one of the plates and then comes to sit next to her on the seat.

They silently eat their meal side by side. After a few bites, Gwen turns to Raven. "Let's start looking for a new place after lunch."

"Okay, if you insist," Raven replies, exasperated.

Gwen smiles and goes back to eating her grilled cheese and ham sandwich, feeling slightly better now that they have a plan of action.

Later that night, after hours of wandering about the slums of New York for a suitable hideout, Gwen and Raven finally head back to the train station for the evening. Their search isn't highly successful, since looking for a new home involves poking their noses where they aren't wanted. Many gangs occupy the area, and although the runaways aren't the least bit afraid of the mortal thugs with their guns and knives, it seems prudent to avoid any confrontation. They don't want to draw too much attention. After all, how would it look if two children took out an entire gang?

Night falls, and all around them the train yard is shrouded in shadows for Gwen. For Raven, the night is a world bathed in the moon's iridescent glow. As the two friends pass the main railway office, everything appears still and quiet.

Gwen hesitates. The silence hangs thick with dread. She looks to Raven, trying to make out his face in the darkness, but can see only dark shadow. By his stance, Gwen perceives that he's in a good mood—obviously, he doesn't share her unease. She decides just to keep her thoughts to herself as they continue to walk on in silence.

They come around the bend to a row of old, broken-down train cars, where their own passenger car rests. With a sniff at the air, Raven stiffens, stopping dead in his tracks. He reaches out an arm to block Gwen's path, making her stop beside him. Alarmed, she looks all about the empty lane, seeing nothing but the ominous shapes and shadows of the train cars along either side of them.

What is it? Raven hears Gwen's voice ask inside his mind.

I thought I saw someone, he answers in his thoughts, knowing Gwen will hear him. Raven takes a deep breath, holds it a moment, then adds, *And I smell something out of place. Cologne, maybe. Someone's been here.*

Maybe they're still here, Gwen counters.

Raven scans the lane with his silvery night vision, looking for a sign of the man he could have sworn was standing half-hidden just a moment ago behind one of the cars on their right. After several minutes there is no other movement.

I think you're just making me jumpy, Raven tells Gwen mentally.

No, there is something out there. I felt it when we passed the ticket office. It's not safe here. We have to leave now. The fervent tone of her thoughts convinces Raven.

Agreed. Try to make as little noise as possible, Raven advises her.

Together they walk backward, waiting until they are behind the shelter of the nearest cargo car before they turn around.

Suddenly, out of the dark, two men spring out before them, blocking their path. One of them flips a flashlight on, shining the bright light directly in their faces, blinding them both. They avert their gazes, shielding themselves with their hands from the painful light.

"Don't move, kids. We don't want to hurt you. Just keep your hands where we can see them!" one of the dark figures commands in a voice used to being obeyed.

"You two are going to take a ride with us down to the station, all right?" the other man holding the flashlight asks, although from his demeanor it is clearly not a request.

Gwen takes one step backward.

One of the police officers puts his hand to his hip by instinct, fingering his holster. "Now don't give us any trouble, kids. We're just here to help you."

"We don't need your help!" Gwen hisses.

Just then, Raven lunges forward, pouncing on the officer with the flashlight. With a shout of alarm, the man hits the ground as Raven pins him in place.

"Run, Gwen!" he shouts, looking over his shoulder. But she's already gone.

Instantly, Raven leaps after her, trying to take this moment while the two officers are caught off guard to follow her. On all fours, Raven runs like an animal in flight over the gravel road around the cargo car in the direction Gwen had fled. Behind him, he hears the two police officers shouting after him, their footsteps pounding down the road.

Raven feels something grab onto his back, taking hold of him. A jolt of pain, accompanied by an electric shock, suddenly shoots through him. His body goes into a seizure as the electric shock continues to shake his frame. Finally, he collapses on the gravel as the pain subsides. His body goes still, leaving him on the brink of consciousness.

The crunch of the gravel beneath their shoe's alerts Raven to the presence of the two policemen standing over him.

"Crazy kids!" The policeman shines his flashlight in Raven's face again.

"You better tell Jensen and Burbank that we lost the girl," the other man says to his partner as he bends down to inspect Raven more closely. The officer pats Raven down, making sure he isn't concealing any weapons before turning him onto his stomach. He removes the Taser from the boy's back and then cuffs his hands behind him. With little sympathy for the boy's physical state, the officer hefts him to his feet.

Meanwhile, his partner unfastens a radio from his belt and talks into the receiver. "Jensen, Burbank. What's your twenty?"

"We're on the northeast side of the train yard, Over," a staticky female voice responds through the radio.

"We lost one of the runaways, a girl about eleven or twelve-years-old, dark hair, about five feet tall, dressed all in black. She should be headed your way. Over."

"We'll cut her off. We'll radio back when we've detained her. Over."

"Ten-four."

With the adrenaline rushing through her veins, it takes Gwen a while to realize that Raven isn't behind her. She finally stops to catch her breath, finding herself on the opposite end of the lane, just two cars down from the passenger car they call home.

Reaching out with her mind, she calls out Raven's name, hoping that he's nearby or perhaps just out of sight. Everything is so dark. Gwen can barely distinguish one shady shape from another. There's no answer to her calls. Suddenly, someone grabs her from behind, picking her up off her feet.

By instinct, Gwen goes limp in the stranger's arms, slipping out of his grasp and falling to the ground at his feet. She takes off running, making her way in between the cargo cars.

"Raven!" she screams into the night, not caring if the man pursuing her hears her or not.

A dark female figure appears just ahead of her with a flashlight in hand. She lunges forward, missing Gwen as she easily sides steps, maneuvering around the female police officer and running ahead. The woman spins around to chase after her. The partner joins her, both officers hot on Gwen's tail.

Ducking behind one of the coal trains, Gwen gets down on her belly and crawls underneath the train to hide. A split second later, she hears the sound of footsteps approaching. Gwen stays still, barely allowing herself to breathe as the police officers' feet hurry past her. She listens intently as the sound of their running recedes into the night and all is silent around her once more. She waits there for several minutes before she finally crawls out into the open.

Staying in the shadows, she creeps back the way she came, toward where she last saw Raven. She ducks out of sight several times, almost being spotted by the male and female partners as they search the area for her.

With her mind scanning the area, Gwen senses Raven ahead. Dropping down on her belly once more, she crawls underneath the cargo car, sensing Raven on the other side. Peering from under the shadows of the cargo car, Gwen sees a police cruiser pull up in front of her. One of the officers who first stopped them steps out of the car. He goes to the back door, opens it, and waits. Gwen hears gravel crunching under feet as the policeman's partner comes into view, pushing a disoriented Raven in handcuffs before him. The man pushes Raven into the backseat of the police cruiser. His partner closes the door behind him.

A voice breaks through the silence, coming from the radio on the taller police officer's belt. "Ericson, Moore, we've lost her. Does anyone have eyes on the girl? Over."

"Negative. We'll head back your way. Maybe we can catch her between us, over." one of the officers suggests over the radio.

"Copy that."

One of the officer's heads to the left, back toward the other officers. The driver locks the police cruiser before he takes off in the opposite direction.

Gwen waits there under the cargo car for several minutes before she quietly emerges into the open. Moving with all the stealth she possesses; she creeps toward the police car and reaches her hand out to place it on the glass of the back passenger window. On her lips is a spell that will shatter glass. Out of nowhere, someone grabs a hold of her.

"I've got her!" a voice shouts into the night.

Gwen struggles to get free, screaming and cursing at the man. She tries to calm herself to enchant the man with the command of her voice, but her heart is racing out of control, her thoughts too wild and disjointed.

"Let go of me! Let me go!" Her voice sounds shrill and hoarse. No power comes through it. Her words have no effect. Through the glass she sees Raven hunched over, defeated. Frustration, anger, guilt, and fear surge through her.

"Raven, wake up! Raven!"

Around the corner, her captor's partner hears the struggle. Gwen is just about to lean forward and flip the man over her back when his partner comes to his aid. Between the two of them, they restrain Gwen. One slaps handcuffs on her wrists. One takes her feet, the other her torso, and together they haul her around the vehicle to the other side. Gwen thrashes and screams. They throw her in the backseat with

Raven, slamming the door in her face as she makes one last attempt to flee from her captors.

"We've apprehended the girl. We'll take the runaways back to the station. Over." The flashlight cop radios the information to the other officers.

"Copy."

Before getting into the car, the partners exchange a look of bewilderment.

"Did you see that boy running on all floors like some kind of dog?" Officer Moore asks his partner in a thick New York accent.

"Yeah, what was that? I ain't ever seen an eleven-year-old girl run that fast!" Ericson replies.

"She's strong, too. You think maybe they're on drugs or something?" Moore ponders aloud.

His partner shrugs. "Could be. We'll have them tested at the station."

They nod to each other in agreement and then climb into the police cruiser. Reversing the car until they find a suitable place to turn around, Officer Moore leads the car back out of the train yard and on toward the police station.

In the back seat, it takes Gwen a while to settle. Her anger spills forth in unintelligible profanities toward the two police officers, who choose to ignore her on the other side of the metal partition. Finally, after all her strength is spent, Gwen relaxes. She turns her attention instead to Raven, who sits slumped in the backseat next to her.

"Raven?" Gwen whispers.

At first Raven seems without comprehension. Slowly, he turns to look at her. "You were right," he says in a sad little voice. "You shouldn't have come back for me."

"Don't be stupid. You wouldn't have left me behind, would you?" she admonishes him.

"No, I guess you're right," he answers.

"I'll always come for you, Raven, no matter what. They can't keep us apart," Gwen proclaims softly so the officers can't eavesdrop.

"No whispering back there," the driver orders. His partner Ericson turns in his seat to give Gwen a stern look. Gwen gives the officer a dark glare in response. Officer Ericson shakes his head at her in disbelief.

"Little girls should have better manners. What will your parents think?"

"We don't have parents," Raven replies in a quiet voice.

"We're not even human!" Gwen adds, relishing in the surprised and confused looks upon the officer's faces.

For the remainder of the car ride, they sit in silence, each of them deep in their own thoughts.

* * * * *

Arriving at the police station, Gwen and Raven are immediately separated. Countless questions are asked, and reports are written up. Gwen is kept in the chief's office handcuffed to a chair. One of the female officers tries to get them to take the handcuffs off Gwen, but Ericson and Moore refuse.

"That little cupcake is a lot more dangerous than she looks," Ericson explains. Moore laughs in agreement.

"What are you going to do to us?" Gwen asks the police chief.

"We are handing you over to child services," he replies, lounging back in the chair behind his desk. "Your friend's lucky that Officer Moore isn't pressing charges, otherwise he'd be going to juvie."

"Press charges for what? We didn't do anything wrong!" Gwen replies.

"For attacking an officer of the law, or how about resisting arrest." the chief answers curtly. "For running away and for squatting illegally on private property. We're not the enemy, sweetheart. We're just trying to help you." He uses a gentler tone to placate her.

"Maybe we don't want your help!" Gwen replies, earning a disapproving look from the chief before he leaves her.

After what seems like an eternity of waiting, the door opens. Gwen looks up, and instantly, red-hot rage boils up inside her. Doctor Renee Thompson stands in the doorway. Behind her, a man and woman in business-causal clothes from the child protection agency enter, followed lastly by the chief.

"This is your fault!" Gwen spits the words out at the doctor, who crosses the room toward her.

"You behave now, girl," the chief warns Gwen.

"It's all right, I'd like to talk to her a moment," the doctor says.

The chief nods in agreement.

The doctor takes a seat next to Gwen. "This is Mr. Wentworth and Mrs. Shoemaker from child services. They've come to help you. I want you to know, Marianne, we're all just trying to—"

"My name is Gwenevere!"

"Now we've been over this before, girl. Your legal name is Marianne January, and that's what they're going to call you. When you turn eighteen, you can change it then," the chief informs her impatiently tucking his thumbs behind his belt loops.

Gwen glares at him.

"You followed me, didn't you, Doctor?" She already knows the answer but wants to hear the woman confirm her suspicion.

"Yes. I had to. When I saw you, I was shocked. You've been missing for three years, Marianne. Everyone in the state looked for you two. We all thought you died out there in the woods or something worse. Is this how you've lived all this time, on the street?"

Gwen nods in confirmation.

"Why? Why wouldn't you go home to the orphanage? Why be homeless and starving if you had a place to go?" Mr. Wentworth asks.

Gwen looks up at him. "First off, St. Paul's Orphanage burnt down. Secondly, that place was never my home. And I'd rather live in the gutter than with you people. We're not like you. We don't belong with your kind. Didn't the nuns tell you anything about me? About all the strange things I made happen when I was their prisoner?" Her voice is cold and stealthy.

"I read the report. You can't expect us to believe all that superstitious nonsense. Besides, you're not going back to the orphanage, Marianne," the female child services agent, Mrs. Shoemaker, informs her.

"That's not my name!" Gwen screams.

"We're putting you in a foster home as soon as possible. I think a small family environment would be a much more suitable arrangement for someone like you," the male child services officer announces.

"That is, of course, if you do well in a group home first," Officer Wentworth adds without skipping a beat.

"What's going to happen to Raven? Will he be with me?" Gwen asks, concern for her friend apparent on her pale face.

"No. He's going to a separate home. You two need to be free of each other's negative influences," his female partner replies.

Gwen laughs. "You people don't know anything. He never would have survived that place if it weren't for me. We belong together. We're the same!" she shouts at the two agents.

"Please, Marianne, try to be reasonable," Renee pleads. "We know you are fond of each other, but this is for your own good."

"My own good?" Gwen asks incredulously, turning a hateful glare on the Doctor beside her. "Was it for my own good that you infected me with that disease?" Gwen asks.

The doctor's face goes ashen.

"I almost died because of you and your curiosity!"

"I'm sorry, I thought I could help. I'll go now," Renee says to no one in particular, jumping out of her seat and dashing across the room for the door. She opens the door and walks out, but before she closes it behind her, she looks back at Gwen.

"I really am sorry, Marianne. I was only trying to help," she says.

"Next time you want to help someone, don't. Just do yourself and the rest of us a favor and keep your nose out of other people's business!" Gwen hisses venomously.

The hate and the anger in Gwen's eyes shock Renee to the core. Without another word, she closes the door and walks away, leaving Marianne behind her. She will never forget her, or the girl's words now forever burned upon her conscience.

Dear Lord, I hope I did the right thing, she thinks to herself as she exits the police station. She hurries down the stone steps to the curb to wait for a taxi. One will be along soon, and she'll finally be able to return to her sister's apartment. *Hopefully, I can make it up to Racheal by taking her to dinner tomorrow night,* the doctor tells herself as she climbs into her cab. The cab returns Renee to her own safe, snug existence, completely unaware of just how much she's ruined two children's lives.

Throughout history many so-called do-gooders, like Renee, with their good intentions, have brought such misery and woe to those who might have lived normal, contented lives had it not been for the intrusive meddling of others.

CHAPTER THIRTEEN

Living Without

"**I** am not crazy," Gwen explains in a flat tone to the grey-haired, horn-rimmed-glasses-wearing psychiatrist sitting patiently in the leather armchair across from her.

"No one is saying that. We're just trying to discover the root of this delusion you have that you're not human," Doctor Monroe replies as he scribbles a quick note in his ledger.

"I'm not. It's no delusion. It's a fact." Gwen sighs in exasperation, trying to keep her hands folded calmly in her lap and sit erect on the green plaid loveseat, ordained as the psychiatrist's couch.

Mrs. Shoemaker from child services brought Gwen from New York City to Scranton, Pennsylvania, a flourishing city with an old-world charm nestled at the foot of the Poconos Mountains. Her escort dropped her off here at the group home, handing her over to the care of Deanna Fairbanks, Social Worker.

After a quick interview with Miss Fairbanks, Gwen had been shown to a spare solitary room in the home to spend the night. This morning she was shown to the cafeteria and allowed to eat breakfast with the other children under the watchful eye of an attendant. Gwen did not enjoy her breakfast. The loud eating in public places reminds her of St. Paul's. She instantly lost her appetite. She received several curious and hostile glances from the other delinquent children, but thankfully, no one approached her.

After breakfast, the attendant, a tall bulky Samoan named Tuapo whom she prefers to think of as her prison guard, escorted her to Dr. Gregory Monroe's office for her psychiatric analysis. So far, the interview with the doctor is not going well. She has already lost her temper twice, raising her voice and shooting indignantly to her feet upon hearing the remarks the police officers back in New York wrote in their report about her. Both times the doctor threatens to have Tuapo, who waits just outside the door, come in and restrain her if she doesn't settle down and behave herself. Gwen forces herself to stay calm and behave like a good little girl, just to get through this ridiculous appointment.

"And when did you first start believing you were a Witch?"

Gwen tries not to sneer at him and his emphasis on the word 'believe.' *He's just a doctor, after all. People like him don't believe in the supernatural or the unexplained,* she reminds herself.

"I've pretty much always known that I was different, but I found out for sure I was Wiccan back in New York a couple years ago."

"I see. And what happened at that time to make you certain of this?" The doctor's condescending tone sends a jolt of lightning up

Gwen's spine, but she holds back the urge to smack his dorky glasses right off his face.

"Raven and I were attacked by a family of Witches."

"A whole family of Witches? Really?" He makes a priceless little expression as he looks down his nose at his notes and writes his thoughts. "Why do you assume they were Witches?"

"Oh, I don't know. Maybe it was the fact that they said they were, or the balls of fire they shot from their hands, or maybe the appearing out of thin air that did it," Gwen answers sarcastically.

"Don't talk to me that way, young lady," Dr. Monroe chastises, making yet another note in his book.

"Sorry," Gwen says flatly.

"If these people were in fact Witches and attacked you with fire balls—" The Doctor raises his eyebrows at this. "—then how did you and Adam escape?"

"You mean Raven," Gwen corrects.

"Adam Mathews is the young man who took you away from the orphanage. I have no record of a Raven."

"He didn't take me away. If anything, I took him with me. And we escaped from the Witches because Raven turned into a wolf and I hypnotized them," she confesses, aware of how ridiculous it sounds the second the words leave her lips.

"Oh…I see."

Again, there he goes with his stupid little pen. Gwen imagines ripping the book out of his hands and thumping him on the head with

it. She smiles inwardly.

"What's so funny, Marianne?"

"You are."

"Excuse me?" His voice and face become hard.

"This whole thing is hilarious. No matter what I say or do, you'll chalk it up to delusions and prescribe the latest drugs to cure me. I don't need your help. All I want is my friend back. We were just fine on our own."

"Just fine stealing food and pickpocketing? Were you doing 'just fine' living on the streets in gang-infested neighborhoods?" the doctor asks snidely.

"We did what we had to. You would, too, if you had to survive," Gwen answers stiffly.

"What about the orphanage? You had a place to live, people to care and provide for you, shelter, and an education. A home, really. You didn't need to survive on your own. You chose to run away and hide."

"I had to leave. I didn't have a choice. We couldn't stay there anymore."

"Why, because of your attack on the Mother Superior?"

"I defended myself!" Rage boils within her. Gwen digs her fingernails into the fabric of her jeans.

"Just like you did with the Witch family. With magic?"

"Yes. I didn't mean to hurt the nun, but the Witches were going to kill Raven, and I had to do something." Gwen's voice grows dark.

"And what about Sister Whitmore? Claiming to have visions of her deeds, pronouncing her a child molester?"

"Yes, visions that were proven true."

"Suppose you didn't have a vision at all." The doctor checks his file. "Suppose this boy Douglas told you a wild story and you made it up about the others to condemn someone you didn't like."

"And the others all lied, too, just for the fun of it?"

"She was the one responsible for disciplining the children at St. Paul's, was she not?"

"Sure," Gwen answers curtly, her nostrils flaring.

"If she wasn't popular with the children, then it wouldn't surprise me if the others simply went along with those same allegations for revenge."

"Yes, revenge for being molested," Gwen emphasizes the last word with venom and disgust.

The doctor gives her a cold look and then writes in his book again. Gwen fights the urge to steal his pen and fling it across the room.

"What about the visions of the fire, hmm? If you're so smart and I'm making all of this up, then how did I know about the fire?" Gwen asks back, mocking him by mimicking his tone of voice.

"I ask the questions, young lady," he tells her sternly, tapping his black pen on his notepad in agitation.

"Fine, then ask the question." Her voice is ice, her face stone.

Doctor Monroe takes a moment to regain his composure, reading over his notes and pretending Gwen hasn't spoken. "Paranoid episodes happen to someone in your situation. You become convinced that everyone is out to get you and begin to see things that aren't there to support these feelings so you can justify your actions."

"You're an idiot," Gwen announces with cool disdain. "I'm done talking to you. Write your stupid little notes in your stupid book and let me go already. I've got better things to do with my time than to sit here wasting it talking to you."

Doctor Monroe looks at her aghast for a moment and then, angrily clenching his jaw, the middle-aged doctor pulls out a prescription pad from his shirt pocket and scribbles away. He makes one final note, irritated, before he closes his book and rips the prescription from the pad.

"Tuapo!" the doctor calls. Gwen stands as her menacing Samoan attendant enters the room, looking Gwen over with suspicion before turning his attention to the good Doctor.

"Give this to Miss Fairbanks and make sure to have that prescription filled and administered to Miss January here immediately." Dr. Monroe hands the attendant his written diagnosis and the prescription slip. Standing, he regards Gwen coldly. "You have my permission to treat her as hostile. Get her out of my sight."

Tuapo gestures to Gwen and she crosses the room to follow him out the door.

"Oh, and Marianne?" Gwen stops and looks back at the Doctor. "You better get used to talking to me, because if you want to get out of this place or see your friend ever again, you'll need to get my approval. I suggest you lose the attitude and appeal to my good side."

The man and the young girl stare at each other a moment. Gwen smiles callously. "My name is Gwenevere." With that, she slams the door behind her.

* * * * *

The rest of the day goes by in a drug-induced blur. Gwen's prescriptions are administered at lunch with her meal, and they leave her disorientated. To her horror, they make it impossible for her to summon even the slightest hint of magic. In her current state, she can't even control her telepathy and catches disjointed thoughts and images from everyone around her. Her head is splitting in two by dinnertime and her stomach is turning summersaults.

In the midst of all this, a teenage boy touches Gwen on the shoulder to get her attention. Startled, Gwen reacts violently, shouting, "Don't you touch me! Nobody touches me!" into the den of noises in the cafeteria. Tuapo hurries to restrain her. He drags her kicking and screaming out of the room, creating a great first impression for the other kids on her first day.

After a few choice words from Miss Fairbanks, Gwen is escorted back to her room and locked up for the rest of the night. Sleep eludes her. Even as dazed and drugged as she is, she can't seem to find rest from her anxious mind. All her fears rise to the surface, forcing her to face things she's spent a long time suppressing. Her every mistake plays before her mind, her weakest and darkest moments relived as she struggles to find sleep in her lonely room. Her thoughts find their way to Raven, and her heart aches with a lifetime of pain and longing.

She doesn't want to relive their last moments together, their painful parting, but it's so fresh in her mind. Back at the police station, Gwen waited a long time for answers, handcuffed to a chair in the police chief's office, waited for adults to decide about her fate, waited to see Raven again. Several possible escape plans crossed her mind, but she dismissed them all. She couldn't leave Raven, and she had no idea where they held him. Even if she could have gleaned that sort of information from one of the police officers, how could she leave the station without resorting to magic or possibly hurting someone?

Finally, Mr. Wentworth and Mrs. Shoemaker came for her. In a cold, dry voice Wentworth told her what would happen next. She wasn't going back to Maine as she originally thought but to Pennsylvania to live for a probationary period in the group home. If she behaves, she will go to a foster home. Raven, he told her, will end up going somewhere else entirely. His violent attack on the police officers convinced everyone that he was dangerous. They placed him in a group home for troubled children. If he doesn't behave, they'll ship him off to juvie without a second thought.

All of Gwen's attempts to reason with Wentworth and Shoemaker came to naught. They turned a deaf ear to her. At their instruction, the chief of police unlocked her handcuffs.

"Come on, it's time to go. I'd like to get on the road. We've got a long drive ahead of us and it's getting late." Mrs. Shoemaker took

Gwen by the arm and led her toward the door.

"I'm not going anywhere without Raven," Gwen retorted, digging in her heels, and yanking her arm free of the woman's grasp. She and her partner shared a look of two people long used to tantrums and adolescent rebellion.

"You can say goodbye but then we have to go," Shoemaker conceded. Neither of them tried to take Gwen's arm again. Instead, they led her out of the office and into the main corridor of the station. Gwen followed close on their heels, her mind still grasping for any way out for her and Raven.

They walked down the hall turning several times before coming to the overnight holding cells in the back of the building. An officer sat behind a desk across from the cells watching the motley crew of prisoners. He nodded at the two agents and stood.

"We'd like a few moments with Adam Mathews, please?" Wentworth asked respectfully.

The police officer looks around the two agents at Gwen with a look of understanding. "Sure, he's been pretty quiet, almost hate to leave a nice kid like that in the cell with the others but Ericson and Moore insisted on it," the officer said as he led the way to one of the last cells and took out his keys. He opened the cell, standing back to let the child service officers in.

Gwen entered the small, cramped cell behind them. A handful of men dotted the cell, yet her eyes locked on Raven instantly. He sat on a bench in the corner handcuffed. His whole demeanor appeared crestfallen, but at the sight of Gwen, he lit up. His whole attitude changed and before anyone can stop them, the two friends bolt toward each other. They met in an embrace in the middle of the cell amongst the criminals, neither one of them the least bit afraid. At that moment, no one existed but them.

"Gwen, are you alright? I've been so worried. Where were you?"

"Are you okay? You don't belong in here. What did they do to you?"

They both laughed nervously as the spoke at the same time.

"I'm fine," Gwen answers. "They had me in the chief's office."

"I'm still a little shook up from the Taser but I'm okay," Raven replied. "They haven't been rough with me. They asked me a few questions, made me take a drug test, and threw me in here."

"What kind of questions?" Gwen asked, aware of the two child services officers hovering in her peripheral.

"They seem to think I kidnapped you or something." His face reddened at the admission.

"What? That's ridiculous!"

"There's been no official charge made. The police were just looking at every possibility," Mrs. Shoemaker assured Gwen.

"Arrangements are being made for Adam to have a police escort to the group home tomorrow. He'll have to stay here overnight but he faces no criminal charges," Mr. Wentworth added over Gwen's shoulder. Gwen sensed that the two agents were nervous and uncomfortable with the youths' physical contact. Gwen reluctantly took a step back, breaking the embrace.

"Tomorrow? But where will Gwen stay the night? You can't put her in a cell! I won't let you." Raven's voice rose in agitation. The two agents tensed.

"Hey, keep your voice down!" the police officer yelled from the cell door, crossing his arms over his chest, planting himself in front of the door like an immoveable sentinel in case Raven should try to make a dash.

"No one's putting Marianne in a cell," Mrs. Shoemaker soothed. "We're taking her with us now."

"What? I don't understand."

"They're separating us, Raven. They're going to drive me to Pennsylvania tonight." Raven was stunned by Gwen's words. "Apparently they think we're a dangerous influence on each other."

"Maybe they're right." Gwen gave him a hurt look as Raven stammered on. "I don't mean you, Gwen, I mean me. Maybe I am dangerous. Maybe you'd be safer without me. If I ever lost control and something happened to you because of me, I…I wouldn't be able to live with myself."

"That wouldn't happen. I wouldn't let it. I'm in control. As long as we're together, I can keep us both safe. Don't say—"

Raven grabbed Gwen's hand and took a few steps away from the agents, speaking in a hushed voice so they couldn't overhear. The agents reluctantly gave them their space.

"Look, Gwen, I've been sitting here thinking. You've got to stop trying to protect me. I've got to learn to control myself, and it might not be so bad if you tried to fit in, to try and have a normal life. So, what if we're different? Maybe we're better off not knowing why. Maybe we don't need to know where we're from. What if I'm the last of my kind, and your kind is evil like the family we met?"

"Raven, you can't give up on me now. We're not alone—I can feel it. You don't know what you're asking. I can't be normal! Neither of us will ever be normal. Things look bad now, I know, but just wait and I'll come up with a way to get us out of this, I promise."

Raven took her slender little face in his two large hands. "Please, Gwen, try taking care of yourself for a while. I can't have you risking your life for me anymore."

"But, Raven, I can't—"

"Okay, that's enough. It's time to go, Marianne." Mr. Wentworth walked over to them. Raven released her face, and Gwen gave the man a hostile glare.

"Just go, Gwen. Don't resist. Everything's going to be okay. We'll be together again. I promise." The resignation in his voice scared Gwen and her heart fell into a pit of helplessness. Numb, Gwen let Mr. Wentworth lead her by the arm back toward the holding cell door, his female counterpart taking up the rear. The police officer locked the door behind them.

"I love you, Gwen," Raven called through the bars of his cell as Gwen walked away, her head turned to watch him.

"I love you, too," she called back with a shaky voice. Her eyes teared up, but she blinked the tears away as Raven faded from her sight.

The tears come now in full force as she lays awake in her bed, not knowing how many miles separate her from her only friend. Not knowing when, if ever, she'll see him again. Unbearable anguish rolls over her in crashing waves as violent sobs rack her body. Not caring if anyone hears her, Gwen gives into it, releasing all her turmoil until at last, her body is exhausted. Her mind reaches absolute fatigue and sleep finally takes her into its dark embrace.

* * * * *

After being diagnosed by Doctor Monroe as troubled, delusional, and suffering from violent episodes, Gwen finds her life full of anti-anxiety medications and constant supervision. Mrs. Fairbanks has Gwen put in lockdown in the "troubled" ward. An attendant, Tuapo more often than not, stands guard to make sure Gwen takes her medication every morning. He is only permitted out with the other children if she is accompanied by another attendant.

Gwen realizes now that she has taken the orphanage for granted. Compared to this place, it was paradise. The drugs affect not only on her mood and her impulses, but also her ability to embrace the magic all around her. The ancient, pure tongue doesn't obey her when she tries to cast a spell. Even something simple that she's done thousands of times like turning the lights on and off or making an object levitate.

The medication impairs her, making her feel as though her brain is stuffed with cotton balls, muffling all natural feelings and instincts, leaving her empty. She can't concentrate in group therapy or in the classes the center offers. She can't even read a book without losing track of her place on every page, and she often finds herself reading the same sentence over and over again before finally giving up. On top of this, she is physically weak, as though her own body is lifeless, moving as slowly as a zombie in an old-fashioned horror film.

When let out for group therapy, or to interact in activities with the other children, Gwen often says something to offend someone and then finds herself being ganged up on by a group of the more violent children. Without magic, she's helpless, and her body is lethargic. One day Gwen takes quite a beating before a social worker intervenes.

All of this would be bearable if Raven were here to go through it with her. For the first time in her life, Gwen feels truly alone, and it hurts down deep in the pit of her heart. She cries herself to sleep every night, calling out Raven's name. Longing for his silent, reassuring presence. She misses his simple ways, his brooding manner, and even his unruly black curly hair. She misses watching him shave his beard every morning, and how it would always grow back by the next day just as thick, as if he had never shaved at all. She misses the way his golden eyes would glow whenever he was excited.

She spends many nights worrying about him, wondering where he is, and hoping he's better off than she. After several weeks, Gwen finally gets Deanna Fairbanks to admit that she knows how to contact Raven.

"Raven has done very well in therapy, Marianne," she informs Gwen. "In fact, he just left his group home and has been placed with a foster family somewhere in Delaware."

"Where in Delaware is he? Can I call him?"

"With good behavior and considerable improvement on your part, Marianne, I might let you write each other. I won't give you his address, but I can make sure it gets sent to him," the social worker replies. "But that's all I can promise. If you try to run off to find him, it won't bode well for either of you. I can promise you that."

Gwen clings to this one hope, this raft in a torrential river onto which she holds for dear life. She lives through each day hoping that soon she'll be able to communicate with Raven, and then they'll be that much closer to reuniting.

Gwen learns to pretend to swallow her medication and spit it out later, hiding it until she can flush it down the toilet during bathroom breaks. With her head clear again, she begins to participate in activities, behaving as respectfully and cordially as she knows how. She forces down every natural impulse to use magic, every survival instinct to keep a distance between her and the other children and even loses her aloof persona so she can better melt into the crowd.

Dumbing down her personality for others is against everything she believes in, yet if it will get her out of this prison and bring her closer to finding her friend again, she'll endure it. She forces herself to smile and be polite when all she wants is to break through a wall and make a run for it. If she tries to escape, she may never find Raven on her own. Gwen considers just forcing the information out of Miss Fairbank's mind but worries that, if she should escape, the authorities will just be waiting for her to contact Raven and capture her all over again. No, she needs to do this legitimately. She needs Doctor Monroe and Miss Fairbanks' help. She needs to appear to the entire world as reformed.

The children who've already taken to harassing her never resist the urge to gang up on her, only now Gwen is no longer helpless. She frightens each and every one of them away by cursing them when no one's around, predicting terrible calamities that happen later when Gwen's otherwise engaged and nowhere nearby. The bullies begin to fear her, calling her a Witch, going as far as to complain to the social workers. Since they have no physical proof and no one hears Gwen threatening them, they are dismissed. After all, the bizarre happenings they report are purely coincidental, and can't be caused by an ordinary eleven-year-old girl.

Doctor Monroe is pleased with Gwen's improvement and recommends that she be placed with a family immediately. A few weeks later Gwen finds herself packing her belongings so she can live with a foster family named the Kellers.

The New York police had searched the train yard and found her and Raven's home in the old passenger car, confiscating all their belongings. When it came time for the child services agents to take her to Pennsylvania, the police allowed her to retrieve her things, including her old red duffle bag. Gwen stuffs the last of her paperback books in amongst her clothing into the duffle and zips it up, barely able to close it over the bulge of all her possessions. She looks about her room and sighs with satisfaction. She has done the impossible: acted normal. Sure, the whole thing is a charade, but still, the right people believe she is repentant and rehabilitated. She is so impressed with her performance that she wonders if maybe she ought to be an actress.

She smiles to herself mockingly at the idea and leaves her bedroom. Outside, Tuapo waits, his arm crossed over his chest in a menacing stance. Gwen smiles radiantly up at him, and the demeanor melts away as his face breaks into a responding smile.

"Your chariot awaits you, my lady." He gives her a little bow. Gwen gives him a sideways smirk, rolling her eyes good-naturedly as they walk on down the hall.

"Thanks, Tuapo. Please don't start crying on me now."

"I'm not the crying type. Besides, you act all tough, but we both know you're going to miss me, Gwen." He speaks softly so that no one can hear them as they pass down the hall.

Gwen smiles to herself. Tuapo is the only one in this place she had convinced to call her by her real name. The big fella turned out to be a really nice guy, a big softy actually. He was perhaps her only friend in this joint. She doesn't admit it, but she will probably miss him after all.

Tuapo leads her to Miss Fairbank's office at the front of the building. Doctor Monroe waits inside with the social worker as Gwen enters. Tuapo waits outside the door. He has other duties but waits to walk Gwen out, nonetheless.

"Ah, there she is." Doctor Monroe gives her a polite little nod as Gwen takes a seat in the chair before Deanna Fairbank's desk. Deanna, in her late thirties, is a pleasant-looking, average-sized woman who always looks as though her clothes are just bought off the rack or fresh from the dry cleaners. Every strand of hair is in place in a tight bun atop her head, her makeup flawless. Everything about her is always crisp and clean.

"Well, here you are, Marianne. Are you ready for this opportunity? The Kellers is a very good family. You will behave yourself, won't you?" she asks in a forced, good-natured tone, sitting erect in her chair as stiff and formal as can be.

"Of course. I realize now that I've been self-destructive, and my only enemy is me. I'm learning to be positive and more outgoing." Gwen regurgitates this lie with a sweet little smile.

"That's great, Marianne," the social worker replies with an equally fake smile of her own.

"Remember, if you need to talk or feel you're lapsing into old habits, please don't hesitate to come by and make an appointment to see me," Doctor Monroe adds with a genuine and cheerful smile of his own.

"Thanks, I'll do that," Gwen replies, smiling back at him with all her charm.

Despite their first disastrous meeting, Gwen and her elaborate charade somehow completely won over the psychiatrist. It is with his glowing recommendation that Gwen is sitting here now about to gain her freedom.

Yes, maybe I should go into acting, Gwen thinks again as she shakes hands and says goodbye to the doctor and the social worker. She exits the office and heads toward the front door, red duffle bag in hand with Tuapo at her side.

Somewhere out there Raven is waiting, Gwen reminds herself. Looking forward to the challenge ahead of her. Gwen promises herself, now that she is free that at last, she can find a way back to him again.

Over the past several months, Gwen learned to live without a lot of things: her headstrong demeanor, her sarcastic biting wit, Raven, and even magic. Now she will return to the one thing she needs most of all: her freedom. It is the one thing she can't go on living without.

CHAPTER FOURTEEN

Victims of Denial

*G*wen stares down at her plate, mindlessly pushing the mashed potatoes, roast beef, and green peas around in interesting designs with her fork. She can feel four separate pairs of eyes on her, their curious stares causing her skin to prickle in a most uncomfortable fashion.

"Aren't you hungry, Mary?" asks Mrs. Judy Keller, a thin, frail, plain-faced brunette woman in her late thirties.

Gwen looks up at her foster mother. "No, I guess not," she replies, exasperated. "And please don't call me Mary, or Marianne for that matter."

"Don't you talk to her like that, girl!" Mr. Dennis Keller warns, his thick New England accent adding a belligerent quality to his chastisement.

Gwen looks at him blankly for a long moment, challenging him with her eyes. The two begin a staring contest, each willing the other to be the first to accept defeat, to look away. Finally, after several minutes in awkward silence, Mrs. Keller reaches out a hand to place it over her husband's. He notices this move and gives her an annoyed look, moving away from her unwanted touch. Judy Keller responds as though he has struck her, shrinking back, her face burning red. She avoids the children's eyes as she returns her attention to her plate. Mr. Keller goes back to eating his supper, shoveling a spoonful of peas into his tobacco-lined mouth.

The Kellers' two other foster children, Aaron, and Cara, sit on either side of Gwen. With deliberate malice, Aaron stomps on Gwen's foot abruptly, causing Gwen to fling her fork in the air in surprise, crying out in pain. Everyone looks at her, alarmed.

"What'd you do that for?" Mr. Keller asks, his expression suggesting that Gwen might be a bit unbalanced.

"Aaron stepped on my foot," Gwen replies, shooting a look of warning at her foster brother. He looks at Mr. Keller with an innocent expression on his face.

"Nonsense, he didn't touch you. Now shut up and eat your food!" Mr. Keller commands.

Gwen reluctantly does as she is told, making sure to casually elbow Aaron in the ribs in such a way as to seem purely accidental. Aaron grunts in pain at the contact but says nothing.

Gwen, having flung her fork somewhere, picks up her spoon and scoops up some mashed potatoes. As she eats, she returns to her own thoughts, pondering her bizarre foster family.

Aaron, the oldest foster child, is twelve. Unfortunately, Gwen has several of the same classes as him at the local middle school. He is an ugly redheaded boy with a large, broad nose and a constant glare on his freckle-littered face. From day one he's made it noticeably clear that Gwen is not welcome in their home. He's gone as far as to harass her at school, at home, and any time any adult isn't looking. Gwen hates everything about him.

On the other hand, there is Cara, the youngest, who is only seven. She is a shy, timid little mouse of a thing with deep-red hair flowing to the middle of her back and a sweet, pale, China-doll face. Cara has instantly become Gwen's shadow. As bothersome as that sometimes can be, Gwen has become fond of her. Every day when Gwen and Aaron come home from school in the afternoon, Cara will sit on Gwen's bed, waiting with her sketchbook or a storybook in her lap. Gwen has been helping Cara improve her reading skills while tutoring her in drawing on the side. Gwen found it hard to believe that Aaron was Cara's biological brother, two siblings couldn't be greater opposites.

As for Mr. and Mrs. Keller, it took only a day for Gwen to decide that they are not to be trusted. Mr. Keller is a two-faced, lying crook who is beloved by all the community as an honest guy. He acts one way in public, treating his wife and foster children with respect and kindness. In the privacy of his home, he is someone else entirely. He is abusive to his wife and short-tempered with the children, always proclaiming how useless they are. He is an alcoholic, and Gwen suspects that there might be some drug abuse as well, but she has no proof.

Both Aaron and Cara seem a bit frightened of their foster father.

Gwen has yet to see Mr. Keller strike both of them, yet she senses there is something else that makes them cower the way they do. Something in her gut tells her that Dennis Keller is capable of unspeakable violence and evil.

From the outset, Gwen hoped to find an ally in Mrs. Keller, believing that maybe she had a kind soul like Sister Mary Shaw back at the Orphanage. Clearly, though, she is mistaken. The second day after coming to live at the Keller's, Aaron stole the sketchbook out of her duffle bag and ripped half of the pages out. Gwen had been tempted to use her magic against the boy but soon thought better of it.

Instead, she went to Mrs. Keller for help, finding her at the kitchen sink, cleaning up after lunch. After listening to what Aaron had done, the thin woman replied anxiously, "Just leave it alone, Mary. You children mustn't fight. It will only upset Mr. Keller. He'll take a whip to you both." Without another word, Judy Keller went back to washing dishes like nothing had happened, her eyes distant as if trapped in her own little world.

After that, Gwen decided to take matters into her own hands. She went to Aaron's room and knocked on his door. When he opened it, Gwen punched him right in the nose without hesitation, sending him stumbling backward. Stepping over Aaron as he groaned in pain, his hand placed protectively over his injured bleeding nose, Gwen retrieved her sketchbook from his dresser. She gathered the pages he took from it and then turned and walked back out without speaking so much as a word.

Gwen was surprised that Mrs. Keller didn't come knocking on her door to chastise her or demand that she apologize to Aaron, but she didn't let it bother her. She spent the rest of the afternoon in her room, far away from Aaron.

That night, around six o'clock, Mrs. Keller had dinner made and the table set. Aaron and Cara sat at the table waiting for Mr. Keller's arrival. Judy asked Gwen to join them, but she declined, choosing to stay in her bedroom instead. She wasn't hungry, and besides, she didn't want to stay in the same room with that obnoxious Aaron, let alone having to sit next to him at the table.

Around a quarter after six, Mr. Keller walked in the front door. He was dressed in his work uniform; a mechanic jumpsuit covered with oil. He owned his own auto body shop, and preferred working with his hands in the shop alongside his employees instead of being stuck behind a desk filling out paperwork all day.

Gwen heard him in the kitchen, stomping around. Aaron spoke her name and then immediately Mrs. Keller's little voice chirped in trying to deny the whole incident from earlier. Apparently, Mr. Keller didn't pay any heed to his wife, for immediately his stomping footsteps came quickly up to Gwen's door. Only then, at the last moment, did Gwen realize that she had not locked her door. Furious,

Dennis Keller flung open the door and burst into her room.

Gwen was sitting on the bed reading *Jane Eyre*, the book still open in her lap. Staring her down with a dark look in his eyes that sent a shiver through her flesh, Dennis hovered over as he stood beside the bed. For what felt like an eternity, Gwen was at a loss for how to react. She sat perfectly still, waiting for him to speak.

Then, just as suddenly as she punched Aaron, he backhanded her across the side of her face. The impact flattened her to the bed. A brain-shattering headache exploding from the pain in her bones and flesh. She temporarily lost her comprehension of the world around her.

By the time the pain started to recede into a numb ache, Gwen found herself alone in the bedroom, her door wide open. Through the open doorway, she could see across the hall to the kitchen and dining room. The entire family sat at the table, eating dinner, ignoring her. She could see Aaron, though, shooting a self-satisfied smirk in her direction.

Gwen was so shocked by the incident that the very next day, after school, she took the bus over to the child services office to speak to her social worker, Deanna Fairbanks.

The child services office was adjacent to the foster care facility. It made Gwen's skin crawl to step foot into that building again, even though it had only been a couple of days since she was released. Remembering her time there, she found herself wondering if maybe taking so much abuse from Mr. Keller would be preferable to returning to this hellhole again. Yes, she found a way to make the best of her situation, but she had no desire to return here. *Maybe Deanna could simply find me another family. Maybe I can just move from the Keller's to some new place without having to spend another night here in the group home.*

Upon entering the child services office, the receptionist recognized Gwen immediately, a look of dread crossing her plump Hispanic face. Obviously, she had never been one of Gwen's biggest fans.

"I need to see Deanna Fairbanks, please?"

The receptionist sighed, brushing a tendril of her short wavy brown hair behind her ear. "Do you have an appointment?"

"No, but this is an emergency," Gwen insisted.

The receptionist rang Deanna's office on the phone. After a quick exchange, the receptionist hung up. "You may go in," the hefty receptionist conceded, waving Gwen on down the hall.

Gwen entered without knocking, finding the social worker sitting behind her desk.

"Mary, what brings you to my office?" she asked kindly, but Gwen could tell that the woman was already wary of her visit.

Gwen had long since learned that, at the group home, insisting that everyone call her by her actual name only got her disapproving looks and marked her for being difficult. Some of the children made fun of her by asking her where Arthur and Merlin were and how life was at Camelot. Gwen fought the urge to correct the social worker about her name.

"I'd like to be placed in a different foster home, please," Gwen requested, in an as calm and polite a manner as she could manage.

"May I ask why, Mary?"

"The Kellers are unfit foster parents. That's why," Gwen replies a bit tersely.

"On what grounds do you make this judgment?" Deanna Fairbanks asked in her usual superior, detached manner. It made Gwen want to scream and wring her neck.

"On the grounds that Mr. Keller hit me!"

"And why would he do that?"

"Because I hit Aaron, my foster brother. But he deserved it, and Mrs. Keller did nothing to help the situation at all. I think she's scared of Mr. Keller or something. She goes out of her way to avoid upsetting him, like she's afraid he'll react violently if she does."

Deanna listened patiently to Gwen's recounting of the events of the night before, but by the look on her face, Gwen could tell she was not convinced.

"Mary, I see you're back to your old ways again. Making wild claims and using violence against others to get your way. This is precisely the kind of behavior that will lead to your ruin someday. I hoped you were past all that, but perhaps I released you too soon. I can't put you with another family, Mary. You'll only find some way to cause mischief there as well. Instead, I could bring you back to the center for a while until you—"

"No! I'm being serious! He slapped me! Is that the kind of thing you allow now in foster homes? I mean, are there so few people actually willing to be foster parents that you'd let just about anyone take kids into their home?"

"Mary, calm down," Deanna warned.

"No, I won't! Why don't you believe me?"

"The Kellers are very well-respected in the community. They can't have kids of their own and they can't afford to adopt, so they became part of the foster care program. Mr. Keller has no prior history of violence, child abuse, or sexual harassment. In fact, he has no criminal record at all. His wife is active in many local charities and runs food drives for the homeless and fundraisers for the needy. She's an angel and her husband a real gentleman. I've known Dennis and Judy since grade school. They're good people. And neither of them has a history of delusional, violent outbursts, or paranoid behavior. Unlike you, Mary. You have a record of violent behavior. You have frequently gone as far to claim you have special powers and that you aren't actually human. You are a chronic liar and a kleptomaniac. I'm sorry, but due to your past behavior, I am prone to disbelieving this fantastic tale!"

"What? So, I'm just supposed to let him beat me, then? What about the other kids? What about Cara? She's only seven. Are you going to let him get away with abusing her?" Gwen knew that she was raising her voice, but she couldn't help it. She was outraged and insulted that the woman dared call her delusional. Granted, she had stolen from time to time, but only to survive and it was something she never enjoyed doing. She didn't like her own behavior thrown back in her face as some commonplace cry for attention.

"Have you actually seen Mr. Keller hit either Aaron or Cara?" the social worker asked, keeping a professional air and tolerant yet condescending tone to her voice.

"Not yet, but I have no doubt he's done it before," Gwen replied.

"You've only been in their home for a couple of days. How can you make this kind of assumption?" Deanna paused for a moment to take a deep breath. "Really, Mary, I expected more from you. I'm only going to ask you this once. Are you prepared to go on record that he assaulted you? Because if you do and no one else in the Keller family supports your claim, I'll have no choice but to bring you back to the center for treatment."

"And if the others confirm that he struck me?" Gwen asked, although she already knew the response Deanna would give her.

"They won't, Mary, because nothing happened. Both Aaron and Cara have been interviewed on several occasions about their living conditions and neither of them have ever hinted at anything remotely similar to what you're describing."

Gwen clenched her jaw shut, holding back the urge to call Mrs. Fairbanks a few choice words and dirty names. Gwen grasps the arms of her chair, holding tight to the wood until her knuckles turn white from the strain. Gwen could tell she needed physical proof before she would ever get through to Mrs. Fairbanks and knew she would have to step down. Still, it took her a bit to suppress the tumult of emotions raging within her. Eventually, she found the determination to calm her nerves. Only then did she look up at Deanna Fairbanks who sat before her with a concerned look upon her face.

"Are you all right, Marianne?" Deanna asked.

"I'm fine. I can see now that coming to you for help was a mistake. I was under the impression that your job is to help children in need. Silly me." With that, Gwen relaxed her grip on the chair. Without another word or so much as a backward glance, she left the room. Deanna Fairbanks was stunned to silence but did not call after her.

* * * * *

In the months that follow, Gwen has more than Mr. Keller to occupy her time. She also learns how to survive middle school. Since her only prior education had been at Saint Paul's, she finds herself completely unprepared for the harsh reality of public school.

First, she is placed in special classes for children with learning disabilities, because she is so behind in her studies. She tries to explain to the guidance counselors that she had been learning at a seventh-grade level, but the school is inclined to think that the nuns at St. Paul's did not have nearly as rigorous a program as their own. By the end of the first week, however, her teacher requests that Gwen be given the chance to test at a Seventh-grade level. The request is granted, and Gwen passes with flying colors, proving that she is indeed more than capable of attending classes with children a year older than herself.

Gwen hopes things will get easier, but ever since she was bumped up to the seventh grade, the sixth graders resent her, and the seventh graders make fun of her. She is not only the smartest kid in her grade, but she is also taking a few classes at an eighth-grade level, which only adds insult to injury. She is considered the prettiest girl in school, outranking even the physically mature thirteen-year-olds despite Gwen's lack of feminine curves. This, of course, makes her very popular with all the boys and hated outright by just about every girl in the school.

The boys are only nice to her as long as she doesn't show them up in class with her superior intellect or say anything too smart at lunch. A constant entourage of boys hover around her at lunch and in between classes. One of them offering to carry her books or walk her to her next class. Sometimes this results in quarrels between the boys because someone else wanted the privilege. All this attention makes Gwen uncomfortable and anxious. She tries to discourage them from following her, insisting she can carry her own things, but this doesn't seem to matter. The boys continue to hang about like a swarm of flies.

It appears to the female students that Gwen enjoys all the attention. They believe she is just playing her part, only pretending to be modest and shy, and that all her actions are carefully orchestrated to attract the opposite sex. Nothing could be further from the truth. Gwen hasn't the faintest idea how to be alluring or flirtatious. She has never really thought about boys that way or ever really noticed them before now. Still, her popularity earns her dirty looks from her female classmates, who shout insults at her in the halls.

Whenever she enters the girl's bathroom and someone is already in there, everyone immediately stops talking and stares at her. On one occasion, while she was in a stall, someone reached over and swiped her book bag from the hook on the door. When she came out, the restroom was empty. She finds her bag in a sink full of water. Her books are ruined, her homework destroyed. After that, she waits to enter the restroom only when she knows no one else is around. Unfortunately, a particular group of eighth graders have been watching her. They wait until she is already in the stall before they enter. One of them goes into the stall next to Gwen's and, standing on the toilet seat, looks over the top of the stall at Gwen. Other times, they throw things at her or spit on her. Once, they even reach under the stall and stole all the toilet paper. After that, she stops using the restrooms at school entirely.

On top of all this, Gwen also has to deal with Aaron Keller and all of his friends. They are the only boys in the school who aren't her ardent admirers. Aaron hates that she is the same age but has advanced to the grade above him. He hates that everyone knows her name. Even the popular kids know who she is while he remains invisible. He is considered a loser— one of those awkward, over eager, obsessive fanboy, role-playing types who never gets invited to parties, or gets any attention from any of the girls. His little group of friends are all just as unappealing as him. They are the dirty kids, already suffering from acne, with poor hygiene and even poorer social skills. Aaron grew up in the area and had been in the same elementary as most of the popular crowd, yet still they never remember his name or acknowledge his existence.

In Aaron's eyes, for Gwen to come in halfway through the school year and find instant popularity without even trying is the greatest injustice of all. Whenever her crowds of male admirers aren't fussing about her, Aaron and his nerd posse call her names, throw trash at her, and generally grate on her nerves.

One day, the entire posse blocked the door to Gwen's math class, refusing to move or let her enter. Gwen was about to make them move with physical or magical force when a boy named Kyle approached. He was a big, tall eighth grader who plays on the school basketball team. He took Gwen by the hand and pushed his way past the puny, little sixth graders, making sure to knock Aaron out of his path.

Later, Kyle asked, "What was all that about?" and Gwen filled him in, telling him all about her foster brother Aaron and his friends. After that, Kyle personally escorts Gwen to all of her classes. Soon after, Kyle's little sister, Kayla, started going out of her way to befriend Gwen, too.

Gwen is grateful for their friendship but constantly reminds them that she is fully capable of taking care of herself. She doesn't need Kyle's protection. However, Kyle would only smile and nod in agreement yet still remain at her side at all times. Kayla turns out to be a really sweet girl, shy and timid, but exceedingly kind and easy to talk to. In Kayla, Gwen finds her very first girlfriend.

Kyle and Kayla Hamilton live just a couple blocks away from the Kellers. Gwen starts getting off at their bus stop to avoid hanging around Aaron as much as possible. She spends most of her afternoons at the Hamilton house doing homework with Kyle or listening to rock music with Kayla, who shares Gwen's love of music and books. Kyle and Kayla show Gwen about town, taking her to all the popular spots. Their family loves to hike in the mountains and goes camping on a regular basis when the weather isn't too cold. Kayla the bookworm takes Gwen to all the local museums, libraries, and historical sites in Scranton.

The city is rich in history and has an old-time charm that really appeals to Gwen. She enjoys the atmosphere and the architecture. In the libraries, she finds a slew of new books on Wicca and the occult. Kayla always gives her strange looks when she sees the titles of the books Gwen checks out but never says anything about it. She tells Kayla that she enjoys reading fantasy novels because of the wizards and all things magical in them. Later, Kayla suggests to her family that they should take Gwen with them to the Houdini Museum.

* * * * *

In a hundred-year-old building just off of Main Street in Scranton, the Houdini Museum holds a collection of historical items once used by the renowned magician and illusionist, including rare film reels of

Houdini's marvelous escapes. The tour of the museum also doubles as a magic show by a professional illusionist.

All the antiques fascinate Gwen as well as the old films, but mostly she is impressed by the magic show itself. The Hamilton family enjoys the entertainment like the rest of the audience. Meanwhile, Gwen watches every move the illusionist makes. Picking apart every trick she's able to tell how they work.

These ordinary people who, through simple tricks and the art of misdirection, were capable of appearing to make magic. It fascinated her. Suddenly, she had an epiphany: if these mere humans could make *others* believe they were gifted in the supernatural, then why couldn't Gwen do the same thing? The only difference is that she is authentic; and she didn't need smoke and mirrors to achieve the same effect as these performers. However, she would need to appear as if she were using magic tricks to levitate and use hypnosis. She would have to find a way to disguise the truth, find a way to use the pure tongue without giving herself away in case another Wiccan should happen to see.

Gwen leaves the Houdini Museum with a new purpose in life. She now has a way to provide for herself; to make an honest living without having to steal or use her gifts to manipulate others. She will dedicate herself to learning the art of magic, to become a professional illusionist. This way, she can hide in plain view. She wouldn't have to endure being called a freak, a liar, or delusional. She could even call herself a Witch and no one would bat an eyelash. It's perfect.

When Gwen comes home that evening, she is in an

uncharacteristically good mood. Everyone notices, even Mr. Keller.

"Why are you so happy?" Mr. Keller asks in his usual gruff manner.

"I'm going to be a magician!" Gwen announces without hesitation, her face beaming.

Both Mr. Keller and Aaron make jibes at her, saying she's too old for such childish things. Ignoring them, she goes to her room to get ready for bed. A few minutes later, just as she finishes putting on her nightclothes, someone knocks at her door.

"Come in."

The door opens and little Cara's red head pokes into the room.

"Can I sleep with you tonight?" Cara asks in her usual little voice.

"All right, but that's the third time this week. You're getting too old to be afraid of the dark," Gwen replies teasingly.

Cara hurries inside closing the door behind her. She's dressed in a pair of pink thermal pajamas with white and pink polka-dotted slippers. Cara jumps onto Gwen's bed with a giggle.

"It's not the dark I'm afraid of. It's being alone," Cara replies before letting herself fall backward onto the twin-size bed.

Gwen digs into the top drawer of her nightstand, retrieving her sketchbook and art case which Douglas gave her so long ago. She sits next to Cara on the bed. The younger girl instantly cuddles up to Gwen, resting her little auburn head on Gwen's shoulder. Gwen opens the sketchbook, and taking a pen from the case, she begins sketching an image of a magician standing on stage and a personage hovering before them.

"Why are you so scared? What do you think will happen if you're alone?" Gwen asks Cara casually, as she draws.

Cara is silent a long time before answering. Then in a voice so soft Gwen can barely hear her speak, Cara says, "He'll come to my room."

Gwen pauses, her hand caught in the air, mid stroke. Has she heard her little friend, right? "Who, Cara? Who comes to your room?" Gwen asks in a whispers, hoping the little girl will trust her enough to confide in her.

"Dennis." Suddenly, Cara scoots away, lying down on the bed with her back to Gwen. This signals that the conversation is over.

It takes Gwen a moment to recall that her foster father's first name is Dennis. As soon as that realization hits her, a cold sensation spreads through her body, accompanied by a sense of dread. She sits there in silence, pondering the implications of Cara's words. Only when Cara begins to snore does Gwen come out of her contemplation.

She gets up, puts her sketchbook and drawing case away, and turns off the light on her way to bed. Careful not to wake the sleeping Cara, Gwen slips under the covers. She lies down and tries to close her eyes and go to sleep. After several minutes, Gwen feels sleep beckon to her. Her eyes become heavy, and her body relaxes.

Footsteps creak down the hallway toward her room. Suddenly, Gwen is wide awake. Instinctively she utters a word in her own tongue willing the lock on her bedroom door to turn, but it won't budge. In a flash, Gwen is out of bed and at the door. Quickly, she locks her bedroom door from inside, feeling relief wash over her as soon as it's done. A moment later, the footsteps stop outside. Underneath the doorway, Gwen sees the kitchen light show though, until the shadow of feet blocks it out. She stands there, motionless, waiting.

The door handle jiggles twice. Suddenly the door shakes as the presence outside tries to force its way in. After a few minutes, it stops. Gwen dares not make a sound or move a muscle. It seems like an eternity before the shadow finally moves on, passing her doorway and continuing on down the hall to Mr. and Mrs. Keller's bedroom.

Gwen has never been more afraid in her life, which she realizes is strange, considering the things through which she has already lived. That doesn't make it any less true. There is something unpredictable about Mr. Keller; his mind is always muffled from the alcohol and his mood and temper are both erratic. He frightens Gwen because she can't read him, and the way the others respond to him obviously doesn't improve things.

Gwen knows there are still many great evils in the world that she doesn't yet understand, and Mr. Keller represents one of those evils, of which she has no doubt. *What did he do when he went to Cara's room at night? And why had he tried to force his way into my own room just now?* Gwen ponders this as she walks slowly in the dark back to the bed and climbs in next to the still-sleeping Cara.

She knows it hadn't been Aaron at her door, for his room is on the other end of the hall, closer to the living room, and Cara's room is the one next to hers. The fourth bedroom is the master bedroom at the far end of the hall. It had to be Mr. Keller.

* * * * *

Gwen has been living in the Keller household for three months now, and though she makes it a point to stay away from Aaron and avoid any confrontation, she still manages to anger her foster father no matter how hard she tries otherwise. It seems that everyone offends him at one point or another, incurring his wrath for the smallest of trespasses.

His wife upsets him daily because of her poor cooking, which Gwen thinks is just fine but knows better than to disagree with him. Aaron irritates him by trying too hard to please him, or by playing video games for too long, or by not being more athletic or popular in school. Everything Aaron does disappoints Dennis Keller. Cara makes the mistake of crossing his path and not getting out of his way fast enough. He yells at her for talking too softly or for mumbling her words.

What seems to bother Mr. Keller most about Gwen are her eyes. He constantly accuses her of staring at him or following him around with her creepy eyes, as he calls them. He says she reminds him of a black cat, high and mighty and cursed with bad luck. He calls her names, claiming that Kyle Hamilton is her boyfriend and that no one would spend time with a girl like her unless she was giving him sexual favors.

This she knows is partially Aaron's doing, He constantly complains to Mr. Keller that he is getting a bad rap at school because everyone knows that his foster sister is a troublemaker. He makes these outrageous claims at the dinner table in front of the family just to provoke her, but Gwen refuses to be manipulated by such an ugly boy, instead she sits still, boring a hole into his face with her haunting yellow-green eyes. Most the time Aaron will shrink back when she looks at him this way. When he remembers he doesn't want his foster father to call him a wimp, he pretends to not be afraid of her.

Once in a while Dennis Keller's foul mood will result in more than just raising his voice or name-calling. He often doles out punishment in overtly physical manners, whipping Cara with his belt for spilling a whole carton of milk on the kitchen floor or slapping Aaron around repeatedly for talking back to him. Gwen will watch as he sometimes chases his frightened wife into their bedroom, after which a tumult of sounds will follow, like broken glass, or heavy objects being flung about, accompanied by Judy Keller's screams and his cursing and shouting.

Always Mr. Keller will emerge from the room and march out of the house and won't return again until later that evening, if at all. Hours later, when Mrs. Keller finally comes out of her room, she is always jumpy and quiet. She will have few visible cuts or bruises and will walk with a limp and have trouble using one of her arms.

During these incidents of marital strife, Gwen will often take Cara for a walk down to the corner convenient store or out to see a movie, just to keep Cara from crying. She will even invite Aaron to come along, just to be nice, but he never joins them.

Gwen tries her best not to suffer the same fate as the rest of her foster family, but it seems that no matter how much she tries to stay out of the way or hold her tongue, Dennis Keller still finds fault with her. Luckily for Gwen, she spends most of her time at the Hamilton's and the little time she spends at home she locks herself away in her bedroom, practicing magic or reading a novel. Yet whenever he sees her, at family dinners or just around the house, she somehow offends him and he will shove her, hit her upside the head, or slap her.

It takes everything in her power not to react to these undeserved punishments. She reminds herself that no one will believe her anyway, that speaking up will only upset Dennis Keller further. And the social worker, Mrs. Fairbanks, will only believe she is paranoid. She needs Deanna to believe she is on her best behavior because Deanna is her last known connection to Raven.

More than that, she knows it's a hopeless cause, because every time a member of the Keller household is abused, Gwen will look at Mrs. Keller, Aaron, or Cara as if saying, "Well? Am I the only one who's seeing this?" And every time, they will look away without answering and then leave the room.

Finally, Gwen decides that she's had enough. Mrs. Keller is crying as she hunches over the kitchen sink, cleaning the remaining dishes from supper. Most of the dinnerware lies broken and shattered on the floor at her feet, the aftermath of her husband's latest outburst, when Gwen approaches her.

Uncertain how to start, Gwen gets a broom and sweeps up the broken pieces of ceramic, dumping them into the tall kitchen trashcan. Judy doesn't look at her once, but her sobs quiet to sniffles. With the floor all clean Gwen takes a dry towel and begins drying the clean dishes. They stand side by side in silence for several minutes before Gwen finds the courage to speak.

"Why don't you say something? Just tell someone. If you let people know what's going on, they can stop him. It will all go away," Gwen encourages in a low whisper.

Judy Keller seems shocked by Gwen's words. Quickly she looks over her shoulder to make sure they are alone. "I don't know what you're talking about, Marianne. After all Mr. Keller does for us, you should be more grateful," she retorts. In a huff, she turns and storms off, ending the conversation.

Gwen watches her in disbelief. *What's wrong with these people?* They all cower before him, like slaves before their angry master. Gwen refuses to be a victim, refuses to be afraid of anyone. She moves over to the other side of the sink and finishes cleaning the dishes.

After all the dishes are clean, Gwen starts drying them off and putting them away in the cupboard, silently plotting in her head. She has suffered enough. Mr. Keller has pushed her around and shunned her more than most children could bear, and still she hasn't caved. It would take more than a bully like Dennis Keller to break Gwen's spirit.

Just then, Cara walks through the front door, returning from a neighbor's house after her play date with Stephanie Cooper. Cara runs to Gwen and gives her a hug, her head coming just below Gwen's shoulder.

"Where's Judy?" Cara asks.

"She wasn't feeling well so she went to lie down," Gwen lies. "Hey, I got a book from the library I think you'll like. You want to go read it?"

Cara follows Gwen across the hall into her bedroom. She hops excitedly up onto the bed while Gwen retrieves the book from her backpack. She hands Cara a large, illustrated children's book. On the cover is a fire-breathing dragon and a stone castle in bright colors.

"Wow!" Cara exclaims as she makes room for Gwen to sit on the bed. "Will you read it to me, Gwen?"

"Why don't you read it to me?"

"You're better at doing all the character's voices," Cara protests.

"Practice makes perfect," Gwen answers.

"Okay," Cara concedes, opening the book. She starts to read.

Just then the front door slams shut. Gwen looks up to see Dennis and Aaron in the kitchen. Quickly, she crosses the room and closes her door, locking it from the inside.

Cara waits for her to sit back down before she continues reading the story. Gwen half-listens to Cara's voice, distracted by her own thoughts.

Mentally she takes note of every cross word, every beating, making a tally of wrongs that someday she'll make right. One day when she's finally reunited with Raven, she will set her trap. Someday when they've all forgotten about her, that's when she will strike. Sometime or another Dennis Keller will find himself walking down a dark alley and will never be heard from again.

Until then Gwen bides her time and waits, hoping for better times. If she plays by the rules and acts the part of the good girl then she'll be out of this place and back with Raven, where she belongs. She'll live her life day by day with as much dignity as she can muster whilst living amongst cowards in a home full of victims of denial.

CHAPTER FIFTEEN

Fleeing From Reality

To her surprise, the Keller's house is entirely empty when Gwen gets home from the Hamilton's house. Usually, Gwen isn't home from her study sessions with Kyle and Kayla Hamilton until eight o'clock on Tuesdays and Thursdays. However, today Kayla had begun to feel sickly, and Mrs. Hamilton, had cut their study session short to put her daughter to bed. Kyle and his father had dropped Gwen off at the Keller's just after seven o'clock. Tonight, Mrs. Keller was at a fundraiser and wouldn't be back until eight or later. Gwen had expected to find Mr. Keller and Aaron lounging about the family room watching some sporting event on TV. Cara would most likely be reading in her room or drawing at the kitchen table. Yet, after doing a quick sweep of the house, she doesn't find any of the Kellers present. Dennis's car is in the driveway so they should be around somewhere.

Maybe they're in the backyard? A quick peek out the back

window into the yard proves that this is not the case. *Maybe they're visiting the Coopers? Cara is best friends with the Cooper's youngest daughter, after all,* she reminds herself. *However, it seems unlikely that they would all be at the neighbor's house.* Dennis doesn't like the Coopers much as they are staunch Christians who never drink alcohol, and Aaron thinks they're boring because they are against video games as well.

But Mrs. Cooper tells her that she hasn't seen Cara or the Keller men at all today. Gwen goes back to the house to see if someone left her a note, but alas, she finds nothing. Gwen grows concerned. It is eight o'clock on a weeknight and it's getting dark out. *There's probably a totally normal explanation for their absence*, Gwen tells herself. *You're just being paranoid.* But somehow she can't shake the feeling that something is terribly wrong. Gwen decides to walk around the block. *Maybe they've gone for a walk?* This seems rather doubtful, but still worth a shot. When her survey of the neighborhood leaves her still without answers, Gwen takes one more stroll around the outside of the house, just to be sure. She is just about to go back inside to wait for everyone to return when she hears a noise coming from the shed behind the house.

Cara knows better than to play in the shed, doesn't she? Gwen asks herself, walking around the side of the house toward the red and white barn-style shed—Dennis Keller's personal retreat and workshop. None of the family is allowed in that shed except for him. He has often warned Gwen never to go in there. More out of fear of incurring his wrath than out of respect, Gwen has listened and kept her distance from her foster father's personal oasis. That is, until now. She reaches out with her mental feelers and senses that Dennis and the kids are inside. *Why didn't I think to do that before I got myself all worked up?* She self-chastises. Gwen realizes that she should feel relieved but instead she feels an overwhelming sense of dread. The rational thing would be to just walk up and knock on the shed door. Something in her gut councils against this action.

Quietly, she creeps up to the side of the shed to peek through the dirty glass window. There are several cans of paint stacked on a shelf just below the window, blocking Gwen's view of the room within.

"*Gainien Raisa,*" she whispers under her breath. She becomes weightless as her feet float off of the ground. Her body rises upward, suspended in midair. Now, from her elevated vantage point, she can see over all obstructions inside.

She can see three workbenches; one lined up against each of the outer walls. Tools and auto parts strewn about on their surfaces except one. A kind of video recording and editing station is set on the desk on the farthest wall. Sitting in a swivel-back-office chair is Dennis himself. Before him, a digital video camera is set up on a tripod. Thirty-something Dennis watches the flip down screen before him, enthralled with the images before him. She sees Mr. Keller first and his behavior makes her look around the room, curious what Aaron and Cara were doing, and why he would be recording it.

Then she sees them. Gwen gasps, putting a hand over mouth to stifle the noise, afraid the three occupants of the shed might be alerted to her presence. At first, Gwen doesn't believe what she is seeing. After several minutes, the shock wears off and a sense of revulsion and anger creeps up her spine into her skull. She knows there are a lot of things about life that she still is too young to understand. She knows without a doubt, that what is happening now is the very reason Mr. Keller wanted her to stay away from the shed.

Aaron stands in the middle of the room looking uncomfortable. His pale face is blank, as if he is trying to keep his mind off of what is happening to him. Kneeling directly before him is Cara, crying and shaking, wearing only her underwear.

"Go on, Cara. Don't make me ask again," Mr. Keller commands in a dark voice, promising violence if she disobeys.

Cara turns to look at her foster father, a pleading look in her eyes. Through her whimpers, she shakes her head "no." A dark look crosses Dennis's face as he gets to his feet. Pouncing, he crosses the five feet between him and the little girl.

Terrified for her friend, Gwen accidently releases her hold on the spell and falls abruptly to the ground below. She hits the dirt with a jarring thud but wastes no time recovering from the impact and jumps to her feet. Inside she hears Cara screaming and crying while Dennis Keller curses and shouts at her. Panicked, Gwen races to the door. Reaching out, she takes hold of the door handle and tries pulling the door open. It's locked and won't budge. With a guttural growl, Gwen yanks on the handle with all of her superhuman might. The door squeaks and groans as the wood breaks off of its hinges. She rips the door clean off and throws it aside.

Without thinking, she enters the shed. She finds its three occupants frozen in place, staring at her in shock and amazement. Dennis Keller has the frightened half-dressed seven-year-old Cara by the neck. Welts and cuts on her shoulders, his other hand still in mid-air, raised for another blow.

Filled with a murderous rage, Gwen flies at the six-foot tall grown man. Shouting in the pure tongue, the eleven-year-old Witch charges into Cara's attacker, hitting him square in the chest. He releases the child in his grasp instantly. The force of the impact sends Dennis flying. He crashes into his video editing station, with a cacophony metal and wood screeching, cracking, and breaking. Dennis hits the ground, out cold. Her head spinning, Gwen takes a moment to catch her breath. She looks up to see Aaron and Cara's pale faces staring at her.

"What are you waiting for? Go! Run! Get out!" Gwen shouts, startling the two children out of their stupor. Aaron looks both embarrassed and relieved, but he avoids looking at Gwen as he fumbles to pull up his pants, zipping up his zipper as he hurries out of the shed and into the night.

Turning to look at Cara, the little girl throws herself into Gwen's arms, almost knocking her off of her feet. Sobbing, Cara buries her face in Gwen's chest, hugging her tightly. Taken aback, Gwen stands there a moment, then, awkwardly, begins stroking her friend's auburn hair in a soothing gesture.

"Where are your clothes?" Gwen asks in a hushed whisper, trying not to further upset the little girl.

Sniffing back the tears, Cara looks up at Gwen, a bit confused until realization dawns on her. Looking around the room, Cara locates her clothes in a heap upon a table on the far wall. They are amongst the tools and motor oil. Cara points to them.

Separating herself from Cara, Gwen crosses the room cautiously, giving the unconscious Dennis a wide berth as she retrieves Cara's clothing. Quickly, she returns to the little girl, handing her the apparel. Cara takes them and begins to dress herself.

Gwen turns away, choosing to keep a watchful eye on her foster father sprawled on the floor. From the front of the house Gwen hears high heeled footsteps click up the cement stairs, and the front door opens and shuts.

"Hello? Where is everyone? Dennis? Kids?" Judy Keller's muffled voice calls out from within the residence.

Suddenly, Mr. Keller begins to stir. Gwen turns and makes for the door, grabbing Cara by the hand and leading her out behind her. Stopping in the doorway, Gwen pauses, and looking back, sees Dennis sit up with a groan. He holds his head in his hands, fighting back the dizziness. Gwen looks between him and the video camera on the tripod and decides to risk it.

"Run! Get Aaron and Mrs. Keller and go to the Coopers' house now!" Gwen orders, pushing Cara out the door.

Gwen wastes no time to see if Cara has obeyed her. She turns on her heels and makes a sprint toward the video camera. Out of the corner of her eye, she sees Mr. Keller on his feet, lunging toward her. Grabbing hold of the camera, she yanks it off of the tripod with all her might. A second later, she turns and makes a dash for the door, fully aware that Dennis is just behind her.

He grabs hold of her coat and yanks her backward. Gwen reaches out her free hand for the doorframe. Grabbing hold, she pulls against Dennis's grip to free herself. Suddenly, he steps forward and catches her up in his arms, pulling her away from the door. He squeezes the breath out of her lungs, holding tight as she struggles to get free.

Barely able to utter the words, Gwen casts a spell.

Objects all around the room begin to float into the air, then project themselves at Dennis Keller's head and body. An alarmed, yet determined, Dennis holds tight to Gwen as he attempts to dodge the objects hurtling themselves at him. A chainsaw breaks itself free off its hook on the wall and magically powers up the engine, roaring to life. To Dennis's horror, it flies toward his head. He releases Gwen and dives to the floor, barely making it out of the deadly tool's way. Missing its target, the chainsaw embeds itself into the wall next to the gaping hole where the door had once been.

Gasping for air, Gwen forces herself to her feet. Just before she leaves, she reaches out her hand toward the light bulb in the fixture in the ceiling and simultaneously she makes a fist with her hand and crushes the glass bulb with her mind, chards of glass fall to the floor casting the shed in utter darkness.

Gwen stumbles out of the shed and into the black night. Although she is relieved to hear Mrs. Keller and the children fleeing the house, she is still terrified of being alone with Dennis. It is a dark night outside, and without a light from the house, the backyard is pitch black and almost eerie to Gwen. Dennis Keller will be fast on her heels. Forcing her legs to keep moving, she stumbles and trips over her own feet in the dark. She finds the side of the house and uses it as a guide. Moving as quickly and silently as she can, she manages to make her way along the side of the house toward the front. The light of the lamp post down the street gives off a dim glow, allowing Gwen to make out the silhouette of Dennis Keller's car in the driveway.

The sound of rock crunching under foot alerts Gwen to Dennis's presence not far behind her. Stepping away from the safety of the house, Gwen runs across the front lawn toward the driveway. She reaches the car and with the video camera tucked under one arm, pulls at the door handle with her free hand. The car is locked.

Looking over her shoulder Gwen sees Dennis running toward her, his face half-cast in shadows from the streetlight. Gwen tugs at the handle frantically as she mentally goes through the list of magical words she knows, trying to produce an unlocking spell. With Dennis closing in on her, suddenly she chants...

"*Sha iter!*"

The driver side window bursts, the sound of shattering glass echoing loud in the silence of the still neighborhood.

Gwen reaches in through the broken window and unlocks the door from inside. Quickly, she yanks the driver side door open and throws herself inside, managing to shut the door behind her seconds before Dennis Keller comes upon her.

The look of malice upon his face frightens Gwen. She heaves herself into the passenger seat in an attempt to put distance between herself and his deadly grip. The camera falls onto the floor under the passenger seat beneath her.

"Give me the camera, you little bitch!" Dennis Keller shouts at her as he violently yanks the door open.

"Leave me alone!" Gwen shouts, willing her voice to take on its entrancing tone. Her heart is racing too fast, her mind in too much of a panic to calm her nerves and say the words properly.

Dennis Keller sneers as he climbs into the car. Gwen presses her back up against the passenger door, retreating from him. Reaching out, he takes a hold of Gwen's foot and pulls. With a yell of defiance, Gwen struggles to get free while she is dragged out of the passenger seat toward Dennis. Frantically, she grabs at anything that she can hold onto, taking hold of the door handle. Dennis continues to yank on her leg with all his strength as Gwen hangs on for dear life.

Do something, Gwen! You're stronger than him. You have to do something! Gwen wills her nerves to calm down and to concentrate on her escape. Grasping at anything she can think of, she suddenly shouts out a slew of magical words hoping that one or all might do something to help her in her predicament.

Suddenly, the car engine revs to life. Both Gwen and Dennis Keller respond in surprise.

What did I just say? What did I do? Gwen thinks, baffled that any of the words from the true tongue could command any type of vehicle. She is fairly certain that there aren't any cars where she came from, if only because she had never laid eyes on one before she came to live in Maine. Her desperation seemed to work in her favor, and somehow, she started the car. *It stands to reason I could drive it with magic.* She hopes she's right since she neither knows how to drive a car nor is she tall enough to reach the pedals. *Maybe she should use her powers and force the car to drive itself?*

Dennis tries to climb farther into the car to get a better hold of her. As soon as he crawls over the driver seat a piece of broken glass cuts through his pants. Cursing he jolts backward out of the vehicle; releases her leg in the process. Frantic now, he hurries around the car to the passenger side. Taking the opportunity, Gwen utters a spell that sends the shards of glass off the driver seat and out of the car onto the driveway. Gwen then lunges toward the driver side door and pulls it shut. She sees Dennis almost at the passenger door. She looks around the car, willing it to work. She can barely see the dashboard in the half-light.

"I need to turn on the lights," she tells herself aloud.

Dennis is at the passenger door, tugging on the knob. To her relief, Gwen sees that the door's locked. Frustrated, Dennis hurries to the side garden, coming back with a large rock in hand. With all his frustration he throws his projectile at the window. The smooth, clear glass breaks into thousands of different-sized shards, spreading glass all over the inside of the car, all over her legs and shirt. The sound of the window breaking startles her. She screams purely out of fear.

Still, she knows she has to keep it together. There is no way she is about to lose her grip, not now, not when it matters most.

"Luminous!" Gwen chants, and both the dashboard and the headlights instantly spring to life. She has no time to celebrate her good luck because Dennis is reaching in through the window and fumbling at the door lock.

Just then, Gwen remembers the video camera lying on the floor of the passenger side. She can't let Dennis Keller get his hands on it. *I finally have what I need to prove that I'm not paranoid or delusional, that everything I've said about him is true.* Her freedom, Cara's, and the rest of the Kellers' safety depends on her getting that tape to her Social Worker and the police.

Just as Dennis Keller opens the passenger side door, Gwen reaches deep into her mind, reaching out with magic to take control of the vehicle. The automatic gearshift starts to move on its own and switches into reverse. An unseen force presses down on the gas, and suddenly, the car lurches backward.

Dennis Keller throws himself into the car as it backs out of the driveway. He lunges at Gwen, momentarily snapping her out of her trance. The car sputters and stalls, the engine cuts off, and the headlights go out.

Gwen struggles to fight off her attacker, the two of them struggling against each other. Neither of them aware that the car, still in reverse, is slowly rolling backward onto the street.

The vehicle gains momentum as the street slopes downward on a hill. The world passes by them, the car completely out of control as they continue speeding backward. Frantically, Gwen reaches for the wheel and for her magic simultaneously, forcing the car to come to an abrupt stop. The force of the momentum sends both of them lurching backward, momentarily freeing Gwen from Dennis's violent grasp.

"Are you trying to get us killed?" Dennis shouts at Gwen. Without warning, he punches her square in the jaw. Pain shoots through her skull, a blinding light explodes inside her head, blurring her field of vision. Gwen's body slumps over, her head rolling to the side as she crumples under the sheer pain of the impact.

As Gwen slips out of consciousness, the car immediately begins to roll again, the weight of the heavy automobile responding to the force of gravity. Dennis Keller yells in alarm, reaching for the steering wheel and trying to maneuver his leg around Gwen's body to step on the break.

Luckily for both of them, they now reach the bottom of the hill, the street behind them leveling out. Managing to step on the brake, Dennis brings the vehicle to a full stop. He heaves a sigh of relief and then glances at the lifeless figure sitting next to him in the driver seat for any sign of movement. He reaches for the gearshift and puts the car in park.

Suddenly, Gwen springs into life. "Get out!" she commands. With a powerful kick to his midsection, she sends Dennis flying backward. At the same time, she commands the passenger door to swing open, hurtling the helpless Mr. Keller out. He lands on the asphalt with a bone-crunching thud.

With her mind Gwen starts up the car. She shifts the gear to drive and presses the gas pedal to the floor. Without a backward glance at her foster father, Gwen sends the car speeding back up the hill.

* * * * *

Racing through the streets of Scranton, Gwen heads toward the middle of town to the child services office. She isn't sure if Mrs. Fairbank's office is closed, but it was pretty close to nine o'clock at night. Gwen prays that she might catch Deanna at the office. If she does not, then she doesn't have the slightest idea where else to turn. Gwen is still fairly new in town, and doesn't know where the police station is, but none of that matters. Her own sense of vindication demands that Mrs. Fairbanks—the woman who had listened to Gwen's story about Dennis Keller and defended that child-molesting, wife-beating monster—would be the first one to see the tape.

Gwen drives the car with her mind, running a few red lights and nearly getting herself into an accident. Luckily for her, no police cars patrol the streets she traversed. After losing her way twice, Gwen finally spots the familiar child services building up the street. Just as she pulls up to the curb in front, she sees Mrs. Fairbanks and a couple of her colleagues descending the white granite steps.

Gwen stops the car and reaches under the passenger seat for Dennis Keller's digital video camera. Afraid she won't catch Mrs. Fairbanks before she gets to her car, Gwen rushes from the vehicle, not even bothering to switch off the headlights, leaving the driver side door wide open.

Deanna Fairbanks says goodbye to her companions and is about to make it to her car when she notices the Kellers' vehicle parked on the curb with Gwen running toward her.

"Mary? What on earth are you—" Deanna began but is immediately cut off as the eleven-year-old orphan nearly collides with her in the middle of the parking lot.

"I caught you. I thought you'd have gone home already!" Gwen exclaims between breaths.

"Nope, not yet. Did you drive yourself here?" Mrs. Fairbanks asks in astonishment.

"Yes, I have to show you something!"

Deanna notices the video camera in Gwen's hands. "What is this all about?"

"You wanted proof, remember? Well, there it is. Watch it and then see how you feel about your buddy Dennis Keller," Gwen answers. The dark tone in her voice gives Deanna a feeling of dread.

"Marianne, would you please just tell me what's going on? Where are Judy and the kids? Do they know you have their car?"

"I have to get back to them. They might need me." Gwen turns back toward the Kellers' abandoned car but then stops and turns back to Deanna Fairbanks. "Call the police, will you? Send them to the Kellers to pick up Dennis Keller. Tell them that the rest of us are spending the night at the Coopers' house."

Without another word, Gwen hurries back to the car. Deanna hurries after. "Wait, Gwen. I can't let you go in that car. You're not old enough to drive! Let me take you home or go with me to the police station!" She tries to reason with the agitated adolescent.

"There's no time. I have to get back to Cara!" Gwen insists, hopping into the car, shutting the door swiftly.

"Gwen! Gwen, get out of the car right now!" Deanna pounds on the hood of the car.

Gwen, ignoring her, revs the engine into life and drives away, leaving a dumbstruck Deanna to watch as the eleven-year-old drives off in Dennis Keller's Buick.

Fumbling with her purse while still holding the camera in her other hand, Deanna retrieves her cell phone. Switching it on she dials 9-1-1. After a few rings, the line picks up and a female voice speaks on the other end.

"9-1-1, what's your emergency?"

Minutes later, after telling the emergency operator all the pertinent information about the situation, the woman on the other end assured her everything would be handled by the police. Hanging up the phone, Deanna comes out of her stupor and finds Dennis Keller's video camera in her hand. Shaken, she walks around to the driver's side of her car. She puts her keys in the lock and opens the door. Her mind still reeling, she climbs into her Saturn, tossing the camera down on the passenger seat beside her. She puts her hands on the steering wheel and takes a deep breath, staring out through the windshield at the empty red brick building. *In all my years working for child protection I have never encountered anyone as strange as Marianne.*

She doesn't know what to think about the girl, or her sudden appearance at her office late tonight. She'd been speaking nonsense, driving a stolen car, and babbling on about Dennis Keller and a videotape. Deanna decides that the only way to make sense of it all is to go ahead and watch the tape.

With a sigh of resignation, she turns and reaches over, picking up the small, gray digital camcorder. She finds the power button and switches it on. Opening the flip screen, Deanna locates the control buttons on the side of the video recorder. She shakes her head, still in disbelief, not sure what to expect. She presses the rewind button, and the machine gives off a mechanical whirring sound as the tape rewinds. It signals with a loud click that it has reached the start of the tape. Locating the proper button on the side panel, she takes a deep breath and pushes "play."

* * * * *

Gwen's return to the Keller residence is much more successful,

her nervousness eased by the knowledge that soon everyone would know the true nature of Dennis Keller.

Mentally, she drives the car around the corner and onto the street where she's lived for the past three months. She slows her speed down to a crawl and shuts the headlights off. Up ahead, the Kellers' home is dark and empty. She can see no sign of Mr. Keller in the yard or anywhere else in sight. With a huge sigh of relief, she silently pulls the car over and parks by the curb, three houses down from the Kellers.

Not quite sure what to do next, Gwen sits in the car, a sense of foreboding creeping through her spine. She needs to check on Cara, to make sure she and the others are safe at the Coopers' house. That means she would have to walk past the Kellers' house to get to them, and for all she knows, Dennis Keller could be waiting out there somewhere in the night, ready to pounce. The thought gives her a chill.

"Come on, Gwen. You can't sit here all night," she instructs herself. Squaring her shoulders, Gwen slowly opens the door and creeps silently into the night. Crouching down, she stays close to the cars parked along the side of the road as she makes her way down the street. The street is empty, and the neighborhood is quiet. Not many cars drive down this street at this time of night, and Gwen is glad of it. While she lacks the gift for seeing in the dark the way Raven does, she's determined to use the night and the shadows to her advantage. Creeping from one shadow to the next, Gwen makes her way safely to the Coopers' home.

Snugly hidden between two cars, Gwen peers out for any sign of life. No one is there. The Coopers' porch light is on, and the windows of their modest home illuminated. Gwen makes a dash for the front door, nearly stumbling as she runs up the front steps and onto the porch. Anxiously, she raps her fist against the wooden door, impatiently waiting for someone to answer.

Mrs. Cooper, a plump kindly woman in her early forties opens the door. Recognizing Gwen, she ushers her inside.

"There you are, Mary. Everyone's been worried about you. Where have you been?" Mrs. Cooper asks, the tone of concern in her voice soothing Gwen's frayed nerves.

"I'm fine. I'll explain everything later." Gwen looks around the front entry and the adjacent living room, seeing only Mr. Cooper and their two young children sitting on the sofa. "Where are Cara and the others? Are they upstairs?"

"Oh, no, Mr. Keller just stopped by fifteen minutes ago to pick them up," Mrs. Cooper explains, as though it's the most natural thing in the world.

"What? And they left with him? Why would they do that?" Gwen asks in disbelief, almost angry at Mrs. Cooper for letting them go.

"Why? What do you mean, Mary? Because Dennis had the house checked and it turns out the gas leak was just a false alarm, honey. He said you got scared and ran off. That he looked everywhere for you. He and Aaron are out searching the neighborhood for you right now," Mrs. Cooper tells her, placing a hand on Gwen's shoulder, "Why did you run off, Mary? A gas leak is dangerous but once you're out of the house there's really nothing to be afraid of." The older woman speaks to her as a concerned adult would speak to a naive child.

"Who told you there was a gas leak?" Gwen asks, impatiently shaking Mrs. Cooper's hand off her shoulder.

"Your foster mother did, of course. She said she smelled gas. She got the other children out of the house, but her husband was out back in his shed, and she sent you to tell him about the leak."

"And you believed this? I mean, what did Mr. Keller say when he showed up?" Gwen asks, perplexed. She can't for the life of her fathom why Mrs. Keller would lie. Was she so afraid of her husband that she would lie for him even when he hurt Cara and Aaron?

"He said he was here to get his family, that it was time to come home. It was Judy who asked if he'd called the authorities about the gas leak. He said that it was just a false alarm, that everything was fine. Then Cara asked where you were, and Mr. Keller told us all that you had run away."

How can I protect Cara and the others if they willingly put themselves back in harm's way? After all she's gone through, she now has to return to the Kellers' house.

A voice in the back of her head tells her not to bother, that this isn't her fight, that she should just take Dennis's car and drive away and never look back. She can't do that, not only because she has no place to go or because she still doesn't know how to find Raven. Because she can't leave Cara, and Judy, or even ugly old Aaron in Dennis Keller's hands. She needs to get them out of there. Where they would go or what they would do afterward isn't important now. She just has to convince them to leave with her.

Thanking Mrs. Cooper for her help, Gwen leaves the house. Slowly, she walks across the lawn toward the Kellers' rambler-style home. She stops at the bottom of the steps leading up to the porch and stares up at the front door. There are no lights on inside, no sign that anyone is home, yet it makes sense that Mr. Keller would leave his fragile wife and foster daughter at home while he and Aaron searched for her. He knew that his wife would do anything he commanded her, and that Aaron was both too afraid of him and too much in awe of him to disobey him in any way. Likely Aaron had forced himself to forget the incident in the shed. As Gwen is certain he had trained himself to do many times before.

She knows now that the scene she witnessed in the shed had likely been recorded on Dennis Keller's video camera many times before. Perhaps it was another form of punishment that he enjoyed inflicting on Aaron and Cara.

Gwen can't help but wonder why her foster father had never tried to force her to perform for him. The reason, of course, was because he was afraid of her. He said before that she had evil eyes, that they followed him and stared at him as though she could see into his soul. What Dennis Keller didn't know is that Gwen *could* read minds, but that his mind was too irrational and sporadic. Maybe she never saw any indication of sexual abuse in the children's thoughts because they are in denial, probably used to suppressing the memories so they could function in their lives. Mrs. Keller likely knows nothing about what was going on in the shed out back and didn't dare ask. Most likely she is too afraid to stand up for herself, let alone two defenseless children. Gwen feels sick to her stomach, disgusted.

There is no way to avoid it, she decides. If Cara is in there, then Gwen has to go inside the house and bring her out. Maybe she can convince Cara to run away with her. Maybe there was some way to find Raven, or maybe she could even break into Mrs. Fairbanks office and steal his address? These thoughts give Gwen hope as she slowly climbs the steps and walks through the front door.

* * * * *

Inside, the house is devoid of light. The kitchen smells strongly of alcohol. Gwen hesitates. *Why are all the lights off? Where is everyone? Are they already asleep?* She knows someone is in the house. She can hear the hum of multiple minds nearby.

Gwen clings to this idea, moving blindly but silently through the kitchen, using the walls to guide her toward the hallway and on to the bedrooms. She is about to step into the hallway when suddenly the kitchen light comes on in the room behind her. A moment later the front door slams shut.

Gwen freezes, the breath caught in her throat. Terrified of who she might find standing behind her, Gwen slowly turns to face them.

Dennis Keller stands next to the front door, his hand still hovering over the light switch.

"Look who's back." He shakes his head ruefully. Dennis's voice has a thick drunken slur. She notices that there are several beer bottles scattered on the opposite end of the dining room table.

This must be what he's been doing while he waited for me to return.

He saunters over and plops down into the head chair, reaching for the nearest bottle. "Why don't you come sit with me, Marianne?" he asks, indicating with a double slap on the chair next to him which seat she should take.

Gwen stands still, not moving a muscle. "Where are Cara and the others?" she demands in a flat tone.

"I knew you'd come back for that girl." He gives her a smug smile.

"Where's Cara?" Gwen asks again, ignoring his statement.

"They're out looking for you. You ran away, remember?"

He's lying. I can feel someone else here. Gwen quickly searches the house with her mind and finds an unidentifiable presence nearby. She can't distinguish who it might be. This confounds Gwen, further unravelling her already frayed nerves.

"Cara? Judy? Hey, Aaron? Is anybody here?" Gwen calls down the hallway, first one direction and then the other. She looks into the darkness and neither sees nor hears a thing.

"There isn't anybody here but you and me," Dennis informs her then returns his attention to his beer, attempting to drink. He gives a disappointed grunt when nothing comes out. Annoyed, he tosses the bottle aside carelessly. It hits the kitchen floor with a crash, shattering to pieces. Gwen flinches, her attention back on Dennis.

"You like that Cara, don't you?" Dennis Keller looks at her, a strange glint in his eyes. "I've seen how she follows you around. I know she spends most of her nights in your room and not her own. She's been saying things about me, hasn't she?" Dennis Keller demands an answer, his voice rising in agitation.

Gwen can't think of what to say.

"Whatever she's saying, it's all lies. You hear me?" Dennis shouts.

"What about what I saw? She can't be lying about that," Gwen feels compelled to ask although part of her fears angering him in this state.

"I don't know what you're talkin' about." A bit wobbly, Dennis stands and walks slowly around the table toward her.

Gwen scoffs, "I have proof, remember?"

"Oh, right. You stole my camera. Where's it at anyhow?" His nonchalance puzzles her.

I would think that someone whose been caught in the act would have the good sense to be worried. But he's not afraid of being caught. The realization turns her skin cold. Gwen shivers involuntarily.

"It's in the car," Gwen lies quickly, not entirely certain why.

"I'll tell you what, why don't you give me the camera back and we'll forget the whole thing ever happened. How's that sound?"

"And you'll leave Cara alone?"

"I bet you'd do anything for your little friend, huh? What do you say?" Slowly, he approaches her.

"I can't. I already gave it to Deanna Fairbanks." Gwen watches him, ready to defend herself if he attacks.

Dennis leans against the table suddenly and burst into a peel of drunken laughter. The sound is just as unsettling as his behavior. After a moment, his mirth subsides.

"Well, that was stupid," he declares, standing up straight again. "You just lost your bargaining chip."

"Why? You don't actually think Deanna is still going to think the world of you once she sees what's on that tape, do you? I bet she's already called the police. They're probably on their way here right now."

"Maybe, but they're not coming for me. I ain't on the video." He puts his hands on his hips in a look of self-satisfaction.

"What? What about your voice? I heard you talking to Cara just before I broke into the shed. Obviously, they're going to realize that you made the tape, that you made them…"

"That camera is old; it hasn't been able to record audio for years." He shrugs cutting off her words.

"But… that doesn't matter," Gwen stammers, her voice weak. "It's your camera. Obviously, someone is making them do those things. Who else could it be but you?"

"Why?" His question astonishes her. Before she can respond he continues, "I've never done anything to make anyone think me capable of such things. Unlike you."

"What?" Gwen rocks back flabbergasted. "You can't expect anyone to think I did this. That's nuts!" Gwen feels a tingling all over her body at the sheer ridiculousness of the notion.

"You're a known thief and a liar. You have a history of violence. You're delusional and you've made claims like this before. Why on earth anyone believed your word against a nun, I can't understand." He takes a step toward her. Gwen instinctively takes two steps back.

"How did you know?"

"Deanna told me all about your past. I'm not sure she was supposed to share all that info with the new foster parents, but she felt she needed to warn me. We have known each other all our lives." He advances toward her again.

"What I said about Sister Whitmore was true. And dozens of witnesses said the same. She's a monster just like you. And just like her you're going to answer for what you've done." Gwen creeps backward trying to keep out of arms reach from him.

"No one will ever believe you."

"Cara and Aaron will tell everyone the truth."

"They will say what I tell them to say." Dennis lunges at her. Gwen tries to turn and run only to find herself caught against the hallway wall. He grabs her by both arms turning her to face him. He shoves her flat against the floral wallpaper, pinning her in place.

"Let go of me!" she screeches, between frantic breaths. She tries to calm her racing heart to get control of herself. She stares into his eyes speaking in her haunting resonating tone. "Take your hands off of me!"

"I don't take orders from you little girl," Dennis snorts. His eyes do not glaze over; his body does not go stiff. His attention is not rapt upon her, willing to follow her every command.

Gwen curses under her breath. *I guess that trick doesn't work on drunks.* Even so Gwen still delves into his mind and tries to take control of him from within. What she finds is a tangled mess of half thoughts and incomprehensible images. The effect it has on her own mind is disorientating. Gwen quickly retreats back into herself.

"Now when the cops get here, I'll tell them all about the sick things you've been doing to poor Aaron and Cara. How you assaulted me and stole my car when I found you out." He shakes his head making a tsk sound. "They'll send you right to juvie, where you belong. I'll be rid of you and those spooky-ass eyes for good."

"Dasae windah," Gwen chants putting all the power she can into the words. As if summoning the wind from deep within her lungs, a gust of air brakes forth from her hitting Dennis directly in the face.

Caught completely unaware, Dennis is knocked backward by the force. With a shout of alarm, he flies across the room crashing into the kitchen counter. The impact makes him fall to his knees in pain, gasping and groaning.

"How did you do that? You made all those tools fly at me in the shed, too, didn't you? So, it's all true, all that crazy stuff about you being evil, it's true." He stumbles to his feet and rushes back toward her.

"I'm not the one who's evil. You are!" Gwen yells defiantly. When Dennis is almost upon her Gwen leaps out of the way, hopping onto a chair she climbs on top of the table. Walking across the wooden surface to get around Dennis Gwen then jumps off dashing toward the door.

He tackles her from behind, pinning her to the floor beneath his weight. Gwen's face is pressed against the linoleum. The full force of his body knocks the air out of her lungs. She can hardly breathe.

Dennis laughs in her ear and then scrambles to his feet. Instantly, Gwen tries to squirm away from him, but he won't let her get away so easily. Forcibly flipping her onto her back, Dennis turns Gwen to face him. Quickly, he deals her two quick shots to the face with his fist. Pain shoots through her skull, exploding deep inside her brain. She tastes blood. Her lip is split, and her nose is bleeding. She makes a weak coughing sound from the back of her throat.

Laughing, Dennis climbs on top of her again, pinning her arms to her side, securing her in place by straddling her. He begins to undo his belt.

The pain fading to a dull pounding headache, Gwen watches her foster father remove his belt from his jeans. Realization puts her into a panic. She bucks and wriggles beneath him, thrashing about like a wild animal.

"Gainien raisa, lun che!" Gwen shouts. A second later the kitchen cabinet drawers open, and objects hurtle through the air at Dennis. He curses as he attempts to dodge and swat away wooden spoons, a rolling pin, a can opener, and several pieces of silverware. He screams in terror as a half dozen steak knives dislodge themselves from the woodblock rocketing toward his chest. Dennis flattens himself on top of Gwen, narrowly escaping being impaled. The knives hit the hallway wall with chorus of loud thuds.

"That's it, I've had enough of that." With a cold, hollow look in his eyes, Dennis slips the leather belt behind Gwen's head, grabbing one end and wrapping it around her throat. Threading the end through the belt buckle, he pulls tight. His movements so swift she can't get another syllable out. Gwen's airway restricted.

Gwen gasps as the leather belt tightens, pressing into the flesh of her neck. Her eyes widen. She struggles for air, unable to utter a word or cast a spell.

Her ability to think fades as the oxygen is cut off from her brain, her lungs, and her fragile mortal body. An inky darkness encroaches around her, as she feels herself become weightless. Her spirit floating into the darkness as the light fades. She feels no pain, she feels nothing. She is nothing.

You are dying, Gwen. A strange voice echoes through the ocean of ink around her. *You are dying!*

No! Not here, not now. Not like this! The strong thought penetrates through all other sensations, fighting violently against the darkness that threatens to overtake her. Gwen thrashes toward the last bit of light left.

Her inner spirit reaches out for the source of all creation, for the power that gives God control over life and death. Gwen sees a vibrant pulsating light within her grasp. With all the mental capacity left in her, she pushes towards it, attempting to command it without words. She hauls herself out of the abyss of death to the surface. Only to find herself stuck, as if trapped under a thick wall of ice. Meanwhile the dark waters grow heavy, wrapping around her, trying to drag her downward away from the light. She can feel life and consciousness on the other side of that frozen barrier.

She focuses all her energy, all the power of creation into breaking through. Clawing, kicking, scratching at it until at last, it shatters. The blinding light on the other side rushes over her. It engulfs the darkness sweeping her up into white nothingness.

* * * * *

"You can't hurt me if you can't speak, can you?" Dennis chortles down at his unconscious preteen foster daughter beneath him. Suddenly, he feels something take hold of him. An unseen force surrounding him, restraining him. He shouts in alarm; his eyes open wide in shock as it lifts him off of the ground and into the air several feet above Gwen's motionless body. Suspended there, helpless to fight against the invisible assailant, Dennis feels the force surrounding him, crushing him.

All of the air leaves his lungs. Every joint and muscle forced inward upon itself. He lets out an inhuman screech. All while his bones shatter, his flesh tares, and the life is squeezed out of him. His agony seems endless. Soon the world goes black, and life leaves his mortal frame.

* * * * *

Gwen awakens to the sounds of screams and other mysterious noises that puzzle her. Suddenly, an object falls on her legs, the weight pinning them in place. Something is around her neck. Reaching up with shaking hands, she unfastens the leather belt around her throat tossing it aside. She coughs and gasps for air. She sees the old, white, cottage-cheese kitchen ceiling above her. She lies there for several minutes letting her lungs fill with air and the ache in them subside.

Where am I?

Her head throbs. Her vision is blurry. White specs of light dance before her, making everything seem vague and surreal. She sits up slowly, not wanting to aggravate the feeling of nausea in her stomach. The room spins around her; she forces her eyes shut. After several minutes, her equilibrium returns.

It's safe to look around now, she tells herself.

She was wrong.

She tries to get up and move but remembers the weight on her legs. Gwen goes to shove the obstruction off. Her hands stop mid-air as her face contorts in an expression of horror. A twisted mass of bones, flesh, torso, and limbs lay upon her. The face of the deformed corpse stares at her with bulging eyes, looking petrified in the attitude of pain and agony. As disfigured as the creature is, she still knows that face.

Panic and revulsion wrap her in its icy grip. Screaming, she wiggles her legs free of the dead man. Gwen scurries backward across the floor until she backs up against a kitchen cabinet.

She takes one more look at the remains of Dennis Keller and the blood-splattered kitchen. Turning her face away, Gwen vomits. When her stomach is empty, Gwen starts to cry uncontrollably. She lets all of her fear, pain, agony, hatred, and guilt pour out through her tears. She cries like a scared, little girl. And, for the first time in her life, she truly feels like a child. There is no one here to impress with her fearlessness. No Raven for whom she has always been strong. No Cara who needs to be comforted. There is no one to witness her breakdown but a dead man. A man she just murdered.

Clarity comes and Gwen realizes it is not safe to live amongst normal people anymore. She has to flee. She can't explain how Dennis Keller died to the cops, to Mrs. Fairbanks, to his wife, or even to Cara. No one would believe her. No one would understand. She is a murderer now and nothing can change that, no matter how much he deserved it. Gwen sniffs back the tears, and dries her eyes, feeling weak as she gets to her feet.

Rumbling laughter fills the silence. Startled, Gwen looks up as a well-dressed man steps out of the darkness at the end of the hall and into the kitchen. In his eyes she sees a blackness that is darker than anything imaginable. He smiles brightly at her. Gwen feels a chill all over her skin. The man with the soulless eyes, from the woods stands before her.

"That's my girl!" he chuckles and then vanishes—back into the darkness.

Gwen stands there, frozen in shock before absolute terror sends her fleeing from the room. Careful to avoid eye contact with the corpse and give it wide berth, she rushes to her bedroom. With the practiced air of someone used to fleeing at a moment's notice, she gathers all her belongings. She grabs her mangled sketchbook, her art case, her new clothes, and her favorite books, including the ones about Wicca and the art of illusion. She stuffs them into her duffle bag. Quickly she strips her bedding from the mattress. Wrapping her pillow in the center, Gwen creates a bed roll. Grabbing a scarf from her closet, Gwen ties the bundle together, threading her arm through the scarf to drape the bedroll on her back.

With all her things packed, she starts to leave but stops short when she remembers her mother's locket on the nightstand. She hurries back to retrieve it, pausing a moment to look at a drawing she did for Cara just yesterday. It depicts a white stone castle, and a city made out of mountains, hills, and trees. Beyond it lay a meadow of multi-colored flowers. In the meadow stands a mysterious blonde-haired, blue-eyed boy, staring out of the picture as though he were looking right into Gwen's soul.

The picture is an illustration of her recurring dream, the one she's had since that first day in the hospital. She'd had frostbitten feet from wandering barefoot for days in the snow-covered wilderness. She had been running from something then, and she is running from something now. She recalls the boy's all-too-familiar warning. Over the years nothing in the dream has changed but the boy himself. He's grown from the boy she first saw, aging while she herself aged. He now seems several years older than she.

"Go, Gwen. Run. It's not safe for you here now. There are those who will stop at nothing to hurt you. You must vanish." His words are truer now than they have ever been before.

She leaves the drawing for Cara, a memento of their brief but special friendship. Turning the paper over, Gwen writes a quick message.

To my little Cara,

I can't explain what happened. I can't tell you where I'm going. I don't even know that myself. However, I want you to know that I did what I had to, and I did it for you. You don't need to be afraid of sleeping alone. No one will disturb you anymore. I may never see you again, so I want you to know that you deserve better than what you've had. Don't settle for anything less than what you deserve. I wish I could promise you that your life will get easier from here on out, but that would be a lie. The world is a dangerous place. Don't let that stop you from living your life. I believe in you, Cara. Take care of yourself. I will never forget you.

Gwen

She turns the paper over; the drawing faces up. Concealing the note with the hope that only Cara will see it. With that, Gwen turns toward the bedroom door and stops.

Although she senses that the black-eyed man is gone, she still can't force herself to go back into the other room. She cannot face the carnage which awaits her in the kitchen, or the reality of what she has done. It will haunt her for the rest of her life. But she did what she had to, to protect herself, to survive.

"I'm not evil. I'm not *his* girl!" she tells herself, squaring her shoulders.

A police siren wails nearby. However unlikely it is that the police car is headed to the Keller residence, the sound still forces Gwen into action. She turns and goes to her bedroom window. Kicking out the old, dirty screen, Gwen tosses her red duffle bag out into the dark night. She hears it land with a soft thud in the grass. Quickly, she climbs onto the window frame and leaps out herself. She manages to land next to her bag, the impact of her landing, sends a momentary shock through her tennis shoes, feet and up her calves.

She once ran from her past into this civilized world, and after all these years, she still finds it less than civilized. She isn't safe amongst mankind. She knows this now without a doubt. She knows that she is different. If not human, she is at least mortal. She can die, she can get sick, bleed, and be just as vulnerable as any human being. Yet, she also is special. Her uniqueness will always set her apart. It's time now to flee civilization and return to the wilderness from whence she came.

Gwen turns her eyes toward the Poconos Mountains looming nearby. Their peaks and crests illuminated by the full moon's pearlescent glow. She hasn't been successful finding her own kind in the cities of men. The few she met tried to do her and Raven harm. Perhaps she has been looking in the wrong place all along.

Her mind made up, Gwen hefts her duffle over her right shoulder and sets off toward the mountains, cutting through the suburbs and the downtown streets of Scranton. A couple of hours later, she finds herself standing on the outskirts of town. Behind her, the city is oddly quiet in the late-night hours. Before her, the mountains loom above, mighty, and strong, promising refuge for her weary heart.

I could use some solitude, Gwen tells herself. No one to judge her, no one to blame her, hit her, hurt her, or leave her. It will be her alone with the earth, the water, and the sky. The thought encourages her, giving her a new sense of purpose.

Someday she will return to this world and seek out her brother the wolf. Their two hearts will be whole once again. For now, Gwen has to move forward, with the mysterious boy's words from her dreams to guide her.

Adjusting her duffle bag and her bedroll on her back, and with the grim determination with which she has faced life head-on all this time,

Gwen leaves humanity behind, disappearing into the night, alone and friendless, leaving cruelty and fleeing from reality.

CHAPTER SIXTEEN

The Forsaken

*T*he white, glimmering palace looms high above her, surrounded by the wild forest city. The quaint little houses and shops along the streets and the main square of the city are all hauntingly vacant, like an old western ghost town.

Someone has to live here, Gwen thinks absently. She can't remember how she got here, but all at once she finds herself standing before a strange castle in a mysterious kingdom. And someone is waiting for her somewhere within.

Taking a deep breath, Gwen tentatively ascends the stairs up to the entry. Apprehensively, she raises her fist to knock on the gilded door. Before she can make contact, the doors swing inward to open. Pausing just a moment, Gwen slips inside. In the bright entry hall, the walls around her are a brilliant pearlescent white. Her bare feet find a white and grey marble floor beneath them. A magnificent crystal chandelier hangs from a vaulted ceiling above her. In front of her, a massive, curved stairway winds upward with gold scroll railings, carpeted in red velvet.

Having no other option, Gwen decides to take the stairs and see where they lead. A strange sensation comes over her as she takes each step upward, coming that much closer to the mysterious personage who awaits her. She can feel this presence beckoning her onward, leading her as if she were following the sound of a voice or a particular scent.

At the top of the stairs, she comes to a landing where the steps split in two directions, one leading to her left, the other to her right. Before her on a golden pedestal stands a sculpture of a man's head, beautifully chiseled out of white marble. Gwen walks up to it so she can examine the sculpture more closely. It is the face of a young man in his teens, delicately boned and handsome. His lips and eyes are large and round like a child's. His nose long and straight, his jaw line sharp with a pointed cleft chin. Something in the stranger's visage hits a familiar chord somewhere within her.

"How do I know this face?" she asks aloud, her voice echoing endlessly off the elegant walls and floors, bouncing deeper into the castle and the winding stairways beyond. Suddenly, she feels vulnerable standing out in the open like this. Tearing herself away from the oddly familiar sculpture, Gwen hurries off to her right, taking the velvet-covered steps upward to the next story.

She comes to another landing, the stairs winding off to the right again and a long hallway with many arched doorways leading off to the left. While she stands there in deep contemplation, her eye is caught by the large tapestries hanging from the wall above her.

A royal family crest with an emblem made up of a hawk encircled by a ring of thorns is brightly woven into the fabric. Beneath it in golden shimmering thread is a single word: Hawthorne. After a moment, she feels the need to move and continues onward. Following her gut, she takes the stairs again.

This time, when the stairs come to the next floor, she notices a painting displayed before her. It takes up the whole wall, maybe ten feet high and four feet wide. Portrayed within it are two women, both of them strikingly beautiful. They are obviously sisters. They bear the same high cheekbones; the same strong features; matching almond-shaped eyes; high, inquisitive, arched eyebrows; full pouty lips; and proud, noble chins. Their demeanor is so marked, so opposite, that their personalities seem to radiate outward through the paint and canvas, almost as if they will suddenly come alive and step out of the painting to introduce themselves.

The older, taller sister looks thirty-something, with long, platinum white hair piled on top of her head in a massive heap of curls and ringlets cascading in strands about her shoulders and long feminine neck. Her eyes are violet with a hint of gold around the pupil, her gaze fierce and commanding, and her mouth tight in a grim yet contrived smile. Adorned in cascades of fine jewelry with diamonds, sapphires, emeralds, and rubies, she looks as regal as a queen. Dressed in a flowing Grecian-style gown of scarlet, her slender lanky figure sits erect upon an ornate gold and ivory armchair.

The younger sister appears to be in her mid-twenties. She is also golden-skinned and blonde, only her hair is like spun yellow gold, brilliant in its radiance. It hangs straight over one shoulder like a curtain of gold silk falling down to her tiny waist. Her eyes are a dazzling jade green, with a golden sunburst around her pupil. They seem to smile with a warmth that touches her budding red lips in a mischievous half grin. She is similarly dressed in a deeper shade of green that matches her eyes, and gold sandals that lace up her long, beautiful legs. She wears no jewelry except a golden chain locket, which hangs seductively between her ample breasts exposed by her garment's deep neckline.

She stands just behind her sister, one delicate hand resting on the chair, the other hand grasping a red-tipped white rose by its long and thorny stem. The austere sister holds an identical rose tightly in her strong, boney hand, almost crushing the barbed stem into her flesh. Looking more closely, Gwen notices that the younger sister's hand is bleeding from the prickly thorns, but she seems oblivious to the bloodstains on her dress and the droplets gathering on the floor by her feet.

The painting makes Gwen's skin crawl. Something about the one sitting upon the ivory chair makes her uneasy, as if she might reach out her large hand and take Gwen by the neck or stomp her underfoot. The other woman has quite the opposite effect upon her. She seems almost flesh and blood. Her smile reminds Gwen of a warm summer day. She imagines her voice is as clear and sweet as a freshwater spring.

Again, a familiarity rings within Gwen's mind, some distant part of her mind trying desperately to remember something long forgotten and hidden away. Finally, she shakes off this feeling and follows the winding staircase to the right and upward once more, still feeling the unseen presence compelling her up. This time the stairs do not break off into further landings, hallways, or passages. They keep climbing onward and upward into the uppermost heights of the palace. Finally, Gwen reaches the top of the stairs, which end abruptly in front of an old decaying wooden door.

In this exquisite palace of white and gold finery, this door seems oddly out of place. It belongs on an old log cabin or a ramshackle barn than a castle. Hesitantly, Gwen reaches out to push it open. It moves of its own volition, swinging inward before she can touch it. With a deep breath, Gwen steps into the doorway and into the room beyond.

Peering around the door, Gwen notices a small room of dark, dank stone, bare of any furniture save for a large, golden, jewel-encrusted mirror leaning against the far wall. The only light in the room comes from the two arched stone windows, devoid of glass windowpanes, throwing the strange room into half sunlight. It only illuminates parts of the chamber; the room seemingly made of sunlight and black shadows.

What I need is in this room. What I came for is here waiting for me, Gwen reminds herself. She wills her frightened body forward, ominously, deeper into the room. She takes one step, then another, and then another until she finds herself standing before the beautiful antique mirror.

She looks into her reflection and gasps. Where she expects to see herself—a slender, petite eleven-year-old girl with a pale face, flashing green eyes and long, straight, jet-black hair—she instead sees a woman, beautiful, tall, curvy, and long-legged, reminding Gwen of the kind of woman one sees in Victoria's Secret catalogs. The woman in her reflection has pale skin, flashing yellow-green eyes, and long, straight, black hair. This woman, however, sports a hard expression, with a bitter tilt of her head, and an angry glint in her eyes. The hostility and coldness radiating from her through the glass are almost overpowering. Gwen quickly looks away, not wanting to meet that gaze or to see the hate in her eyes.

She turns her head and finds a young man standing before one of the arched windows, his back to her as he stands in the bright morning sunlight. Gwen knows it is him even before he turns his piercing blue and gold eyes to look upon her. His golden hair catches the light, looking ablaze in the sun. His face is just as his marbled sculpture depicted him, striking and beautiful as only a boy about to become a man can be. He smiles at her, and Gwen feels as though she is basking in the sun herself. For he is the sun. He is the day. He is the light of everything that is good and beautiful.

"Gwen, there you are." As he speaks, her heart aches. Now she knows with certainty that this is all a dream. He always comes to her in her dreams, and as real as this castle and this room seem, she knows that this, too, is all in her mind and may fade away in an instant.

"It's you, isn't it? Who are you? Please, for once tell me," Gwen pleads, her voice trembling with frustration and childish hopes.

"Don't you know by now? Haven't you always known me?" he asks in his warm, clear voice, turning to fully look at her, standing straight and tall, his arms folded behind his back. He wears a white tailored suit with gold trim and gold buttons, looking as dashing as a soldier in the uniform of the royal guard.

"I don't know anything. You never tell me anything. You kind of just fade away. Where are you? How do I find you? What is this place? I know it's real. I've seen it a hundred times in my dreams, this white palace surrounded by the kingdom grown out of the trees and the flowered meadow just beyond the forest. It's a real place, and if it's real, then so are you!" Gwen takes a few steps toward the handsome young man. He takes a few steps back, keeping his distance from her. Gwen looks at him with pain in her eyes.

"I can't give you the answers you need, Gwen. You aren't ready yet. You can't come here. We're not ready for you either. It's much too soon and you've got a lot to learn before the end." He speaks to her softly, trying to comfort her with his words.

"The end? The end of what?" Gwen probes. The boy only shakes his head in response. "You can't tell me? Fine! Then what do you want? Why do you come to me like this? Are you some kind of ghost from the future?" Gwen asks bitterly.

The boy smiles. "Yes and no. I come this way because this is the only way I can protect you, the only way I am able to move in this world at all," he admits.

"Why? Are you dead? Are you really a ghost?"

"No, I'm not dead. Not quite, anyway, but I fear I may not last until you finally return home."

Her breath catches in her chest. "What do you mean, return home? What home?" Gwen asks.

"I can't tell you. All I can tell you is that you are not an orphan, Gwen. Your life is not worthless. You are far more important than you comprehend. You will touch the lives of countless souls, but you must be careful of the roads you travel in the years to come." Gwen opens her mouth to speak, but he raises a hand and cuts her off. "You have to turn back, Gwen. Don't go into the wilderness. Go back where you came from," he pleads, his voice showing the first sign of fear.

"I can't go back. It's impossible. I have to flee. It's my only chance to survive," Gwen retorts.

"I fear you may not survive the evil that awaits you in the mountains. Be strong, Gwen. Don't let anything break you. No matter what, remember that I am waiting for you, that I am a part of you, and that when all else fails and all seems lost, in your dreams I will always be here. You are not forsaken." He turns and starts toward the arched window.

Gwen can't let him go, not now. There is so much she needs to know and only he can give her the answers she seeks. A wave of panic propels her forward. She hurries after him, reaching out her hand, her fingers barely missing his coat sleeve as he steps out of the high- tower window and into the air.

* * * * *

With a jolt, Gwen shoots up from her bedroll and stumbles into the snow beyond her little camp beneath an evergreen. She looks about for a moment, still half-dazed as the fogginess of her dreams slowly dissipates, and the real world becomes tangible once more. She takes a moment to steady her erratic heartbeat, returning back to the warm shelter of the tree and her blankets and pillow.

The full moon high above the forest reflects off the snow as if a natural nightlight. The trees glisten in the silvery light, surrounding her, watching silently over her like sentinels of the dark. Gwen considers lighting a fire but decides to conserve her energy for tomorrow instead.

Gathering her bedding around her, Gwen wishes she had a real tent and a nice air mattress and a kerosene lamp. She could pretend that she is camping for the weekend or hanging out with some friends in the woods. Perhaps even that she was going on a little vacation with her large, loving family who enjoys spending time in nature doing outdoorsy things.

"It's much too cold and way too late to delude myself," she says aloud. She fights off the gloom that threatens to overtake her, resolving that she will not break down sobbing, shivering in the cold, crying out for a mother she barely knows. "There's no one to cry out for, Gwen." Her words this time feel oddly comforting as the sound of her own voice rings in the still of the night.

She looks up at the full moon and thinks of Raven, wondering if he's somewhere out there in a forest just like this, prowling the night on all fours, with fur on his back and a beast in his heart. She mentally turns away from the thought, knowing that thinking of her lost friend will only make her feel even more wretched.

Everything would be so much easier if he were still with her. If they had never been separated, no harm would have ever come to her. They would have protected each other, he would have saved her from Dennis Keller, and together they would have fled into the wilderness. Right now, she would have a big, warm, cuddly boy to snuggle up against in the bitter winter night. But no, these thoughts aren't going to help her. They will only make reality all the more bitter.

Nearby an owl screech into the night, its mournful cries echoing the sorrow Gwen feels inside that threatens to overtake her.

Lying down, Gwen closes her eyes and concentrates on the last images of her surreal dream: the boy's handsome, sweet face, his warm, rich smile, and his brilliant blue-gold eyes. But most importantly, she tries to recall his words. She smiles and falls back into her dreams, hoping that if she tries hard enough, she might summon him again. As she drifts away, she hears his voice in the wind.

"I will always be there. You are not forsaken."

A sneak peek at

THE THIRTEEN TRIBES OF CAIN SERIES

Book Two

The Offspring

All at once she finds herself wandering through a monstrous cave with hundreds of corridors and passageways in every direction. The only light comes from the dim glow of the lanterns carved into the rock along the walls. They cast eerie shadows across her path. The dull, hollow echo of her footsteps bounces off the walls before her, along the unseen tunnels beyond. She shivers as a cold, acrid chill permeates from the dark stone walls and floors, penetrating her slender frame. She feels the daunting sensation of being trapped in a never-ending maze, deep in the ground as if buried alive. Panic grips her, caressing with icy fingers down her spine.

Her instincts tell her to turn back, to get out as fast as she can. Yet something compels her forward, as though someone—or something—has summoned her, but why she cannot fathom. She continues on, even when the corridors become smaller, and the walls begin to close in on her. Claustrophobic panic creeps into her flesh, tempting her to turn back.

"What was that?" She stops to listen. A muffled sound of someone crying and whimpering comes from somewhere just beyond the bend.

The voice seems eerily familiar. Alarmed, she hurries around the bend, following the faint crying down a long, steep stairway, heading into the depths of the cave-like fortress. The stairs, carved out of the rock, end abruptly, leading into a small, dimly lit chamber; empty, except for a hole in the floor on the far end.

"Is somebody there?" she calls out. Fearing a trap, she hesitates by the entry, ready to bolt back up the stairs at the first sign of danger.

"Help me!" a small trembling voice answers. Timidly, she follows the sound of the voice to the dark hole in the cave floor. Kneeling down, she looks inside. Below her, a pit drops straight down into pitch-blackness. She can hear water trickling down the sides of the walls and dripping into a body of water somewhere below, but she sees nothing.

"Who's down there?" She leans closer to the edge, waiting for the mysterious voice to reply. There is a long silence.

"You better leave, he's coming!" The voice sounds far away as if the pit is very deep. The woman starts to sob, the sound echoing off the walls of her prison. "It's too late!" the woman cries out.

"Who? Who is com--" she begins, when suddenly she hears a sound in the chamber behind her. It starts as just a whisper, like someone breathing very softly, and then, as it grows in volume and proximity, it becomes a hiss in her ear.

A jolt of fear shoots up her spine as the sound comes closer, creeping up on her. She wants to run, to turn and flee, but she is paralyzed by fear. She hears a crunching of rocks just behind her.

Holding her breath, she slowly stands up but does not turn around.

"Who's there?" she asks aloud, her voice shaking.

Again, she hears the hissing inches from her ear, as well as a cold, metallic breath that touches her neck with a bone-shivering chill. Abruptly, a hand grasps her by the throat. Her windpipe is squeezed shut; she desperately gasps for air. Her hands fly up to claw at the icy-cold hand choking her. But the stranger is too strong, his iron grip impenetrable.

She tries to call out for help, but her voice leaks out as nothing more than a scratchy whizzing croak. She begins to panic, thrashing about wildly in an attempt to shake off her attacker, but to no avail.

"You're so weak and pathetic," a terrifying voice airy as the wind laughs in her ear. Her vision blurs and the room begins to spin about her. Suddenly, her captor releases her.

Wheezing and coughing, she collapses to the floor, sucking in sweet breaths as she fights against bitter nausea. A moment later a cold hand takes her by the chin and hauls her to her feet, forcing her to look into her attacker's eyes. She looks into a pale, malicious face, gaunt and strikingly angular. His eyes are a piercing whitish silver which seem to bore holes into her soul. His skin is as white and lifeless as a corpse. His wavy hair, eyebrows, and eyelashes are all platinum blonde, adding to his overall ashen appearance. He towers above her, thin as a rail with broad, bony shoulders. Just from looking into this stranger's eyes she somehow knows that he truly is a man with a heart black as the pits of hell.

He gives her a taunting smile. She sickens at the sight of dried blood clinging to his white teeth and razor-sharp fangs. He laughs, and as he does, fresh blood oozes out from between his teeth and drips like molasses from his lips down to his chin.

He reaches his bony hand toward her, beckoning her to him. Revolted, she shrinks back from his grasp. He steps toward her, bringing her to the edge of the pit's opening. Without a word, he grabs her by the shoulders, his long fingernails digging into her skin. Giving her a mockingly sweet smile, he thrusts her violently away. Startled and frantic, she tries to hold onto him to keep from falling. But he just laughs and steps back, out of her reach.

Helpless, she stumbles backward and topples over the edge.

Her screams echo off the walls of the chasm as she plummets into the black abyss below. Everything grows darker as the dim light from the chamber above fades, until finally she is engulfed in complete darkness. She hits the pit's watery bottom with the force of a brick wall. Pain shoots through her body as she is engulfed by the bitter-cold spring water which chokes at her lungs. Frantically, she tries to swim to the surface, but something pulls her downward, deeper, and deeper into a dark oblivion.

Writers Depend on Their Readers

Thank you for taking the time to read my book! The Forsaken
is book one in The Thirteen Tribes of Cain series. To keep up to date
on the releases of future volumes in this series you
can follow me at any of the following:

www.rjcraddock.com

http://rjcraddockauthor.blogspot.com/

https://www.goodreads.com/RJCraddock

www.facebook.com/RJCraddockAuthor

https://twitter.com/RJCraddockwrite

https://www.instagram.com/r.j_craddock_author/

Your Feedback Is Appreciated

A story not read is a story not realized. You the reader, give
my words life. Your imagination brings them one step
closer to reality. If you enjoyed getting to know Gwenevere
and reading about her world, please leave a review on the
following sites:

https://www.goodreads.com/RJCraddock

http://www.amazon.com/dp/B00DQA9OZI

http://www.barnesandnoble.com/w/the-forsaken-r-j-
craddock/1115287679

ACKNOWLEDGMENTS

Credit goes to my mother, Jane Harris,
for her constant support over the years. To my
friend, Adrienne Monson, for encouraging me to get
involved in The League of Utah Writers and inviting me to
join her critique group. Also, I must give credit to the other
ladies of that group: Roxy Haynie, Karyn Patterson, Rebecca
Rode, Karen Pellett, and Mary King. Thanks go to Jessica
Bradshaw for her excellent advice. To my first edition
editors, Liana Markel, and D.W. Lundberg. Thanks go
to my final draft editor/proofreader Julie Caldwell.
Last but not least thanks to all my beta readers
whose input helped my story reach its
full potential.

R. J. CRADDOCK

Born Ruth Jerraisetti Harris in Oka Tamuning, Guam, Ruth is the youngest of eight children. As a young child, she began telling stories, developing unique characters, and conjuring fantastical worlds in her mind. As she grew older, a thirst for reading overcame her and she devoured all kinds of books, finding kindred spirits in classic novelists such as Dickens, Bronte, and Fitzgerald. She started writing her first novel at age eleven. After high school, she attended the Art Institute of Phoenix to pursue her other great passion: Art. Ruth now lives with her husband, four sons, daughter, and their cats in Kaufman County, Texas.

www.ingramcontent.com/pod-product-compliance
Lightning Source LLC
Chambersburg PA
CBHW030547260626
47157CB00006B/2221

* 9 7 8 0 6 1 5 8 0 6 4 8 8 *